DATE DUE

OCT 12 '99			
OC 14 '99			
OCT 19 '99			
OCT 28 '99			
NOV 11 '99			
NO 22 '99			
DEC 6 '99			
DEC 20 '99			
MY 21 '02			
GAYLORD			PRINTED IN U.S.A.

PARIAH

BOOKS BY THOMAS ZIGAL

INTO THIN AIR
HARDROCK STIFF
PARIAH

PARIAH

A KURT MULLER MYSTERY

by

THOMAS ZIGAL

Delacorte Press

Published by
Delacorte Press
Random House, Inc.
1540 Broadway
New York, New York 10036

Delacorte Press® is a registered trademark of Random House, Inc., and the
colophon is a trademark of Random House, Inc.

Library of Congress Cataloging in Publication Data
Zigal, Thomas.
    Pariah : a novel / by Thomas Zigal.
      p.   cm.
    ISBN 0-385-31930-4
    I. Title.
    PS3576.I38P3   1999
    813'.54—dc21   99-32900
                                         CIP

Manufactured in the United States of America
Published simultaneously in Canada

September 1999

10 9 8 7 6 5 4 3 2 1

BVG

*For the three people
who have put up with me the longest:
Billie, Frank, and Frances*

pariah (pə rī′ ə) *n.* **1:** a member of a low caste of southern India and Burma; **2:** any person or animal generally despised; **3:** an outcast.

PERSPIRING THROUGH HIS rented tuxedo, Sheriff Kurt Muller stood on the dais in the hotel ballroom and smiled gamely at the audience murmuring under dimmed chandeliers. From the soft-glowing dinner tables Aspen society women were raising their jeweled hands, bidding on a date with him, and the banter between parties was lively and contentious.

"Ladies, please. We're at two thousand dollars. Two thousand," said the auctioneer, a former *Playboy* centerfold presiding over the benefit.

"Three K!" waved a waxen grande dame whose young husband had perished the previous spring in a hang-gliding accident. She wiggled her fingers at Kurt and flashed a naughty smile, and in that moment he understood why the gigolo had chosen to sail into a rock wall.

Corky Marcus was sitting with his wife at a table near the dais. He gave Kurt a sympathetic shrug that said *Hey, whatever.* Corky was the department's legal counsel and this appearance was his brilliant idea.

To beat the recall vote you'll need more visibility, Kurt. A boy-next-door image. You'll have to throw Frisbees in the park and kiss the rich gals on the cheek and show up at all their charity fundraisers. The numbers are too close to call.

Over the summer a popular county commissioner named Ben Smerlas had circulated a petition to recall Kurt as sheriff, and the movement had received the four hundred names needed to place the issue on the November ballot. In two weeks the people of Pitkin County would decide by a simple majority vote if they wanted Kurt Muller to remain in office.

"I hear three thousand dollars!" acknowledged the Playmate. Notorious for her gaudy '70s apparel, she nevertheless appeared modestly contained tonight: silk turban, slinky white gown hugging her celebrated body, pearls dipping into deep cleavage. "Come on, ladies! Is that the final offer for a night of bliss with this studly gentleman of the law?"

She hooked the auction gavel behind Kurt's neck and pulled him closer, shoulder to shoulder. "You know what they say, girls. Cops know how to drive their unit."

There was a bawdy howl from the audience. Kurt glanced again at his attorney. Corky Marcus was history.

Two aging matrons with more tucks and lifts between them than the Gabor sisters began bartering in hundred-dollar increments. Kurt felt like a sofa at a yard sale. He raised his eyes and prayed for a hotel fire to end this misery.

"We're at three thousand eight hundred," the Playmate said after a lull in the bidding. "Is that all I hear? Three thousand eight hundred."

The silence lingered. She looked from one bidder to the other and lifted the gavel. "Okay, ladies. Three thousand eight hundred going once—"

"Ten thousand dollars."

The husky female voice had come from a dark table in the rear. Heads turned. The entire ballroom grew quiet. Kurt thought he might have been hallucinating. The Playmate stepped to the edge of the dais and gazed out over the stirring patrons. "Hel-*looo*," she said, shielding her eyes from the chandelier glare. "Was that a serious bid or were you trying to buy Carbondale?"

A ripple of weak laughter. Everyone had shifted to stare at the woman sitting alone at an unlit table.

"The offer is ten thousand," replied the woman.

Kurt recognized that bourbon-rich voice. Nicole Bauer, the town's most infamous recluse. She was wealthy, she was eccentric, she had pushed her lover off a redwood deck twenty years ago and got away with murder.

The Playmate turned and whispered in Kurt's ear. "Do yourself a favor, hon, and hold on tight to the railing," she said with a wicked smile. "It's a long drop to the bottom."

AFTER THE LAST prize was auctioned off, a weekend for two at an Arizona mud spa, the orchestra swung into an old Big Band favorite and couples dispersed to the dance floor. Corky caught up with Kurt before he could sneak off to the men's room. "That wasn't so bad, now, was it?" the attorney said, clapping Kurt on the shoulder.

"You're fired, Marcus."

With his unruly mop of hair and sagging, beaglelike face, Corky looked more like a Catskills comic than a lawyer. "I'm trying to keep you in office, man," he said, his eyes small and shrunken behind the thick horn-rimmed glasses. "You don't seem to grok the situation here. Smerlas has the mo'. When five percent of the county signs a petition to kick your tush out, you've got some serious problems with public image."

The issues were simple. Smerlas contended that Kurt was too soft on drug crime, that he had lost control of the Latino immigration problem in the county, and that his department was uncooperative with the DEA, the INS, and other federal agencies who were struggling to clean up the Roaring Fork Valley. Smerlas also maintained that two high-profile murder cases in recent years had hurt tourism in Aspen. A local newspaper poll revealed that a significant number of voters agreed with the commissioner.

"Roll the fucking dice," Kurt said. "I like my chances. The people of this county have elected me three times. They know who I am. I don't care who his friends are, Ben Smerlas had better watch his own ass in next year's commission race."

Corky shook his head. "Smerlas has higher ambitions, Kurt," he said. "Next year he'll be running for the House seat that's up for grabs, Third District. You're his whole platform. He takes you down, his reputation is made."

"He's not taking me down."

"Wake up, man, it's the nineties. The old ski bums you used to party with are wearing Rolexes and driving BMWs. They're pissed about the Hispanics using up county services and becoming a burden on the tax base. And guess who they blame for not cracking down on all these scary illegals riding the valley buses? In case you haven't noticed, everyone but you and me is sending their kids to private schools, where they still teach in English."

Carole Marcus approached, wineglass in hand. Kurt welcomed her intrusion. She was a petite, attractive woman with short dark hair gelled and glistening. Standing with her husband, a man barely five feet six, she looked like his matching miniature partner on a wedding cake.

"Jesus, Kurt. Nicole Bauer," Carole said, her small heart-shaped mouth teasing a smile. "Wonder what she'll do with your body when she's done with it?"

He could already hear the jokes from his deputies in the department: *Remember to practice safe sex, Kurt. Pack your Glock.*

"Sheriff Muller?"

A handsome young man dressed in a dark blue chauffeur's uniform had materialized out of the dancing crowd. "Miz Bauer would like to speak with you in private."

Kurt glanced over at the empty table where she had been sitting.

"Would you come with me, sir."

"Oh, this is perfect," Kurt said, raising his brow at the Marcuses.

"Enjoy yourself, Studly," Carole said with a bye-bye wave.

2

AN UNSEASONABLE OCTOBER snow had begun to fall earlier in the afternoon, dusting the city streets. Behind the Hotel Jerome a limousine was waiting for him, its roof and hood mantled in a soft white powder. When the chauffeur opened the back door, clinging snowflakes whirled off the window glass. Kurt watched a pair of long tanned legs shift under fur in the dark interior. "Get in," she said. "I've warmed it up for you."

He hesitated, then lowered his shoulders and slid onto the seat beside her as the chauffeur shut the door. The motor was idling and there was a warm, pleasant hum from the heating system. The air smelled like roses and oiled leather. "You're an expensive date, Sheriff," she said, offering him a fluted glass of champagne. "I hope I get my money's worth."

"I can't imagine what ten thousand dollars will buy you."

She leaned forward and kissed him gently on the mouth. "You underestimate yourself," she said.

She was even more beautiful now, in her mid-forties, than when her pretty face had headlined newspapers two decades ago: BAUER HEIRESS ON TRIAL. Tonight her thick auburn hair was brushed back behind her ears, revealing small amber bears dangling from each lobe. She had a strong, classic jawline and a delicate complexion that freckled lightly in the sun.

"I thought you were anti-fur," he said, running his hand through the soft, sensuous pelt caressing her shoulders.

"It's faux, darling," she said. Her warm fingers touched his face as she pressed closer, kissing him again. "Real animals bite."

He knew he shouldn't give in so easily, but he felt powerless to pull himself away. His entire body tingled, aroused by the bare heel locked around his calf. Her teeth found his bottom lip, nibbled him, then bit down hard enough to break the skin.

"Bastard," she said breathlessly. "Why didn't you return my phone calls?"

He touched his lip and rubbed a trace of blood between his fingertips. "It wasn't going to work out, Nickie," he said.

"Was there someone else?"

He shook his head. The truth should have been obvious to her. No one in this town could afford to be associated with Nicole Bauer. Especially not a man in public office.

"You didn't give it enough time, Kurt," she said in a husky whisper. "You should've trusted me. God knows, I can be discreet. I've had lots of practice."

He inhaled deeply, catching his breath, searching his pocket for a handkerchief to daub the blood. "We're very different people," he said.

"All I wanted was your company, Kurt," she said, tugging at the upturned collar of his overcoat. "We didn't have to go public. I've never cared about that."

He had known that sooner or later he would have to face her for the way he'd handled their affair. "It's been a year, Nickie," he said. "Let it go."

A silent teardrop raced down her cheek. He felt like a prick. "I'm sorry," he said, touching the sleeve of her fur.

She snatched the handkerchief from his hand and wiped at a

dark smudge under one eye. "Someone is trying to kill me, Kurt," she said. "Otherwise I wouldn't be making such a fool of myself. I need your help."

He stared at her. This was how they had met. A year ago some crazed young Courtney Love look-alike had broken into Nicole's mansion, bent on avenging the death of the mythic rock star who had plunged from her deck.

"Come back to Starwood with me," she said, drying her tears. "I'll show you the letters. This isn't just another strung-out junkie."

"Nickie," he said, "if it's a police matter, there are proper procedures for handling the case. I'll assign an investigator."

"I know about police procedures, Kurt. And investigators. If you'll recall, I've had some experience in that area. I could write a fucking book on the subject. I don't want anybody but *you* seeing these letters."

A ten-thousand-dollar date was an expensive way of getting his attention. But the cold terror in her eyes told him she wasn't playing games. Something had scared her badly.

"He's alive, Kurt," she said, dropping her gaze into her lap.

"What are you talking about?"

"Rocky," she said, her voice quavering. "It's him."

Rocky Rhodes was the legendary blues guitarist who had dropped forty feet onto the boulders below her bedroom deck. They were having a fight, she'd told the sheriff's department and the news media at the time, and her bruised face, the scuffle tracks in the icy slush on the deck, sustained her statement. She testified in court that Rocky had lunged at her, lost his balance, and crashed through the railing. The tabloids didn't believe her story, but twelve Aspen jurors let her walk.

"The letters are very—" She considered her words. "Intimate," she said. "Explicit. There's only one person who could possibly know what went on between us."

"No," Kurt said. "I've seen the coroner's photographs. He was dead, Nickie. Very dead."

Because Rocky's body had been stolen from the funeral home and never recovered, rumors had persisted for years that he was still alive. Like Elvis and Jesus, he had been seen among the living.

"Then how do you explain this?" she said, offering her hand. "It was in one of the letters."

He examined the tarnished ring on her middle finger. Engraved in the gold face were interlocking yin-yang symbols encircled by several codelike marks, each one a variation of three broken lines.

"It's the ring I gave him for his thirtieth birthday," she said. "The eight trigrams of the *I Ching*. He was wearing it when . . ." She paused, collecting herself. "When he died."

Kurt held her hand longer than he should have. "Somebody's playing with your head, Nickie," he said. He was surprised she wasn't accustomed to this kind of harassment by now. "If you want me to be a cop and put a stop to the threats, I'll be happy to. It's my job."

She withdrew her hand and straightened her posture. "Oh yes, your *job*," she said. He could hear an entire year of resentment in that single word. "That's how we ended up in bed, wasn't it? Your *profession* brought us together."

He closed his eyes and tried to empty his mind of those memories, the sweet nights he'd spent in her arms at the Starwood mansion. "We're going to have to get past this, Nickie."

"Money is my therapy," she said, raising her chin with the pride of a baroness. "I've just spent ten thousand dollars to deal with a chronic problem I can't seem to resolve. Men in my past." She lifted the champagne bottle from a silver ice bucket and refilled her glass. "Like it or not, you're the only one who can help me, Kurt. I don't care to have some young joker in a uniform reading about my sexual proclivities and laughing it up with his pals in the department. Especially when the descriptions are amazingly . . ." She hesitated, studying him with equal portions of sensuality and fear. "Accurate," she said.

He retrieved his glass from the limo floorboard. The cold champagne stung his cut lip. "You've bought an evening with Kurt Muller." He shrugged. "You want to spend it reading crank letters, that's your call."

She surprised him with another kiss. "And if I want to spend it in other ways," she said, her hand resting warmly on his thigh, "is that my call, too?"

He smiled. "Depends on what you have in mind."

With her fingertip she smoothed the broken skin on his lip. "You ought to show more gratitude," she said. "I've saved you from a night in hell with some aging bondage queen."

"To think," he said, "I might've gotten hurt."

She smiled mischievously and pressed a console button. The window whirred and a gust of snow danced into the warm vehicle. Outside in the darkness, large wet flakes floated in the orb of amber light from a corner streetlamp. "Take us home, Kyle," she said to the young chauffeur standing at attention beside the driver's door.

3

A HOME IN Starwood was a promise of protected anonymity. Yet the guardhouse and electronic gate and round-the-clock surveillance patrol had not prevented one lone young woman with a carving knife from making her way on foot to the Bauer mansion, where she'd hoisted herself over the stone wall and smashed a patio door with her fists, screaming obscenities, before the security system had finally registered her on the grid. Kurt remembered how frightened Nicole had been that night, how he'd set aside his department notepad to hold her shivering body, consoling her with hot tea and brandy until she'd pulled herself together. Those hours late into the night were the beginning.

"You've added more lights," he said as the limousine climbed the private drive flossed with snow. Even through tinted glass the Bauer mansion looked ablaze. When the automatic gates swung open, he could see strategic new floodlights illuminating the stone walls and garden. Snowflakes drifted like flaming ash through the harsh beams. It felt like Christmas in a prison yard. Maybe that's what this place has become for her, he thought.

"I took your professional advice and put in some extra bells and whistles since the last time you were here," she said, glancing at him with mild reproach. "I get that way when there's no man in my life."

Kurt smiled skeptically. There was always someone in Nicole Bauer's life. *L'homme du jour.* Their identities remained the best-kept secret in Aspen.

With her family inheritance Nicole had built this sprawling split-level palace of glass and lodgepole pine long before Starwood had acquired guards and gates. Her parties up here in the early '70s were legendary. Kurt's older brother had once crashed an all-night bacchanal, when Rocky Rhodes and his band were at their peak, and his brother talked about the scene for years. Group sex with French film stars, electric Kool-Aid in the bathtub, Rocky's melancholy guitar riffing out over the dark valley. Two decades later Kurt was still hearing stories about those Bauer bashes. Graying yuppies around the grill, sighing wistfully, pining for the wild old days in Aspen.

The chauffeur opened the limo door, and when Kurt stepped out after Nicole he bumped the young man, confirming the bulge under the jacket. "You have a permit to carry that piece, Kyle?" he asked.

"Yes, sir."

"You know how to use it?"

"Yes, sir, I do."

Kyle appeared to be a spruced-up snowboarder she'd dragged off the slopes to play butler and bodyguard. Probably her rainy-day boy toy as well. Nordic, mid-twenties, deeply tanned, lank blond hair hanging below the blue chauffeur cap. He looked very familiar.

"We've met before, haven't we?" Kurt said. "Refresh my memory."

Kyle's eyes darted nervously below the tipped-down bill of his cap. "It's a small town," he said.

Kurt stared at him, trying to remember his case. "You've

been one of my county guests," he said. "Remind me of the occasion."

The young man turned dutifully to Nicole, as if he owed the explanation to her. "I cut a fence," he admitted with a petulant shrug.

Of course, Kurt thought. Kyle Martin. The self-proclaimed elk defender who had cut down a section of ranch fence near Owl Creek because the fence had long obstructed an elk migratory run. A ranch foreman had wrestled Kyle to the ground and hog-tied him with a cattle rope until the deputies arrived.

"Kyle's a dear," Nicole interceded, hooking her arm around Kurt's and huddling against his body as they trod through the snow toward the bright entrance. "He's always close by when I need him."

They crossed the front deck, leaving tracks in the light powder, and Kurt felt a sudden, unexpected affection for the secret nights he'd slipped in out of these formidable double doors. It occurred to him that perhaps she was a very clever actor indeed, as the tabloids had always portrayed her, and that her entire story was a deliberate lie to lure him back here to those velvet memories.

When the doors opened before them, another young man stood waiting in the rectangle of warm light. "Good evening, Miz Bauer," he said.

"Good evening, Lyle," she said, slipping out of her faux fur and dropping it into his arms. In her heels she was six feet tall, her legs unforgettably long and shapely. Tonight she was wearing a black evening dress with thin straps, and her bare shoulders were still brown from a summer tan.

"Kyle and Lyle," Kurt mumbled, glancing at Nicole. "These boys haven't killed their parents, have they?"

Lyle could have been Kyle's dark twin, the domestic version. Hand-woven sweater, suede slippers, his black hair pulled back in a ponytail. Three bead-gems were implanted in the soft cartilage of one ear. Like Kyle, he seemed eager to please his employer. Their behavior struck Kurt as the phony solicitude ex-cons always paid to parole officers.

"Would you like a drink?" Nicole asked Kurt with a tantalizing smile. "Or is this going to be all work and no play, Sheriff?"

"Let's see the letters," he said, surrendering his overcoat to Lyle. "I may need a drink afterwards."

She led him up the spiral staircase to her bedroom, a large open space made cozy by earth tones, Navajo fabric, and Mexican folk art. How well he remembered the comforts of this room. He found himself staring at his own reflection in the glass doors leading onto the deck where that hapless young fool had crashed through the railing on a wintry night like tonight, snow clinging to the panes.

"Make yourself at home," she said, sweeping her hand across the room in a grand gesture. "The letters are in a safe. I'll get them for you."

He sat in a plush reading chair near the bed, removed the tuxedo bow tie, loosened his collar. Slipping off his damp patent leather shoes he rested his feet on the ottoman and listened to the logs crackling in the fireplace. Several large-scale paintings of animals in the wild, richly layered canvases with thick brushstrokes and dazzling colors, decorated the walls. Kurt had always been fascinated by the one in which a huge howling bear was fending off an attacking bighorn buck while other rams looked on in the blue Rocky Mountain landscape.

I prefer animals to people, Nicole had once told him. *They settle things out in the open. Without lawyers.*

The night table was only an arm's length away. He opened a drawer and remembered her private world of lotions and lubricants and that pull-string dope bag of potpourri, the jasmine and sandalwood she always sprinkled on the sheets before making love. He found a plastic vial of pills and read the label. WARNING: DO NOT DRINK ALCOHOLIC BEVERAGES WHEN TAKING THIS

MEDICATION. It was something called Risperidone, prescribed by Dr. Jay Westbrook—her ex-husband and Aspen's most prominent psychiatrist. The date indicated that the pills were two weeks old. Apparently Westbrook was still her shrink, though they had been divorced for at least five years.

Kurt found something else at the back of the drawer—a small Beretta hiding like a black scorpion among her effects. He made sure the safety was on, then slid the pistol back under a silk sleeping mask and shut the drawer.

Closing his eyes, listening to the wind crying underneath the terrace doors, he thought he could hear echoes of the room's many secrets, ex-husbands and otherworldly voices, animal spirits. They should have conducted this business in another part of the house.

"You look comfortable," she said, reentering the room. "Should I have Lyle bring you a pipe and slippers?"

"You don't want to spoil me," he said.

She handed him a small stack of envelopes bound by a red ribbon, six letters altogether. "Here they are," she said. "I'll be back in a minute. Sure you don't want that drink?"

It was nearly midnight and he was beginning to tire. "I could use some coffee," he said.

"Sorry I'm not more stimulating company," she said, frowning at him over her shoulder as she walked to the door. "Maybe the letters will provide better entertainment."

He untied the ribbon. Aspen postmarks, which meant they'd been mailed within a few square miles. Judging by the dates, they had arrived at her P.O. box every few days for the past two weeks. The writer had used an old manual typewriter, pica face, maybe an Underwood like the one that had belonged to Kurt's father, a heavy black antique gathering dust now in the book-lined study at home. A quick glance through the first letter disclosed numerous strikeovers and spelling errors, dropped words, a breathless urgency. Glued to every page were cutouts from hard-core porno magazines and lingerie catalogs, scantily clad women and couples engaged in various sex acts. Large single words spliced from magazines—REAM, GASH, NAIL—had been pasted at random. The pages took on the messy look of a '60s pop collage. He was prepared to dismiss them as a deranged prank, someone getting off on talking dirty to a one-time celebrity with a scandalous past. Until he began reading.

Rocky and Nicole's stormy romance had been well documented in tabloids and rock magazines over the years, so the allusions to violent public scenes, legendary recording sessions, and Moroccan holidays did not surprise or impress Kurt. What finally forced him to sit up and take notice was the sex itself. The descriptions sent a shock of recognition through him. Her rituals, her peculiar tastes. Kurt raised a page close to his face and smelled the scent of jasmine, the fragrance that clung to his body for hours after he'd made love to Nicole Bauer.

The door opened and she walked in bearing a silver tea tray with a service of coffee. When she saw the blush on his face she stopped to study him. "Well," she said, raising an eyebrow. "I see you've got past the foreplay."

Without comment he read on. Whoever had written this wasn't making wild guesses. In the third letter there were graphic details only someone who had been Nicole's lover would know. *Before i kill you im going to mount you from behind,* it said, describing with disturbing precision the way Nicole liked to come pressing her partner's finger against her. *You dont know how much i miss that in the grave. Nothing but worms to fill my void.*

"Black?" Nicole said. "Isn't that how you take it?" She was pouring coffee from a silver pitcher.

"What's going on here, Nicole?" He felt caught up in some perverse game, the object and rules of which she would reveal at her own leisure.

"I was hoping you would tell me. You're the cop."

Despite his suspicion that he was being played for a fool, he opened the last envelope. The tone had turned darker, more desperate. She had betrayed him, the letter said. She was fucking everyone, even the guys in his band. She was going down on women. *Wasnt i enough for you?* The final passage was a recounting of that tragic night. How he'd found her in bed with *that bitch Pariah* and it was *her* fault that he and Nicole had fought. He didn't mean to hurt her. He didn't mean to strike her face. But now she would have to die for what she and Pariah had done to him.

Nicole set the coffee cup on a side table next to Kurt's tuxedo sleeve. She gave his shoulder an affectionate tug and turned to retrieve her Scotch.

Kurt scanned the last paragraph again. Nickie and Pariah, the letter said. They had pushed him through the railing. They had murdered him. *Evil fucking cunts.*

He refolded the letter, slipped it into its envelope, and placed the stack on the side table next to the steaming coffee. She was staring at him now, trying to gauge his reaction, her face gravely troubled. He understood why she was reluctant to allow the police to examine these documents.

"Is any of this true?" he asked.

A smile brushed her lips. "You must have a poor memory, Kurt," she said. "I suppose I should feel insulted."

"Rocky's death, Nickie. Who was Pariah?"

Her smile vanished. "There was a groupie named Mariah who hung out with the band. Rocky didn't like her, so he nicknamed her Pariah."

"Cute."

"Rocky was ever so cute," she said dryly. "A real wordsmith."

Without touching the coffee, Kurt stood up and went to the doors facing the deck. Starless and heavy, the night pressed against the glass with a palpable force, the cold seeping inside, chilling his stocking feet. Snow floated at him on dark currents, tapping the glass like insistent moths.

"Was she here the night he was killed?"

He could see her reflection in the glass. Sipping Scotch, sauntering toward him in a slow, languorous motion. "Are you asking me as a friend?" she said. "Or are you asking me as a cop?"

Like everyone in Aspen, he had followed the trial twenty years ago and was fairly certain there had been no testimony about a third party present at the time of Rocky's death. He would have remembered something so dramatic.

"You want my help, Nickie," he said, turning to face her, "you've got to be straight with me."

She was so close he could smell the Scotch on her breath. If she was taking the medication in the drawer, she shouldn't be drinking like this.

"It was a long time ago, Kurt. I've spent half my inheritance in therapy trying to forget that night. Hell, I even *married* my shrink so I could get free home care. Until that blew up in my face, too."

A few months after the trial she'd married Jay Westbrook, the man her family's defense team had hired to testify that she was mentally unstable at the time of the incident. Kurt remembered that a newspaper editorial had cynically diagnosed the marriage as a form of the Stockholm Syndrome—a prisoner falling in love with her captor. Another bizarre turn, but by that time Nicole Bauer had no reputation left to protect.

"Was Mariah here, Nickie? Was she involved in what took place?"

She stepped past Kurt and stared through the glass doors into the night. Wind jiggled the brass handles. "Rocky was beating me up. It wasn't the first time," she said in a calm, distant voice, exhaling a weary sigh. "He lunged at me and I fell down and he went through the railing. That's what I remember, and that's what I testified at the trial. Nothing else matters."

Her back was bare in the evening dress, fine smooth muscles he had massaged many times with her oils. "The D.A. might disagree," he said. If she had perjured herself, or withheld evidence, such a disclosure could nullify the original trial and re-open the case.

"I don't want to go through that nightmare again." She turned, her eyes pleading with him. "I'm not a very strong person right now. Isn't there some way you can take care of this without the whole fucking world peeping through my windows?"

He understood what she wanted. Her own private cop on the case. Professional, personal, discreet. A cop who had compromised himself a year ago and was vulnerable to this emotional blackmail.

"Harassment by mail is a federal crime," he said. "This is a case for the FBI. They're very good at tracking down creeps who write dirty letters."

"Don't be clever about this," she said with a quick burst of emotion. "He's going to kill me. I don't need some pencil-neck showing up next month with a postal form to fill out. I need help now, Kurt. Tonight."

"You're being a bit melodramatic, aren't you?"

"You've read the letters. How could anyone know those things but Rocky?" She leaned into him and kissed his neck. Her body was warm and her hair smelled like an Asian garden, the bouquet from the letters. "Help me, Kurt."

This felt familiar, her fear, her unexpected kiss. When they'd first met she was living alone and frightened by the memories in her own house. He had lost someone dear to him, too, and was haunted by his part in the woman's death. They both knew what it was like to live through sorrow and blame. He and Nicole had needed each other, if only for one brief consoling moment.

"There's a simple explanation, Nickie," he said, his face against her ear. "One of your old lovers has gone off his rocker. Somebody you've told too many secrets to. He's pissed and crazy and getting back at you."

She pulled away from him and took a long drink of Scotch.

"You have a warped view of my love life," she said irritably. "You and the rest of this town."

"It's going to be someone you know. Someone very much alive. I'm sure you can come up with a short list of names if you give it any thought at all."

She gazed past his shoulder into the snowy darkness. "I'm afraid names are a problem," she said, careful not to meet his eye. There wasn't a man in Aspen willing to have his name linked with Nicole's.

"That's where any cop would start. A list of unhappy boyfriends."

He watched a smile take shape and turn wicked. "There are no *unhappy* boyfriends, Kurt," she said. "Only the ones who lost their nerve."

He felt the sting of her remark. She was right, of course. He had stopped seeing her, stopped returning her calls, because their stolen hours together were changing into something deeper and he feared exposure, talk, public ridicule.

"There's one boyfriend we can eliminate, though, isn't there?" she said, nuzzling his neck.

"And how can you be so sure of that?" he asked, teasing her.

"Because you're the only one I didn't disappoint."

He smiled and wrapped his long arms around her. No, she hadn't disappointed him. If she had had another past, another reputation to live down, perhaps they would still be together.

"How is your lip?" she asked, kissing the swollen skin where she'd bitten him. "Would you like some ice for it?"

"It doesn't hurt so much when you do that."

"Mmm," she said. "Then maybe this will help."

She kissed him again and they fell into it the way they had the first time, their bodies drawn together in a desperate rush. This ember-lit room had once been their refuge against the world on the other side of the glass, cold and dark and stalking with strangers. Now they were back in each other's arms as if there had been no year apart.

When they were undressed and lying in bed, she opened the night table drawer to search for her potpourri. The stock of the Beretta had slipped out from its hiding place underneath the sleeping mask.

"What's the gun for?" he asked, sliding his hand along her bare back.

"Nothing to worry about, darling," she said. "Just an extra precaution."

They performed her exotic rituals the way he remembered them, as if the ceremonial oils and incantations were preparation for some sacrificial act. But as their lovemaking slowly unfurled, he couldn't rid his mind of the letters and their crude suggestions. He felt trapped in someone else's fantasies, his rhythms ruled by a force larger than his own will. Nicole whispered encouragement, goaded him on, a hoarse sigh in his ear. This was how she liked it, she said, and they writhed on her scented sheets with a frightening abandon. Deep in the throes of their passion, at the moment she rubbed his finger against her wetness and moaned, he had an eerie feeling they were being watched.

Afterward they lay entwined like broken branches, her hand resting warmly on his belly. The room was overheated from the fire and he could smell their sweat mixed with an aroma of jasmine and piñon. As her nails raked sleepily through the wet hair below his navel he could feel the cool gold band she had shown him earlier. *Take the ring back you unfaithful bitch,* one of the letters had said. *My finger has rotted and it wont fit me now. Wear it to your own grave.*

"The ring," he said, his lungs laboring in the heavy air. "It can't be the same one."

She raised her fingers to look at it. Her hand glowed like a pink shell, backlit by the fire. "It's the same one," she said in a quiet voice, studying the yin-yang symbols.

"Did you actually see it on his finger? After—you know—after the undertaker had prepared him for the casket?"

She shook her head back and forth across the pillow. "They stole his body right out of the funeral home. I didn't have a chance to see him at all."

Members of the band. Roadies, groupies, hangers-on. Legend had it that they'd cremated his body in Canyon de Chelly, Arizona. No one was ever prosecuted for the ghoulish crime.

"There's your answer," Kurt said. "Somebody pocketed the ring as a souvenir before they . . ." He hesitated, struggling to express himself tactfully.

"Before they set his body on fire out in the fucking desert," she said, slipping off the ring to examine it closely. "I have no idea why I've been *wearing* the goddamned thing."

She hurled the ring at the fireplace. There was a thump against the hearth screen. "Hold me, Kurt," she said, burying her face in his neck. "I'm having trouble keeping myself together. Those letters have got me spooked."

He held her close, listening to the hiss of the fire. In their long, exhausted silence he could feel the tension leaving her body as she slowly settled into sleep. "Whatever happened to her?" he asked, giving Nicole a slight squeeze.

She seemed startled by the sound of his voice. Her eyes struggled to open. "Who?" she groaned, lifting her chin from his shoulder.

"Pariah," he said. "Where is she now?"

Nicole inhaled, the air whistling in her nostrils. "God knows," she said. "OD'd or found Jesus, like all the rest of them."

"You haven't heard from her in all these years?"

She closed her eyes and burrowed into him, her face pressed against his jugular. "No, darling, I haven't," she mumbled. "Not a single Christmas card. Now can we please go to sleep?"

He lay still for a long time, her body curled against him, warm and smooth and smelling like a rare flower. As the firelight faded and the air grew cooler, the room seemed to contract around them, shrinking the distance between shadows. He thought he could hear someone speaking softly in another part of the house and wondered if the bedroom door was locked. He wanted that pistol in the drawer to be closer at hand.

He had no idea how long he'd been asleep when the wind woke him, a fierce howl high in the rafters. The glass doors had swung open and an icy gale was sweeping the room, billowing the overhead canopy like a sail. Snow swirled around them, rocking the bed as if it were a small bark in a winter squall. Kurt sat up quickly. The terrace doors were banging like loose storm shutters. There was a human silhouette on the deck, long tendrils of hair whirling in the wind. *Rocky,* he said, *is it you?* The figure watched them silently, ominously, his robe rippling in the frozen moonlight. Or was it a woman standing out there? *Come in,* Kurt said, leaning over the sleeping Nicole for the Beretta in the drawer. *Let's finish this once and for all.*

"Kurt," she said. "Wake up, darling." She was shaking him, drawing his head to her bosom. "You're having a nightmare."

He was lying beside her in a pool of sweat. There was no gun in his hand. The terrace doors were shut tightly, the room untouched by the storm outside.

"Are you okay?" she asked, kissing his forehead. "You were talking in your sleep."

He pulled away from her and got out of bed and walked naked to the glass doors. The carpet was dry under his footsteps. When he tested the door handles, they were locked securely. He peered out onto the dark deck at an unblemished layer of snow. There were no tracks of any kind.

"What's the matter, Kurt?"

"I thought I saw someone out there."

She propped herself on an elbow. "Come back to bed," she said. "You were dreaming."

He returned to the chair where he'd discarded his tuxedo and found his watch. It was two A.M. "I'm sorry, Nickie," he said, "I've got to go. My ex is bringing Lennon back home early in the morning."

It was a lie, but not the first one he'd ever told her. His son wasn't coming home until Sunday morning.

"Convenient," she said tersely. Kurt had never stayed with her until daylight. He wondered if any man had.

"I'll call you around lunchtime and we can talk more about the letters," he said, slipping on his trousers. "Let me see what I can dig up."

He needed to puzzle this thing out. It wasn't going to be an easy investigation. He suspected that eventually he would have to turn everything over to the FBI.

Nicole rose and found her robe. She helped him button the studs on his starched shirt. "I suppose there's no point in trying to entice you to stay a little longer," she said, kissing him gently on the chin.

"I'm sorry. I can't."

"Call me before two o'clock," she said. "I have a meeting with my brothers. The boring quarterly family foundation meeting."

He was surprised that she was involved in such matters. At one time her family had disowned her.

"Decisions, decisions," she said, reading the bewilderment in his face. "Father made it so my vote counts, too. They can't piss away all the money unless I let them."

She held the tuxedo jacket while he settled his arms into the sleeves. "The Menendez brothers," he said, glancing at her hall door. "Are they live-in help?"

She nodded. "I'll wake Kyle. He'll take you home."

"Do they have security experience? I can assign one of my deputies to watch your house."

"The boys take good care of me. They're better than they look."

In their final embrace he felt the soft contours of her breasts and thought he must be insane to walk out on this woman and into the cold night.

"You said his name in your sleep," she whispered close to his ear.

"Who?"

"You know who," she said in a cautious voice, as if someone might be listening. "You were shouting his name."

"It was just a bad dream," he said. "Rocky is dead, Nicole. He didn't write those letters."

She kissed him one last time. "I'll be waiting for your call," she said.

4

WHEN KURT TROD down the steps to the parking circle he found Kyle slouched against the limousine in a half-conscious state of sleep deprivation. The young driver had traded his uniform for a quilted down parka and battered hiking boots, and he'd tucked his long blond hair into a fleece ski cap. Kurt's appearance seemed to startle him awake. With a grudging sense of duty he opened the back door for his passenger, but Kurt walked on past him and opened the front door for himself. "Why don't we get acquainted," he suggested.

"This time of night I'm all out of party chat," Kyle grumbled.

Either he was a very cautious driver or he was seriously stoned. On the dark mountain road curving down from Starwood to McLain Flats the limo crept along at twenty-five miles an hour, its high beams like searchlights sweeping the snowy night.

"You gonna drive like this all the way to Aspen?"

"We're in *their* world now," Kyle said, breaking his sullen silence. "We're intruders here. This is their hour."

Kurt looked out the tinted side glass. "Don't tell me you're expecting a UFO," he said.

"The animals, man. God's creatures. This is when they cross

the road and we slaughter them. The highways are a bloody ho-
locaust."

Where had Nicole found this young loon?

"How long have you been working for Miz Bauer?" Kurt
asked, lowering his voice to what he hoped was a sedative level.

"Since the spring," Kyle said, his eyes swollen from sleep.

"What did you do before this? Besides sawing down fences to
free the elk."

Kyle glanced sidelong at him, then back to the road. "Mostly
carpenter work and some gardening," he said.

Nicole's armed chauffeur-bodyguard was apparently a converted yard boy. If she feared for her safety, why hadn't she hired
professional security? They were easy enough to find. Every
wannabe VIP in Aspen employed a knuckle-dragger with a neck
full of steroids to trail them around the slopes.

"So why the hardware under your jacket?" Kurt asked. He
wondered if the live-in help knew about the letters.

"When that wigged-out chick with the knife broke in to the
place, it freaked her." He studied Kurt's reflection in the windshield. "It's a sick world out here. She likes extra protection. You
ought to know."

An uneasy silence lingered between them for the next two
miles of darkness. They passed the lurking shadow of Red Butte
and turned off Cemetery Lane, coasting like a long soundless
cutter toward the bridge over Castle Creek. The snow clouds had
drifted southward and silver threads of moonlight glimmered
through the rushing water.

"What about Lyle?" Kurt said after the long interval. "What's
he do besides answer the door and hang up coats?"

Kyle slowed the limousine for the dramatic curve onto Main
Street, Aspen. "He's handy with a wok," he said, offering Kurt a
nasty little smile. "Maybe you ought to ask him. He's been at her
service longer than I have."

Kurt wondered if either young man was capable of sending
those letters to Nicole. They had access to her private domain;

they may have even shared her bed. That would certainly explain the intimate sexual descriptions. But why would an overpaid, underqualified employee do something to jeopardize such a posh gig? Anger, jealousy, revenge? Blackmail? Or maybe one of them got his rocks off on the dirty talk. Kurt intended to run a background check on Kyle and Lyle as soon as he could sit down at a department computer.

"Looks like you got something cooking tonight, Sheriff," Kyle said.

Kurt turned to the driver and dropped his voice even deeper, saying, "Listen, Kyle," prepared to threaten him physically if he mentioned to a living soul what time he'd left Nicole's bedroom. Then he saw the police lights swirling in the dark street ahead and realized that the young man had meant something else.

"It's that sushi bar," Kyle said. "Might have yourself a grease fire."

A flashing Aspen police cruiser was parked in front of the establishment, an old Main Street home remodeled into an upscale restaurant with Japanese decor and tatami seating. Kyle pulled the limousine over to the curb as a Pitkin County Sheriff's unit sped past. The vehicle skidded to a halt behind the police cruiser, and two of Kurt's deputies, Muffin Brown and Joey Florio, leaped out with weapons drawn and raced toward the bright entrance. Kurt could see two municipal cops squatting behind a snow-laced hedge that ran the length of the original front porch.

The burglar alarm was ringing. Someone had broken in.

"I'm getting out," Kurt said, opening the limo door to the frigid night air. He stepped onto the frozen pavement and then ducked his head back inside. "Kyle, I'm sure Miz Bauer has given you strict instructions about her privacy," he said.

There it was again, that nasty little smile. "I know the rules, Sheriff," the driver said. "Tonight never happened."

Kurt straightened his shoulders and stared at him. The

young man had delivered that line before. Other nights, other limo rides in the snow.

"We'll talk again," Kurt said.

"It could get to be a habit," Kyle said with a mock salute. "Adios, chief."

Kurt waited for the limousine to edge off into the darkness, then hurried across the street to the Pitco unit. He used his master key on the trunk, where a spare twelve-gauge shotgun was latched into a safety holder. Pumping a shell into the chamber, he jogged toward the restaurant with his head low. Deputy Florio and an Aspen cop had forced open the front door and three officers were inside now, but there were no shouts or audible voices, only the alarm ringing above the eerie silence.

"Kurt, is that you?"

Muffin Brown crouched by the door with her Glock raised, a sheriff's department cap tucked tightly over her brow. She watched him lumber up the steps and slide to his knees next to the long picture window.

"Hey, must've been a bitchin' party," she said sarcastically.

He looked down at his clothes. The striped tuxedo pants were visible below his herringbone overcoat. The rented patent leather shoes gleamed under the restaurant burglar lights.

"What's the situation?" he asked.

"Broken window in the rear. The surveillance cameras picked up movement in the kitchen area."

"Still in there after all this noise?"

"Only one way to find out," she said.

Knees bent, scuttling like a crab in sand, she led the way into the dim interior. He followed her past the hostess station and through a dining room where straw mats were spread around floor-level tables. Kurt had only been here on one occasion, a birthday party last year with friends.

Muffin signaled him to halt and they crawled behind a liquor bar while she spoke quietly into her walkie-talkie. "Joey, come in. Where are you, man?"

The radio squawked. "Kitchen doors," the voice responded. "Sounds like he's tearing up the place."

Kurt could hear Muffin's shallow breathing. "Some asshole on angel dust," she said to him.

They moved swiftly through the darkness until they spotted flashlight beams crisscrossing in the rear of the building. The three officers were stationed near a pair of swinging doors that led into the kitchen.

"*Police!*" shouted a burly red-headed cop Kurt recognized as Mike Marley from the Aspen force. "We know you're in there! Give it up and come on out where we can see you!"

There was a commotion of crashing pots and pans. Marley stood up and flattened his wide back against the wall next to the swinging doors, gripping his .38 with both hands. "Cover me," he said to the others. "I'll kick the door."

"Hold on, Mike!" Kurt said, slipping to the other side of the doors with the shotgun braced across his chest. He had caught a whiff of something and it wasn't raw fish. At least not in any palatable form.

"Recognize that lovely smell?" He turned to Muffin, who was down on one knee fifteen feet away with her Glock 9 aimed at the doors.

She sniffed the air, considered, and sniffed again, like a connoisseur with a wine cork. "Eww, god, yes," she said.

Kurt laughed. He knew that smell too.

Inside the kitchen something heavy and metallic banged to the floor. They could hear a liquid leaking like a slow dribbling faucet. Kurt slowly nudged open the door with his knee and peeped in. Thirty feet away, under pale burglar lighting, the black bear raised its head from an overturned bucket of slop and stared back at him. It had made a mess of everything in view.

"Pretty good-sized female," he said. "Two-fifty, two-eighty."

Muffin slipped up behind him and peered around his shoulder. "Holy bear scat," she said. "It's eating all the sushi."

"Maybe we ought to put a couple of rounds in her before she

totals the place," Marley said, scratching his huge, moon-shaped face.

"Relax, Mike," Kurt said. "We'll take care of it from here."

Technically this restaurant resided in the municipal jurisdiction, but Kurt knew that Marley and his partner, city cops, had no experience with bears. For the past two years there had been a rash of black bear sightings in the Aspen area and Kurt's department had assisted the Colorado Department of Wildlife rangers on several occasions. This was the first bear to break into an Aspen restaurant. The lure of raw fish must have been overwhelming.

"Joey, who's on duty in the squad room?" he asked the deputy hiding behind a service cart. All he could see of the man's face were his bushy black eyebrows below the bill of his cap.

"Linda Ríos," Joey called out.

"Radio her and tell her to bring the Cap-Chur rifle. Pronto."

The bear had entered the kitchen through a window above a large industrial sink. Glass shards and fragments of wood frame were scattered over the aluminum sideboard and the tile floor. A shelf of cooking pots had been pulled over and a tray cart lay upended near the Hobart dishwasher.

"A sushi-eating bear," Marley said, shaking his head. "Wonder if it drives a Volvo?"

Everyone had bunched together at the swinging doors, trying to see the bear without venturing inside the kitchen. She ignored them and shoved her nose deeper into the slop bucket.

"Muffin," Kurt said to the young deputy stepping on his toes. "Get on the horn to Rick Keating and tell him to bring a cage."

Keating was a tall, lanky, agreeable DOW ranger who lived in Woody Creek, five miles north of Aspen. It was nearly three A.M., but he could always be counted on to show up within half an hour of a bear call, day or night.

Extracting a pack of cigarettes from his shirt pocket, Marley walked away from the door and took a seat at one of the dining tables. "Is this the smoking section?" he asked no one in particular. "Waiter, I'll have the yellowtail and some warm sake."

Kurt propped the shotgun against the wall and waited for the others to move out of the doorway so he could keep an eye on the creature. The smell was horrendous, a mix of putrid fish remains and the animal's foul breath and the scat it had left somewhere in the room. As she raised her head from the bucket, licking her yellow teeth, Kurt could see a plastic DOW tag clipped to the bear's ear. She had been captured once before.

These small black bears lived in the higher elevations of the valley, but developers were building monster homes up there now, each one at least ten thousand square feet on five acres of cleared land. The construction activity was not only scaring the bears, it was depleting their food sources. Over the past three years they had been coming down to civilization in alarming numbers, marauding through garbage cans, occasionally breaking into a home while the occupants were away. Though everyone in the county had been warned repeatedly not to feed the bears, some misguided fools were still setting out food in the hope of befriending the creatures. It was spoiling them, eliminating their natural fear of man.

The Department of Wildlife's response was clear and straightforward: They tranquilized bears found wandering in populated areas and transported them back to the wilderness. But the bears kept returning. The bolder ones had lost their inhibitions and the DOW was concerned that humans might get hurt, perhaps a child. So now they ear-tagged captured bears and employed a "three strikes" policy. A bear caught for a third time was euthanized by lethal injection.

Kurt watched the animal knock over another garbage can and devour a slew of fine bones. He hoped this wasn't the beginning of a new pattern of bear behavior. The local restaurateurs weren't exactly tree-hugging naturalists. They would poison every bear in Christendom to defend a single serving of poached salmon in white wine sauce.

"Here's Linda," Joey said, mashing out his cigarette in a tea-cup.

Deputy Ríos trotted into the dining room with the CO_2-powered Cap-Chur rifle, which fired a small tranquilizer syringe filled with a muscle relaxer called Rompun and the anesthetic ketamine hydrochloride, a potent combination. First it made the bears happy, then it knocked them out.

"Who's been eating my porridge?" Linda said, handing the rifle to Kurt. She was a robust young woman, early thirties, with thick muscular thighs and a strong upper body. "What have we got here, boss?"

"A mama bear without reservations," Kurt said.

He held the door open with his knee, cocked the lightweight rifle, and took aim. When he sighted down the barrel, scanning the far corner of the kitchen, all he could find was the bear's plump backside protruding from under a sink. He pulled the trigger and the rifle popped like a boy's .22 rabbit gun. The bear yelped, spun around in circles chasing her tail, and crashed against a tall column of container shelves, toppling them to the floor. Then she stopped suddenly in her tracks and studied Kurt, her small black eyes blinking like an old drunk's at closing time. In less than sixty seconds the animal rolled onto her side, snorted mournfully, and began to nod off.

"She'll be snoring in five minutes," Kurt said. "But Rick may have to shoot her up with another dose before we start moving her into the cage."

The six officers gathered at the swinging doors, waiting for the bear to fall asleep. Once the animal's breathing had slowed to a somnolent rhythm, her jaw slack and drooling, Kurt entered the wrecked kitchen with the others close behind. They circled the animal where she lay sleeping in the broken glass. His first guess had been right: she looked to weigh 250 pounds, a smooth black coat with no apparent signs of scarring or trauma. No one spoke as they stared down at this beautiful creature who had lost her fear of humans.

"Wonder if she's carrying cubs?" Muffin said. "It's that time of year."

Joey Florio knelt down next to the animal. "Well, old girl," he said, running his hand affectionately across her bristly pelt as if petting his favorite collie, "you got in over your head this time." Stroking her leg, he gazed about at the destruction. "The Man won't let you mess with his sushi."

With no forewarning the bear lifted her wobbly head, growled weakly, and was suddenly on her feet. Joey rolled away as the unsteady animal swiped at him with her paw, missing his face by inches. Everyone scattered. Kurt fumbled with the breech of the Cap-Chur rifle, trying to load another tranquilizer dart. The bear fell over, still woozy from the drug, then reared up on her hind legs, pawing at the air and growling in a fierce angry roar. Muffin and Linda Ríos were cornered behind the dishwashing machine.

"Hang on!" Kurt shouted, working the jammed rifle bolt. "I'll take her down."

Two quick shots rang out and the animal's head exploded, spewing blood and skull fragments against the tile wall. It dropped deadweight to the floor and writhed for several seconds in a bloody spasm, then lay still, panting hard.

Kurt looked over at Mike Marley, crouched beside a grill. His .38 was still poised in the shooting position, smoke curling from the barrel.

"Goddammit, Marley!" Joey said, crawling out from under a sink. "You didn't have to blow the poor fucking thing away!"

"She almost took your face off, Florio," Marley said in a calm voice.

Kurt finally had the rifle loaded. "Step back, people," he said. He aimed and fired a dart into the animal's huffing chest. She wasn't going to survive those head wounds. The ketamine would put her to sleep before she suffered any more agony.

"Kurt had another tranq," Joey said, coming at Marley. "You didn't have to do that, asshole!"

"I saved your life, man," Marley said, holstering his weapon. "So back the fuck off!"

Joey Florio was a small scrapper with a quick temper. Though a head shorter than the Aspen cop, he grabbed Marley by the shirt and ripped off three buttons before Kurt could step in and lock an arm around his deputy's neck and pull him away. Muffin and Linda Ríos rushed over, restraining Marley from throwing a punch, and then helped Kurt hustle Joey out of the kitchen.

"Let go of me!" Joey said, fighting to free himself from their grasp. "I'm going back in there and kick his fat ass!"

"No, you're not," Kurt said, gripping his arm and shaking him. "You're going to the courthouse with your partners. If I catch you back here, or I hear you're hassling Marley later on, I'll suspend you for a month without pay. Is that understood?"

"The guy's a trigger-happy dickhead, Kurt!" Joey said. "He wanted to shoot her from the git-go."

Kurt motioned to the two deputies to take him away. "Get the fuck out of here, Joey. You're making things worse."

Once they were gone Kurt collected himself, straightened his bow tie, and shoved through the swinging doors into the kitchen. Marley and his partner were standing over the dead bear. Her face was destroyed. Blood had pooled around the animal and a long, thin stream was snaking toward a floor drain. The kitchen looked as if it had withstood four hours of hand-to-hand combat at close quarters.

"Hey, man, I'm sorry. I thought she was going to hurt somebody," Marley said, avoiding Kurt's furious glare. The two cops stared down at the creature with pity and remorse. "The situation was out of control."

Kurt was angry at Marley but also at himself. If he hadn't fumbled with the Cap-Chur rifle, maybe this would have ended differently.

"It was a tough call, Mike," Kurt said, shaking his head sadly. "You took the sure way out."

Marley looked officially contrite. "I appreciate that, Kurt. I hope you won't forget to say that in your report."

Kurt gazed down at the bloodied animal. "Rick Keating from the DOW will be here in a little while with a cage truck," he said. "Tell him the whole story, start to finish. He'll probably have to write something up for the Wildlife Department."

"You leaving now?"

"That's right. But I'll call the owner. He's got some serious cleanup."

"Who's gonna lug this big fucking thing to the truck?"

"You are, John Wayne," Kurt said. "You shot her, didn't you?"

AFTER CHECKING IN briefly with his deputies at the courthouse and making the phone call to an irate restaurant owner, Kurt went home and collapsed onto his bed without even removing his rented shoes. He was exhausted but still too edgy to sleep. Nicole was on his mind. Seeing her again after nearly a year. The letters. It was all too confusing to sort out.

He doubled the pillow beneath his head and clicked on the TV at the foot of his bed, channel-surfing the usual early-morning fare for insomniacs: old black-and-white movies, hand-wringing ministers, belligerent political wonks, satanic music videos, laugh-track family episodes from his childhood. He had almost achieved that blessed state of cool white cathode bliss when something caught his eye on the VH-1 channel, a grainy video of a blues band playing on a dark smoky stage back in the '70s. When the camera moved in for a closeup, Kurt could see that the young man under the spotlight was Rocky Rhodes. His long graceful fingers were crawling up the Rickenbacker neck like a willowy spider. He was tall and ruggedly handsome and slightly bowed at the shoulders, unruly bangs of thick brown hair falling across his tightly closed eyes, sweat dripping from a youthful beard. Kurt had seen him perform at the Wheeler Opera House here in town, '74 or '75, and this was the way he would always remember the rock star, lost in the ecstasy of his music. A handheld camera captured shadowy glimpses of the other players—the classically trained Gahan Moss arched over his keyboard, and their bare-chested drummer pounding frantically on the skins—but they were peripheral to Rocky himself, luminous at the center of the stage. Kurt listened on, sleep-dazed and slightly mesmerized, as the singer slipped back into his lyrics, a gravelly moaning blues, and for an instant he felt something stir deep inside him, something that had lain dormant for many years, the raw hurt and longing of those times.

Later he realized he must have drifted off to sleep listening to Rocky perform. He thought maybe the phone was ringing, but he was too far gone to lift the receiver. Somewhere in the smoky shadows of a dream he heard the drummer's relentless beat, pounding louder and louder, until he was awake again and he didn't know why.

It was still dark outside when he opened his eyes. The digital clock said 5:32 and the television screen hissed gray static. The pounding was louder now, more persistent, and he gradually understood it wasn't a tom-tom but someone knocking on the door of his house. He threw on the overcoat he'd used as a blanket, retrieved his flashlight and Smith & Wesson from the bedside drawer, and rumbled down the stairs.

"Who the fuck is it?" he said in a sleepy voice.

"Open up, Kurt."

It was Muffin Brown. She had come to tell him that Nicole Bauer's body had been found on the rocks forty feet below her redwood deck.

5

KURT STARED AT her body in the cold pale light of dawn. She was lying on her side, wedged between two boulders. Snow had formed a crust over her twisted limbs. Her mouth was open, her teeth bared in a hideous grimace. One arm was lodged out of joint behind her broken neck. He knelt down to cover her exposed legs with the bloody flap of her robe. "Haven't you taken enough pictures?" he asked the coroner, a dour Canadian named Paul Louvier who was standing among the icy rocks with a camera bag slung over his shoulder.

Dr. Louvier nodded. "Okay, let's get her to the morgue," he said. "Nothing else I can do down here."

Kurt was still in shock, unable to locate his personal anguish amid function and duty. He felt himself floating above it all, in some remote and dreamlike state, certain he would wake soon in Nicole's arms and she would assure him this was just like the other dream. But when he leaned closer and brushed the cold crystals from her face, peering into those dead eyes, he knew this moment was as real as darkness itself.

"Are you okay, Kurt?" asked Muffin Brown, standing beside him.

He couldn't speak. He sat back in the snow and began rocking slowly with both arms locked around his knees.

"Come on," she said, trying to lift him to his feet. A deputy named Dave Stuber stepped over to give her a hand. "Let's go inside. The guys can help Dr. Louvier take care of this."

THE FIRE HAD burned itself out in the bedroom hearth and a deep chill filled the room, its terrace doors left open while the deputies tromped in and out. They had taped off a narrow area from the doors directly to the railing, a path where footsteps disturbed the snow.

"Two sets," Muffin said, crouching to point out the different prints. "Around four-thirty Miz Bauer's chauffeur, Kyle Martin, heard a scream and rushed up here. He found these doors wide open and came out on the deck. His are the bigger skid marks right through here."

Kurt walked around the tape to the railing. Morning light seeped over the ridge of Red Mountain, revealing hunky, snow-shrouded formations in the ancient boulder slide below, where two deputies were now shifting Nicole's body into a long black zipper bag under the watchful eye of the coroner. A few years ago, while digging through the department files in an unrelated case, Kurt had discovered photographs from the Rocky Rhodes crime scene and he'd seen what those boulders could do to a body.

"Miz Bauer's footprints are slightly smaller," Muffin said. She was kneeling now, pointing with her gloved hand, talking to Kurt as if he were actually listening. "She was barefoot, and she must've been running."

He turned to glance at the tracks. "Running?" he said.

"On the balls of her feet," she said. "Look at the spacing. A longer stride, no heel marks." Muffin was always right about detective work. "Pardon the expression, Kurt. It looks like she took a flying leap."

"Two makes?" Kurt said, curious now. He squatted beside his deputy to study the tracks, which had hardened in the snow.

"Right. Kyle has identified himself as the other one."

"Where is he?" Kurt asked.

"Dotson's talking to him downstairs. Florio's with the other Bobbsey twin, Lyle Gunderson."

They walked back into the bedroom. He had never been here except at night, and now, in the stark morning light, cold and harshly white, the place felt stripped bare, devoid of human history. It wasn't the same room anymore. Her death had reduced the space to the sum of its furnishings.

"The chauffeur said you were here last night," Muffin said, raising an eyebrow. She was a small woman with deep brown eyes and a wholesome alpine tan. Over the summer she'd cut her hair shorter than Kurt's and it was only now growing out, a thick tuft protruding from the back of her department cap. "I didn't realize you knew Nicole Bauer," she said.

"She won the date with me at the Les Dames benefit."

Muffin stood next to the bed, regarding the tossed sheets and rumpled quilt. "Some women have more money than good sense," she said.

He had hired her six years ago, when she was only twenty-four, a graduate of the police academy in Casper, Wyoming. He'd watched her develop into a first-rate cop, but more than that, she had remained his most loyal friend through some very difficult times. A couple of years back, when he'd nearly self-destructed during a murder investigation, Muffin was the only one who hadn't given up on him.

"The receiver was off hanging, above the floor," she said, pointing to the telephone on the night table. One of the deputies had set it back in place. "I'll check with the phone company to see if there were any calls."

She bent down to read the label on an empty bottle of Macallan Scotch. Ice melted in a tumbler with a trace of lipstick on the rim. "Looks like she was hitting the sauce pretty hard," Muffin said. "Did she seem inebriated when you left her?"

Nicole had enjoyed expensive single malts. During their brief affair she'd tried to make a Scotch drinker out of Kurt.

"No," he said. He thought about their last embrace, her body soft and warm. An hour's sleep had sobered her. "A couple of drinks, that's all."

He opened the night table drawer. Among Nicole's tubes and fragrant vials lay the Beretta .25 and the amber bear-shaped earrings she had worn last night. He pushed them aside and rummaged through her effects. "There were some letters tied with a red ribbon," he said. "They were on this table. Has anyone taken them?"

"We haven't touched anything."

He opened the container of Risperidone with its sticker forbidding alcohol. Only four pills remained.

"Why don't you leave everything alone," Muffin advised, stepping closer to have a look at the contents of the drawer. "In case there's more to this than a simple suicide."

He stared at her with a dazed expression, more surprised at his own conflicted feelings than by what she had just said. In spite of all the evidence, it hadn't sunk in yet that Nicole had taken her own life.

"Those letters are very important," he said, returning the pills to the drawer and closing it.

"What letters are you talking about?"

"Hate mail," he said. "Somebody was making obscene threats and she wanted me to do something about it."

He suddenly remembered the ring. Nicole had thrown it against the hearth screen. He walked over to the fireplace and knelt down to search the carpet, sweeping his hands through the thick sand-colored piling.

"Are you looking for this, Kurt?" Muffin opened her glove and the ring appeared in her hand as if she were performing a magician's trick. "I noticed it earlier and wondered what it was doing on the floor."

He stood up and took the ring from her, studying the *I Ching* engravings, running his finger along the inside of the band. The gold was as smooth and worn as his mother's wedding ring. It had worked itself around someone's finger for more than a few years.

"How did you know it was there?" Muffin asked with a strangely accusatory tone, as if she'd caught him in a compromising lie.

"The ring was in one of the letters," he said, gazing into the cold fireplace. "She got angry and threw it."

"You seem to know your way around this room pretty well. Kyle says you were here until two A.M., when he drove you into town."

He knew where she was going with this. She wanted him to tell her the truth. Every detail. He had tried to keep something from her in another investigation and the lie had nearly destroyed their friendship. It had nearly ended his career.

"I don't know what time it was," he said, the slipknot of another lie. "We left the Jerome around eleven and came here. The date was an excuse to show me the letters. She was upset about them and wanted to know what could be done."

Muffin crossed her arms and leaned against a bedpost. "You're in the woman's bedroom until two in the morning," she said, her eyes following the path to the glass doors. "A couple hours later she jumps off her deck. Call me old-fashioned, Kurt, but it doesn't look good. What do you think the newspapers are going to do with this? Especially with the recall vote coming up."

He lifted the poker from its rack and stirred the ashes in the hearth. Had Nicole tossed the letters in the fire? "They've been looking for an excuse to take Smerlas's side," he said. "I guess they've got one now."

Muffin chucked back the bill of her cap. "Jesus, Kurt," she

said with an impatient sigh. "Better get Corky on the line to do some quick damage control."

He churned the ashes, searching for shreds of paper. He felt his emotions surging to the surface, a tightness in his throat. Nicole had asked for his help and he had doubted her and treated the entire matter lightly and now she was dead.

"The letters pushed her over the edge," he said, groping for an explanation.

He tried to imagine how it could have happened. Nicole lying in bed, rereading the letters by candlelight after he'd gone, fretting over the threats, frightened that Rocky was alive and coming for her. A shadow crosses the room. Wind rattles the glass doors. Something makes her panic and leap to her feet. Something makes her run.

"They were written by a very sick individual," he said.

The poker turned up a small ragged square of paper ash. He bent down and examined the charred fragment, less than a quarter of a page. The word GASH, cut and pasted from a magazine, was all that remained.

"She burned them," he said, staring at the word. Nicole was dead, but whoever had written the letters was still very much alive. "Get one of the guys to bag these ashes. Let's salvage as much as we can."

Muffin sat down on the edge of the bed and gazed absently at the scuffed toes of her boots. He didn't like the hard set of her jaw. Anger or disappointment usually followed that expression, sometimes both.

"You'll have to take yourself off the case, Kurt," she said.

He wasn't willing to do that.

"When is the recall vote?" she asked, looking up at him. "Two weeks?"

He nodded.

"You might go down," she said without a trace of sentiment. "But I'm not letting you take the department with you."

6

As MUFFIN ESCORTED him down the stairs Kurt noticed Kyle sitting near the fireplace in the great room, his long blond hair snarled around his face as if he too had awoken in a blizzard dream. His coloring appeared more gray than tan now and he stared at the cherrywood floor, troubled and remote, his body slumped into sharp angles under a wrinkled white dress shirt and chauffeur pants, his handsome cheekbones hardened by what he'd witnessed from the deck. Deputy Gill Dotson was interrogating him, scribbling on a notepad.

"I'd like to ask Kyle some questions," Kurt said.

"No," Muffin said firmly, taking his arm.

Kyle heard their voices and glanced up, his eyes dark and hollow and unforgiving. "Why don't you ask *him*?" he said to the deputy. "He was the one partying with her half the night."

Kurt stopped to stare at the young man. "Come on," Muffin said, her nails pressing into his arm. "That's exactly why you don't belong here."

"I want to hear what Kyle has to say," Kurt said, trying to shrug her off.

"Let Dotson do his job," she said, steering him toward the double doors with surprising force.

In the parking circle outside the front entrance, three department cruisers sat at the end of long, curving tire trails in the snow. "I'm not sure what happened to her," Muffin said, "but if the coroner finds something hinky, Smerlas and the other commissioners will want to know why the last man to see her alive was poking around the crime scene. I imagine the family would question that, too."

The formidable Bauer family. "Have you notified them yet?"

"As soon as I get you out of here," she said.

The Bauers were one of the wealthiest families in Colorado. Suddenly Kurt saw every dime he'd saved for Lennon's college education, and every dollar he would earn hereafter in this lifetime, deposited directly into a Bauer bank account because of some tenuous legal technicality proving his negligence in Nicole's death.

"That kid Kyle has been in trouble before," he said, blowing into his cupped hands. "Run a background check on him. The other one, too—Lyle."

Muffin signaled to Linda Ríos stationed at the front gate. "Don't worry, Kurt, we'll cover it. You'll have a prelim by the end of the day." She walked him to the nearest cruiser. "Linda will drive you home. Lie low for a while, okay? Take a few days off. I'll keep you posted, as things shake out."

He watched Deputy Ríos stride up the hill, her boots crunching in the fresh snow. "You'll have to take my statement, too," he said to Muffin. Now that the shock was wearing off, he was beginning to recognize the extent of the damage. To him personally, and in turn to the reputation of the office he had struggled so hard to improve.

Muffin opened the car door and gave him a slight push, lowering his head with her hand until he was seated. Now he understood how this gesture felt from the other side. "I'll do my best to keep your name out of the papers," she said.

"Don't waste your time. Half the town knows she bought a date with me last night."

Muffin closed the door and rested her forearms on the window frame. He could smell her minty mouthwash. "Is today the day you're doing that town hall thing with Smerlas?"

In all of the confusion he had forgotten. This afternoon he was scheduled to debate Ben Smerlas at the Wheeler Opera House. Another public relations event arranged by Corky Marcus.

"My advice, develop a sudden case of laryngitis. Tell Corky to cancel," she said. "This thing is going to hit the streets running, and by six o'clock it'll be on everybody's box. Nicole Bauer has always made good copy."

He dropped his head back against the seat rest and closed his eyes. He felt exhausted and sick to his stomach. A sharp wind was blowing snow off the cruiser's hood. He could hear the two women conversing quietly outside his door and he imagined they were deciding what to do with him. When Linda Ríos slid behind the wheel she refused to look at him or speak, and he had the feeling she'd been instructed to drive him over a cliff.

7

As SOON AS he got home he phoned Corky Marcus and woke him with the news. Corky muttered something unintelligible in Yiddish, cleared his throat, and began to groan. He sounded like Kurt's aging mother. "I'm sorry, man," Corky said after several seconds of guttural noises. "How in God's name did it happen?"

"We don't know yet. It looks like a suicide."

"And you were there till when? How late did you say?"

Kurt told him and Corky moaned again. "The recall vote is two weeks away," he said, "and a woman commits suicide after one date with you. This is not a strong endorsement."

"You're such a caring guy, Corky."

"Okay, okay," he said, excited now, fully awake and irritated. "You want sympathy—here, talk to Carole. I'm getting up. I've got to save a man from himself."

He could hear the fumbling sounds of a telephone being passed off, and then Carole's voice, deep and sleepy: "Mmnh? What's going on, Kurt? What, uh, what happened?"

Corky was complaining in the background while he dressed, and the tension rose in Carole's voice as she tried to conduct a three-way conversation. "She's what, Kurt? *Dead?*" He could hear her gasp. "Oh my lord, that's horrible." She caught her breath. "Are you okay, hon?"

"I'm not sure," he said, comforted by the sound of her morning voice. He liked Carole Marcus in more ways than were sensible.

"Start the coffee," she said. "We'll be right over."

"You don't have to do that, Carole. I'm fine."

"Would you stop being such a fucking pain!" she shouted, then giggled at Kurt's shocked silence. "Sorry, Kurt. Not you, dear. Corky is driving me crazy with his goddamned kvetching."

"Tell him to chill. I don't care about the recall. It doesn't matter."

She muffled the telephone and said something to Corky. "Eww, that man . . . Listen—you need me, I'll be there. Okay? I'm going to put some clothes on—if Corky will let me."

Kurt smiled. He didn't think he would ever smile again. "Sorry I ruined your Saturday morning."

There was a slight pause. "Oh." Carole laughed. "No, no," she said, "I didn't mean it that way. Are you kidding? We don't have Saturday mornings anymore."

They had three boys: eight, ten, and twelve years old.

"If you need any help with Lennon," she said, "I'll be happy to take him. Josh and Seth are always thrilled when he comes over."

"He's with Meg today," he said. "Let's wait and see if reporters start swarming around our house."

After he hung up, he lit a fire in the woodstove and made his way to the study with a cup of strong coffee. The blinds were open and the morning appeared gray and cold, more like a sullen winter's day back east. He couldn't remember the last time an early snow had stayed on the ground until ski season.

Sitting down at his computer he clicked on an Internet search engine and typed the word *Risperidone*. There were three hits. According to the first article, it was an antipsychotic drug prescribed for people who suffered delusional depression and various personality disorders. "Antipsychotics such as Risperidone have sedating effects," the article said. "But their major effect is to reduce psychotic thinking and behavior."

He sat back in his chair and gazed numbly at the screen. Nicole was being treated for mental illness. Perhaps he should have recognized the signs. But her behavior had been no more erratic than that of the other pampered rich women he knew in Aspen.

The article was a highly technical treatise on symptoms, medication, and side effects. He printed out the eleven pages and read them a second time, slowly absorbing the language. One passage stated that if Risperidone were mixed with alcohol, the psychosis would become more acute. "Potential side effects include insomnia, agitation, akasthisia, and anxiety." He wondered if mixing Scotch and Risperidone could have conjured up a ghost from the past.

Reaching into his pants pocket he retrieved the ring Muffin had found on the bedroom floor. He studied the eight trigram symbols, some ancient code of the *I Ching*. If Muffin knew he had kept Rocky's ring, she would be all over him right now, reciting proper procedure, demanding its return. He didn't give a damn. The ring was the only link to those letters, and he was certain that the letters had led to Nicole's breakdown.

On a shelf below his father's library of moldy German tomes, the family Underwood typewriter sat hiding beneath its original cloth slipcover, untouched for countless years. The machine was as awkward as an anvil, but Kurt carried it back to the desk and blew dust off the keys. He scrolled a sheet of typing paper into the carriage and pecked out a few phrases. *Now is the time for all good men* . . . The ribbon was weak, in need of replacement. Did they make these ribbons anymore? *It was the best of times, it was the worst of times.* . . . The typeface was as he remembered it—and identical to the one used in the letters to Nicole. But unless the deputies recovered more pages from the ash, there was no evidence that the letters had existed at all.

He rose from the chair to get another cup of coffee and noticed the message light blinking on the recorder. There was a single call waiting for him. He tapped the play button, remembering the phone ringing in his sleep.

"Kurt! Are you there, darling? Please pick up! Please, Kurt."

It was Nicole. The sound of her voice sent a shiver through him.

"It's him—he's alive! I've heard his voice. Please pick up, I need you! You've got to stop him, Kurt. He says he's going to kill me!"

She began to cry, a husky choking sob, and then the line went dead. After a moment's pause the recorder's mechanical voice intoned "Four-oh-eight A.M., Saturday."

He stared at the machine, shaken by what he'd heard. Kyle had told the deputies that Nicole's scream woke him around four-thirty. She had made this call only minutes before she ran out onto the snowy deck.

He played the tape again, forcing himself to listen. Was she hallucinating—blown out of her mind on booze and pills? Or was there something to what she was saying? *I've heard his voice. . . . He says he's going to kill me.* They had found the receiver hanging off the telephone.

Kurt dropped deadweight into the chair and dialed Muffin's beeper. Then he called the office and left word on her voice mail: "Hey, this is Kurt. You've got to access Nicole's phone records ASAP. Something has come up. Call me right away."

He slumped back in the chair and picked up the ring lying on the desk. In his trembling hand the tarnished gold coil felt as heavy as a bolt. He closed his fist and squeezed hard, imprinting the symbols into his palm. There was no doubt in his mind that the letters had shattered her fragile psyche. They had uncovered a past she had wanted desperately to bury.

*I've spent half my inheritance in therapy trying to forget that
night. I even married my shrink so I could get free home care.*

The name on her prescription container.

He lifted the receiver and dialed directory assistance. Within
moments he had reached a young female voice, fully awake and
beaming good cheer. "Elk Mountain Wellness Center," she
chirped. He could picture the rosy glow of her cheeks. "How
may I help you?"

"This is Kurt Muller, Pitkin County Sheriff," he said, hearing
the sharp contrast of his own voice, all hoarseness and fatigue.
"I would like to speak with Dr. Jay Westbrook, please."

"Do you want to schedule a session with Dr. Westbrook,
sir?"

"Yes, I do," he said. "But not for the usual reasons."

8

THE JEEP TIRES streaked through the thin layer of snow on Highway 82 as Kurt steered downvalley toward Watson Divide. Five miles past the access to Snowmass Village he turned west onto a two-lane county road that hugged the creek on its course down from Elk Mountain. At the mouth of this small green valley, ice crystals sparkled on the ponderosa pines and the overnight snow clung to antelope brush. The road led onward past the abandoned geodesic domes of the Star Meadow Holistic Institute and the groomed pastures where clever hobby ranchers grazed alpacas and miniature show ponies. In another mile he had reached the stark archway that signaled the entrance to Elk Mountain Ranch. There was no fence of any kind to mark the property line, only a sign that said POSTED: NO HUNTING and 150 acres of open land.

Kurt could see the old pine lodge tucked into the spruce grove at the base of the mountain. The lodge had been built by a group of pioneer entrepreneurial outdoorsmen in the late 1930s, a full decade before Aspen opened its ski area to the public. Elk hunters, Olympic bobsled racers, maverick venture capitalists had been lured to the Maroon Bells Wilderness by a local silver miner looking for investors. But the men quickly lost interest in what was deep inside the earth once they'd explored the pristine backcountry snow and the breathtaking vistas of the Colorado Rockies. One of them had ties to Sun Valley and knew that America would soon discover the great winter sport so popular in Europe. He convinced his partners to build here, less than ten miles from the sleepy, run-down village of Aspen, where they could retreat for the necessities—groceries and mail and an occasional drink at the only tavern in town. Above them in this hidden valley rose the magnificent Elk Range, 3,600 feet of vertical drop down some of the most rugged, unspoiled slopes in the West. They knew this terrain would challenge the best skiers from around the world.

The private ranch road curved off toward Snowmass Creek, its clear gleaming waters running shallow over ice and broken rock. A huge bull elk was tasting the snowmelt not fifty yards upstream. At the sound of the Jeep engine the animal lifted its grizzled head, gazed implacably in Kurt's direction, then resumed drinking without concern. Several single-room cabins were spread along the near bank, leftover ski huts now serving as visitor housing for the soul-searchers who had come to Jay Westbrook's retreat seeking peace and solitude. Except for smoke curling from one galvanized chimney pipe, there was no sign that any of the cabins were occupied.

As Kurt approached the lodge he counted a dozen sport utility vehicles parked out front under the trees. Dr. Westbrook's assistant had explained that the psychiatrist was conducting weekend group sessions this morning, and she resisted calling him to the phone until Kurt informed her that he had urgent news.

In the muddy parking lot he found a space between a Pathfinder and a Geo Tracker and got out to look at the old lodge. The building had been boarded shut the last time he was here, with his brother and their friend Jake Pfeil when they were teenagers, but that hadn't stopped them from breaking in to explore the infamous old thirty-room blunder.

Before the Second World War expert skiers from the university clubs back east had stayed here, braving the untested cirques and couloirs high in the backcountry beyond. But in the winter of 1940 three shining stars from the Dartmouth Ski Club were swept away in an avalanche near Mount Daly, and the word soon reached the ski world that this spur of the range was too unstable for even the most experienced Tyrols.

The war closed the place, and afterward Aspen, the sleepy mining village down the road, quickly developed into the most commodious resort in Colorado. The Elk Mountain Lodge was too remote, too extreme. Within a few short years the investors had abandoned their project and sold the entire piece of land to the Bauer family of Denver. Nicole and her two brothers still owned the 150 acres.

Kurt walked up the split-log steps to a wide porch beset with wicker rocking chairs. Pushing open the heavy Bavarian door, he found the old lobby in considerably better shape than the last time he'd seen it, when the building was deserted and stank like animal urine and these polished pinewood floors were as dirt-packed as a potato cellar. Now the room had presence: the quaintness of its original intention. Logs burned in the large stone fireplace. Deep, overstuffed reading chairs were arranged in a circle around an adobe pueblo surface rug. The sign-in desk was fully restored, with its original porter's gate and wall of pigeonhole boxes for room keys and messages. There was no one in the chairs or at the desk counter, and with little imagination he could believe that the lodge was inhabited entirely by hospitable ghosts.

He wandered into the cozy pine-beamed room, drawn to the sunlight glistening through the modern sliding glass doors that opened onto a rear deck. It was public knowledge that in their divorce settlement Nicole had given Jay Westbrook this lodge for his practice, along with the use of the grounds. Judging by the handsome renovation, his practice was doing well.

Kurt heard what sounded like a woman weeping somewhere down the long corridor leading to the private rooms. The eerie strain unsettled him. He was still carrying the weight of Nicole's sobbing phone call like a stone in his pocket. At a stairwell to the upper floor he stopped and listened with more concentration, trying to make out her pleading words.

Soon the weeping began again. He followed the voice down the narrow corridor off the lobby until the woman's distress grew louder and he could hear her clearly: "I can't let go, dammit! Don't you think I've tried? I've been working through this my entire adult life!"

A group therapy session was taking place in a carpeted space that may have been the billiards room in the old days. Kurt paused at the open door. People were sitting cross-legged in a circle, mostly middle-aged clients listening sympathetically to the distraught woman.

"I endorse that," said Dr. Westbrook, a bearded, barrel-chested man with squared shoulders and impressively erect posture. Kurt recognized several other faces as well. Local people with money to burn.

As soon as he saw Kurt, Westbrook nodded to a young woman, who rose alertly and hurried over to the door. "You're the sheriff, aren't you?" she said in a low voice, taking Kurt's arm and walking him back down the corridor away from the gathering. "I recognize you from the newspapers. You're a lot taller in person."

"I have to be," he said, offering no resistance. "Are you the young lady I spoke with?" He recognized the chirp in her voice.

"Uh-huh. The session will be over in a few minutes. Jay will see you then."

Her name was Tanya and she seemed less officious in person than on the phone. Late twenties, a turtleneck sweater complementing her full Teutonic figure, a long blond braid down her back.

"Is there anything I can do for you while you wait?" she asked once they'd reached the lobby. "Some herbal tea?"

"I'm fine, thanks. Unless you want to listen to some of *my* problems."

She was slow to smile. Her responsibilities were important to her. "If you're serious, I will be happy to arrange something."

"It may require electroshock."

She started to formulate a sincere reply, then caught herself, realizing he was joking. "Jay will see you shortly," she said with a dismissive frown.

Kurt watched her return down the corridor to the therapy session, then he ambled across the lobby to the glass sliding doors. Out on the deck the pine benches were dark and wet. Snow was dissolving in the morning sunlight, trickling into the roof gutters. In the distance a spruce forest belted itself around the rocky lower terrain of Elk Mountain, and Kurt could see more of those cabins nestled in the trees. Someone was sitting on the steps of a small hutch hidden within the shadows a hundred yards away, and when Kurt gave him a friendly wave the man stood up stiffly and went back inside.

Stepping over to the deck rail, Kurt cupped his hands around his eyes and gazed up the steep southwest chute into the white glare, where an alpine wind was blowing snow smoke and the ice shimmered on fir branches. The tower poles for that old T-bar lift still ran like a tight black stitch up a thousand feet of rock face. The investors had abandoned their dream before the lift was completed.

When they were seventeen, eighteen years old, Kurt and his brother and Jake Pfeil had been outlaw skiers restlessly searching for adventure, another boundary to cross, untrammeled slopes and virgin powder. They had skied in this valley since they were children and had mastered Aspen and Highlands and had even grown bored with the extreme outback of Maroon Bells and Hayden Peak. They knew the old stories about the Dartmouth skiers, and more than anything else it was that tragedy, and the boys' morbid curiosity, that had brought them to this doomed range. Arrogant, fearless, fit as Sherpas, they truly believed they were the best skiers in the Roaring Fork Valley and that no mountain could lay them low.

So one morning in the early spring of 1964 they drove the Pfeil family pickup truck to this obscure valley, where deep snowdrifts beckoned beneath the glorious sun. The county had plowed the road only up to the old ranch fence, and they had to park the truck and snowshoe a half mile to the uninhabited lodge with backpacks and skis slung over their shoulders. Those were the days before avalanche probes and Tracker DTS transceivers. They didn't even carry a rescue shovel.

After breaking in through a window and exploring the dark, feral-smelling rooms, scaring off a family of foxes holed up in the old kitchen area, they stowed their gear on this same deck where Kurt was now lost in memory and followed a trail thirty degrees uphill through the draw, tracking over deadfall and icy rocks for two hours until they topped the first summit. The view was magnificent. In the distance rose the peaks of two mountains, Daly and Clark, and between them one of the deepest, most perfectly rounded bowls of white powder they had ever seen, like a snow-filled crater of the moon.

"That's what ate them," Bert had said that day, meaning those bold young men from Dartmouth. Kurt would always remember the basin as unblemished and blessed, like the face of a sleeping child.

Jake looked at his two friends, their poles knifed in the snow. "The bitch spread her legs," he said with a scoff, "and they jumped in. Fucking amateurs."

Kurt stared into the bowl below, his lungs laboring hard after the thousand-foot climb. "It wouldn't happen to old pros like us," he said, only half serious.

The boys considered the statement in silence. They were

tempted to traverse the spiny ridge and slice down into the immaculate purity of that basin as the other skiers had done nearly twenty-five years earlier.

Minutes passed in the chill wind while they studied the unspoiled beauty. Finally Bert said, "We'd be crazy to trust her. She'll swallow us alive."

They all knew he was right. That stunning bowl was an avalanche waiting to happen.

"There's a whole world up here." Kurt had pointed with his pole, breaking the spell with more sober possibilities. "Let's go check it out."

For the next two hours they crisscrossed the terrain near the bowl, discovering other cirques and rugged paths splitting down through the fir forest. A cluster of small frozen lakes flashed sunlight off blue ice. The country felt so new and untouched they wondered if any human had ever left tracks in this snow. Cut by slash they were claiming these ridgetops as their own breathless secret.

Later it was impossible to say for certain what had triggered the slide: thawing sunshine, seismic pressures, a ski blade or the sound of their voices.

It was the end of their day and they were resting on a ledge overlooking the final plunge down three hundred yards of unknown chute toward the lodge somewhere below. They had breathed the thin air too long, enthralled with themselves and their discoveries, overcome by testosterone and hubris and the maniacal competition between teenage boys. They were out of water and Bert's stomach was cramping, Jake's lips were sticky from dehydration, Kurt was exhausted. His quads twitched uncontrollably, a raging fire from his heels to the base of his spine.

"Come on, ladies. Up on your feet," Jake had barked like a weary master sergeant. "Let's go for it."

They were only sixty yards down the chute when they heard the roar behind them. Kurt looked over his shoulder and saw the white cloud and huge chunks of snow hurling downward, sluicing the narrow rock channel carved into the mountainside. Panic-stricken, Bert waved his pole at his younger brother, entreating Kurt to catch up. Each boy raced for survival now, the avalanche bearing down on their strapped heels.

"Sheriff Muller," someone said. "I'm sorry we have to meet under these circumstances."

A bone-chilling vapor swirled around them. They could feel the snow giving way beneath their strokes, set off by the noise echoing through the chute. They poled faster, skiing for their lives, but the avalanche kept roaring after them.

"Sheriff Muller?"

Kurt turned around to face a short, stocky man wearing wire-rimmed glasses and a cardigan sweater, brown corduroy trousers, Rockport dress boots. He appeared to be in his late fifties now, his trim gray beard streaked with red. Twenty years ago, when the Bauers had brought him into Nicole's defense team, his beard was as red as a Norseman's.

"Jay Westbrook," the psychiatrist said, offering his hand.

"Sorry," Kurt said, grinning apologetically, shaking hands. "You caught me daydreaming, Doctor."

With a warm smile Westbrook cupped his other hand firmly over the top of their mutual grip, the sympathetic double handshake of a minister or undertaker. "Memories," he said. "They trap us all."

"Or worse," Kurt said.

He noticed the clients milling about the lobby on break, making their way toward the deck for fresh air. "Is there somewhere we can talk in private?" he asked.

Westbrook led him through a deck entrance to his office, a large converted space, two lodge bedrooms with the common wall removed. Pine paneling, bookshelves filled with hefty volumes, file cabinets side by side in an orderly row, a majestic walnut desk arranged with tidy stacks of notes and pink message slips. Against the opposite wall sat the requisite couch, a glass coffee table, and a stately high-backed chair. The wall above the couch was arrayed with dozens of small amateur artworks, the kind rendered for doctors by their patients.

"Thank you for agreeing to meet with me," Kurt said. "I know you're a busy man."

"Your phone call came as quite a shock," Westbrook said, directing Kurt to the couch while he stepped over to a hot-plate nook and placed tea bags in two decorative mugs. "Forgive me if I seem a little dazed. I'm having a hard time processing this," he said, pouring water from a steaming kettle. "We were married for fifteen years."

He brought the two mugs of steeping tea to the coffee table and sat down in the high-backed chair across from Kurt.

"I'm aware that Miz Bauer had a history of psychiatric care," Kurt said. "Had she ever attempted suicide before?"

Westbrook laced his fingers and stared at the steam curling from the two mugs. Time passed while he was lost in contemplation. "Yes, she had," he said finally. "Soon after the Rocky Rhodes trial."

Kurt could see that this was still delicate ground.

"Unfortunately, over the past year she seemed to be regressing to that painful period in her life," he said, "reopening old wounds. I was concerned for her stability."

"Is that why you prescribed Risperidone?"

His eyes widened, showing surprise that Kurt would know about her medication. "Nicole had been on and off antipsychotics for many years," he said, bending forward to dip the tea bag up and down in his mug. "She was experiencing a relatively long period of equilibrium when that disturbed young woman tried to break in to her house. The incident sent her into a downward spiral."

"I'm familiar with the case," Kurt said.

"Yes, that's how Nicole met you, isn't it?"

Now it was Kurt's turn to show surprise. Until this moment he hadn't considered the possibility that Nicole might have revealed their affair to someone else. Say, her longtime therapist and ex-husband. Suddenly he felt ill at ease. He shifted about on the couch, searching for a more comfortable position. Instead of two professionals, cop and shrink, examining the motivations of a suicide, the conversation had taken a strange, more personal turn.

"The break-in left all her vulnerabilities exposed," Westbrook added. "She was grateful that you gave her case so much attention. You must be a very conscientious police officer, Sheriff Muller."

Although the compliment appeared straightforward, Kurt felt the slightest undertow of another man's envy.

"She discussed it with you?" he asked, unsure himself if he meant the break-in or the affair.

Westbrook nodded. "Even after the divorce I was always there for her. An emotional crutch," he said. "She knew she could confide in me."

"So you continued to be her therapist? She came to you for counseling?"

"That's correct." His round bearded face grew animated. "Why let a bad marriage ruin a good relationship?"

A bad marriage. At the time of their divorce the Aspen gossip mill had circulated the story that Westbrook could no longer tolerate Nicole's infidelities. But Nicole herself had once mentioned to Kurt, during their own brief affair, that the divorce was her idea. She had told Kurt that living with a psychiatrist was like living in a laboratory where every utterance was examined and dissected. Their life together had become too claustrophobic, she'd said. Too confining.

Restless, Kurt stood up from the couch and wandered over to the wall where the doctor's diplomas were hanging in frames. "Did she tell you about the letters?" he asked, reading the inscribed parchment. M.D., Tulane School of Medicine. Alpha Psychiatric Institute of Denver.

"Which letters, Sheriff?"

Kurt bent down to watch a lone fish gliding in the green-glowing aquarium below the diplomas. It was an exotic golden creature with delicate tendrils floating about like ribbons. "The ones she started receiving a couple of weeks ago," he said.

"Can you be more specific?" Westbrook said.

"Death threats," Kurt said, turning to face him. "A half dozen in all, the same sender."

The psychiatrist's eyes shrank behind the wire-rimmed glasses. He issued another comprehending nod. "Nicole received hate mail for years, Sheriff. Deranged fans of the late Rocky Rhodes. Every time a new generation discovered his music and learned how the great rock star died, they turned on the person they thought was responsible. And then the letters came. Angry, obscene, threatening," he said, his face conveying pity for the kind of people who sent them. "They blamed Nicole for killing their god."

The vicious words flashed through Kurt's mind: *evil fucking cunts.* "She showed me the latest ones," he said. "They were very convincing."

"Is there any reason to believe they were different from all the others?"

"Nicole seemed to think so," Kurt said. "They were from Rocky Rhodes himself."

The psychiatrist sipped his tea and raised an eyebrow, as if he'd been told a joke in poor taste.

"Someone claiming to be Rocky," Kurt explained. "Nicole was certain it was him. She thought Rocky was alive and planning to kill her."

Westbrook took some time to respond, then spoke in a measured tone. "Nicole was a delusional paranoid, Sheriff Muller. She had suffered a long acquaintance with the imaginary," he said, his voice dropping into a solemn confidentiality. "Some of the persecution was real, of course. The occasional harassment, the bad press. And she certainly had been shunned by Aspen society."

His face softened, as if he himself had endured the same rejections. Despite the popularity of his practice, their fifteen years together must have forced him into an awkward social isolation. "She had fantasies about Rocky all the time," he said. "A recurring nightmare that lingered with her throughout her waking hours. She always believed he would come back someday and take revenge."

"The letters were for real, Dr. Westbrook. Whoever was pretending to be Rocky did a damned good job."

Suddenly it occurred to him that the person most familiar with Nicole's bedtime rituals—and the intimate details of her relationship with Rocky—was the husband-psychiatrist sipping tea from his arty ceramic mug.

"It was someone who had known Nicole extremely well," Kurt said.

Westbrook stifled a smile. "Yes, my friend, you're certainly right about that," he said, removing his glasses and fogging a lens with his breath.

Kurt was losing his patience. "Those letters were probably what tipped the balance," he said. "They may have been responsible for her suicide."

The two men stared at each other in silence.

"Sheriff Muller, I know exactly what the letters say." Without his glasses the psychiatrist looked older, hollow-eyed, worn. "Whatever else is in them, they eventually make their way to Nicole's sexual proclivities—what turned her on and what made her climax. There are explicit descriptions of the pagan goddess rituals she surrounded herself with when she was aroused and ready for her mate. Am I correct?"

Kurt swallowed dryly. "Close enough," he said. "Do you know who wrote the letters, Doctor?"

"Yes, I do," Westbrook said, working a lens with his handkerchief. "Nicole wrote them herself."

The hairs stood up on the back of Kurt's neck.

"She played that game for years. I have to admit I fell for it myself the first time."

Westbrook rose and went to his desk to retrieve a set of keys, then unlocked a file cabinet and rolled out a drawer. After a few moments of thumbing through the dividers he found the folder he was looking for and held it up as evidence. "I've collected some of her more creative missives," he said, dropping the folder onto his desk blotter. "She pretended they were from old lovers. Usually anonymous, but once or twice she used Rocky's name to get my attention." The psychiatrist gazed across the room at Kurt and smiled sadly. "I agree with you that her writing skills were quite convincing."

Kurt was having difficulty finding his voice. "May I see them?" he asked.

"I'm afraid not, Sheriff. Client confidentiality. Even a dead woman has a right to privacy."

"Why did she write them?"

"She was a very disturbed woman. There are no simple explanations," Westbrook said. "She resorted to this game when she was desperate and in fear of losing someone. And frankly, she enjoyed the melodrama. The letters gave her a rush."

He studied Kurt with bemused pity. "Nicole was a very alluring woman," he said, smiling sympathetically. "Feel flattered that she chose you to play the game."

It wasn't flattery Kurt felt but anger and humiliation. Nicole had wrapped him around her finger. She had used the break-in to seduce the naive cop who had symbolically rescued her. He imagined it had happened the same way twenty years ago with her psychiatrist, the stable authority figure assigned to rescue her from a prosecutor bent on sending her to prison for murder. Kurt knew that if they trusted each other, he and Westbrook, this would be the moment when they faced their own complicity—how the holding of her hand and a few consoling words had quickly led to the sweet scent of jasmine and sandalwood.

But what about the phone message? If Nicole had written the letters, why had she called with such terror in her voice? *It's*

him—he's alive! It couldn't have been an act. Unless she was
. . . what? Completely deranged. As truly psychotic as Westbrook had diagnosed her.

Kurt reached into his pants pocket and found Rocky's ring.
"Have you ever seen this before?" He crossed the room and
dropped the ring into Westbrook's hand.

The psychiatrist examined the *I Ching* symbols. "No, not
that I recall," he said. "Should I have?"

"You never saw it in Nicole's possession?"

He studied the ring more closely, measuring its weight in his
palm. "It's a man's ring, isn't it?"

Kurt nodded.

Westbrook shrugged and returned the heavy gold band. "She
had so many things like this," he said. "There were dozens of
baubles that meant something special to her. I would venture to
say she collected jewelry like she collected companions. Something new and dear every week."

Kurt felt the psychiatrist's eyes follow him as he turned
toward the deck doors and the morning sunshine warming the
glass. Gazing outside, he could see the old T-bar framework and
the deep draw through the mountains and the narrow seam that
had been his escape from that snow slide in 1964. Today it
looked like a thin white tributary branching off course at forty-
five degrees, but back when they were racing for their lives the
opening seemed as wide as a canyon. Bert had spotted the fis-
sure ahead and waved them over, and they had shredded
through the cutoff while the avalanche thundered past them
down the main chute toward the valley floor. If the side trail
hadn't been there that day, the Mullers and Jake Pfeil would now
be distant memories in the local lore like those daring Dartmouth boys whose bodies hadn't surfaced until the summer
thaw.

"The way it happened, it could've been an accident," Kurt
said, forcing himself back to the present. He turned to stare at

Westbrook. "Something frightened her and she bolted for the doors." A voice from her past on the telephone? "She didn't seem to be fully aware of where her actions would lead her."

"Yes," Westbrook said thoughtfully, nodding, agreeing with Kurt's observation. "It sounds like the behavior of a very disoriented person."

"I discovered the Risperidone in her drawer. Had you cautioned her not to drink alcohol while she was taking it?"

Westbrook appeared wounded by the question. "Nicole was well informed about her medication," he said defensively. "She knew the rules."

Kurt wanted to make his point. "But as you know, Dr. Westbrook, she'd had problems with substance abuse and alcohol in the past. She dearly loved her Scotch. Did you consider the possibility that she would drink while she was on Risperidone, and that the results might be dangerous to her?"

"She gave me her word she wouldn't drink," the psychiatrist said, disappointment smothering his words. "I can't count how many times I tried to persuade her to enter a rehab program to get help for her addictive behavior."

"I've done a little research on Risperidone. Mixed with alcohol it can cause hallucinations."

Westbrook held up his hand, a gesture calling for patience and sound judgment. "Let's wait for the autopsy report—shall we?—before we rush to any conclusions about her physiological condition."

There was a knock at the door. Someone in the corridor spoke Westbrook's name. "Yes?" he said with a faint note of irritation.

The door cracked open and Tanya's smiling face appeared. "The break is over, Jay," she said. "Will you be joining us, or should I tell them you're delayed?"

He took a deep breath to calm himself and gazed across the room at Kurt. "Yes, darling, tell them I'll be right along," he said. The soft intimacy in his voice made Kurt wonder if Westbrook and Tanya were lovers. "I believe the sheriff and I have reached the end of our discussion."

He searched his desk drawer for a pencil, a notepad. "Thank you for driving out to speak with me personally," he said, jotting something on the yellow pad. "Nicole's death is a loss we all must bear. Those of us who loved her will always feel guilty that we didn't do more to help."

Kurt understood the guilt. He could still hear Nicole's desperate voice on the message recorder: *Are you there, darling? Please pick up, I need you!*

He took one last look around the pinewood office. Every inch of space was carefully arranged to provide a warm, safe haven for the troubled souls seeking Westbrook's guidance. "You've got a nice place here, Doctor," he said. "Will you be able to hang on to it now that Nicole is dead?"

The psychiatrist's head snapped up from whatever he was writing and he straightened his shoulders. The question seemed to annoy him. "Under the circumstances I haven't given it much thought," he said.

"I hope you get along with her brothers."

Westbrook bristled. "I do," he said, visibly offended. "We've been family for quite a long time."

Kurt nodded. Meg's brother still called him every now and then from California. "Right," he added with a smile. "Why let a bad marriage ruin a good relationship?"

He slid open the glass door, the way he had come in. The outside air was cool and sweet with woodsmoke. Wind rustled the spruce trees at the foot of the mountain.

"One final question, Doctor," he said, pausing at the doorway. "In those letters you've collected, did Nicole ever mention the name Pariah?"

Westbrook regarded Kurt with professional curiosity. "Yes, I'm familiar with Pariah," he said, not entirely surprised that Kurt knew the name.

"Who is she? Or should I say, Who was she?"

The psychiatrist studied him in silence, his face suddenly pale and drawn. "Pariah was the bad girl. The one Rocky hated. The femme fatale the whole world blamed for killing a legend," he said. "Sheriff Muller, whenever Nicole had sunk to the depths of her depression and was feeling persecuted, Pariah was the secret name she called herself."

9

KURT DROVE BACK down the ranch road to the creek and got out
of his Jeep to throw rocks in the stream. As a boy he had learned
to calm down by walking along Hunter Creek in total solitude
and hurling rocks at whatever floated by. His own personal therapy. The hourly rate was considerably cheaper than Westbrook's.

He brushed the snow off a chunk of sandstone and hummed
it at a frozen tree root embedded in thin ice, remembering what
Muffin had once observed about the women he had become involved with: "It's none of my business, Kurt, but these past few
years since your divorce you've covered some pretty rough
ground in your private life. I imagine it's enough to make you
wonder about yourself."

They were fly-fishing together not long after Kurt had tried
to save his boyhood sweetheart from dying violently in a Las
Vegas parking garage.

"It's the life," Muffin had said, standing thigh deep in the
Fryingpan River several yards downstream from him. "Let me
give you some cheap advice you don't want to hear. Stay away
from the women you come across on the job. They're halfway
gone by the time you meet them. Busted luck, heavy baggage,

some kind of Oprah tragedy making every one of them miserable. You need to find yourself a nice stable lady who loves dogs and children and putters around in her garden. Somebody who isn't beaten up by her past."

Kurt picked up another rock and watched a harem of elk emerge from the dense stand of willow trees on the opposite bank, a dozen cows with their calves meandering upstream. It was the rutting season and the old bull he had seen earlier was trailing close behind, 700 pounds of meat and 40 pounds of antler, sniffing Kurt's scent in the wind and barking to warn the others of danger.

The cell phone chirped in the Jeep, disrupting the serenity of the moment. He chucked the rock into the stream and jogged back to respond to the call.

"Hey, Kurt, got your message," Muffin said. "I filed the request for Miz Bauer's phone log. We could have it by the end of the day."

Within these mountains where the elk roamed unharmed, the line connection was weak and her voice wavered in and out.

"Lean on them. I want to know if someone called her around four A.M., just before she jumped."

"What makes you think that?"

He wasn't ready to tell her about Nicole's message. Not yet. Without corroborating evidence Muffin would dismiss the call as the rantings of a madwoman. "The phone was off the hook," he said. "I've got a gut feeling."

"Okay, whatever. I'm on it."

"What did you find out about the Menendez twins?"

"The chauffeur, Kyle Martin, has two priors," she said. "Destruction of property in Pitkin—that fence he sawed down—and criminal trespass last year in Utah. He and two accomplices tried to free fifteen hundred minks at a fur farm near Provo. They were apprehended by the owners and turned over to the local sheriff."

Mink. Elk. "Another animal rights freak," Kurt said.

"Which explains how he and Miz Bauer found each other."

Rumors had persisted for years that Nicole Bauer had secretly financed the 1990 antifur initiative, a proposal to ban the wearing of dead animals on your person in Aspen. The initiative ultimately failed at the ballot box, but the volatile debate had left its mark on the town's conscience. Few women wore furs in public anymore, even to the ritzy ski-season galas. And when they did, they could be overheard explaining, *It's an old family heirloom, darling, left to me by my grandmother. I just couldn't throw it out.*

"It so happens she was the one who paid Kyle's fine for the fence damage and bailed him out of the county tank," Muffin said.

Kurt gazed upstream. The elk had found their way to an aspen grove, where they were busy stripping the bark off the slender trees. "Any idea what kind of relationship they had?" he asked, trying to conceal the resentment behind his question.

"He says she was like a big sister to him. Poor kid lost it when he told us how he looked over the railing and saw a white form on the rocks below."

Kurt closed his eyes. He didn't want to see Nicole's body the way they'd found her. "What about the other one—Lyle?"

"Lyle Gunderson. He grew up here. No sheet. Seems pretty clean," she said. "You know his parents, don't you? Gus and Marjie, local art crowd. They sent Lyle to Reed College a couple of years ago but he flunked out or something and came on back home."

Kurt had crossed paths with the Gundersons over the years. Gus taught ceramics at the Anderson Ranch Art School and Marjie had conducted seminars in New Age healing at Star Meadow before the center closed down. She was a friend of Kurt's ex-wife, Meg.

"Did you bag those ashes in the fireplace?" he asked.

"Yeah, we brought it all down to the department for a closer look. Murphy is sifting through it right now. It's a mess, Kurt. He hasn't found anything you didn't."

If they were able to recover a few pages he would show them to Westbrook and verify if the language and typeface matched Nicole's earlier compositions.

"Burned letters are the least of our worries," Muffin said. "The wolves are knocking on our door."

"The press?"

"Worse. The Bauer family."

He knew this was coming.

"Her two brothers will be in soon, Learjet from Denver. They're bringing their own medical examiner. They insist that he be allowed to observe the autopsy."

"Is that some kind of religious conviction?" Kurt asked.

"They make the rules as they go," Muffin said.

The Bauers had money, they had political clout, they had strong ties to the religious Right. Their dynasty had begun four generations ago with hardrock mining in Colorado. Great-grandfather Walter Bauer, Sr., was the one who had hired goons to shoot up striking miners in Telluride and Ludlow. Over the next eighty years the family had branched into banking and real estate, and had even produced a popular soft-drink beverage called High Country Delight. Nicole's early lifestyle had mocked everything the Bauer name stood for.

"Why don't you come in and write up your statement," Muffin said. "Get it out of the way before the Bauer boys show up and start asking hard questions."

He could hear the misgivings in her voice. She didn't know if he had done anything wrong, but he was her friend and partner and they had been through hell together more than once. She would do everything she could to protect him, whether he deserved it or not.

"And Kurt," she added, her words ringing loud and clear through the static: "Do us both a favor and bring back the ring."

10

HE KNEW SOMETHING was wrong as soon as he opened the storm door and heard the music. Loud, haunting guitar chords, the stereo turned up to full volume, vibrating the glass in the windows. There were no vehicles under the parking shed, so it wasn't Meg and Lennon. He unzipped his leather jacket and withdrew the Smith & Wesson .45 from his shoulder holster, then quickly crossed the mud porch and nudged open the front door, dropping to one knee and pointing the pistol into the dusky living room.

Someone had closed all the blinds. The air reeked of marijuana. Kurt could see the refrigerator door hanging open in the kitchen, the light shining. If he didn't know better, he would have guessed his eight-year-old son had hitchhiked back home transformed into a metal-head teenager.

"I have a gun!" he shouted, his words drowned by the music. He shouted again, louder this time, trying to make himself heard: "Let me see you with your hands on your head!"

No one stirred. At first glance nothing appeared to be out of place. The house remained intact, a dated still life of flower vases and knotty pine paneling and old furniture that hadn't changed since his mother had left it to him a decade ago. Gripping the pistol with both hands, he stood up and ventured into the living room, his eyes searching for sudden movement. He knew the song booming from the stereo. He had listened to this album a million times when he was younger. Rocky Rhodes singing his heart out behind his wailing Rickenbacker guitar. "Blue Midnight," his signature piece.

Every pore in his body opened up, streaming sweat. The .45 felt slippery in his hands. "Come out and show yourself!" he barked. In the back of his head a small edgy voice began to whisper what his body already knew.

On the floor near the stereo Kurt's ancient collection of tattered, taped-together album covers lay strewn about like a game of 52 Pickup with a large deck of cards. The intruder had shuffled through them looking for this record to play. With one eye on far doorways and dark corners, Kurt lifted the lid on the turntable and removed the needle with a clumsy scratch, and the house fell into a deafening silence. But his ears were still ringing and his heart kept pounding to the heavy beat of Rocky's drummer.

There was a cool draft through the house, a sure sign that someone had left the door open to the rear deck. He made his way across the living room with his arms extended, the pistol raised, his finger on the trigger. Skirting past the counter that cordoned off the kitchen area, he noticed a crushed beer can next to a bag of tortilla chips split open and spilled across the tiles. The son of a bitch had certainly made himself at home.

The sliding door had been smashed by a two-by-four from Kurt's unfinished construction project out on the deck. There was a clear trail of footprints in the slush, leading to and from the door, but the sun was strong and the prints were already evaporating, spreading wide and leaking through the cracks. He hurried over to the rail and gazed in both directions, first at his backyard and then down the hill toward Red Mountain Road. There was no one in sight.

He went back inside and checked the house thoroughly, the closets, the showers, the narrow spaces underneath the beds. Then he walked back through each room and checked everything again. By the time he had holstered the .45 his wrists were aching from the strain. Exhausted, his energy depleted after the heavy adrenaline rush, he dragged himself into the study to phone the department and request assistance.

The first thing he noticed was the smell. The marijuana was stronger in this room. When he sat down at the desk in front of the old Underwood typewriter, he saw that something had been typed on the sheet scrolled into the platen:

she chose death over life, me over you. her bodys cold & hard but i can still make her squirm with my slide finger.

He caught his breath. It was the bastard who had sent the letters. He was for real. Nicole hadn't written them.

The phone rang, sending his heart into his throat. He lifted the receiver and waited several seconds for a voice to speak. He sensed a lurking presence on the line, someone listening to his shallow breathing, measuring his sudden fear. Someone who enjoyed playing games.

"It's you, isn't it?" Kurt said. He had broken into a sweat despite the chill in the room.

The laughter was deep and wheezing, a smoker's blackened lungs. The sound caused Kurt's own chest to tighten. "Tell me who you are," he said, struggling to speak calmly.

Another gale of dark laughter, then the line went dead.

Kurt slammed the receiver and stared at the sheet of paper in the Underwood. His hands were trembling. He read the final typewritten lines: *everybody that fucked her while i was gone will soon join us in the grave. think about it fool. you never meant shit to her.*

Nicole had had good reason to be frightened of this man. And now he was threatening Kurt as well.

His mind groped through all the possibilities, trying to visualize the face that matched the raspy laugh. There was something deep in the laugh itself that sounded unused, sealed off, neglected. A shut-in, a prisoner in solitary, a monk in his cloister. A dead man risen from the grave.

11

SHORTLY BEFORE THE deputies arrived, the phone rang again. Kurt hadn't left the chair. He lifted the receiver and waited silently, expecting the sinister laugh.

"Prepare yourself for a potential shitstorm." It was Corky Marcus calling to tell him that he'd met with reporters from the two local newspapers. "They're asking for an interview with you. According to these vultures, the public has a right to know every detail of Nicole Bauer's final evening. I did my best to shoo them off, but you can bet they'll hunt you down."

"No press conference. I'll talk to them when I have time."

"And let's cancel this town hall debate with Ben Smerlas," Corky said. "I'll tell the speaker committee there's been an emergency. You're involved in a case that needs your full attention. Not a total fabrication, by the way."

"No," Kurt said. "This thing's been planned for weeks."

"You're distraught, Kurt. You don't know how shaky you sound right now."

"I've been here before." A couple of messy homicide cases in years past that Ben Smerlas had accused him of botching.

"If the media decide to focus on you in the Bauer story, your career is over. The recall is a done deal."

Kurt read the last line in the typewriter: *you never meant shit to her.* "Tell the committee I'll be there," he said.

"Goddammit, Kurt Muller! Are you listening to me? *Carole!*" he howled away from the phone. "Carole, come talk to this stubborn ass! He's doing his best to self-destruct!"

Kurt sighed, waiting for Carole to pick up. "He's right, you know," she said when she came on the line. "You're in no shape to sit on a public stage and defend your reputation."

HE HATED TO withhold evidence from the two deputies he had summoned to his house, but he wasn't prepared to show the typewritten message to anyone but Muffin and right now she was preoccupied with the Bauer brothers, walking them through the death scene at the Starwood mansion. So he played the break-in as a random crime.

"The guy busts in the county sheriff's home, lights a reefer, pops open a brew, and grooves on some sounds," chuckled Joey Florio, shaking his head. He was down on one knee, dusting the handle on the broken sliding door for fingerprints. "He's gotta be a fucking moron."

"Or a misguided youth snorting crank," said Dave Stuber, browsing through the scattered albums. "Bitchin' collection you got here, Kurt. What will you take for this *Yardbirds' Greatest Hits?*"

"I've got to go down to the office," Kurt said. He assigned Stuber to watch the house for a few hours. "Joey, don't forget to dust the typewriter keys on that old Underwood in the study."

"What's that about?" Chewing on his thick black mustache, Joey Florio shrugged at him. It was the second time Kurt had made the request. "The bad boy sit down and write you a poem?"

Kurt tried to smile, tried to pretend it was a clever remark. "And the needle arm on the turntable," he said. "I touched it, but his prints might be there, too."

"Hey, you chauvinist pigs," Stuber joked. "How do you know it's a *he*?"

12

FOR MANY YEARS the basement of the Pitkin County Courthouse had served as the coroner's examination area, but now the long narrow space housed department records, an archive of old case files, and a disorganized evidence cage with an outdated catalog system. When they saw Kurt coming down the dimly lit corridor, the three deputies who were tagging items in the cage halted their conversation abruptly and he suspected that they had been talking about him.

"Morning." He nodded at them.

They mumbled good-mornings, avoiding his gaze. He was well past the cage, heading toward the east corner of the building where the dead cases were stored, when Mac Murphy raised his voice.

"Whatever we can do, Kurt."

By now the talk had spread throughout the department. Everyone knew he had been with Nicole Bauer until two hours before her suicide. It was only a matter of time before the rest of Aspen knew as well.

"I appreciate it," he said over his shoulder. Then he stopped and turned back toward the deputies, realizing they were logging in evidence from Nicole's place. "Murph, did you find anything in those ashes?" he asked.

"No, sir. Not a thing. Just carbon and crumbles."

The letters were a dead issue. Gone.

"Do a clean job, people," he said. "The press and her family are going to be all over this thing."

At the far end of the building he switched on a bare bulb dangling from a long black cord and searched the case drawer marked Q–R–S, finding the folder he had come across once before. A few steps away, below a conjunction of exposed water pipes, sat a wooden table with a goosenecked desk lamp. He spread the contents of the folder across the table's dusty surface.

A dozen glossy black-and-white photographs documented the misshapen body of Rocky Rhodes lying naked where he had fallen into the boulder garden below Nicole's deck. The photographer had shot the corpse from various angles but only one image, a ground-level close-up, revealed any portion of the face, a bloody mass of bone splinter buried partway in the snow. Kurt picked up the magnifying glass in a tray of chewed pencils and loose paper clips. Even under close scrutiny there was no way to verify the identity of the dead man.

He dug through the folder and found more photos. Morgue shots, the corpse stretched out on an autopsy table. Fully exposed, the face was in no better shape. The degree of damage made it difficult to distinguish his features.

This was not easy for him. His own brother had died in a fall from Maroon Bells six years ago and Kurt had viewed the body stuffed inside a zipper bag. Bert had looked even worse than this, but crushed bone was crushed bone, and dead was dead.

Flipping through the photographs, he eventually found what he was looking for. The victim's hands lay slackly by his side, palms down, a large ring clearly visible on one finger of his left hand. Under the magnifying glass Kurt could make out the yin-yang engraved in the gold. It was the same ring.

He knew two things for certain now. The letters were from someone other than Nicole and not the fabrication of her disturbed mind, as Westbrook had suggested. And the ring was either authentic or an impressive facsimile. Nicole hadn't contrived any of her story. She had had every reason to believe that the threats were from Rocky Rhodes.

He wondered if Rocky's family had been called in to ID the body, or if Ted Brumley, the crusty old coroner at the time, had simply taken Nicole's word that the long-haired decedent was who she said he was. But what if Nicole had been involved in some elaborate hoax from the very beginning? What if the unidentifiable corpse wasn't Rocky Rhodes after all? Surely Bumbling Brumley, as he was known affectionately by his colleagues, had fingerprinted the dead man. Kurt skimmed through the paperwork but couldn't locate the prints.

Brumley's handwritten report told him nothing new—massive injuries, alcohol level 0.21mg percent, high content of cocaine and THC in the urine. The police account was straightforward and produced no startling revelations. The forensics of the case had been thoroughly scrutinized during the trial.

The letters had mentioned *that bitch Pariah,* blaming her for the fight that had led to Rocky's death. Was Pariah Nicole's alter ego?—Westbrook's explanation. Could the name have been some sort of double-talk code word between two psychotic lovers, a name Rocky had given to Nicole's bad-girl persona? Or was Pariah a real woman? Had she been there that night? Had Rocky caught her in bed with Nicole? The letters implied that the two women had ganged up on him during the altercation. Kurt looked carefully through the report for a reference to a third person at the crime scene, another woman, but there was no mention of one. What he found instead was the transcript of an interrogation conducted by Kurt's predecessor, Sheriff Joe Stanton, two days after the incident.

STANTON: You were partying pretty hard, isn't that correct, Miss Bauer?

BAUER: I don't know what you mean.

STANTON: Your friends say you two had been holed up in the house for several days.

BAUER: Rocky was cooling out. He'd just come off tour, two months on the road. He was fried.

STANTON: Were you doing drugs?

BAUER: Drugs are illegal, Sheriff.

STANTON: The autopsy showed he had cocaine and marijuana in his blood. And too much alcohol.

BAUER: I don't keep track of what people ingest in their bodies.

STANTON: How about you, Miss Bauer? Weren't you loaded when it happened?

BAUER ATTORNEY: Don't answer that.

Kurt read quickly through the next part of the deposition, which covered the familiar territory of the fight and its aftermath. Nicole had told the authorities exactly what she later testified in court—and what she had steadfastly maintained for twenty years.

STANTON: What were you two fighting about?

BAUER: I don't remember.

STANTON: The fight ended with a man falling to his death and you don't remember what started it?

BAUER: What difference does it make how it started? Take a look at my face. This is why I tried to get away from him.

STANTON: Did you go down to the boulders and see what happened to *his* face?

BAUER ATTORNEY: If you make another inappropriate remark like that, Sheriff, this session is over. I will not allow my client to be badgered.

STANTON: I'm sorry, Miss Bauer. I apologize. Let's go on.

BAUER: Yeah, whatever. But I've already told you people everything I can remember.

STANTON: And we appreciate your cooperation. You've been very helpful. Just one or two more questions.

BAUER: Okay. Do it.

STANTON: Did you go down to the boulder slide to check on Mr. Rhodes after he fell?

BAUER: I could see him from the deck.

STANTON: You didn't go down to see if he had survived?

BAUER: No. I couldn't. I heard the— (Pause. Witness asks for tissue.) I heard the sound his body made against the rocks. I knew he was dead.

STANTON: You stayed in your bedroom?

BAUER: I don't remember what happened after that. My face was numb from his punches. My mouth was full of blood. Every bone in my body hurt. I think I passed out. The next thing I knew there were cops all over the house. I don't even remember calling them.

Kurt leaned back in the folding chair and tried to envision the scene the way it had always been portrayed in counterculture circles, by word of mouth. Nicole and Rocky had been boozing and mixing drugs for days on end. They were wired, strung out, gorging on junk food, playing music nonstop, fucking each other dry. How did their fight start? Stoned paranoia, jealousy and wild accusations, shattered nerves? A bloated ego wounded by something she'd said? There was a flashpoint, a moment when the debauchery turned violent and they'd tumbled out onto the snow-heaped deck in a flurry of fists and kicking and bloody screams.

Is that how it had really happened? Or was there an entirely different scenario?

He read the list of items confiscated at the crime scene. What surprised him was not what was on the list but what wasn't. The sheriff's deputies hadn't retrieved a syringe or a joint or even a stray marijuana seed. No drug paraphernalia whatsoever. He wondered why no one at the time had asked the question that seemed so obvious now: Who cleaned up the place before the cops arrived? Nicole was in no shape to do something that coherent. No, Kurt thought, someone else had taken care of the dirty work and then called the police. A close friend, a confidante. Maybe someone who was already in the house that night.

He thumbed through the file folder and found a second

crime report, dated 3/8/77, the day after Rocky's death. It was the mortician's statement disclosing that the body had been stolen from his funeral home.

Over the years the incident had acquired the aura of myth. The stories varied wildly. That Rocky's keyboard man had rented a hearse and posed as a driver sent by the family to claim the body. That band groupies had loaded the corpse into an ice-cream freezer truck and had shot their way past highway patrolmen in two states, making their dramatic escape. Kurt's favorite tale was the one in which grieving followers had borne their god by a horse-drawn travois for forty days and forty nights through icy mountain passes, trekking southward to the desert floor of Canyon de Chelly, where a blind shaman cremated Rocky and scattered his ashes across an ancient Anasazi kiva.

The mortician's account was limited to actual events and his story was far less sensational. In the middle of the night someone had broken into his Victorian funeral parlor by smashing the French doors. The mortician complained to the officer in charge that the body had disappeared before he'd finished the extensive cosmetic work requested by Rocky's mother in Texas. According to the report, the Pitkin County Sheriff's Department had issued a statewide all-points bulletin and dispatched deputies to interview the known associates of Rocky Rhodes living in the Roaring Fork Valley. There were no debriefings in the folder describing the results of the interviews, but Kurt found a list of names scribbled in the margin of one report sheet. He recognized the name Gahan Moss, the keyboard player who still lived on the outskirts of Aspen near Buttermilk Mountain. His eyes ran down the column until he discovered a name that grabbed his attention.

Mariah Windstar.

He stared at the two words for several moments, frozen in silence. *There was a groupie named Mariah who hung out with the band,* Nicole had told him. *Rocky didn't like her, so he nicknamed her Pariah.*

Mariah Windstar. Was this her? Pariah. A real woman and no alter ego.

He copied the dozen names on a sheet of paper and returned the Rocky Rhodes folder to its drawer, then switched off the light and walked back down the corridor. The deputies were gone and the evidence cage had been locked. On his way to the stairs he stopped to have a look around the former examination chamber, its drain trap still embedded in the cement floor like an old high school shower room. The place was now filled with file cabinets and discarded office furniture, but Kurt could recall vividly how it had looked for so many years: the mobile body cart, the hoses and scales and fluid-collecting tanks. In the center of the room he stood over a stack of chairs where the autopsy table had once been located. With little imagination he could smell the blood, the unforgettable stench of death. He had witnessed too many dissections here, the coroner explaining what had happened to a mother's careless teenager while he placed a liver on the scale like a butcher weighing meat. Too many lessons in the cold calculus of tissue and bone.

Closing his eyes, alone and isolated from the world above, Kurt could picture Rocky's body stretched out on the stainless steel table. He could see the violent protrusions, the disfigured face and long, blood-matted hair. Something bothered him about this dead man. Maybe it was the lack of fingerprints and the impossible ID. Struggling to work through his doubts, he remained motionless in the dreamlike grayness of the room, his mind retracing every bruised inch of the corpse. Was a gold ring enough to prove that the body in the photos was indeed Rocky Rhodes? But what if Nicole was right—what if Rocky was still alive? That would mean the dead man was someone else. Would it also mean that Rocky and Nicole had pushed the man off her deck to fake Rocky's death?

13

KURT EMERGED FROM the courthouse at the same moment that a TV satellite truck was arriving from a network affiliate in Glenwood Springs. He knew why they were here and hurried off down the alley behind a strip of commercial buildings before the news cameras had a chance to track him down. At the end of the alley he looked back to see if he was being followed, then walked quickly across the brick plaza and entered the new county library.

The library computer listed only one biography of Rocky Rhodes, published in 1987, the tenth anniversary of the guitarist's death. Kurt located the book on the shelf and took it to a secluded reading area, where he sat at a small cubbyhole desk and skimmed through the pages written by the same gonzo journalist who had covered the trial for *Rolling Stone*.

By now everyone in Kurt's generation knew the sketchy details of Rocky's life. A country boy from East Texas, he'd run away from home as a teenager to apprentice at the feet of his two blues idols, Lightnin' Hopkins in the bars of Houston's Fourth Ward and Mance Lipscomb on his porch overlooking a dusty Texas cottonfield. In the mid-'60s Rocky had played lead guitar with various Houston bands, cut a legendary live album jam-

ming with Freddie King, and eventually found his way to
L.A., where his life unraveled in one long rock 'n' roll cliché.
Groupies, drug busts, troubled recording sessions, disastrous
tours, fired sidemen, broken contracts, dead friends, the Cha-
teau Marmont. But in Kurt's memory Rocky Rhodes had been
the real thing, his growling voice and soulful guitar work as close
as any white boy ever got. The only surprise was that he'd lived
to see thirty.

Kurt didn't know how Nicole had entered the picture, so he
skipped to the last chapters in the book and read about the
"Denver deb" in her wild early twenties. She was described as a
spoiled rich girl from a prominent mining fortune, a dropout
from Scripps College who had slept her way through valleys of
L.A. musicians and hip young movie stars in the early '70s. With
her inheritance she was able to build the house in Starwood and
still maintain a place in Laurel Canyon, where she threw extrav-
agant parties and carried on turbulent affairs with a series of in-
dustry stars exposed in the book. Rocky had wooed her away
from a notorious B-movie director when she was only twenty-
three, "perhaps the worst mistake of Rocky's mistake-riddled final years," the biographer had written.

Several pages of photographs occupied the center of the
book, a visual history of Rocky Rhodes from dirt-poor childhood to his last days in Nicole's mansion, a puffy, drug-addled
junkie staring bleary-eyed at the camera with a cigarette dangling from the corner of his mouth. Kurt hardly recognized him.
The tall, handsome lady-killer had put on fifty pounds of candy
bar chunk and another twenty years of hard time. He was thirty
going on fifty. The lines in his face were as deep as razor scars.

Studying the photos, Kurt noticed that one of the pages had
been torn from the book, leaving a ragged fringe in the gutter.
He turned to the permissions page to read the list of credits and
found that the missing page contained four photographs, two
on each side, including "Rocky with Aspen friends, 1976." The
copyright symbol was followed by the photographer's name—

someone Kurt had known for many years. It struck him as suspiciously coincidental that the only ripped-out page in the book showed a photo of Rocky in Aspen.

He checked the index at the back of the book for the name *Mariah Windstar* and discovered two references: "p. 196; *see also* photo number 27." Mariah Windstar was pictured in the Aspen group shot on the missing page. These coincidences were beginning to irritate him.

The passage on page 196 mentioned Mariah in a string of humorous countercultural names, the "druggy young pseudonymous hangers-on in Aspen, members of Rocky's entourage who could be found day and night at Nicole's Starwood pad, stoned out of their minds, listening to music and cavorting in ever-shifting daisy chains."

He closed the book and pulled the sheet of paper from his shirt pocket, reading the police list. Several names matched the ones in the biography. *Crescent Moon. Boogie Downes. Wolfgang P. Gursted. Maggie Mae Turner.* He remembered those days in Aspen with a fond smile. Everyone was young, naked, and stoned. Where had all the beautiful people gone? Where was Mariah Windstar now? *OD'd or found Jesus,* Nicole had told him. He turned toward the library window and examined his reflection in the glass, knowing how much his own features had changed in twenty years. Softer chin, crow's feet, hair going gray. If he'd slept with Mariah Windstar in 1976, he probably wouldn't recognize her today if she walked up and sat in his lap.

Glancing at his watch, he saw that it was nearly one o'clock. His debate with Smerlas would begin in another hour. He went to the front desk and checked out the book, then found a pay phone near the library entrance and placed a call to Miles Cunningham's remote cabin in Castle Creek Valley. He waited while the answering machine played Nixon's voice insisting *I am not a crook.* After the beep Kurt said, "Hey, Miles, I heard you were back from R and R."

His old photographer friend had spent the past month in the

Betty Ford Clinic, drying out from various chemical dependencies.

"Hope everything went okay. I've been meaning to call you."

Kurt had been putting off the phone call because the idea of conversing with a sober Miles Cunningham left him utterly speechless.

"I need to talk to you about a photo you shot in 1976. Your favorite subject—rock groupies. Give me a call."

With his last quarter he dialed Meg's farmhouse in Basalt. Her new husband, a Zen master named Bhajan, answered the phone.

"How are things going?" Kurt asked.

"Things are harmonic," Bhajan said, deadly earnest.

"You haven't shaved my son's head yet, I trust."

Bhajan giggled. He was a serene, likable fellow with thin graying hair gathered in a knot at the back of his head and a penchant for hemp clothing. Kurt's extensive investigation had revealed that the man's given name was Robert Goldsmith and that he'd once taught comparative religions at City College, New York. He had been married once before and his children were grown. There were no skeletons in his closet, as far as Kurt could tell.

"Lennon's been helping us clean the rabbit cages all morning," Bhajan said. Their household of six hippie Buddhists made their livelihood breeding pet rabbits. "I'll bet he's ready for some private space of his own."

Meg came on the line in a cheerful mood. She had been annoyingly cheerful ever since her elaborate Buddhist wedding last May.

"Is it okay if Lennon stays with you the rest of the weekend?" Kurt asked, concerned about the break-in and the note in his typewriter. Even with round-the-clock police surveillance he didn't feel comfortable with his son on the premises.

"Sure, that's fine, Kurt. We always love to have him with us. Is everything all right there?"

"Somebody broke into our house. Probably a kid," he lied. "He didn't take anything but I want to be sure he's not coming back."

By her long pensive silence he knew what she was thinking before she expressed the words: "This isn't anything like last time, is it?"

A couple of years ago four hired killers had broken into the house in the middle of the night and kidnapped Kurt. Lennon hid under his bunk bed for over an hour, crying his heart out until Kurt escaped and returned for him.

"It's nothing like last time," he insisted. "It's just some kid fucking around."

"I thought you were going to install a burglar alarm."

"I did," he said. "I just can't get used to turning it on."

"You're the county sheriff, Kurt. That makes you an easy target for every nut with a bone to pick. Turn the goddamn alarm on at night and when you leave the house."

Meg had always been emphatic about protecting Lennon from the world of law enforcement and the ugly realities of Kurt's job. The kidnapping had made her understandably more concerned. If she knew the truth about this break-in, he would have a nasty fight on his hands bringing the child home.

"One of my deputies is watching the house," Kurt said. "It's no big deal, Meg. But keep Lennon another night just to make absolutely sure."

"Maybe we should consider a longer stay. I can take him to school this week."

"Let's talk about it tomorrow. Right now I've got to run. Let me say hello to him first."

His son greeted him in his high, bright, eight-year-old voice: "Hi, Dad. When are you coming after me?"

"I have great news," Kurt said exuberantly, employing the usual positive-reinforcement technique. The one that never worked. "You get to spend more time with Mom! I'll be there tomorrow night."

A long silence. "I'm sick of rabbit poop," Lennon groused. "And I'm dying for a cheeseburger."

For nearly two years Lennon had happily accepted the peculiarities of his weekends at the farmhouse in Basalt, but lately he had begun to complain. Mom made him eat too many vegetables. There were no children to play with, no television, no video games.

"How is our bunny?" Kurt asked, hoping to reroute his attention.

Lennon had picked out a beautiful white Himalayan with gray ears to be his pet. Kurt had promised they would bring the rabbit home as soon as he finished the large screened-in hutch he was building on the deck.

"She's old enough to come home with us, Dad. When is her place going to be ready?"

"Soon, I promise. I just need to stretch the screen and then nail on some mink wire."

"Make sure nothing can get in and hurt her."

"Don't worry, she'll be the safest bunny in Colorado," Kurt said.

He told his son he loved him, and Lennon said he loved him too. "Oh, and Dad," he added, whispering into the receiver, "when you come pick me up, bring some fries and hide them in the Jeep."

14

OLD DOC BRUMLEY was still alive at eighty-five, still picking up the newspaper every morning on the lawn of his run-down baby Victorian on Aspen's West End, one of the few stately homes left ungentrified in the quaint, overpriced neighborhood. His wife had died decades ago and his children and grandchildren were all living in California, and the only time he appeared in public was at VFW meetings. During the Second World War, Brumley had served as a medic in the 10th Mountain Division, which had trained at Camp Hale near Leadville. He and his fellow troopers had spent their weekend passes in dilapidated Aspen, skiing Ajax and drinking their nights away in the rustic Hotel Jerome. Enamored of the Roaring Fork Valley and its sun-filled winter days, many of the soldiers had returned to live in Aspen after the war. When Kurt was growing up, Ted Brumley had been their family physician. For thirty years he'd volunteered as the county medical examiner because no one else in the small mountain village had witnessed as much death as Lieutenant Theodore Brumley fighting his way up 2,500 feet of Riva Ridge to overtake German artillery emplacements.

Kurt banged the knocker on the front door of the Brumley residence and waited. The old doctor was notoriously hard of hearing, so he banged again. Finally the door opened wide and the man who had once sewn three stitches above Kurt's eye stood gaping at him with his mouth parted slightly and a look of utter bewilderment on his pale, sagging face.

"My god, son," he said in a near shout. "I thought you were dead."

Kurt smiled at him. "Do you know who I am, Doc?" he asked, extending his hand. "Kurt Muller, Otto and Hanne's boy."

Brumley was holding an uncapped tube that oozed something thick and clear, possibly petroleum jelly. He offered Kurt a sticky handshake. "Yes, yes, of course," the old doctor said, the confusion slowly lifting. "I mistook you for your brother. Albert, wasn't that his name?"

"Yes, sir."

"The one who died in the climbing accident."

Everyone close to the incident suspected it had been a suicide. "Yes, that was Bert."

"The local football star."

Kurt smiled fondly. "Yes, sir."

"Your mother asked me to look after his body, you know. I went down to assist Dr. Louvier."

"Yes, sir, I know."

"Nine hundred feet of rock," the old man said, picking at a dark substance on his fingertips. "As bad as I've ever seen it."

Every night for the past six years Kurt had seen his brother's body, too, just before he drifted off to sleep. He didn't want to see it anymore.

"I've come to ask you some questions about another accident like Bert's," he said. "A fatal fall that happened twenty years ago."

Brumley gazed at him with a slack expression. "What kind of trouble are you in?"

Trouble, Kurt thought. Let me count the ways. "I'm not sure what you mean, Doc."

"You're the sheriff now, aren't you? They're trying to get rid of you."

Kurt nodded with a haggard sigh. "There's a recall vote coming up."

"Whatever they're saying about you, it's crap. Don't let the bastards get their way. I'm going down to the schoolhouse to vote for you. These newcomers, they want to change everything. We oldtimers have got to stick together."

Kurt smiled. "Thanks for your support, Doc. I appreciate it. Do you mind if I come in?"

"Certainly," the doctor said, waving the tube, which Kurt now recognized as bonding cement. "I don't get many visitors. Yes, please come in."

The house reeked of peculiar odors, flammable solvents and split-pea soup and something old and fleshlike, perhaps soiled laundry. Brumley had spent his entire life around foul smells and was no doubt oblivious to them. A tall man who had towered over Kurt when he'd poked and probed him as a boy, scratching his arm with the polio vaccine, shining a light in his ears, the old doctor now walked stiff-limbed and slightly hunched, his jet-black hair gone to baldness. Wearing a maroon buttoned sweater and loose slacks, he led Kurt through an archway into the formal dining room, where a stuffed owl perched with spread wings on the antique dining table under a blazing chandelier.

"Hope you don't mind if I do a little touch-up while we talk," Brumley said. "Can't afford to let the glue dry."

Kurt remembered now that Ted Brumley was an amateur taxidermist specializing in birds. The moldy owl was so old its feathers had begun to drop off. The doctor had arranged the strands of fallen plumage on a newspaper and was in the process of gluing them back on.

Slipping on his half-moon reading glasses Brumley bent over a dull brown wing feather, applying cement with an unsteady hand. "Were you the boy whose appendix I removed?" he asked.

"No, that was Bert."

The old man glanced up with an affectionate smile. "Then you were the one who caught that fly just above your eye," he said, studying Kurt's face. An accident while fly-fishing the Roaring Fork with his brother and Jake Pfeil. "What were you, twelve, thirteen years old?"

"Good memory," Kurt laughed.

"It comes and goes," Brumley said, shrugging, squinting at him. "I can't see a scar. You must've healed up pretty well."

Kurt had been inside this house many times back in the old days, when he was a classmate of the youngest Brumley boy, Tim. He remembered the china cabinet with its delicate wine-glasses and the stuffed pheasant on the mantelpiece and the em-broidered insignia of the 10th Mountain Division under framed glass. This was the kind of house he had wanted his parents to own, gabled and majestic and recognizably American, instead of the hay-barn Swiss chalet that had suited their quirky bohemian taste.

"Dr. Brumley, I've been looking into the Rocky Rhodes case and I have some questions about his autopsy," Kurt said.

The doctor was leaning into his work with great concentra-tion, but his body sagged noticeably at the mention of Rocky's name. "I should have guessed," he said, pausing, lifting his head slightly. "Everyone wants to know about that poor young man."

Kurt knew that Ted Brumley had been interviewed exten-sively by the Rhodes biographer. "I'm sorry, Doc. This is very important or I wouldn't bother you with it. I looked through the case file and couldn't find his fingerprint card. Do you re-member taking them?"

"Fingerprinting is standard procedure in an autopsy," Brumley replied without hesitation.

"I understand that. But the card isn't in the file. Can you say for certain you took his prints?"

"Son, for thirty years I examined every corpse in this valley," he said, peering hard at Kurt over the top of his half-moon glasses. "And step four of each and every autopsy was always the same—fingerprints. If records are missing, it doesn't surprise me. I housed my reports with the sheriff's department, but they weren't terribly security-conscious back then. Too many people had access to the files without supervision."

Misplaced. Scrapped. Stolen. After decades of shoddy filing practices, anything was possible.

"I've looked at the photos," Kurt said. "There was a lot of trauma to his face. Did someone ID him for you?"

Brumley carefully fit a glue-daubed feather into a gap on the owl's outspread wing and held it in place with his finger. "I don't recall how I made the determination," he said, wrinkling his mouth. "I believe I consulted his girlfriend—the Bauer girl—but I can't say for sure."

Nicole had told Kurt she hadn't viewed the body. "I don't mean to be rude, Doc, but is it possible you just assumed it was Rocky Rhodes?" he asked. "Nicole Bauer told the cops he was the man who fell from her deck. All the evidence pointed in his direction."

Brumley was clearly annoyed by this idea and raised his voice even louder. "I can assure you I verified his identity," he said. "Fingerprints, distinguishing marks, personal affidavits. Are my notes in the file, for heaven's sake? Read my goddamned notes."

The high shrill screech of a smoke detector sounded in the kitchen. Kurt caught a whiff of something burning. "Are you cooking, Doc?"

"Oh, my word," Brumley said. "Hold your finger here, please. I'm burning my lunch!"

Kurt held the glued feather in position while the old doctor padded off to the kitchen. An oven door banged, a utensil clanked against Formica, a window shuddered open. The detector continued to scream as heavy smoke drifted into the dining room. Through the doorway Kurt could see Brumley drag a chair across the linoleum and step up onto the seat with wobbling legs. He reached high over his head, opened the plastic cover, and yanked the battery loose from the alarm. The silence was sweet relief.

Satisfied that the feather would hold, Kurt eased his finger away and walked into the kitchen, where dark smoke swirled around the overhead light fixture. Brumley was stirring something charred in a casserole dish.

"Leftover stew," the old man announced loudly. "Have you had lunch, Bert?"

"Yes, I have, thank you," Kurt lied.

Brumley opened a cabinet door and began searching through stacks of vintage porcelain. "I don't know why everyone is so obsessed with that poor boy's death," he said. "You'd think by now they would let him lie in peace."

"Are you looking for this, Doc?" Kurt pointed to a large earthen bowl sitting on the counter near the sink.

"Ah yes, there it is," he said, sliding the bowl next to the casserole dish and spooning in burned stew. "Like I told that lady—when was it? Last week, I think," he said, pausing to stare off into space. "I stand by my work. If I declared it was Rocky Rhodes, it was Rocky Rhodes. No one paid me to say otherwise."

Kurt watched him pick through the dark crust, choosing the more recognizable chunks of meat and potatoes. "Somebody else was asking about the autopsy?"

"Oh yes. Just last week a woman came knocking on my door late one night. Nice-looking gal. Anyone else, I would've told them to go to hell. But she was very polite. I figured her for a reporter writing another damn story, but now I'm not so sure."

Kurt pictured Nicole showing up on the old coroner's doorstep after dark, frightened and overwrought, determined to discover the truth about the letters she was receiving. "Was it Nicole Bauer?" he asked.

Brumley frowned. "No. No, I remember Miss Bauer quite clearly. A tall, striking redhead. Beautiful young woman, in spite of the drug abuse. This lady was middle-aged." He seemed to have lost track of the years and hadn't considered that Nicole had aged, too. "Forty, forty-five, I would guess. An attractive woman but much smaller than the Bauer girl. One hundred and ten pounds. Dark hair, dark eyes. Small-chested, but real nice calves."

Ted Brumley still had an eye for the human body. "What did she want?" Kurt asked.

The old doctor tasted the ruined stew, added seasoning. "She danced around it awhile, but when it came down to it she was asking the same question you are. Was I certain the body I cut on was Rocky Rhodes?"

Kurt looked at a camper jay sitting quietly on the windowsill as serene and unruffled as the day Doc Brumley had stuffed and mounted it. "Your visitor," he said. "What was her name?"

Brumley put down the spoon and closed his eyes, thinking hard, his face like a crushed cigarette pack. "Something that reminded me of a song I used to know," he said, struggling, frustrated with his poor memory.

"A song?"

"Frankie Laine," Brumley said, beginning to hum a melody that Kurt thought he recognized.

"Mariah?"

"Yes, that's it!" the old man said with a grateful smile. "Good old Frankie Laine."

"Mariah Windstar?"

"That's it! Nice-looking gal, very polite."

Pariah. She was still in Aspen after all these years.

"Did she give you a phone number? A way to contact her?"

Brumley shook his head. "No, I'm afraid not. We sat in the living room and talked for a good long while and then she left all of a sudden. I thought she was going to interview me for another story, but after she was gone I got to thinking she wasn't the reporter type."

Kurt checked his watch. He was due at the Wheeler Opera House in five minutes. "Do me a favor, Doc," he said, slipping a business card from his wallet and leaving it on the countertop. "If she contacts you again, give me a call right away. I want to meet this lady, too."

Brumley picked up the card and read the information. "Thanks for coming by, uh, Kurt," he said. "By the way, how is your father doing? A gentleman of the old school. Not many like him around these parts anymore."

Kurt patted the old man affectionately on the shoulder. His father had been dead longer than Rocky Rhodes. "Don't forget to reattach that battery," he said, nodding at the smoke detector.

15

WHEN KURT ROUNDED the corner at Mill and Hyman he saw the TV satellite truck parked in front of the Wheeler Opera House and a crowd of reporters surrounding Corky Marcus at the entrance to the elegant building. Deputy Gill Dotson, posted near the doorway, spotted Kurt approaching on foot and hurried down the sidewalk to escort him through the gathering.

"The sharks are circling," Gill said, placing his hand at the small of Kurt's back. "Get ready to get physical."

Gill was a large man like Kurt, six four, 220 pounds, his waves of thick dark hair beginning to gray, matching the soul patch below his bottom lip. People sometimes mistook him for Kurt's brother.

"There he is!" someone shouted. The reporters quickly abandoned Corky and rushed Kurt with a barrage of questions. Gill forearmed his way through the swarm, saying, "Make a hole, people. Sheriff Muller is late for the forum."

"Good to see everybody," Kurt said with a politic smile. He recognized two staff writers from the Aspen newspapers. "I'll talk to y'all later, when there's more time."

The reporters followed them through the Tourist Information Office on the ground level and stayed hard on their heels up the thickly carpeted stairs to the second-floor lobby, tugging at Kurt like terriers with a pants cuff: *Tell us about your evening with Nicole Bauer! Did you spend the entire date at Starwood? What did you talk about? How late did you stay? What kind of mental state was she in when you left?*

"Didn't you hear the sheriff?" Gill snapped, pushing a cameraman out of their way. "He'll answer your questions later."

He led Kurt by the jacket sleeve across the lobby to the theater doors, leaning close to whisper, "We'll find you a back way out when this thing is over." Then he turned to block the doorway with his large body, allowing Corky through but restraining the reporters from entering the seating area.

Inhaling a lungful of the stale, vaultlike air of the old theater, Kurt passed down the aisle aware of hostile glances and furtive whispers, the packed audience mostly friends of Ben Smerlas. The only receptive smile he encountered was from Carole Marcus, who waggled her fingers at him in a mimelike greeting. But in the corners of that smile he saw her warning that this whole event was a very bad idea.

Behind a velvet curtain in the dark wing of the stage, two men were going over the notes attached to a clipboard. They looked up as Kurt approached. "Hello, Muller," said Matt Heron, the former movie star turned New Age wellness guru whose brainchild was the now bankrupt Star Meadow Holistic Institute. "We weren't sure you would show."

"I'm here. Let's get it on."

"The speaker committee has asked me to moderate the discussion," Heron said. "I hope that's cool with you."

Matt Heron was synonymous with Aspen. Wholesome, outdoorsy, superficial. Kurt neither liked nor trusted the pretty-boy narcissist, with his helmet of golden hair and ice-blue eyes. He suspected that Heron had had an affair with Meg just before the divorce, when she was spending night and day at Star Meadow *working through the changes*, as she had explained at the time.

"No, you're perfect for this, Heron," Kurt said. "Absolutely perfect."

"Copacetic," the actor said with an uncertain grin. "Then we're ready to rock."

Onstage Ben Smerlas greeted Kurt with a virile handshake and a gangster's smile. Smerlas was a short man, maybe five-eight, gym-built and bronzed like a Mediterranean god. His thick black hair was combed back with a hint of oil and his face was perfectly structured, his nose and strong jaw modeled after classic Greek sculpture, his teeth expertly capped and gleaming. There was little doubt he had provided a Princeton education for the children of some expensive cosmetic surgeon from the Coast.

The story on Smerlas was that he'd been a young L.A. cop when Watts exploded in the summer of '65. Being shot at in the streets had convinced him to quit the force and move to Orange County, where he eventually made his fortune in used cars, waste management, and industrial properties. Rumors persisted about mob ties, Vegas debts. He was a fierce skier and workout fanatic, and since his arrival in town fifteen years ago he'd gone through two trophy wives and assorted bimbo girlfriends. Still, his splashy parties had endeared him to the older social set, who had supported his campaigns for county commissioner. From his earliest days in office he had championed growth and development in the valley, and he was a strict law-and-order man, openly attacking Kurt at every opportunity for the way he ran the Pitkin County Sheriff's Department. If Corky was right—and Corky was always right about such things—Smerlas was using the commission seat to springboard into higher office.

"Have you met my wife, Sheriff?" Smerlas said, introducing the attractive woman at his side. "Don't get too friendly. She's also my research assistant and it's her job to dig up dirt on everybody in town."

"I'd hate to guess what you have on me," Kurt said, shaking hands with Dana Smerlas.

"Some targets are easier than others," she said, challenging him with a clever smile.

She was older and less glamorous than the women Kurt had usually seen Smerlas with, and it occurred to him that maybe the bastard was running short of flexible cash and had bagged this unfortunate woman for her Cayman bank account. She resembled the other wealthy middle-aged society women of Les Dames d'Aspen, charming and well-bred and pampered by the men in her past. Like her husband, Dana Smerlas showed signs of reconstruction, not in what was detectable but in what was not. The natural wrinkles were missing from the corners of her eyes, and her deeply tanned face had the skin-stretched quality of a surgical lift. But she looked good in jeans and a colorful handmade sweater from some third world sweatshop, and her short-cropped hair appeared its own natural color, graying at the temples with hints of red, an unfashionable statement in this town.

"It's nice to meet the infamous sheriff at last," Dana Smerlas said with a derisive glint in her eye. "I've heard so much about you. But let me get out of the way and leave you two gentlemen to your stage."

KAJX radio had arranged to air the discussion live. A ponytailed studio engineer hunched over his soundboard in the orchestra pit, adjusting knobs, issuing cryptic hand signals to the young female techie clipping a microphone to Kurt's flannel shirt. Trapped by wire and ceremony, he gazed out at the quiet audience and noticed Muffin Brown slipping into a seat in the rear of the theater. She must have completed her walk-through with the Bauer brothers at Nicole's mansion. Sooner or later he would have to meet with them himself, an unsettling thought he tried to force out of his mind.

When the houselights dimmed and the engineer motioned for Matt Heron to begin the program, Kurt stared out at the ghostly silhouettes and remembered his afternoons in this old theater as a boy. His father, an Austrian composer and the creator of the summer music festival, had often dragged him and Bert in here to watch chamber rehearsals on this same stage where he and Smerlas were now seated behind a cafeteria table with notepads and dripping pitchers of water.

"There are two main charges Commissioner Smerlas and his recall movement have made against Sheriff Muller," explained Matt Heron after brief introductions. A proliferation of illegal drugs in the valley. A proliferation of undocumented Latino service workers.

"Give me a few minutes and the list will grow," Smerlas said, eliciting laughter from the audience.

Kurt couldn't bring himself to focus on the discussion at hand. He was still processing the thought that Mariah Windstar was a real woman walking the streets of Aspen. After twenty years why was she suddenly curious about Rocky's autopsy? Did she know about the letters to Nicole? Had they remained friends all along?

"Okay, Commissioner," Matt Heron said, "let's begin with your remarks."

Smerlas wasted no time launching his attack. He claimed that the DEA had brought in their own agents to work Pitkin County and the Roaring Fork Valley because the sheriff's department was either incompetent or unwilling to investigate drug trafficking among the Latino service workers in the Aspen area. "My sources inside the DEA tell me that Sheriff Muller and his staff are so unreliable the agency routinely excludes them from their investigations," Smerlas said. "I would like this county to have a sheriff's department that doesn't embarrass the good people who live here—one that works hand in hand with the DEA to stop the illegal drug activity running rampant everywhere you turn. But let me assure you, folks. As long as Kurt Muller is in office, the drug dealers know this is the sweetest place on the planet to set up house and do business."

There was a hum of low voices in the theater. "Sheriff Muller?" Heron said, inviting him to respond.

A door opened in the dark balcony above the audience and the flash of light caught Kurt's eye. Something long forgotten surfaced in his memory. He suddenly recalled sitting up there many years ago, just after he'd come home from the army, passing a joint among friends while Rocky Rhodes and his band blew out the fuses down here on stage. It may have been the same concert he'd seen on VH-1. He wondered if Nicole and Mariah had been in the audience that night.

"Sheriff Muller, it's your turn," Heron repeated, grinning boyishly at Kurt's inattention.

Kurt sat up straight and tried to refocus his thoughts. "I have no problem with, uh, the DEA," he said, doodling on the pad in front of him as if making a note to himself. "Our department has cooperated with them on a number of warrants. But I think the agency needs to, uh, improve its percentages. Last year they busted one apartment for possession of tortilla mix, and a farmhouse in Old Snowmass for trafficking in herbal tea." A snicker from the audience. "The DEA should do their homework before they pull weapons and raid a place. Thank god nobody was hurt in either incident. But I would suggest," he said, a sudden inspiration, "that somewhere in their basic training these agents should learn the difference between cocaine and tortilla mix."

Everyone laughed. Even Smerlas seemed amused by Kurt's comment.

"What about that, Commissioner?" chirped Heron. "The DEA has blown it themselves a couple of times, haven't they?"

Smerlas's long sputtering response sounded circular and defensive, as if he himself were responsible for the agency's actions in the valley. Kurt made no effort at following the lame justifications. He could see that people were lining up in the aisle behind a microphone stand, eager to ask questions. He suspected they were all Smerlas plants.

"Thank you, Commissioner. It looks like there are several audience members who want to participate in our open forum today," Heron said. "Go ahead, young man. What's your question?"

"Yeah, first off I'd like to point out that Man is totally destroying this valley with his fences and mini-malls and monster homes. You so-called civic leaders up there onstage don't give a rat's ass, so long as you're making some jack off your development deals on the side."

Squinting into the hot stage lights, Kurt leaned forward in his chair to see who was saying these things. The Gen-X voice sounded familiar.

"Take a look at what's going down all around us, people. The elk can't migrate from the snow country to the warmer meadows 'cause all your ranch fences are blocking their runs. And now the bears, man. What're the bears supposed to do?"

It was Kyle Martin. He kept raking the long blond hair out of his eyes and gesturing dramatically.

"Do you have a specific question for the speakers?" Heron asked with a patient smile.

"I got no fucking specific question, dude. But I got some serious advice for you all." He reached down into a backpack at his feet. *"Stop raping the wild!"* he shouted, hurling a fat round object toward the stage. The balloon was intended for Kurt and Smerlas but fell short, splattering a thick red liquid across the flooring. *"You got blood on your hands, you bastards! You're raping the wild!"*

Gill Dotson and a security guard moved down the aisle after him, but Kyle scooted along the orchestra pit and bolted up another aisle, escaping to the lobby.

"Bye now," Matt Heron said. "And thank you for sharing your thoughts with us."

It looked more like red paint than blood, but Heron called for a short break while two theater attendants wearing rubber gloves rolled out their squeeze bucket and quickly mopped up the mess.

"Back in my day as a cop that kind of behavior would get a man arrested," Smerlas said into his microphone when the radio engineer signaled that they were back on the air. "But Sheriff Muller takes a bean-sprout approach to law enforcement and he'll probably just arrange a massage and some Yanni music for that troubled boy."

The audience laughed. Questions resumed from the floor microphone. Kurt rocked back in his chair, gazing upward again into the theater's gloom. A cigarette glowed in the dark balcony seats. Someone was sitting up there alone, smoking. He thought he could smell the faint drift of marijuana.

"Sheriff Muller, I'm sure you'll want to address that," Heron said.

Kurt hadn't been listening. "I'm sorry," he said. "Too much mike feedback up here. Could the lady repeat her question."

Heron and Smerlas exchanged glances. "She asked about the avalanches last March," Heron explained. "Your policy of search and rescue. Considering what happened to Maggie Turner."

"Oh, right," Kurt nodded. "Maggie Mae." The same aging hippie whose name had appeared on the 1977 police list of Rocky's friends.

"Sheriff Muller, I would like to know why you didn't try harder," the speaker said in an accusatory tone.

Last spring an avalanche had swept over Maggie Turner's small rustic cabin in Castle Creek Valley, and after an initial attempt at rescue, Kurt was forced to call off the search because of whiteout conditions and the threat of another avalanche. Several days later, after Maggie's body had been recovered from underneath the mangled cabin, there were signs that she'd been trapped alive in an air pocket for perhaps twelve hours. The media speculated that she might've been saved if the sheriff hadn't given up so early.

"Let me say something about that," Smerlas interrupted. "I

think what Kurt Muller did last March showed incredible cowardice!"

"Let's give the sheriff a chance to answer first," Heron insisted. "Then you can make your point, Commissioner."

All eyes shifted to Kurt. A moment passed, an eternity in radio time, and he could see the sound engineer remove his headset and peer up from the orchestra pit, impatient with the lull. Kurt glanced into the wings, where Corky Marcus had suddenly materialized like the ghost of Hamlet's father. The attorney was spinning his hands in a frantic circle, imploring Kurt to say something. Anything.

"Sheriff Muller?" Heron prodded.

Kurt consulted the doodles on his pad. He had unconsciously sketched several *I Ching* trigrams like the ones on Rocky's ring. "Hindsight is always twenty-twenty, Mr. Smerlas," he said finally. "In this job you can second-guess yourself forever. You'd do a lot of things differently if you had another chance."

He looked again at the trigrams, then toward the dark balcony. He imagined it was Nicole sitting up there, smoking defiantly, a faux fur draped around her tanned shoulders. He imagined her drinking champagne from a fluted glass and smiling down on his misery. She believed in absolution and second chances. She had known what it was like to seek forgiveness for a mistake.

"You let the woman die!" Smerlas said, his words so emphatic they reverberated down Kurt's spine. Angry and stunned, he turned quickly to face the commissioner, and Heron raised his arms as if he expected a flurry of blows.

"I wasn't willing to risk other lives in that storm," Kurt said, his voice rising. "The men and women who were out there with me poling through the ice had loved ones waiting for them to come home."

Smerlas was livid now, his face flushed and indignant. "Imagine the poor woman lying there helpless for all those hours, thinking you would come to her rescue," he said, leaning forward to glare at Kurt.

Kurt looked away at the balcony again, where the small orange tip of a cigarette burned in a single point of light. *You're the only one who can help me, Kurt,* she had said. He could still feel the terror in her eyes.

"You pulled out too quickly, Sheriff Muller. That's my assessment, and that's the way a lot of voters around here feel about it," Smerlas barked. "You don't seem to have the intestinal fortitude it takes to make responsible decisions. I have serious doubts about your judgment. And that's why I'm urging the good people of this county to recall you as sheriff."

Kurt had gone inside himself to wallow in his own guilt and was only vaguely aware, at first, that someone was applauding from the dark balcony. A measured, echoing clap, muffled and menacing, filled with a palpable contempt. There was a man standing in the shadows near the gilded railing, the cigarette glowing from his lips. Heron stopped midsentence and squinted upward through his rimless glasses, distracted by the haunting clap. The audience was stirring now, shifting about in their seats, searching for the source of the interruption. From the overhead darkness a sudden burst of laughter spread like a black net over the entire theater, a sound so vile it chilled every listener into silence. Kurt stood up abruptly, knocking over his chair. He had heard that laugh before.

"*You!*" he shouted, ripping off the clip mike and pointing his finger toward the balcony. The cigarette burned in the dark like a tiny ember spit from a hearth log. "*Stay where you are! You're under arrest!*"

When Kurt reached the wings of the stage, Corky grabbed at his jacket sleeve. "Kurt! What the hell—?" he said, trying to detain him. "Have you lost your freaking mind? You're live on the radio!"

He shoved Corky aside and thundered up the aisle toward the lobby, scanning the unlit balcony as he ran. He saw a shadow moving swiftly across the upper rows, then a slice of light, the rear door opening. "Muffin!" he yelled, searching the audience for his deputy. "Backup! Bring Gill!"

Like everyone else, she was standing at her seat, gaping at him as if he were the village idiot on the loose.

"Draw your weapon!" he commanded the stunned young woman. "It's him!"

He banged through the theater doors and raced across the lobby in full stride, pounding up the stairwell to the balcony section, his lungs fighting the sudden exertion, his mouth as dry as powder. He was unarmed but too angry to feel fear. It was the joker who had harassed Nicole and broken into his house, and when he caught him he was going to tear him apart with his bare hands.

At the top of the stairs Kurt caught a glimpse of the man retreating through a doorway at the end of the third-floor corridor. He was tall and slightly stooped, with long greasy strands of silver hair falling to the shoulders of his faded black duster. Kurt didn't get a look at his face.

"Stop!" he shouted, running down the corridor toward the closed door. "Pitkin County Sheriff's Department! Come out where I can see you!"

He stood aside the door, bracing his back against the florid wallpaper, listening for movement inside. Where was Muffin with her Glock 9? Where was Gill? There was no sign that they had followed him.

Unwilling to lose more time, he reached over and gripped the doorknob and flung open the groaning door. A musty draft whiffled out from the dark enclosure, a sealed-off smell of yellowing paper and layered dust and, if he was not mistaken, a trace of charred wood that could have dated back more than eighty years to the Opera House fire of 1912. He took a deep breath, cocked a hard fist, and poked his head around the polished mahogany molding. The darkness was spoiled by a high transom window, the gray light revealing bare wooden stairs leading steeply upward to what must have been the Wheeler's storage attic.

Kurt looked back across the quiet corridor and realized that his deputies had taken a wrong turn somewhere. He knew he should wait for them to catch up, but every wasted second gave that creep the advantage, and there was no more time to lose. He pulled the tube of pepper spray from his pocket and stepped inside the closet-like space.

"Hey, you up there! Come down with your hands on your head!" Kurt yelled into the darkness above, a black rectangle that may have been a door at the top of the stairs. He was standing on the first step now, adjusting his eyes to the dim lighting, searching the room for something to wield as a weapon. Noticing a stack of ancient window drapes rolled up and stashed against the wall, he stooped down and examined the spearlike head of a long wooden rod protruding from one of the moth-eaten bundles.

"Hey, pal, this is an official police order! Come back down here immediately!" he said, whipping the rod through the dusty air, testing the wood's durability. What else did he have? He didn't want to get close enough to use the spray.

Kurt issued another loud command and listened to the silence. Gripping the rod like a baseball bat, he climbed the creaking stairs until he reached the black hole that was no door but an open portal into a vast storage attic filled with shadow-looming silhouettes, tall crates and costumed mannequins and the disassembled parts of background scenery from long-forgotten theater productions. The air vents leaked enough daylight to provide an eerie, chimerical definition to the shapes scattered about the dark space. Kurt ventured forth, following a walkway that ran alongside the attic's support beams, his boots rattling loose boards underfoot. He was torn between calling out another official order and inching along in this breathless silence, hoping to surprise the man before the man surprised him. His anger had given way to a sudden fear and uncertainty, the creepiness of this place so visceral it made the hairs stand on his arms. A small tension knot was pressing the nape of his neck. He could smell the man's body odor, a funky tinge of sweat and piss in the mausoleum air, and he wanted to confront the bastard face-to-face.

When he reached the end of the walkway he paused to get his bearing. Stacked wooden crates formed high walls enclosing him on three sides, but he could make out a small opening in one corner, a slender breach wide enough for a body to slip through. He thought he heard something just beyond this row, a low croaking sound, solid weight on a sagging board. He waited, listening intently, the rod seized with both hands. The scant attic light had dimmed into deeper shade, a passing cloud blocking the gray sunlight filtering through the vents. It was so dark now he couldn't decipher the words stenciled on the crates. There was another noise, a soft sound like a hand brushing grit from a wood surface. Brandishing the old drape rod in front of him like a spear, he tucked in his shoulders and squeezed between the crates, slowly tunneling through the dusky passage for twenty feet or more, a cold, foul-smelling draft blowing in his face, the unmistakable odor of human waste. Within moments he'd reached a small clearing where a shaft of meager light shone down on a man standing perfectly still next to a full-length dressing mirror with a long jagged crack. He was tall and gaunt, with a scraggly silver beard and wild-burning eyes. In the pale light he looked like the gnarled husk of what had once been Rocky Rhodes. The man slowly reached into his black duster and pulled a long dull hunting knife from a leather sheath hanging at his side.

Kurt recoiled a step, jabbing the air with the rod. "Drop the knife!" he shouted.

As he retreated another step, his back foot splintered a rotten plank behind him. His ankle twisted, his knee buckled, and he felt himself going down. Losing the rod, he tried to catch his balance against a crate and realized too late he was pulling over the entire precarious wall of boxes. The first one landed across his shoulder blades and knocked him to his knees, and then the avalanche began, a cavernous roar all around him, box upon box, flattening him facedown on the boardwalk.

He didn't know how long he was out. A few seconds, a full minute. When he came to, he realized he was buried beneath the crates and couldn't move. He heard the slow drag of shoe soles, and then a raspy whisper from somewhere above him: "Now you know how it feels six feet under." The vocal cords sounded damaged, ruined. "Dark and cold. All alone. The worms crawl in, the worms crawl out," the man sang in a husky growl, laughing to himself.

His footsteps were shuffling along the perimeter of the fallen crates, moving closer. Kurt struggled hard to free himself and managed to shift a crate off one arm. His belly and legs were pinned and he couldn't reach the pepper spray in his pocket.

"Ain't no use fightin' it, brother," the voice said with that low scratchy laugh. "Sooner or later we all end up thisaway."

A ragged sleeve descended out of the darkness and the knife blade plunged into a crate two feet from Kurt's head. With his one free hand he grabbed the bony wrist, but the man was strong and gristled and jerked the knife away. Kurt braced for another attempt and heard the second slash coming, the long wide blade whiffing near his ear. A snatch of loose sleeve was all he could see of his attacker. He was taking his time, crawling slowly over the crates now, shifting them out of his way, looking for an opening and flesh to cut.

"What did you expect would happen to you, brother," the voice said, strained and winded, "when you fucked my old lady?"

The next slash tore through the thick shoulder pad of Kurt's suede jacket.

"Hey, Kurt, are you up here?" Somewhere in the distance a woman was calling his name. "Deputy Muffin Brown, Pitkin County! Is anybody up here?"

"Over here!" Kurt shouted with all his might, but his voice sounded muffled underneath the heap of boxes. "Use your Glock! He's got a knife!"

Above him the movement stopped. In the silence Kurt could hear only the pounding of his own heart. Where was the attacker?

Suddenly the crates began to collapse all around him. A box edge caught the side of his head. In that final moment before losing consciousness he heard the man's hoarse laughter trailing off into darkness.

16

"KURT, WAKE UP. Are you all right?"

He nestled against Nicole's gentle bosom. She was patting his cheek to rouse him. Running through the snow on her deck, he must have slipped and hit his head.

"Hey, boss, come out of it. Wake up."

Something familiar about the smell of her body soap, a nut-brown fragrance, polished saddles, and baked bread. He had once shared that soap, round and smooth, hanging from a coarse string in her shower stall.

"Don't move him. Something might be broken." A male voice floating in the haze. "EMS is on the way."

Kurt opened his eyes and winced from the harsh light.

"Keep the flashlight out of his eyes, dummy," Muffin said.

"Hey, Kurt old buddy, you're gonna make it," the man giggled. Kurt recognized the high nasal voice of Joey Florio. "Nobody's ever been snuffed by twenty boxes of sequined costumes."

Kurt watched him reach down into a pile of clothing and find a ruffled black teddy, sizing it against his chest.

"Not your color, Florio," said Gill Dotson, who was roaming

around nearby with another flashlight. "You look prettier in pink."

"Fuck you, Dotson," Joey said, tossing the teddy at him. "Here, your old lady left this in my car."

"Knock it off, you two," Muffin said sternly. "Give me a hand. He may have a concussion."

With considerable effort Kurt lifted his head from Muffin's lap and sat up. They had cleared away the boxes, but gaudy costumes were strewn all around them like debris from a wrecked gypsy wagon.

"Did you collar him?" Kurt managed to say, the words echoing distantly through his head.

"Collar who, Kurt?" Muffin asked. "I didn't see anyone."

There was a loud ringing in his ears and he couldn't focus on anything solid. He felt Muffin's muscular arm around his shoulder but her face was a blur. Flashlight beams fluttered in the murk like luminous cave moths.

"Rocky," he said in a weak voice. "It's gotta be Rocky Rhodes."

The flashlights ceased their motion. In the long ensuing silence he heard the men whispering.

"He had a hunting knife," Kurt said. There was a bloody scrape on the back of his head from one of the crates. The feeling was slowly returning to his legs. "He tried to kill me."

"Take it easy," Muffin said, holding him. "Try not to move. EMS will be here soon."

"Where were you, Muffin? I needed your backup."

"Hang on now. Why don't you lie back down?"

"Hey, Kurt, here's your Rocky Rhodes," said Joey Florio, shining his flashlight on a tall figure standing next to the long cracked mirror. It was a mannequin.

"These things are all over the place," Joey said. "Somebody had some fun with this one. Looks like Sonny Bono on black acid."

The mannequin was outfitted in '60s attire. Long-haired wig

and false sideburns, prism sunglasses, strings of cheap beads
and a medallion around its neck, ragged Turkish sheepskin
jacket, bell-bottoms, marijuana-leaf belt buckle.

"Joey, go check on the EMS unit," Muffin said. "They should
be downstairs by now."

She had served as acting sheriff for a year when Kurt was on
R and R and was used to giving orders.

"Aye aye, sir," Joey grumbled, shuffling off into the darkness
with the flashlight beam dancing at his feet. "If I run into Rocky
on the way out, I'll ask him to hit a few power chords for you,
Kurt."

Kurt stared at the mannequin in the gray attic twilight. "Get
a team up here to search the place," he said, gazing around at
the cobwebbed rafters. "He may be hiding somewhere in this
mess."

He pulled himself out of Muffin's grip and rolled onto his
knees, closing his eyes to slow the dizziness.

"You've had a blow to the head, Kurt," she said. "Why don't
we sort this out after you've had some rest?"

She laid a hand on his shoulder, but he shrugged her away
and tried to stand. "It was him, goddammit!" he said, a faint
echo surrounding each word like a man speaking in a long narrow tunnel. "Didn't you hear him up in the balcony? The laugh
gave him away."

Muffin rose to her feet with him, steadying his shoulders.
"Everybody thought you'd lost it," she said. "Running offstage
like a bat out of hell."

He took hold of her wrist and pulled her so close he could
smell that nutbrown soap she always used. Even in the weak
light he saw the surprise on her face. "He tried to stab me with
an eight-inch hunting knife," he said, showing her the gash in
his jacket. "It was the guy who wrote the letters to Nicole. The
same guy who broke into my house."

Her warm breath feathered his neck. "Whoever it is, Kurt, it
can't be Rocky Rhodes. Don't you hear how crazy that sounds?"

Heavy footsteps scuffed out of the darkness and Muffin re-acted quickly, drawing her holstered sidearm.

"Hey, you two lovebirds," Gill said, his flashlight blazing into their faces. "I found something back here. Can you walk, boss?"

Kurt felt strong enough to move his feet and limped along with Muffin's support as Gill led them down a sagging board-walk between mounds of junk. In another small clearing near the rear wall of the attic Kurt caught a whiff of what he'd smelled earlier, just before his encounter with the knifer.

"God, that's not rat shit," Muffin complained, disgusted by the odor. "More like the human variety."

Dotson's flashlight illuminated an old olive-drab sleeping bag spread out in a hiding place behind several crates. The en-closure was littered with fast-food wrappers and tattered maga-zines. The stench was overwhelming.

"Looks like some homeless person's been holing up in here," Gill said. "Good chance he's your heckler, Kurt."

Muffin pulled winter gloves from the pocket of her parka and slipped them on, then stooped down to leaf through one of the splayed magazines. "Hmm," she said, directing her light on a page of pornographic photos. "It's so hard to find a devoted harem nowadays."

The photographs were laughably dated, a gaggle of naked hippie girls lying about in various poses, wearing long straight hair and flower-power body paints. A young man as hairy as a simian appeared in each frame with a stiff erection, the focus of their sexual attention. The magazine must have been at least twenty-five years old.

"Don't ruin the merchandise. I'm sure Florio will want to examine every page in detail," Gill said, toeing at a small brown packet of Zig Zag rolling papers.

Kurt turned a slow circle, gazing out across the dark expanse of attic. "He has another way in and out," he said. "Maybe a window onto the roof. There's a fire escape down the side of the building."

Muffin stood up and pointed her light into the distance, the beam diffusing like a white mist over the prop graveyard. "I'll radio for some more help," she said. "We'll search the place top to bottom."

Dotson's flashlight ray nosed around the sleeping bag like a sniffing hound. He found the pile of excrement and fouled candy wrappers used for toilet tissue. "Looks like it's just some nasty old bum getting in out of the snow," he said.

"Tell our people to treat this one real serious," Kurt said. "He's got a long blade and he's not afraid to use it."

The fog was beginning to clear from his brain, but now he was more aware of the pain. His right ankle throbbed and his shoulders felt as if they were bearing a hundred-pound bag of sand. "Go through these magazines and see if he's cut out any pictures or words," he said, feeling the need to sit down again. "Look around for an old Underwood typewriter."

Gill stopped to regard him with a wide smile. "What, Kurt? You think this freak's up here sending valentines to his sweetheart?"

They heard a racket near the top of the stairs. Joey Florio called out their names. "Yo, where *are* you cowboys? Did the bogeyman get you?"

The EMS team was close behind him, banging through the maze of crates with their oxygen equipment and their stretcher.

"Okay, boss," Muffin said, patting Kurt's shoulder. "Here comes your ride."

17

Dr. Stephen Perry, Kurt's personal physician, was making his rounds at Aspen Valley Hospital and came down to the emergency room to examine Kurt himself. The X rays showed no broken bones. A nurse dressed the abrasion on Kurt's scalp and taped an ice bag to his swollen ankle while Dr. Perry conducted further tests.

"You've had a mild concussion, nothing serious," the doctor said after probing and palpating Kurt's head, scoping his pupils and ears. "No signs of a hematoma. You may feel dizzy and out of sync for a few days. A concussion can make everything seem like a weird dream. Your brain has been shaken up like one of those eight balls with the floating messages and there's no predicting what will surface. You may suddenly remember the lyrics of an old song or a night of bliss with a girlfriend you've forgotten all about."

Dr. Perry smiled innocently at Muffin, who was sitting on a stool in the corner of the examination room.

"Wonderful," Kurt said glumly. "What I need now is more weirdness."

"Just take it easy, okay? Relax for a couple of days. Watch

videos, listen to some good music. And stay off your feet until the swelling goes down in your ankle."

An RN wheeled Kurt to a room farther down the corridor and told him she would return in a short while to remove the ice pack. Muffin stood in the doorway, absently tapping the department cap against her leg, clearly preoccupied with other considerations. He recognized the familiar signs of her restlessness.

"Will you be all right?" she asked. "I'll call one of the deputies to drive you home."

"Sit down," he said.

"Don't have the time, Kurt. Too much going on. One crew's finishing up over at Nicole's place, and now this thing in the Wheeler."

"Tell me about the Bauer brothers. How did it go?"

She stared past his shoulder out the small window. "They brought their lawyer along, some wiseass from Denver. I walked them through the scene," she said. "The younger one, Jeffrey, took it pretty hard. Needless to say, they want to talk to you."

He dropped his chin. The Bauers wouldn't rest until their sister's death was investigated to their full satisfaction. "As the sheriff of this jurisdiction?" he asked, curious how much detail she had already supplied them. "Or as Nicole's last date?"

She regarded him with the superior disdain he'd felt from her on other occasions. Something was bothering her. "I checked in with Louvier," she said. "His examination indicates she had sex last night, Kurt. Is there something you've neglected to tell me?"

She seemed to take dark pleasure in punishing him for his mistakes. She had had plenty of practice at it. But he suspected there were deeper motives, a delicate tension between them they wouldn't acknowledge aloud, the intimacy of that night in her trailer a few years ago. They had decided it should never happen again, but sometimes the memory surprised Kurt, curled around his thoughts at unexpected moments.

"The Bauers are people who got filthy rich sweating the details," she said. "They'll want to know who caused the penetration. You can bet it will be a topic of great interest to them."

"Please sit down, Muffin," he said, softer now, an appeal rather than a command. He nodded to the paper-covered examination table, the only seat in the room besides a small aluminum swivel stool.

"I'll stand," she said, glancing at the table. "Women usually end up on those things with their knees spread wide."

This wasn't going to be easy. He reached across the wheelchair and poured himself a cup of water from the pitcher on the physicians' desk. "About a year ago Nicole and I had an affair," he said, avoiding her eyes. "I got to know her during the investigation, when that junkie chick broke into her house."

He took a deep breath, then another drink of water. He wasn't accustomed to this side of a confession. "The affair didn't last long and we hadn't seen each other in a while, but we were still friends, I suppose. She didn't trust anybody else. The date was an excuse to bring me to Starwood to look at those letters."

"And then one thing led to another."

He didn't want to see Muffin Brown raise another eyebrow at him for the rest of his life. "I liked her," he said, unwilling to admit how strongly he had been attracted to the woman everyone had treated as an outcast. "I knew she'd had her share of problems, but I didn't realize how serious they were. I didn't know she was suicidal."

Muffin ran a hand through her hair, exasperated with him. "Christ, Kurt, the woman killed her boyfriend. She'd slept with half the men in town. Everybody knew she was trouble. What planet have you been living on?"

Kurt didn't believe the rumors. There were men, yes. But Nicole had been discreet, selective. He suspected that over the years she had spent many long days and nights alone.

"She asked for my help," he said. "As a cop. She wasn't fabricating the letters or playing some kind of head game with me. The son of a bitch who tried to knife me in the Wheeler is the one who wrote them."

"How do you know that?"

"He broke into my house and left me a message." He told her about the sentences typed on the Underwood, recounting some of the phrases. "Same attitude, same style as the letters to Nicole. It's him, all right. He even called me on the phone and laughed that sick laugh. The boy wants to play."

He had her attention now. "Jesus," she said, stepping toward him with a grave expression. "Sounds like you might be his new target."

"He may look like a gnarly old freak who sleeps next to his own shit in an attic, but he knows exactly what he's doing."

"We'll get you some extra protection," she said, visibly disturbed by the turn of events. "And I'll put out an APB right away. It shouldn't be too hard to track down somebody that out of place in Aspen these days."

The ice had numbed Kurt's ankle and now the cold was traveling up his leg, chilling his entire body. He crossed his arms to stop the shivering in his chest. "He called her," he said, clenching his teeth to prevent them from chattering. "Sometime around four this morning. That's why she panicked." He tried to calm himself. "The bastard scared her to death."

Muffin saw that he was shaking and threw open the doors of a small white cabinet, searching for something to cover him. She found a blanket and wrapped it around his shoulders. "Are you all right, Kurt? I hope you're not going into some kind of delayed shock."

"She left a message on my machine right after his call," he said, shuddering under the blanket. "I want you to hear it. She thought it was Rocky Rhodes. It's why she freaked out and ran."

Muffin rubbed his shoulders briskly. "I wish you would stop talking like it really could be him," she said. "It's giving me the willies."

"We need her phone records ASAP," he said. "We've got to find out where he was calling from. And while you're at it, run down the calls to my house this morning, too."

Voices echoed in the corridor, swift footsteps approaching. "Knock knock," said Carole Marcus, appearing in the doorway. Corky was behind her, sullen and worried.

"Kurt, honey, are you all right?" Carole said, rushing into the room. "We thought you— Well, we didn't know what was going on, then we heard what happened."

He smiled dumbly and nodded at the ice pack. "Just a sprained ankle," he said. "Otherwise I'm fine."

Before Corky could say anything, Muffin moved quickly across the room and took his arm. "I'm glad you're here, Counselor. I was going to track you down. Can we talk a minute?"

Kurt suspected that Muffin needed to brief Corky about her meeting with the Bauer entourage. "Don't lose any more votes while I'm out of the room," he said to Kurt, then stepped into the corridor with the deputy.

"You're making us crazy, darling," Carole said. She held Kurt's face in her warm hands, staring down into his eyes with deep concern. She was a good friend, but every time she touched him like this, something unwholesome stirred inside him.

"I'm sorry, Carole. You were right. I should've listened to you and stayed at home."

There was a tear on her cheek. Her lovely dark eyes were wet and glistening. "Carole," he said with surprise in his voice. He didn't understand this sudden emotion. "Are you okay?"

"I worry about you."

He knuckled the soft skin of her face, catching the tear on his finger.

"Maybe this recall is the best thing that could happen to you," she said, squeezing the fingers that lingered on her cheek longer than they should have. "I'm thinking about voting against you myself."

He smiled at her. "Now you're starting to sound like Meg," he said.

Carole and Kurt's ex were old friends. The two couples had been in the same birthing class when they were pregnant with Lennon and Joshua Marcus.

"Somebody's got to keep an eye on you," she said, tucking the blanket around his neck.

"If it's any consolation," he said, "I'm probably not going to vote at all."

CORKY AND CAROLE drove him back to the courthouse and helped him into his Jeep, which was parked in his designated sheriff's space.

"Would you like me to drive you home?" Carole offered.

"You're spoiling me," he said. "I feel fine. Really."

"Don't field any phone calls or talk to the media without me present," Corky instructed him.

"There goes my feature on *Hard Copy*."

"This is not an occasion for humor," Corky said peevishly. "Go home and hide under a bed until further notice."

After they had driven away, Kurt sat numbly in the old Willys, the crutches angled against the passenger seat. The deep shadow of Aspen Mountain had crept across town, dropping the temperature. He rested his head against the seat and breathed in the crisp alpine air. There was a strange magnified quality to the surrounding light. He could hear water trickling down a rain spout, slush thawing in the gutter beneath his tires. He remembered this heightened sensation from long ago, this slowed-down rhythm of things unseen. It was what the world felt like after a long toke of Thai stick. It was the sweet vibration all through his body after making love with Nicole in her warm firelit bedroom while the wind howled outside in the night.

"Hey, Kurt, you all right?"

Gill Dotson was squatting down at the passenger window, smiling at him in his good-natured, Minnesota farmboy way.

"How long you gonna be on these crutches?"

"A day or two. It's just a sprain." Kurt glanced at the courthouse windows catching the last rays of afternoon sunlight. "How's it going at the Wheeler?"

"Poor Linda," Gill sniggered. His gruff laugh sounded like an echo from a deep well. "I put her to work bagging that bad boy's stash of dirty magazines and she found some sticky pages. She almost lost her lunch."

Linda Ríos had been in the department for only two years and still suffered from rookie status. She was a burned-out middle school teacher from rural southern Colorado. Muffin had recruited her to help with the county's Spanish-speaking population.

"At least our boy's practicing safe sex," Gill said, laughing harder.

"Let's work up his blood type," Kurt said. "And dust the magazines for fingerprints."

He would ask the lab techs to look for a match with the late Rocky Rhodes. If they ever located his goddamned records.

"Any sign of a typewriter? There might be one lying around somewhere—a prop from an old play."

"Nothing close by his camp," Gill said. "But there's a shitload of junk in that attic, Kurt. We could kill a week looking through it."

"Find the Underwood," Kurt said, cranking the Jeep engine.

Hiding in his house, watching videos until his ankle mended, was out of the question. His head felt clearer now and there was someone he wanted to talk to.

"You've got this guy's description." He nodded toward the downtown shops. "Ask around. Somebody would've noticed him on the mall. You don't see old freaks like him in Aspen anymore."

"Fuckin' A," Gill said wistfully. "Damn place has gone over to the Granola trustafarians."

He stood up to full height and fished for the pack of cigarettes in his shirt pocket. "Ahh, for the bad old days," he said, firing up a Camel.

18

ONE OF THE names jotted in the margin of the 1977 police report was Gahan Moss, the keyboard man in Rocky's band. For many years Gahan had lived at the foot of Buttermilk Mountain in a fabled residence the locals called the Magic Mushroom House. In his wild younger days Kurt had wandered into a couple of parties when the house was owned by a swinging '60s movie star and her architect husband, who had designed the strange lair after reading J.R.R. Tolkien on psilocybin mushrooms, or so the story went. The interior doorways were shaped like warped Dalí clocks, stairwells spiraled upward without destination, and the bedrooms were optical illusions, their rectangular planes receding smaller and smaller into corners where waterbeds lapped in slow undulating waves. As Kurt recalled, it had been a fun place to be stoned—if you didn't get lost in the hall of mirrors.

Neon toadstools decaled the mailbox marking the entrance to Gahan's private drive. Kurt followed the sharp switchbacks uphill through a grove of bare aspen trees until he found a small dirt-packed parking lot and roughhewn stone steps leading onward up the cliff. The climb was strenuous on crutches, and when he reached the outdoor patio at the top of the rise, he paused to rest and take in the view of the valley below. Darkness was falling quickly, a wintry chill. He could see the landing lights at Sardy Field and a steady stream of headbeams on Highway 82. When he turned toward the house, round-roofed like the cap of a giant gray mushroom, he realized that the song he'd been hearing in his head was not a floating memory brought on by the concussion but a real song wailing from speakers somewhere inside the place. It was "Blue Midnight," the same guitar solo playing on his stereo after the break-in.

Crutching his way down the cobblestone path to the main entrance of the house, he noticed high-voltage light blazing through a long, narrow picture window. He stopped to have a look and counted four tall floodlamps placed strategically around the sitting area near the glass. A naked man stood peering into a tripod video camera, patches of coarse hair on his back and shoulders, his short pale body sagging under middle-aged flab, a rat tail braid dangling from the nape of his thick neck. Kurt rustled through the hedge running alongside the walkway and hopped one-footed onto a stone bench for a clearer view. Two nude women were cavorting on a polar bear rug near the window seats, massaging each other and kissing, vamping for the camera. Even at this distance Kurt could see the difference in their ages. The older woman roiled around her partner's small hard body like a sleek, bulbous sea lion sliding off a rock. She tongued her lips and played to the lens, beckoning the man to join them.

Without warning a huge black rottweiler sprang snarling out of the undergrowth and would have taken Kurt's leg if he hadn't swung his crutch full force against the beast's skull. The dog howled and stumbled backward, legs churning, then lowered its nose and charged again. When Kurt swung the second time the dog snared the crutch in its teeth and yanked fiercely, a brutal crunching sound Kurt's bones would make when that animal got to him. In a panic he glanced at the picture window and saw the two women scrambling for their clothes. "Hey!" he yelled. "Somebody come get this fucking dog!"

The rottweiler splintered the crutch, dragging it out of Kurt's hands, then pressed its attack, lunging and retreating while Kurt jabbed at its snout with the other crutch. He managed to pull the tube out of his pocket, and when the dog lurched again he pepper-sprayed the animal's cold black eyes. It barked and rolled around in the dirty snow, pawing at its face, then disappeared into the brush with a wounded howl.

Kurt struggled to catch his breath. His panting left vapor in the dying light. With the crutch still raised like a weapon he stepped down off the bench and cautiously backed his way toward the hedge, prepared for another attack. When he turned, there was a man in a silk kimono waiting for him on the footpath.

"That was the female. She's the sweet one," the man said in a clear British accent. He stared at Kurt with an austere sense of violation. Another rottweiler growled at his side, pulling on its leash, eager to pounce. "But her brother here has a nahsty temper. If you don't leave these premises immediately, I shall be quite happy to release him."

"Pitkin County Sheriff," Kurt said, jerking the leather holder from his hip pocket and raising the badge high in the air. "You sic that dog on me, Gahan, you'll do time in my jail."

Gahan Moss seemed both astonished and flattered that Kurt knew his name. But he was an easy make. The years hadn't ravaged Gahan's face, as they had those of so many rock stars from his era. Though his hair had thinned to long mouse-colored strands and his waist had spread like a soft pudding, the prominent cheekbones and English jaw held firm and his eyes had not yet sunk into the dark cadaverous sockets of a former junkie. Perhaps he had undergone a face-lift, like everyone else past fifty in Aspen.

"I assure you the young lady is of legal age," Gahan said with a wicked gleam in his eye, "if that's why you're here, Sheriff."

Kurt picked up the mangled crutch that had been flung near

the hedge like a rubber bone. "Put away the dog and tell the ladies to get dressed," he said. "I'm here to ask you some questions about Nicole Bauer and Rocky Rhodes."

"Ahh," Gahan Moss said, visibly relieved. "Of course."

By some furtive signal, a subtle yank of the leash, a gentle touch, the rottweiler sat docilely at his feet. "Can't we *shedule* this some other time?" he said, glancing toward the picture window where the floodlights burned brightly over a vacant white rug. "As you have no doubt observed, I'm in the middle of something."

"Re-*shedule*," Kurt said. "The world will have to wait another day for the next Gahan Moss masterpiece."

The musician scratched the top of the rottweiler's head. He seemed to be considering whether to release the dog and take his chances in court. "On the subject of Nicole Bauer I have nothing to say. The woman was a murderous bitch and should've been locked away long ago."

He had used the word *was*. "So you're aware she's dead," Kurt said.

"I am aware," Gahan replied with a scowl. "I can't say as I'm brokenhearted by the news. The slag killed me best friend. They should've burned her at the stake when they had the chance, the sodding witch. Her family bought everyone off."

When Rocky died, so had Gahan's musical career. Kurt knew he hadn't cut a record in nearly twenty years, not even as a studio musician.

"Lose the dog and put on some clothes," Kurt said. "You and I are going to sit down and have a nice long rap about the old days and the way it all went down."

THE INTERIOR OF the house smelled like marijuana and scorched sex. "Blue Midnight" had finished playing and another Rocky Rhodes classic was channeling through the speaker system.

Gahan Moss left him waiting in what had once been the grand room, a circular recessed space as dank and uninviting as a drained pond. The last time Kurt was here, at least twenty-five years ago, this room was a cozy clutter of velvet cushions and wandering plants, the floor-to-ceiling bookcases filled with expensive art volumes and colorful masks from Africa and Latin America. Nearly empty now, Gahan's shelves contained only a scattering of books and stand-up framed photographs of himself and his friends. There was a mounted gold record, other awards. Not enough memorabilia to fill the wide spaces, nor to account for the many lost years since Rocky's death and the end of the band.

Kurt wandered over to Gahan's baby grand piano and lifted the dusty fall-board. The ivories had yellowed and cracked like cheap enamel. He placed his fingers in position and played a soft chord, remembering those childhood lessons from his father. The piano needed tuning. No one had cared for this beauty in a long time.

After ten minutes had passed without a sign of Gahan, Kurt wondered if he should go looking for him in the gloomy warren of rooms. He could hear voices raised in argument somewhere in the back of the mushroom, and he imagined the man caught up in delicate monetary negotiations with the two women, reassuring them, begging for another session. Kurt limped over to the bookshelves and examined a row of ornately framed photographs. Hippie musicians and their retinue, draped around one another in smoky clubs, naked in hot tubs, stoned at ancient monuments in timeless lands. The photos spanned an entire generation, from miniskirted young British schoolgirls with long, ironed-straight hair to tough biker mamas in denim and leather. They all looked familiar, a convergence of faces and attitudes from Kurt's own past. He wondered if one of these young women could be Mariah Windstar. Maybe she was the laughing girl sitting half nude on a speaker amp, over whose ample breasts Rocky and Gahan were pouring streams of wine. Or the Marianne Faithfull look-alike in the floppy hat, pecking a tux-edoed Gahan on the cheek. Or the djellaba-clad groupie wearing dark sunglasses and smiling from the top of a camel.

One photograph aroused his attention and he lifted the frame to study the image. Two young women were kissing un-derneath a jungle waterfall, their hair slicked back, beads of wa-ter glistening on their beautiful tanned bodies. The smaller woman, dark-haired and slender, wore only a black bikini hal-ter. Her companion was a tall shapely redhead with long muscu-lar legs. He was nearly certain that the redhead was Nicole Bauer.

"I'm delighted to see we share the same preferences in women, Sheriff Muller."

As instructed, Gahan had returned without the dog or his porno talent. He looked refreshed, as if he'd taken a quick shower. His Ben Franklin fringe of hair was damp and his face glowed with a ruddy heat. He had dressed in jeans and a flow-ing, puffy-sleeved silk shirt, and his tattered leather boots looked like fashion wear from Carnaby Street circa 1967.

"Don't worry, your secret is good with me," the Englishman said, smiling cleverly.

Kurt glanced at the photo again. The image was strikingly erotic. "Who are they?" he asked.

Gahan came closer and paused near the piano bench. "Hmm," he said, raking a thumbnail across his chin. "Some birds we met on our Hawaii tour in—when was it?—seventy-five or seventy-six, if I'm not mistaken."

"The redhead looks familiar," Kurt said, waiting for him to identify her as Nicole.

"Don't they all?" His laugh trailed off into a wistful regret. "In those days there were enough birds to let a few fly away."

"How about one named Mariah Windstar? Do you remem-ber her?"

Gahan's brow wrinkled, a wave of creases rippling high into his sparse dome. "Mariah Windstar, Celeste Starpattern, Ruby Moonshadow," he said with a hopeless shrug. "I can't remember one from the other, Sheriff. Too many years of inhaling. In my mind they're all the same fuzzy blur of bush."

Kurt was intrigued by the small dark-haired woman in the photograph. There was a butterfly tattoo near her shoulder blade. "Give it some thought, Gahan," he said. "Mariah hung with the Aspen crowd. Rocky didn't like her. He called her Pariah."

He waited for a visible reaction but Gahan's eyes remained steady and unyielding. The musician walked over and took the framed photo from Kurt's hand and placed it back on the shelf, in the same spot outlined in the dust. He seemed touchy about his gilt-framed memories.

"Rocky had a nahsty little nickname for everyone," he said, shaking his head with a distant smile. "He called me Dickweed when he was angry, which was often enough. I loved the bloke but he behaved like a first-clahs prick."

Kurt was growing impatient with this charade. "Come on, Gahan. You remember Pariah. She was with you people when you stole the body." A calculated guess.

The old keyboard man stood back from Kurt and gave him a cold, harrowing stare. "If that's what this is about, Sheriff, you're wasting your time. I wasn't there."

"Funny, that's not what the biography says. I have it out in my Jeep if you'd like to read the chapter where three eyewitnesses—your old running buddies—describe how you masterminded the whole thing."

A dark smile curled around Gahan's mouth. "At what point did cheesy rock bios become the measure of reality in this culture, Sheriff Muller? You'd do better to look into allegations that aliens abducted Elvis."

Kurt slid his hand into his pocket and pulled out Rocky's ring. "You're right, Gahan. It's only rock 'n 'roll," he said, showing him the ring in an upturned palm. "So why don't you tell me what really happened to the body?"

Gahan stared at the ring. His face turned ashen. "Where did you get that?" he asked in a husky voice, his words slow and deliberate.

"The last time you saw this thing, it was on Rocky's finger, wasn't it?" Kurt watched the shock register in the man's eyes. "You look a little surprised, Gahan. Is it because Rocky was dead and you were dragging his body around the Arizona desert?"

Gahan studied the ring. "May I see it, please?" he asked.

Kurt extended his hand obligingly and the musician lifted the ring with great care, appraising its facets as if it were a sacred relic.

"I need some answers, Gahan, and you're the one who's going to supply them. Otherwise I'll turn your ass over to the district attorney and he can decide what to do with a washed-up junkie making skin flicks in his jurisdiction."

Gahan sat down on the edge of the piano bench and gazed at the ring. He still hadn't recovered from the shock of seeing it. "It's impossible," he said in a small weary voice. He stared at the object in his hand. "How can it be?"

"It's his ring, all right."

"Just please tell me how you came by it."

"I was hoping you could tell *me* where it came from, Gahan. That's why I'm here."

The doorbell rang. A wiry-haired young cabdriver appeared in the foyer, announcing his presence to "Mr. Moss" with a genial familiarity. It was clear he had worked this fare before.

"Just a moment, Howie," Gahan said. "I'll fetch your ride."

He left and returned a few moments later with the younger woman. Kurt was relieved to see that she wasn't a local high school girl but some barroom stray well into her twenties, not particularly attractive at close distance, with heavy makeup and teased hair and a Denver Broncos starter jacket concealing the boyish figure he'd observed on the polar bear rug. As she passed by Kurt, leaving a wake of sweet floral perfume, she gave him a naughty smile.

"Yum," she said. "Is he gonna join us for the next shoot, Gay?"

Gahan hustled her through the foyer and stood outside in the gathering shadows, their voices trilling in one last contentious exchange over money. Kurt wondered where the older woman was.

Before long the musician returned inside, rubbing his cold hands and appealing to Kurt with a wordless, shrugging desperation.

"I once saw you play with Rocky at the Wheeler," Kurt said. "You were as good as they came, man. Is this what it's come down to?" He nodded out the window at the young porno queen making her way up the cobblestone path with the cab-driver.

Gahan sighed and dropped his eyes, stung by the question. He was struggling to piece together the remnants of his dignity. "If we're going to dig up skeletons, Sheriff," he said, "I'd like to have a drink first. Care to join me?"

Relying on the one intact crutch, Kurt followed him past a dry indoor fountain and up wide steps chiseled out of dark volcanic rock to the upper level of the house. Gahan's bar was a long gnarled cypress trunk hewed lengthwise and lacquered to a high gloss. Kurt propped his crutch against a tree knob and hoisted himself onto a tall vinyl-topped toadstool. There was a fungal odor in the air, like the underside of a garden stone. He watched Gahan Moss pour himself a shot of Bushmills. The ring lay between them on the glassy brown surface.

"Are you looking to break a story on *Unsolved Mysteries*, Sheriff Muller?" Gahan asked after downing a mouthful of the Irish whiskey. "Perhaps the telly is a good career move for you," he said, amused by his observation. "I understand your future in law enforcement is somewhat in doubt."

He raised the bottle, offering his guest a drink. Kurt ignored the gesture. "I've seen the morgue photos, Gahan," he said. "This ring was on the victim's finger when the medical examiner performed the autopsy."

Kurt picked up the ring and slipped it onto the finger that had once worn a wedding band, forcing it past his large knuckle. Smooth and cool, heavy as a lure weight, a very tight fit. He could feel the blood throbbing in his nail.

"But the man's face wasn't recognizable, my friend. The boulders weren't kind to him. I couldn't tell if it was Rocky Rhodes or some other poor sucker."

Gahan was hunched over the bar, resting on his forearms, the whiskey glass cupped in his hands as if it were a warming candle. After a few moments of silence he poured himself another drink.

"The body you and your pals half-assed cremated down in Arizona," Kurt said. "Are you sure it was Rocky?"

According to the biography, Rocky's mother had made plans to bury her son in a Baptist cemetery in East Texas, against the guitarist's adamant request to his friends that when he died he wanted his ashes spread over Canyon de Chelly. The biographer claimed that three corroborating participants had divulged to him the definitive story of what had happened. They alleged that Gahan and two other band members had broken into the mortuary and loaded the body into a pleasure van full of waiting female groupies and that they'd driven the corpse down to Arizona for cremation. Somewhere on the canyon floor they made camp in the dead of night and buried Rocky in a deep pit of burning coals. The ceremony lasted throughout the next day, and the eyewitnesses described a bittersweet, tearful wake with peyote, marijuana, and wine. On the second night, when the moon was full, they scattered Rocky's smoldering remains across several acres of desert.

Gahan stood up straight, threw back his shoulders, and

tossed down the shot of whiskey. "Forgive my cynicism, Sheriff. There are a million bullshit stories about Rocky's corpse, and by now I've heard them all."

"A few hours ago I got jammed up with an old freak who looked like the shit end of Rocky Rhodes at fifty," Kurt said in a calm voice, though he wasn't sure he believed it himself. "If he's alive, that means somebody else was killed in that fall and the body was stolen to cover tracks. Maybe Rocky arranged the whole thing, but he had to have help. Nicole Bauer would've been deep in it. And right now I'm looking at the guy who was Rocky's best friend and the lead body snatcher, by all accounts. How do you suppose that reads from where I'm sitting? The word *homicide* comes to mind, Gahan. Or at the very least, accessory to murder."

Large beads of sweat appeared high on Gahan's forehead, near the sprigs of his receding hairline. "I'll tell you what comes to *my* mind, Sheriff," he said. "That wonderful American expression *blowing smoke*. I'm afraid your imagination has run away with you."

Kurt had lost patience with the man's denials. "The old freak I told you about—he's acting like a disturbed head case," he said. "His mind is unstable."

He wouldn't divulge that there had been threatening letters to Nicole Bauer, or implicate Rocky in her death. Gahan may have already known these things. If Rocky Rhodes was still alive, Gahan may have known his every move for the past twenty years.

"Let's say it's our boy Rocky Rhodes," Kurt said. "Twenty years on the lam, living god knows what kind of life, it's understandable he's strung out. But he's losing it, Gahan, and I'm going to bring him in. When I do, the walls come tumbling down and everybody involved in the faked death will see the inside of a prison cell."

Gahan daubed his forehead with a puffy sleeve. "If what you say is true," he said, running his hands through his wet hair, slicking the long thin strands against his skull, "then I'm afraid you've missed your bloody best shot to crack this one open, Sheriff. The person you really want to interrogate is a stone-dead bitch named Nicole Bauer."

The bastard was right. Why hadn't Nicole told him everything? Maybe she had helped Rocky orchestrate his own death and twenty years later he had returned to torment her. If that was so, then why had she shown Kurt the letters and asked for his help? Was she prepared to expose the truth if it was the only way to save her life? Or did she think she could persuade her old lover Kurt Muller to turn a blind eye to the law and take care of Rocky on his own?

"Forget about Nicole, Gahan. You better worry about your own ass," Kurt said. "If it's Rocky, I'm guessing you know how to contact him. So here's what I'm offering you, man. Help me bring him in and I'll make sure you aren't charged with what happened in 1977."

Gahan's laughter sounded more weary than bitter. "You've read the biography, my friend. Last time Gahan Moss saw his old droog Rocky Rhodes, the bloke was ashes blowing in the desert wind." He stared at Kurt with a dark intensity. "I've got no clue why you're fucking with me now."

Kurt slowly raised his hand. "If Rocky's dead, then where did this come from?" he asked, showing the ring.

Gahan poured another drink and refused to look at Kurt or the ring. "Damned if I know, old sack," he said, his eyes following the flow of whiskey. "From some grave robber, I should imagine."

"You mean a grave robber back in '77. One of your friends at Canyon de Chelly," Kurt said. "It must have been quite a scene, Gahan. Everybody crying and singing and stumbling around stoned to the gills out in the cold desert night. Rocky's loyal entourage overwhelmed with grief. It would've been easy for some calculating soul to get to the body and stick the ring in a pocket before you loons lit the barbecue."

Gahan gazed into his shot glass, brooding in silence. He seemed angry at the last remark.

"So somebody got themselves a relic. A final souvenir from the great dead rock star," Kurt said, turning his hand over and back, the tarnished gold band catching the faint light. "Yeah, they stole Rocky's favorite ring, all right. The only question is, Was the guy wearing it really Rocky Rhodes?"

Gahan hovered over his shot glass. "We all took a blood oath," he said finally, scornful of the memory. "Pricked our fingers with broken glass and made a vow. Nothing was to leave our little camp. Not a word to the outside world. Complete silence till the end of time."

Kurt remembered one of the foolish promises he had made when he was younger. To love someone *till death do us part.* "It didn't take your friends long to spill their guts to *Rolling Stone,*" he said.

Gahan offered him a tepid smile. "Money is thicker than blood, mate," he said. "Everybody's got their price."

Kurt reached over and screwed the cap back on the bottle of Bushmills. Gahan's recollections were shaky at best. He didn't want the alcohol to further impede his memory. "Who was there, Gahan?" he asked. "Who took the oath?"

The musician finished off what was left in his glass. "You want names, do you?" he said, working the whiskey through his teeth.

"I do," Kurt said, pulling a small notepad from inside his jacket. "I'm guessing that the two other guys in the band helped you steal the body. What were their names? Jack something and Big Boy Lake."

Gahan smiled. "Very good, Sheriff," he said. "You've done your homework."

Kurt shook his head. "I've got three or four of your albums at home."

"Gathering dust, I imagine."

Until someone broke in and put "Blue Midnight" on the

turntable. "Who else?" Kurt asked. "How many people are we talking about?"

Gahan drew in a deep breath and thought it over. "Seven or eight, I suppose," he said, rubbing his sweat-flushed face. "I can't recall the exact number. I'm afraid my brain's burned a few cylinders along the way."

"Names, Gahan. Do your best."

"Look," he said, clearly annoyed by the task, "I can't remember the chicks' bloody names, and it would do you no good if I did. None of them used their real names, understand? They called themselves all sorts of wiggy crap. Mariah Windstar," he scoffed. "How do you expect to find someone like that after all these years?"

"Gay, darling, did I hear you say *Mariah Windstar?*"

A female voice drifted up behind them. Kurt turned to watch her mounting the stone steps on bare feet. It was the older woman from the video shoot. Her soft Botticelli body filled the loose robe with wide swaying hips and heavy unfettered breasts. Her tangled hair was long and yellowish white, the dark roots graying, and her skin was uncommonly fair for this climate, as if she were some fleshy fruit plucked from deep in a rain forest. She stopped beside Kurt and gripped the bar, her round shoulders rocking slightly, and he realized she was wasted on drugs or drink. She gazed at him through eyes as blue as cornflowers, beautiful in spite of their bleary, unfocused state. They looked like something precious left out in the weather.

"Thass a name I haven't heard in ages," she said in a thick, druggy voice. Then she laughed hoarsely. "Let me hear you say it again, Gay. It sounds so poetic in your prissy English accent."

Gahan raised his head and stared at her. "Shut up, you cow," he slurred. "Don't you recognize this bloke?"

With one hand clutching the bar she stepped backward to study Kurt, appraising him from head to toe. "I like your size," she said with an approving smile. "Did we have children together?"

"He's the goddamned sheriff," Gahan explained. "And he's here to bust me for killing someone, or stealing something—I can't remember which. He doesn't seem to know, either."

"Exactly how large are you, Marshal Dillon?" she asked, running her finger along Kurt's thigh.

"Sheriff, please forgive my wife," Gahan apologized, embarrassed by her behavior. "Old habits die hard."

Kurt grasped her roving hand and placed it gently on the surface of the bar, pressing his hand over her soft damp fingers. "Tell me about Mariah," he said. "Did you know her?"

She picked at something on her dry lips and eyed the ring on his finger. "*Know* her?" she said. "Yes, I guess you could say I knew her, Marshal."

"That's enough," Gahan said. "Toddle on back to your bedchamber, dear."

Kurt recognized her now. One of the photographs on the bookshelf. When she was a much younger woman she had sat on a speaker amp backstage at some long-forgotten gig, stripped to the waist, wearing only a crushed velvet skirt while Rocky and Gahan poured wine over each pendulous breast.

"You haven't introduced us, Gahan," Kurt said. "I didn't get your wife's name."

"Gay has no fucking manners whatsoever," the woman said with a hostile smile.

Was she Mariah Windstar? Doc Brumley had described his late-night visitor as a small, demure woman.

"Forgive me, Sheriff," Gahan said. "This is the lovely Amanda, my blushing bride. She was just leaving. Weren't you, buttercup?"

"A gentleman would offer me a drink," she reproached her husband.

"I want to hear about Mariah," Kurt said, uncapping the Bushmills and sliding the bottle toward her.

"Why are you so interested in *her*?" she asked, lifting the bottle straight to her lips. She watched Kurt as she drank, and he had the feeling she was showing him how her mouth could manage something long and slender.

"I'm looking for her," he said. "Do you have any idea where she can be reached?"

She set the bottle down hard on the bar with a sloshing thud, then rubbed a glistening drop of whiskey from her bottom lip. "Mariah Windstar is dead," she said, serious and final.

Kurt wasn't convinced. "How do you know that?"

"Dead as a butterfly that turns into a worm," she mumbled, tracing the tip of her finger over the ring on Kurt's hand.

"Isn't it the other way around?" he said.

She was dreamy now, lost in memory, her attention fixed on the ring. "Not through *my* looking glass," she said, blinking, her eyes losing focus.

"Someone stole this ring when you and Gahan and your friends cremated the body down in Canyon de Chelly," Kurt said. "I'm wondering who it was." He placed his ringed finger softly under her chin and raised her face, forcing her to look him in the eye. "Maybe it was a woman called Pariah," he said.

She jerked her head away, a strand of white hair falling loose across her face. "But that was in another country," she said. "And besides, the wench is dead."

She was fading fast and Kurt knew there was little time left before she became slurringly incoherent.

"So Marshal Dillon is here to bust us for burying our Shelley in the sand, is he, darling?" Amanda said, turning toward her husband.

"He's on a fishing expedition, love," Gahan said calmly. "Why don't you shut your mouth before something nahsty snags that luscious lower lip of yours."

"Don't be a bully, Gahan," Kurt said. "She was just about to tell me how a butterfly turns into a worm."

"It's the oldest trick of nature," Amanda said, helping herself

to another swallow of Irish whiskey. "You flutter your pretty little wings until you get noticed, and when you're in their net you
turn into an ugly flesh-eating grub."

Kurt thought about the photograph of the kissing women
and the butterfly tattoo on the small woman's shoulder blade.
"Is that what Mariah did?" he asked. "Caught Rocky's eye? Or
was it Nicole she was after?"

Amanda's stoned, knowing smile told him more than she
wanted to.

"They were lovers, weren't they?" Kurt said. "Nicole and
Mariah. Like the two women in the photo downstairs." He offered this idea like a small smoking vial of poison placed between them on the bar. "Mariah was there the night a man was
killed."

Amanda clung to the bar, her eyes downcast at her bitten
nails, the strand of hair dangling in her face. Gahan stared into
his empty shot glass. Their silence lingered with its own peculiar
echoes. Suddenly she began to cry.

"Darling pussycat," Gahan said, fumbling his way around
the bar to embrace her. "You've overdone it today, I'm afraid.
Excuse us, Sheriff," he said, beseeching Kurt for his sympathy.
Unable to control her tears, Amanda sagged into her husband's
arms. "I'll only be a minute. My wife needs to crash."

"Would you like some help with her?"

"No, no," he said, leading her away with her limp arm
thrown around his neck. "I'm well practiced at this by now."

Kurt waited on the stool. He stared at the empty page in his
notepad. He could hear Gahan's voice swelling in anger, the
woman's cries growing deep and turning into a long, husky
moan. Then there was dead silence. In time Gahan returned to
the bar.

"Don't think too poorly of her, Sheriff," he said. "She's having a bad time of it."

"She seems a little sensitive about those days."

"When she gets this blown she'll weep over anything."

"Even Nicole Bauer?"

Gahan smirked at him and tried to pour whiskey into his glass, but his hand was unsteady and he splashed a good deal on the bar. "You've got to understand something, man," he said. "We've been trying hard for twenty years to forget that whole crazy nightmare. Nicole, Rocky, the fucking canyon. When I left Arizona I drove straightaway to New York and got on a plane for England. I just wanted to be alone, away from the scene. I didn't even come back for the trial. In fact, I didn't return to the States for two or three years. It was too much to bear. With Rocky gone my whole bloody world had crashed and I couldn't manage to pick up the pieces."

Kurt had felt the same way when Bert died. He didn't return phone calls for six months.

"But you did make it back," he said. "Eventually. You've lived in this place for what—ten years?" He gazed about at the strange fungiform decor. "You and Amanda found each other again."

"Yes, the dear girl never gave up on me."

"What about the others? Haven't you stayed in touch with them?"

Gahan shook his head slowly, thoughtfully. "Big Boy OD'd a couple of years after Rocky died. Jack skipped off to Tibet or India or some such place. I haven't spoken to him in years." He wiped a puffy sleeve across his wet brow. His head appeared to float neckless on heavy shoulders. "And the birds, well . . . All the pretty birds have flown, brother. You and I wouldn't recognize them anymore. They married surgeons and settled down in their lovely suburban ranch-styles and started dropping babies." With a trembling hand he downed the shot and poured himself another, and this time Kurt didn't stop him. "They have their aerobics classes and their book clubs and little Justin's soccer on the weekends. If the old boys knew the dirty secrets I could tell on their wives—" He laughed cruelly, waving off the fragment of thought.

Kurt closed the notepad. He wondered if he could trust anything Gahan had told him.

"The body, Gahan." He stared at the ring on his finger and remembered Nicole's words: *He's alive. It's him.* "Did you see his face?"

Gahan looked as if he could use a good night's sleep. The new video career no doubt required long, exhausting hours of physical stamina.

"He wasn't a pretty sight, Sheriff, if that's what you mean," he said, sweat rolling down his long forehead. "The mortician had done his best to mend the face, but dear old mum down in Texas was advised not to open the casket if there was a funeral. The good neighbors wouldn't have recognized her baby boy."

Kurt studied the musician's heated features. "Two hours ago an old freak tried to stick a hunting knife through my heart," he said, poking his finger into the slit on his shoulder pad, showing Gahan the gash. "I want you to tell me it can't possibly be Rocky Rhodes. I want you to tell me for certain it was Rocky you cremated at Canyon de Chelly."

Gahan canted his head and looked at him with the innocence of a stringy-haired mutt. "I had no reason to believe it was anyone else," he said, and Kurt sensed that the old musician was too worn down to tell another lie.

He slid off the stool and retrieved his crutch. "If you're lying to me, Gahan—if it turns out Rocky's alive and you know where he is—I'm coming back to bust you for everything in the book," he said, dropping his business card on the bar. "Think it over. You want to deal, give me a call at my office. I'll make sure the D.A. offers you immunity for whatever happened twenty years ago."

He found his way down the steps and into the pond room, a hobbled man on a single crutch. The photograph of the kissing women lured him over for one last look, and as he stood gazing at them with shameless curiosity, aroused by that gentle hand resting on the curve of the dark-haired woman's bare ass, he was aware of shadow movement and soft footsteps behind him. When he looked over his shoulder, Gahan Moss was sitting on the piano bench, the whiskey glass in his hand. He watched Kurt with a troubled, faraway expression, his eyes sagging from half a bottle of Bushmills.

"Your wife recognized the name Mariah Windstar," Kurt said. "Why didn't you?"

There was a long silence while Gahan tasted the whiskey. His attention was somewhere else, coiling around those forsaken years. Kurt suspected that the man might be too far gone to respond.

"All the pretty birds have flown," he said finally, his words heavy and slow. "Rich . . . spoiled . . . uppity little whores. Fighting over his limp cock. In the end they took the poor fool down with them. You and I wouldn't recognize them anymore."

Two beautiful young women, hues of red and black, embracing under a waterfall. Kurt set the frame back in its place. "Get some sleep, Gahan. I want to talk to you and your wife again when you're both straight," he said. "I'll call and set a time tomorrow."

Gahan mumbled something and laughed. Kurt could smell the liquor sweat pouring down the man's face, dripping onto his floppy collar. "Tomorrow and tomorrow," he said, lifting the fall-board of the baby grand piano with an awkward bang. "All our yesterdays."

Kurt estimated ten minutes until the old musician would keel over and fall off the piano bench.

"Am I going to make it back down to my Jeep without having to club that rottweiler again?"

"Kill the bitch for all I care," Gahan said, slurring badly. "She's always been too much to handle."

Kurt wondered if he was talking about the dog. When he reached the foyer he heard the man mumble an incoherent tatter of words: "Wha'll you do with it?"

Kurt turned, straining to hear him. "With what?" he asked.

"The ring, mate. Rocky's ring."

Kurt tugged at the band, trying to remove it. He couldn't squeeze the ring over his large knuckle. "I don't know. Donate it to the Rock and Roll Museum in Cleveland," he said, "if I can get it off my finger."

Outside in the snow-fluttering darkness he turned and looked back through the picture window. Gahan was still sitting on the piano bench, staring at the keys. Kurt remembered a much younger pianist hunched over his keyboard, too many years ago now, playing slow bluesy riffs that rocked every soul in the Wheeler. Gahan Moss had once been a magician on the ivories.

He watched the man place his hands limply on the keys. Several seconds passed before he played the chord. The notes sounded sour, dissonant. In a rage Gahan swept his whiskey glass off the piano and it shattered across the floor.

19

BACKTRACKING ALONG THE county road, Kurt swung his Jeep into a glade of cottonwoods and cut the lights. From sixty yards away he could see the Day-Glo toadstool decals shining on Gahan's mailbox at the entrance to his private drive. There was only one way in and out, and if the man went anywhere tonight, as Kurt suspected he might, he would spot the vehicle from this blind of trees.

For half an hour the road remained dark and untraveled. Around his hidden Jeep, islands of snow glowed under the moonlight sifting through the cottonwood branches. The night was clear but cold, maybe thirty degrees. Kurt was glad he'd brought his department cap and an insulated hunting vest. Even with the roof up, the old Willys provided poor shelter against the frosty wind riffling through the trees. After another half hour of hugging his ribs and watching his breath fog the windshield, he retrieved the emergency blanket from the trunk and wrapped himself in a snug cocoon. There was no sign of Gahan, no headlights leaving the access drive.

He had drifted into a delta state of half awareness, half dream, when something stirred the underbrush behind the Jeep. He unraveled the blanket and slipped his hand under the seat for the Smith & Wesson .45 he kept in a holster. The Jeep rocked slightly and then he heard a sniffing sound. A small black bear was rooting around his rear tire. "Shoo," he said, but the bear paid no attention and nosed its way along the Jeep until it reached Kurt's door. He certainly didn't want to shoot the animal, but he didn't want it to paw through the flimsy canvas top, searching for food, while he was sitting behind the wheel.

"Beat it!" he said in a loud whisper.

The bear raised its head at him, stared silently and without fear, and then turned and padded off through the patches of snow. Kurt reached quickly into the glove box for his CB-4 Night Vision binoculars and framed the creature as it crossed the county road and galloped down the hillside toward civilization. With the binoculars he could see two DOW tags clipped to the bear's ears. It had been captured twice by Wildlife rangers and the next time would be its last.

Fully awake now, the adrenaline pumping, he scoped the toadstool mailbox and the dark drive. He began to wonder if he'd been wrong about Gahan. Maybe the old musician was telling the truth and this entire pursuit was a waste of time. Hunkering down for a long night of surveillance, he picked up the cell phone, dialed his home number, and coded his answering machine. "Your box is full," the electronic voice informed him.

Most of the calls were from news reporters, print and television, seeking interviews with him about his auction date with Nicole Bauer. Listening to the messages left his spirits in a place as raw and solitary as the surrounding night. Was there any way out of this? His career was on the verge of ruin. But more important, how would the scandal look from the eyes of his eight-year-old son? He could think of nothing worse than watching Lennon suffer through his father's public humiliation.

The sheer volume of interview requests overwhelmed him. After more than a dozen urgent appeals his mind went numb and the other messages droned past him. His mother in Scottsdale. The Bauer attorney. Muffin Brown. He pulled himself together when he heard her voice. She had finally obtained the call lists from the telephone company: "You were right, Kurt. Miz Bauer received two phone calls just before she died—one at three fifty-two A.M. and one at four fifteen. They were from a phone located backstage at the Wheeler. Same number that called you at ten forty-three this morning. Sounds like our boy the Phantom of the Opera."

How long had the creep been hiding out in the building? The first letters had arrived two weeks ago.

The final message was from Carole Marcus, who again offered to take Lennon for a few days. "You may need some time alone, Kurt. I know this has been rough on you. If I can do anything—anything at all," she ended her message, "please give me a call."

As he bundled himself deeper in the blanket, watching the quiet entrance to Gahan's drive, the soothing rhythms of Carole's voice lingered in his head. He didn't want to dwell on her tonight in this cold and isolate condition. Better to push those thoughts out of his mind. Ever since last summer he had been trying hard, without success, to forget their night together in his tent.

They had taken Lennon and her two youngest boys on an overnight camp-out high into the Collegiate Peaks Wilderness near Lincoln Creek. At the last minute Corky had bailed out on them to work on an urgent legal case and to keep an eye on their sullen twelve-year-old, who refused to make the trip. After a long day of hiking and fly-fishing and the usual campfire meal of hot dogs and S'mores, Kurt had collapsed in his two-man tent and was struggling to read a paperback mystery by lantern light while Lennon whooped it up with the Marcus boys in the larger tent. Around midnight he heard footsteps in the grass. Someone was unzipping the flap.

"Knock knock," Carole said, her face appearing out of the darkness. "I can't take it anymore, Kurt. May I join you?"

"Sure," he said. "Come on in."

"If I hear one more reenactment of a *Simpsons* episode, I will lose it."

"I'm surprised you held out this long," he laughed. "You deserve the door prize. Here," he said, digging into the pack beside his sleeping bag. "I've brought something in case of emergency."

She crawled into the tent and sat on Lennon's unfurled sleeping bag. He offered her the small flask.

"*Schnapps,* Kurt?" He had never heard this laugh of hers. It was girlish and charming, a laugh from her teen years. "I haven't had schnapps since I was in college."

"Me either," he said. "Seemed like a good thing to bring along to the mountains on a summer night. My Austrian roots."

"As long as you don't start yodeling," she said, tasting the liquor. "My god, it's sweet. Too much of this stuff and I'll be bouncing off the tent with the kids."

They sat facing each other in lotus positions, passing the bottle back and forth, laughing and making easy conversation. He had known her as long as he'd known Corky, more than ten years now, and had always been attracted to her. The men in their circle of friends often needled Corky, wondering how he'd been so lucky. She was a beautiful, elegant woman with instant warmth and good humor. Kurt admired her intelligence and her lively arguments, her concern for those larger matters that touched him as well. When he was with her and Corky he always felt a melancholy longing for Meg and their lost moments together.

After an hour of friendly talk they had finished the flask, but the boys were still wrestling around and screeching like wounded birds in the Marcus tent. "I wonder how much longer they can go on like that?" Carole said.

"At our house they usually crater around three A.M."

She laughed and touched his arm. "What a good dad you are. Corky always reads them the riot act at midnight. Whoever gets caught talking after that has to sign a letter of intent to law school."

Her warm hand lingered on his sleeve and he made no effort to move. "Lennon and I lead such a boring life, we both enjoy the chance to go wild when kids come over."

"Are you saying there isn't a romantic interest in your life, Kurt Muller?" she asked with a teasing smile. "I've always suspected you were carrying on a torrid affair with someone in secret."

Her remark had made him blush. He was no longer involved with Nicole but he'd worried that their affair had become common knowledge in Aspen society circles.

"Who has time for romance?" he'd said, eager to dispel her suspicions.

"Don't you read the gossip columns? You're Aspen's most eligible bachelor."

"Men stay eligible bachelors," he'd said, "when their first choice is spoken for."

He didn't know what had made him say this. Corky was one of his best friends and there was nothing in this world he would do to alter that.

Later he would blame the schnapps and the heady mountain air. He would convince himself he'd been overwhelmed by her physical proximity in the dusky, claustrophobic tent. They were so close he could almost taste her peppermint breath.

In response she'd dropped her eyes—demure, embarrassed, he wasn't sure—and he'd felt like a fool. He was prepared to make light of his remark when she raised her eyes and gazed at him with a serious, exploring look. "Be careful what you wish for," she had said, leaning forward to kiss him tenderly on the lips. When she pulled away he saw in her face a mirror of his own confusion and surprise. The kiss had left him speechless.

"Do you want to go to bed, Kurt?" she had asked, smiling behind half closed eyes.

In his memory the tent had suddenly filled with the white sound inside a seashell, as if he were sitting on a beach listening to the roar of wind and surf. "Carole, I—"

"I've kept you up long enough," she said, and he realized her question hadn't been an invitation but an apology.

"I suppose I should go calm the savages," she said. He could hear fatigue and alcohol wrapping themselves around her tongue. "I'll send Lennon back. That'll break up the party."

He caught his breath, worked his jaw to stop the roaring in his ears. "Okay," he had said. He didn't want her to leave, but he didn't trust what might happen if she stayed any longer. "I guess it's time to call it a night."

She handed him the empty schnapps flask and pressed herself against him in a long, limbering embrace. "We're getting too old to keep this up," she said, kissing his lips again before crawling toward the flap. "Good night, bachelor number one," she giggled, slowly sliding open the zipper. "Sweet dreams."

Kurt flopped back deadweight onto his sleeping bag. "I enjoyed that, Carole," he'd said.

Standing outside the tent she blew into her cupped hands. "Me too," she said, stomping circulation into her legs. "I'd forgotten how easy it was."

He wasn't sure what she'd meant. "Getting drunk on peppermint schnapps?" he asked.

"Being with a man. You know, another man. I'm glad it was you."

He propped himself up on his elbows. Chilly night air was seeping through the slit. "Did I miss something?" he'd asked.

She laughed that girlish laugh again. "Your icky schnapps took me back to the days before I became a happily married woman."

"I wish I'd known you then."

"Mmm. What an intriguing thought."

She zipped up the tent flap until all he could see was her small white face floating in the darkness like a luminous moon.

"I'll send Lennon back with a flashlight," she had said. "Sweet dreams, buckaroo."

He had almost settled into sleep when a bright beam flashed across his face. He thought it was his son returning to the tent, but then he realized he was sitting in his Jeep and a vehicle's headlights were zagging down the long private drive, turning onto the county road. He retrieved the Night Vision binoculars and quickly framed the driver of the Ford Explorer as it passed in front of him. Gahan Moss was wearing a beret and a neck scarf and he seemed to be talking to himself while toking on a fat joint.

Kurt pulled out of the cottonwoods and followed the musician down to Highway 82, where he made a right turn and then a squealing left at the traffic signal on Cemetery Lane. The street cut through a suburban neighborhood en route to Starwood and Woody Creek, and Kurt was prepared for a lengthy tail out in the moonlit countryside when Gahan abruptly wheeled off at the dark entrance to Red Butte Cemetery. Kurt cruised slowly past the turnoff and saw Gahan's brake lights fade out beneath the black trees near the cemetery gate. He knew this place. His father was buried here and on Sunday mornings he sometimes brought Lennon to the grave site with flowers and silent prayers.

He drove on for another block, then circled back and found an empty space in the line of cars parked along Cemetery Lane. There was a party going on in one of the large suburban houses on a cul-de-sac side street, and he could hear faint music and the chatter of voices.

Sitting in the Jeep's dark enclosure he caught snatches of conversation from the couples crunching past him in the brittle snow. *Don't you adore these jodhpurs, darling? They're making a comeback, you know.* No one seemed to notice him. It was the perfect cover from which to observe the cemetery entrance. Whatever Gahan Moss was doing in there, he had to come out sooner or later.

A lone figure emerged between cars about thirty yards ahead

and crossed the road. At first he thought the woman was a partygoer returning to her vehicle, until she passed behind a Land-Rover parked near the cemetery fence and pressed farther into the darkness. Kurt grabbed the binoculars lying on the passenger seat and tried to read her before she disappeared into the trees surrounding the headstones. She was wearing jeans and a jacket with a fur-fringed hood, her hands tucked into the pockets as she strode on with an urgent purpose, swiftly receding into the impenetrable forest of dark limbs.

Had Gahan Moss arranged a rendezvous with this woman?

He crawled out of the Jeep and tested his foot. The swelling had gone down in the ankle and there was less pain now when he put pressure on his step. He turned off his beeper and limped across the road without a crutch, slowly finding his way down the gravel drive to the cemetery's entrance gate, where Gahan's Explorer was parked in the darkness. He sought cover behind one of the tall oak trees looming along the lane and peered around the thick trunk, training the CB-4 binoculars on the back windshield. The Explorer appeared to be empty. He waited, listening for voices. Castle Creek streamed past the far boundary of the cemetery, a loud white hiss blocking out all other sounds. Kurt wouldn't be able to hear their words no matter how close he got.

Slipping up behind the Explorer he gazed through the back glass and saw that there was no one inside. He hobbled over to the old iron-spear fence and scanned the deep shadows with his binoculars. The area covered only an acre or two, a few hundred shady plots, postwar family names with lasting attachments to the town, the merchants and small-time innkeepers who had kept Aspen alive during the quiet years before the rebuilding. What were Gahan and his friend doing here at such a late hour?

He found them standing next to one of the tall spired markers in the middle of the cemetery, about fifty yards away. Gahan was gesturing wildly, a flurry of hands and pointed fingers and hostile body language. The woman watched him in silence, her own hands tucked stoically into the jacket. With the hood up it was impossible to see her face.

Who is she? he wondered. A secret affair? One of Gahan's porno queens with an angry boyfriend at home? Or someone from the old days. Someone Gahan desperately needed to talk to about Rocky and a snooping sheriff.

After one final outburst of irritation the musician turned abruptly and stormed back toward his vehicle, leaving the woman alone near the tombstones. Kurt retreated into the foliage and dropped flat against the cold ground, pain shooting up his leg from the sprained ankle. Soon Gahan's headlights were sweeping above him as the Explorer ripped into reverse and sped away in an adolescent fury. What had made him so upset?

In a short while the woman rattled open the cemetery gate and walked back down the dark tree-lined lane. Favoring his ankle again, Kurt followed at a safe distance. He watched her cross the public road and join a small band of latecomers sauntering along the sidewalk toward the party. They all knew one another. Their laughter rang out with the familiarity of friends.

Kurt slid into his Jeep and waited for the group to reach the party site before he raised the binoculars. At the doorway the woman dropped the hood onto her shoulders, revealing the back of her short, stylish hair. Then she went inside with the others.

There were only eight houses in the cul-de-sac—sturdy, two-story suburban family homes that belonged on the outskirts of a large city rather than in a quaint mountain resort. The subdivision bordered the municipal golf course, explaining the country club affect. An avid golfer could walk out his backyard onto a long green fairway.

Kurt shoved the binoculars back in the glove box and rested his head against the seat, listening to music and the hum of voices coming from the house down the street. It had been a long day and he was exhausted. A party full of jolly drunks was the last thing he needed to endure. But he was too curious about the woman to let her go. If he waited for her to reemerge in her fur-lined hood at the end of the evening, that might take two or three more hours. And as staking out Gahan Moss had proved, the Jeep wasn't properly equipped for a long surveillance in the frigid night air.

He got out and walked down the sidewalk to the party house. Furtive smokers huddled in the dark near the triple garage. In spite of the brisk temperature, several uncloaked revelers stood on a second-story balcony with drinks in hand. An older woman called down to him, "You're missing all the fun, Marty. Come back up and fill my glass!"

It appeared to be a casual free-for-all spilling out from its crowded center, the noise swelling toward a frenzied pitch. Kurt wanted to go inside and look for the woman—find out her name, something certain about her—but his face was too familiar and it wasn't possible to mill about unnoticed. He suspected that after the disasters of the past twenty-four hours he would be as welcome at an Aspen society party as O. J. Simpson at a policeman's ball.

His plan was to circle the house a couple of times, glance through windows and patio doors, breeze past the hardy souls gathered around outside, and hope to catch sight of the woman without entering the premises. All he had to go on was an Audrey Hepburn haircut and a brown suede coat with a fur-fringed hood. And she wouldn't be wearing the coat indoors.

Venturing around the east side of the house, he passed the kitchen windows and saw several Latina servants preparing hors d'oeuvre trays around a large oakwood island. As he moved on, the brick exterior gave way to a long glass wall that looked in on a spacious den with a crackling fireplace and grand-scale Japanese paintings of snowcapped mountain landscapes. People stood shoulder to shoulder, snacking, raising their drinks and laughing. The couches were filled with lively conversationalists. Red, white, and blue streamers fluttered from the ceiling around

clusters of balloons. It looked like a patriotic Fourth of July cele-
bration on the wrong day of the year.

He recognized many of the faces: the older, more established
social clique whose photos appeared often in the local celebrity
columns. An aging ex-mayor from the late '60s who had caused
a furor over his antihippie policies was lecturing the daughter of
a famous movie mogul. A professional soldier of fortune who
owned a hotel in Belize strolled arm in arm with the waxen
grande dame who had bid $3,000 for a date with Kurt. Two ar-
chitect partners named Guerin and McCord who specialized in
ski resort hotels stood off in a corner sharing pâté crackers with
the director of the local ballet company. It was all very Aspen.
He studied the scene, searching for a woman to match the haircut he'd glimpsed through his Night Vision binoculars.

A small group trailed out of the room, shifting the body dy-
namics, and in their wake Kurt could see something propped
against the wall near the fireplace, a tall stiff poster the size of a
door. He took a few steps to the right for a clearer view of the
photo image and the words below: BEN SMERLAS FOR UNITED
STATES HOUSE OF REPRESENTATIVES, THIRD DISTRICT, COLORADO. An
enlarged picture of Smerlas smiled at him across the crowded
room. This was a party to announce his candidacy, Kurt now
realized. This was Ben Smerlas's home.

It should have come as no surprise to discover Nicole's two
brothers among the guests; still, Kurt was astonished to see them
at a party on the same day their sister had been found dead. Walt
and Jeffrey Bauer both owned second homes on Red Mountain,
not far from where Kurt had grown up and now lived, and they
often attended Aspen fundraisers and charity benefits. Ben
Smerlas was their kind of politician: a pro-business, pro-devel-
opment water boy who would happily carry their interests to
Congress, if the price was right.

Kurt watched the two brothers and wondered if he was being
too old-fashioned about this. Maybe no one in America believed

in a period of mourning anymore. Maybe it was time for him to give up that quaint practice and move on.

Known by his friends and the press as Walt IV, the oldest Bauer brother was tall, angular, ruggedly handsome, bearing a striking resemblance to Nicole. Though in his mid-fifties he was still fair-haired and buoyant, with the ruddy coloring of a year-round sportsman and a penchant for khakis and waffle-soled hiking boots even at corporate board meetings. Kurt remembered the news clips of the telegenic Walt IV testifying before Congress during the Iran-Contra hearings, proudly defending the Bauer family tradition of patriotic causes. But tonight he was in a relaxed mood, smiling roguishly and sharing a drink with the former Playmate who had emceed the auction benefit last night at the Hotel Jerome.

Shorter and softer in appearance than his older brother, Jeffrey Bauer was sitting on a bar stool behind the Playmate, removed from the conversation and looking noticeably uncomfortable, disengaged, overwhelmed. Muffin had mentioned his emotional reaction to his sister's death, and perhaps that explained why he was staring glumly into the wineglass set beside him on the bar.

Jeffrey was battling a weight problem, fifty years old and furrowed by the awesome responsibility of keeping the family books. With glasses, a double chin, and a bald patch like a monk's tonsure on the back of his head, he looked like a wayward off-breed of the imperial family, some recessive gene a lifetime of Bauer money and upbringing hadn't been able to suppress. Kurt imagined him living in the shadow of his two beautiful siblings, perpetually hurt and ignored. It was enough to turn a young child to numbers.

A cheer rose up from the rear of the house and all eyes turned toward the outside deck. Something was going on back there, and people began to wander in that direction. Curious himself, Kurt left the glass doors and followed a tall hedge glistening with ice crystals until he came upon a twenty-foot fir tree planted at the corner of the house. Hidden within the tree's shadow he could observe the scenario unfolding in the backyard. There was no fence, and Ben Smerlas stood teeing off golf balls deep into the outer darkness, where a fairway lay hidden under a mantle of light snow. Each time he swung, driving the ball like a tiny meteorite into the black void, the audience cheered and whistled from the redwood deck. The bucket of balls at his feet was nearly empty. His face beamed from alcohol and he joked with his audience in a loud, exuberant voice, waving his club triumphantly as he bent over to tee up another ball.

A woman walked out across the flood-lit lawn with a drink in each hand. She was wearing jeans and a wool sweater, and her red hair was cut short and fingered back behind her ears. Smerlas laughed and hugged the woman and took the drink she offered. They clinked glasses, drank, and exchanged a long sincere kiss. The onlookers burst into more cheers, and someone shouted a toast for the next Colorado congressman and his wife.

Kurt scanned the boisterous crowd on the deck. Sitting with one hip hitched on the railing was someone else he hadn't expected to see tonight. Dr. Jay Westbrook was sipping a glass of wine with an arm around his young blond-braided assistant, Tanya. The casual observer might have mistaken them for father and daughter.

Walt IV soon appeared at their side. Tanya smiled at him. He leaned over and said something in Westbrook's ear. The two men laughed heartily and tapped wineglasses in a casual toast.

Smerlas, the Bauer brothers, Jay Westbrook. One cozy little circle of acquaintances. What was it that Westbrook had said? *We've been family for quite a long time.*

In the midst of the raucous cheering a Latina housemaid raced onto the landscaped lawn bearing a bundle of clothing in her outstretched arms. *"Señor, señora!"* Kurt heard the girl say, "You going to catch cold out here! *Por favor,* put on your coats."

Ever the gentleman, Smerlas accepted a coat from the girl and placed it around his wife's shoulders. The coat was brown suede with a fur-lined hood. When she snuggled into it, fastening the buttons with a familiar touch, Kurt had found what he'd come looking for. The woman in the cemetery was Dana Smerlas.

20

SLUMPED DOWN IN the driver's seat, the boot slipped off his sprained ankle, Kurt turned his beeper back on and dialed Miles Cunningham's cabin on his cell phone. He was prepared to hear Nixon's voice again and then leave another message for the photographer; instead, a clear crisp male voice said hello after two rings. Kurt hesitated, confused. No one had ever answered Miles's phone except the eccentric loner himself.

"Is Miles there, please?"

"Speaking. What can I do for you?"

Though the voice sounded familiar, this wasn't the Miles Cunningham he had known for twenty-five years. Where was the slur, the convoluted, incomprehensible scramble of language? Where were the insults?

"Miles, it's Kurt. If this is indeed Miles Cunningham."

"Of course it's me, Muller. Who else would it be?"

"Miles, you're—you're—"

"Sober?"

"Yeeaaah," Kurt said with a puzzled drag to the word. He hadn't experienced this before: Miles Cunningham sober after dark.

"My primary care physician said I was killing myself," Miles said. "Others agreed."

"Congratulations. You did the right thing."

"I've been clean and sober for exactly nine days, four hours, and thirteen minutes."

"Was it rough?"

"Like somebody scraped out my soul with a manure shovel. But it had to be done."

"Incredible, man. Congratulations."

"You've already said that."

"Uh, yeah. Well, anyway, we're all happy for you."

"That's horseshit and you know it. Nobody wants a funny drunk to go straight. It spoils the party."

"You were getting worse these past few years."

"So I'm told."

There was something missing in his expression, something essentially Miles. His peculiar sense of humor appeared to be on hold. When they exorcised the demons at the dry-out farm they may have killed off a few angels as well.

"Did you get my message about the photograph?" Kurt asked.

"Yes, I did," Miles said, the words snapping off his tongue with a brazen self-confidence. "But this sobriety jones has had its side effects. Like for instance memory loss."

"You can't remember my message?"

"I remember your message, nitwit. I can't remember being a photographer."

"Don't take my word for it," Kurt said, rubbing his sore ankle. "Go look in that bunker you built behind your cabin. It's full of photo files. Thousands of them."

"Was I good?"

"You were the best. You won a Pulitzer prize."

"I wondered how that thing got on the mantel."

"Miles, you're joking, right? You're fucking around."

"After Betty Ford there's good news and bad news. The good

news is I'll live another fifteen years. The bad news is I can't remember why I want to."

Kurt glanced at his watch. Ten-thirty. He didn't have time for
counseling. Not tonight.

"You took some photographs of Rocky Rhodes and his
groupies back in the seventies. I want to see what you've got on
file. There's one woman in particular I'm trying to track down."

"Rocky Rhodes the dead rock star?" Miles asked, as if he'd
never spoken the man's name before. "You know, I've always
wondered what it would be like to hang out with a faggy rock
star, eat his primo drugs, and sleep with all the groupies."

"Miles, you did that. For several years."

"You're shitting me."

"I have this feeling I'm being fucked with and I am not
amused. Goddammit, you took at least one picture of a young
hippie chick named Mariah Windstar—a group shot with
Rocky and friends—and I need to see what she looks like. You've
got to dig her out of your files for me."

Gahan's photograph resurfaced in Kurt's mind, the two
women kissing, red and black. The small dark-haired woman
with the butterfly tattoo on her shoulder blade could have been
Dana Smerlas at twenty-five.

"What makes you think I have what you're looking for?"
Miles asked.

"There's a picture of her in the Rocky Rhodes biography but
the photo page was ripped out of the copy I saw. The credit line
had your name on it."

Maybe Gahan had contacted Dana Smerlas tonight because
she was an old friend from the Rocky days, someone who had
been with them at Canyon de Chelly, and he was warning her
that a cop was poking around in their past. Maybe the new Mrs.
Smerlas had once been a young woman called Mariah Windstar.
The elusive Pariah.

"Why don't you phone the publisher, genius?" Miles said.
"The chances are nada to nil I'll find something in that slag pile

out in the bunker. I don't have a clue what's in those file cabinets."

It was the weekend and Kurt would have to wait until Monday to contact the publisher. "How about if I lend you a couple of deputies to help look through your contact sheets?"

"I may be obnoxiously sober at this point in my life, Muller, but I'm not entirely bereft of my old principles. To wit, lawmen of any ilk shall not set foot in my inner sanctum."

"We've known each other a long time, Miles. You know I don't ask for your help unless I'm jammed against a wall."

Kurt heard him inhale, the telltale drag on a cigarette. Or maybe a joint. He could easily imagine Miles Cunningham giving up alcohol but no other drugs.

"I'm not opening that bunker anymore. I go in there, my face gets rubbed in a lot of painful shit I've just spent half my life savings to get free of. In fact, I'm going to take a trowel and a bucket of wet cement and seal that motherfucker shut. Or maybe I'll dynamite it to the ground, I haven't decided yet. All I know is the past is a wash and the present is a cold bowl of sop. But I'm alive, goddammit. I'm alive." He paused for another puff. "Ain't that fucking wonderful."

Kurt could see that their conversation was headed straight into the dead end of denial and self-pity. He had been down that road many times himself. "When you get through being angry at yourself for being a survivor," he said, "give me a call, Miles. We'll sit down over coffee and I'll tell you about an amazing photographer I once knew. He went into places where women and children were being tortured and murdered, and he brought back pictures to show the world that the horrors had to stop."

There was a long silence. Then, with an air of indifference, "I don't think I ever knew that fellow. He sounds so earnest."

Once upon a time they had all been earnest. Miles, Nicole, Rocky Rhodes. Kurt and his brother, Bert. An entire generation. "Before you padlock the door, go into the bunker for one last look at the pictures," he said. "You're right, every one of them will scream at you. But the world needs to keep hearing those screams."

In the awkward silence Kurt tried to imagine the aging war photographer sitting across from him at a latte bar, wearing a pressed cotton suit and a trendy tie, Oliver Peoples metal-rimmed eyeglasses, his nails pared, his bushy gray sideburns neatly razored. Miles Cunningham in the '90s. It did not compute.

"Be well, Miles. Call me if you decide to help. Or if you just want to talk."

Kurt shut off the cell phone and sat watching the party house down the street. The music was growing louder and no one was leaving yet. Ben Smerlas, U.S. Congressman, Third District. A scary thought. Kurt could expect Smerlas to harass him and his department, as he had as county commissioner, only with greater authority and more extensive means of curtailment. Maybe being recalled as sheriff wasn't such a bad idea after all. He wouldn't have to suffer Ben Smerlas any longer.

The beeper sounded. Muffin's desk at the courthouse. He dialed her back immediately. "I've been trying to reach you," she said with irritation in her voice. "Don't you have your beeper with you?"

"I had to turn it off for a while."

"Got a call from Dan the Man." Dan Davenport was the sheriff of Garfield County and a former deputy under Kurt. "He's got Lyle Gunderson in custody. Speeding, avoiding arrest, GTA. Our young friend was booking it at ninety-plus in a stolen car, heading for Interstate 70, when one of Dan's boys tried to pull him over. Lyle wouldn't stop and there was pursuit and the kid rolled the car just this side of Glenwood. He's banged up, but not too bad, considering. Damned lucky to be alive."

"Sounds like he was in a hurry to get out of the valley," Kurt said.

"He was driving Nicole Bauer's Saab, Kurt, with a trunkful of videotapes. They figure two, three hundred, mostly homemade porn. Young Lyle's specialty is what's called 'hiddens' in smut circles—a camera hidden in a closet. Dan the Man thinks we should come take a look at the collection."

Kurt suddenly felt ill. Nicole's houseboy with a hidden camera. Which would explain his eerie sense that someone had been watching them last night in her bedroom. "Has Dan looked at the tapes?" he asked in a small, troubled voice.

"Apparently so," she said. "But he didn't want to discuss it on the phone."

THE DRIVE TO Glenwood Springs took forty-five minutes on average, but with Muffin behind the wheel, pushing the department cruiser to eighty miles an hour on the dark two-lane highway northward through the valley, they were making record time. There was Saturday-night traffic outside the small rural communities of Basalt and El Jebel, but she turned on the flashing overhead lights and forced everyone out of her way.

"I had a creepy feeling about that kid," she said, blazing past the nocturnal lights of a bedroom subdivision built near the highway on century-old ranch land. Somewhere out in that frigid darkness lay a freshly planted private golf course with eighteen holes. And probably another martini party where a swaggering loudmouth was teeing off from his backyard.

"No priors, right?" Kurt said. "Let's look into why he dropped out of college in Oregon."

Soon they were passing the location where Lyle had wrecked Nicole's Saab. The short skid marks on the pavement told them he had flipped quickly. Muffin slowed down, the tires crunching fresh glass. By this time there was only one Garfield County Sheriff's vehicle, a deputy shining his high beams on the two tow-truck men down in a shallow gully hooking cables to a car with a flattened roof.

"So we've got ourselves a peeper with a video camera," Muffin said, slowly pulling away from the scene, "and some crazy old dude living in the Wheeler attic. What's the connection?"

Lyle and Rocky Rhodes. Kurt couldn't imagine it. He didn't know.

"We've gone over the attic pretty good, Kurt, and we didn't find anything new. Just those magazines and some trash," she said. "Joey dusted the backstage phone where the guy made his calls to you and Nicole but all he lifted was a greasy smudge."

"What about my house?"

"Same thing. Stains and smears. Our man doesn't leave anything solid. It's like he's, he's—"

"A ghost," Kurt said.

She cast her eyes aslant at him, showing her annoyance. "Don't start that," she said.

THE GARFIELD COUNTY Sheriff's Department and its attached jail were located in a '60s vintage brick structure on the south side of the Colorado River, three blocks off the main drag through Glenwood Springs. From the parking lot Kurt could see the elegant lights of the old Hotel Colorado across the river, where Teddy Roosevelt had stayed during his famous bear hunts in the territory. Vapor billowed up from the natural hot springs near the hotel. The Ute Indians had revered those springs as sacred ground. Enterprising settlers had built a sanatorium there. Doc Holliday had come here to battle his tuberculosis and was buried on a nearby hill; and some years later, when a doddering Buffalo Bill Cody was lowered into the waters to soothe his aged bones, he lapsed into a coma from which he did not recover.

Dan Davenport was watching *The Tonight Show* on the television in his office. Davenport was a tall rope-muscled cowboy who had wrestled steers in the rodeo circuit before turning to law enforcement. Kurt had inherited him from the previous regime in Pitkin County. But Dan eventually lost his tolerance for the glitzy, fast-track Aspen of the '80s and hired on as a deputy farther north in Garfield County, still the rural West. A few years ago he'd been elected county sheriff.

"Y'all made good time," he said, rising from his desk to shake their hands. His drooping handlebar mustache was streaked with silver, and there was a permanent hat indentation through his short-cropped hair. "The Gunderson boy's gonna be in Valley View for a couple days. His face is cut up some and he's got two busted ribs and a broken leg. One of my deputies is sitting with him. His parents are down there, too."

"Can we talk to him?" Kurt asked.

"He's pretty doped up but you're welcome to try," Davenport said. "I thought you might like to see something first."

He walked over to a stack of cardboard boxes that filled one corner of his office. "The boy was hauling quite a load," he said, retrieving a videotape placed aside from the others. "I've looked at enough to git the picture."

The portable television rested on a mobile cart near his desk. He slid the tape into a VCR and handed the remote control to Kurt.

"Miss Brown," Davenport said, "can I talk to you a minute outside?"

He opened the office door and extended his hand toward the corridor. Muffin hesitated, glancing at Kurt for an explanation. "Is there some reason I shouldn't see this tape?" she asked them both.

Davenport stared at the scuffed tips of his cowboy boots. His embarrassment appeared mannered but genuine. "I think Kurt'll want to watch this by hisself," he said, his jaw flexing sternly.

Behind Muffin's eyes something locked in place. She nodded, agreeing reluctantly, a moment of comprehension. "Okay," she said directly to Kurt. "For now."

After they had left the room Kurt sat down in Dan's swivel chair and pushed the play button. Within seconds his worst fear was exposed before him on the screen. He recognized the bedroom and the two people kissing, undressing each other. Lyle's tape had been recorded from a pinhole camera high above Nicole's bed, possibly through a grate of some sort, the central air duct. The view was partially obstructed, the video quality poor, the sound muffled, but there was no doubt what was going on and when it had taken place.

Everything began to unfold before his eyes in a morbid déjà vu—the thin dress straps slipping off her shoulders, his hands gliding gently across her breasts. The sight of her long sinewy body, freckled and golden, took his breath away. He watched her sprinkle potpourri on the sheets like a flower girl tossing petals at a wedding. *Smell,* she said, raising her upturned palm to his face as if feeding him a strange fruit. *Do you remember?*

I remember, Nickie. His own rough voice was clear and unmistakable.

Reliving those final hours, his thoughts leapt back and forth between a resolve to kill the little bastard who had filmed them making love and a desire to hold Nicole one last time. As the tape rolled on, his anger turned to guilt and regret. He couldn't deny it any longer: they had been a good fit, two damaged souls struggling to fill the empty spaces within them. It was impossible to look at the woman on the screen without feeling a sense of longing and remorse.

Like Dan Davenport, he had seen enough. There was no point in letting the tape run on like this, but he couldn't bring himself to push the stop button. Nicole sat up in bed and lifted his face from her body, whispering something, raking her hands through his hair. He reached over to the remote control and turned up the volume to hear what she was saying. *Do you remember how I like it?* she asked him with a beautiful dreamy smile. She rolled onto her knees and elbows, reaching back to pull him into her, and in that moment Kurt understood how the author of those letters had known the intimate details of Nicole Bauer's sex life. He had seen everything on tape.

21

"I FIGURE THESE boxes belong with you folks in Pitkin County," Dan Davenport said as he escorted them to the parking lot. "I'll git one of my men to write up a quick inventory. Be ready by the time you're finished talking to the boy."

"I appreciate that, Dan," Kurt said.

"Tell you the honest truth, I don't want to mess with it. We've got him on speeding and failing to obey—you and your D.A. can deal with the rest. I don't want that crap sittin' around my office."

When Kurt opened the door of the Pitco cruiser, Davenport gripped his arm and took him aside, facing the dark river so Muffin couldn't hear his words. "Only one deputy has seen that tape besides myself, Kurt, and I've told him he'll lose his job if he talks about it to anybody else, including his wife."

"Thanks, Dan. You're a good man."

There was a shy smile hiding under the heavy mustache that had always made him look melancholy and serious. "You'd do the same for me, hoss," he said.

On their short ride to Valley View Hospital, Muffin's silence grew into a hostile tension and Kurt realized he had to tell her something. "Dan was just being an old-fashioned gentleman," he explained. "He doesn't think a female employee ought to watch her boss make a fool of himself in a compromising situation."

"It wouldn't be the first time," she said.

"Trust me, this is different."

Muffin stared ahead into the late-night traffic. "So he's covering for you. One good old boy doing a favor for another."

"No," he said. "He expects me to do the right thing."

"Are you sure you know what that is?"

She followed Davenport's Jeep Cherokee down the main thoroughfare through the old shopping district, heading south again. Soon they turned off into a modest residential area where few house lights were burning now, shortly past midnight. The hospital looked out of place in the slumbering neighborhood.

"You going to let me see the tape?" she asked as they pulled into one of the spaces reserved for police emergencies.

"Better than that," he said. "I want you to look at them all."

"Hah!" she laughed, rolling her eyes. "Two or three hundred porno tapes? So now I'm being punished for being a nosy girl."

He watched Davenport get out of his Cherokee and wait for them at the side entrance. "Divide them up with Linda Ríos," Kurt said. "Just the two of you, nobody else."

"Why Linda? You figure Nicole can teach us a few moves?"

He frowned at her. "I figure you and Linda will keep the information to yourselves, which is more than I expect from the guys," he said. "Pull an all-nighter if you have to. We've got to see what else is on those tapes."

"Don't you mean *who* else?"

A parade of Nicole's secret lovers. Husbands, men of position. Many of Aspen's most prominent names. Was blackmail Lyle's game? Monetary gain? Or was he in it for the sexual thrills?

Muffin opened her door, letting the dome light shine on them. She wanted him to see her face clearly when she said what was on her mind: "You were a fool, Kurt."

He inhaled deeply, blew air through his nostrils in one quick burst. He didn't disagree with her.

"I've been told that 'hiddens' are a hot property on the Internet," she said. "Better hope Lyle didn't download your bare ass onto the World Wide Web."

DAVENPORT CLEARED THE interview with the attending physician and they proceeded through the maze of corridors to Lyle's room. They found his parents fussing over him, rearranging pillows, adjusting the lighting. The deputy in the room sat reading a magazine, oblivious to their pampering ministrations.

"Kurt!" said Marjie Gunderson, surprised to see him walk into the room. She was holding a sip bottle to her son's blood-dried lips. "Don't tell me they're dragging you into this, too."

Kurt nodded. "Looks like Lyle's got himself in some serious trouble," he said, staring at the young man stretched out on the bed. His right leg was encased in a cast, suspended in traction; his face and arms bore the jagged gouge marks of broken glass. A bandage covered his forehead.

"Should we get a lawyer, Kurt?" Gus Gunderson asked him. He was a tall rawboned man, mid-fifties, wearing paint-spattered bib overalls and a yellowing insulated underwear shirt rolled up past his flinty elbows.

"Yes, you should, Gus," Kurt said, giving him a friendly pat on the shoulder. They were good people who didn't deserve the grief their son was going to put them through. "Why don't you and Marjie go make some calls while I talk to Lyle."

The Gundersons were reluctant to leave the room, but Kurt escorted them into the corridor and Dan Davenport asked his deputy to find them a comfortable place to wait until the interrogation was over.

"Well, young man," Kurt said, returning to stand over the bed. "You've been a naughty boy."

Lyle closed his eyes, revealing large encircling bruises the color of ripe plums. "I'm blown," he said in a groggy voice. "I need to sleep."

"I know you've already heard this from the Garfield deputies," Kurt said, "but to make sure there's no misunderstanding . . ." He recited Lyle's Miranda rights.

"Come back when I've got Johnnie Cochran," Lyle mumbled with his eyes still closed.

Kurt stooped closer and lowered his voice. "Your parents love you, Lyle. But you're breaking their hearts," he said, glancing at Davenport and Muffin standing next to each other on the other side of the bed.

A hidden camera. Someone's most private moments on tape. Kurt wanted to twist the little bastard's suspended leg. How did such a well-loved child like Lyle Gunderson become a peeper?

"Why don't you get the whole thing off your chest?" Kurt said. "Dragging it out will only hurt your parents worse."

Lyle opened his eyes and stared at the ceiling. "I didn't steal the car," he said. "Nicole let me use it whenever I wanted."

"I'm not concerned about the car right now, son. Let's talk about the tapes."

The young man twirled a strand of long blond hair around his finger. "Most of that stuff I bought off the Net," he said. "If that's against the law, I haven't heard."

"It's against the law to hide a video camera in somebody's bedroom and take pictures of them," Kurt said. "I think you know that."

Lyle moved his head, turning away from Kurt to stare at the zipper on Muffin's parka. Dried blood matted the long strings of hair clinging to his thin neck. There was a small encrusted hole in his ear where one of the bead gems was missing.

"What were you going to do with the tapes of Nicole Bauer?" Kurt asked him.

Silence. A blank stare.

"Who else did you show them to?"

Lyle wasn't going to answer him.

"What about Gahan Moss? Does that name ring a bell?" Kurt asked. "He's into porn, too, isn't he? You and Gahan have something worked out together?"

The young man stubbornly held his silence.

"You're pretty messed up here, son," Kurt said with a tight laugh, looking over the bandages and leg cast like a claims adjuster examining a wrecked car. "Broken bones, facial lacerations. Who were you running from?" he asked. "The law? Or was somebody else after you?"

When Lyle didn't respond, Muffin reached down and took his nicked chin in her hand, raising his jaw, forcing him to look her in the eyes. "If you're working some kind of blackmail scam with those tapes," she said, her fingers digging into his welted skin, "you're gonna do time, lover boy. You have any idea how much fun it is in prison for a sweet-looking, sexy guy like you? Everything you've ever seen on those videos is going to happen to you, only you'll be playing the girl."

Lyle jerked his head away. "Get the fuck out of my face!" he shouted, his hand groping awkwardly for the call button. "I want my parents back in here and I want a lawyer!"

"Just tell us who else has seen the tapes," Kurt said, "and we'll let you get some sleep."

Lyle held his thumb to the call button, producing an obnoxious nonstop buzz. When Muffin wrestled it away from him he began to scream at the top of his voice. The nurse rushed in and tried to calm him, admonishing the police officers to leave the room while she administered a hypo full of tranquilizer. A few moments later, when Kurt looked in on him, Lyle was fast asleep.

DAN DAVENPORT EXCUSED himself to return to his office, leaving Kurt and Muffin to wend their way through the silent hospital in search of the cafeteria. Service had closed hours ago, but the glass doors were unlocked and the Gundersons occupied a table under lighting so dim it would have been difficult to read a newspaper. A clock hummed on the wall, the only sound in the room. The couple was drinking coffee they'd purchased from a machine. They appeared haggard and resigned, like prisoners awaiting their sentence. Kurt sensed that they hadn't looked at each other or exchanged a word since the deputy had brought them here.

"May we sit down?" he asked.

"Certainly," Gus Gunderson said with a sweep of his hand. His steel-gray hair was tied back in a ponytail, his strong jaw and chiseled features the source of Lyle's own good looks.

"Can I get anybody another coffee?" Muffin offered.

They declined. Marjie Gunderson's stricken expression revealed the bitter taste of everything they had endured tonight. "What's going to happen to our son?" she asked.

"I won't lie to you, Marjie," Kurt said. "He's in trouble."

She lowered her eyes. Marjie Gunderson was a hefty woman with a large head and neck and a thick mane of hair colored equally auburn and gray. The quintessential Earth Mother, nurturing, amiable, passionate about her causes. She had taught sensitivity sessions at Star Meadow until the place had gone under. In spite of her New Age affectations Kurt had enjoyed their occasional conversations at gallery openings and benefits. But at this moment, sitting in near darkness, clutching the paper cup, she seemed subdued, burdened, reduced by her anguish.

"Sheriff Davenport told us there may be some additional charges," she said, refusing to look at Kurt or Muffin seated across the table. "The videotapes they found in his trunk."

"That's correct," Kurt said. "We'll have to review them all before we can determine the extent of the offenses."

"Did you know your son was into that sort of thing?" Muffin asked, her hands clasped in front of her on the table. "Has he been in trouble before?"

The couple traded glances, their eyes darting quickly and then returning to gaze forlornly at the cold Formica. "Yes, Miss

Brown, I'm afraid he has," Gus admitted with a weary sigh. His small weak eyes swam like minnows behind the thick lenses of his black horn-rimmed glasses. Kurt wondered how he managed to create the intricate, finely wrought metal sculptures that had won him local acclaim.

"There was a problem at college," Marjie said.

Gus lifted his chin and looked directly at Kurt and Muffin for the first time. "Some incidents at a girls' dorm. Apparently he was hanging around outside their windows with a goddamned video cam."

"He was peeping," Marjie said with an undercurrent of anger aimed entirely at her husband. "They caught him at it."

"When the campus police searched his room they found a closet full of porno tapes. And there was some smut on his computer that he'd got off the Internet."

"I suppose it could've been worse," Marjie said, speaking to the tabletop. "They kicked him out of school but didn't press criminal charges."

"I don't know," Gus said, shaking his head. "I thought they were pretty rough on the boy."

"You're in denial, dear," Marjie countered, irritation pinching her soft wide face. This sounded like an argument they had been having for quite some time. "What he did was wrong and he was lucky to get off that easy."

When bad things happen to good parents, Kurt thought. He tried to imagine how he would react if Lennon had done the same thing.

"Has Lyle ever mentioned Gahan Moss?" he asked, still attempting to place the two of them together because of their video interests. "You know who I mean—Gahan Moss the musician. Do they know each other?"

Gus shrugged. "I think Lyle has been to some parties at the Magic Mushroom House," he said. "Most college kids in Aspen have been up there at one time or another."

"God only knows what goes on in that place," Marjie said.

"Oh, right," Gus said with a pained smile. "Like we haven't had some parties of our own, dear."

A child of Aquarius, Kurt thought. Lyle had grown up around his share of tomfoolery.

"You've never seen Lyle and Gahan Moss together?" he asked.

They shook their heads in unison. "No," Gus said, perplexed by the line of questioning.

Marjie dragged a huge flannel-lined poncho from the back of her chair and settled it around her shoulders, bundling against the chill white surfaces of the room. "Lyle has always been a serious child, Kurt," she said. "He didn't make many friends growing up, even though the town was full of wonderful kids. I mean, it was Aspen, for crying out loud. Everybody was special."

"We tried to work it out ourselves," Gus said glumly. "We did everything we could to make him happy."

Marjie looked as if she were going to cry. She reached over and laid her hand on her husband's. "We didn't know what was wrong, but we knew he needed professional help," she said. "Our son has been in therapy since he was fourteen."

"I still don't know what's in that boy's head," Gus said, squeezing his wife's hand, looking away.

"We thought he was doing better," she said, her voice growing husky, trembling. "We thought that business in Portland was behind him. Dr. Westbrook convinced us that Lyle had worked through it."

"Westbrook?" Kurt said.

She gazed at him with tears sparkling in her eyes. "Yes," she said. "Wonderful man. He's been Lyle's therapist since the beginning. What's it been, hon—eight years now?"

Gus nodded.

"I don't know where we would be without Jay," she said with an admiring smile. "Gus and I have gone through some counseling with him ourselves."

Kurt looked at the *I Ching* ring still lodged on his finger. Muffin was staring at it, too, noticing the ring for the first time. "Dr. Jay Westbrook," he said half to himself, slowly curling his fingers into a fist. "Let me guess. That's how Lyle got his job with Nicole Bauer."

Marjie didn't hesitate. "Yes, it was," she said. "Lyle was lying around the house, watching TV all day, feeling sorry for himself. Dr. Westbrook's been trying to get him to do something with his life. He thought the job would give him a sense of purpose."

"What did his job entail?" Muffin asked.

"Keeping house," Marjie said with an indifferent shrug. "Cleaning, grocery shopping. A little cooking on the side. Lyle's always had a domestic streak. And he's mechanically inclined."

Especially proficient in the field of video technology, Kurt thought. Installation, maintenance, upgrade.

"He adored the Bauer woman," Marjie said, shaking her head sadly. "I'm sure it's her death that's got him so strung out. He's not like this, Kurt. Running from the police? He's just not himself."

The Gundersons didn't know yet that their son had been secretly videotaping the woman he adored. Kurt would wait another day, after the thorough review of the tapes, before informing them. They had suffered enough for one night.

"Kurt," Gus Gunderson said, straightening his bony shoulders, showing a sudden strength in his gaunt face. "He might be twenty-two years old but the god-awful truth is he's still a little boy living inside his head."

Silent tears were streaming down Marjie's face. "He's all we've got," she said.

Her husband slipped his long arm around her shoulders. "Please do his mother and me a favor," he said. "If he has to serve time in jail, bring him back to Pitkin County. We know you'll keep an eye on him for us."

In that moment Kurt thought of his own son and how much

he loved him, and how something like this would devastate him, too. He thought about his dead father, how different they had been and how his lack of ambition had disappointed the old man. In the end the only thing that mattered was that you stood by each other, holding hands in the darkness. And he had done that at his father's deathbed.

"I'll do what I can, folks," he told the Gundersons. "If you don't have a lawyer yet, I know a few names. Let's make some phone calls."

22

KURT ATTEMPTED TO sleep on the trip back to Aspen, but Muffin wouldn't let him. "Hey, wake up," she said, shaking his knee. "You're not bailing out on me until you answer a few questions yourself. Like what's the Gahan Moss thing all about?"

"I went to see him at the Magic Mushroom House," he said. "I thought he might know something about Rocky."

"I'm not sure I want to hear any more of this," she said, catching his eye in their reflection on the dark windshield glass.

"I also paid a visit to Jay Westbrook."

She threw back her head, groaned, and slapped the steering wheel. The car veered across the white stripes but she quickly guided it back on course. "Didn't I tell you to stay out of the investigation?" she said.

"They're both protecting secrets," Kurt said. "I don't have any answers, but I know the two of them are in this up to their short hairs."

"If you don't stay out of this case, Kurt Muller, you're going to fuck it up so bad the D.A. won't get near it."

Kurt gazed out the side window at the muted lights of Car-bondale. "You haven't told me about the autopsy yet," he said, working hard to blot out what he knew had happened to Nicole's body on the stainless steel table. The Y cut, the organ probes.

Muffin shrugged. "No surprises. It was an uncontrolled fall, with fatal damage to her skull and neck. No signs of other trauma."

Kurt breathed deeply. "Tox?"

"She was legally drunk, Kurt. She must've kept drinking after you left. And there was definitely antipsychotic medication in her system. The stuff in her drawer."

He pounded his thigh with a clenched fist. "Westbrook knew she had a drinking problem," he said, "yet he prescribed a drug that can make you see little green men if it's mixed with alcohol."

Muffin glanced at him, then back to the highway. "So what are you saying?"

He hadn't thought it through with any precision. "He gives her shit to make her even more paranoid than she already is. He sends her a fucked-up kid he knows will spy on her with his video camera," he said. "You tell me, Muffin. Is this his idea of an amicable divorce?"

"You think Lyle was making videos for his shrink?"

"It's possible."

She was silent for several moments, considering the possibilities. "So Westbrook's the crazy jealous type who likes to keep a close eye on his ex-wife? Like the notorious Heisman Trophy winner."

"Maybe."

"Or maybe he gets off watching her do it with other men," she said. "Maybe that's his thing."

The tapes as a command performance for Jay Westbrook and god knows who else, Kurt thought. The idea made his skin crawl. "But why the drug?" he asked, thinking aloud. "What does that get him?"

"And what about the letters?" she said, lost now in the labyrinth of conjecture. "And our man with the hunting knife? Where does he fit in?"

Kurt massaged his forehead. "This is giving me a headache," he said.

Muffin reached over and rubbed his shoulder. "It's probably the concussion," she said. "You've been pounded pretty hard today, my friend. Why don't you go ahead and catch a few winks. We'll be home soon."

The car climbed the steep roadway, hugging curves above the dark valley. Snowflakes swirled in the high beams. Kurt relaxed his head against the seat rest and briskly rubbed his face. The cool ring raked his jaw. He lifted his hand and stared at his spread fingers.

"Why the hell are you wearing that thing?" she asked him. "It should've been logged in the evidence cage with her other stuff."

"I'm stuck with it," he said, tugging at the band. "I can't get it off."

"Here," she said, gripping the ring, pulling. There was a tug-of-war, her strength, his resistance, the ring gnawing into his knuckle.

"Muffin," he said, wincing from the pain, "what if somebody showed those tapes of Nicole to a jealous lover? Not to Westbrook, but to a psychopath completely off his rocker. What if somebody showed them to Rocky Rhodes?"

With one hand steering the wheel, her eyes fixed on the dark highway, Muffin continued to pull. "Come on, Kurt. You've got to stop talking like he's alive."

"The biography said he was always insanely possessive. Seeing the tapes would make him so crazy he'd want to kill her. Plus everybody else he thought was sleeping with her. And that's exactly what he typed on my typewriter."

She was jerking the ring now, rubbing his skin raw. "Okay,

so where has Rocky been all this time?" she asked. "And why is he coming out of mothballs now?"

Kurt withdrew his hand before she managed to pull the finger out of its socket. "Damned if I know," he said, sucking on the broken skin.

He thought about the man's haunting, strangled laugh—how it had sounded like someone who hadn't used his voice in a long time. Maybe someone shut away for his own good.

"Did you use a lubricant?"

"What?"

"Your *finger*," Muffin said, raising an eyebrow. "Have you tried Vaseline or liquid soap? I'm sure there's a tube of K-Y lying around your bedroom somewhere."

They were passing the airport, only a few miles outside Aspen. The radio hissed, alerting all units. The dispatcher was reporting an alarm at the architecture offices near Rumpf Park, the firm of Guerin and McCord. An image flashed through Kurt's mind, the stylish Ben Guerin and Andy McCord eating pâté crackers at Smerlas's party. "Christ, I hope it's not another bear," he said.

"What would a bear be after in an architect's office? Glue Stick?"

"Let's pick it up," he said. "One of the architects working late probably forgot to disarm the system."

They arrived in ten minutes. A Pitco Sheriff's Department car and a flashing Aspen police unit were parked in front of the place, an old mining-era Victorian home that had been converted into an elegant design studio with offices. The structure sat on the same knoll as a quaint bed-and-breakfast next door, and up the hillside between them rose a stair-step path made from railroad ties. Muffin and Kurt got out of their vehicle and she shone her flashlight on the sloping lawn. The only tracks were human, a crisscross of footsteps in the light snow, arcing toward the top of the knoll.

"They've gone around back," she said.

The railroad ties were aglaze with ice and Kurt couldn't set his footing on the weak ankle. They abandoned the stairsteps and trailed up the frozen rise, discovering a backyard garden area with prim trellises and redwood picnic tables. Tonight's snowfall had powdered the split-level decks, dusting the flower boxes and planters. In another month the alpine winter would bury this entire gardenscape beneath deep white drifts, leaving only a handrail poking out here and there to mark the architects' ambitious design.

From the foot of the wooden stairs they could see three uniformed officers roaming around in a high-ceilinged studio with glass walls facing the decks. The track lights were turned on, burnishing the blond wood paneling to a golden umber. When Kurt and Muffin reached the sliding doors, they noticed that the lock had been jimmied by crude means, possibly a crowbar. The break-in was not the work of a professional.

"Gentlemen," Kurt said, entering the studio. "What have we got?"

"Looks like simple vandalism," said Gill Dotson, the only sheriff's deputy on the scene. The other men were from the Aspen municipal police.

"Somebody gave the place a good trashing, Kurt," said Mike Marley, his second busy night in a row. "But this time it was a two-legged beast."

Several file cabinets had been jerked open, their folders emptied onto the gleaming hardwood floor. Sketches, blueprints, handwritten notes, memoranda, correspondence typed on embossed letterhead. The officers were weaving around the clutter, careful not to disturb the debris.

"Get the owners on the phone," Kurt said, surveying the chaos. "They'll have to sort through this themselves. It's probably some disgruntled employee they fired recently. Somebody pissed off and making a statement."

"Could be a greenie," Gill said. "They hate these guys." He

was stooped over a slanted drafting table, examining an X-acto knife angrily impaled in the wood. "Guerin and McCord, you know their rep. Condo builders, nature rapers. Glitzy hotels hanging off a mountain."

"Whoever it was," Marley said, pointing at a scale model dominating one of the tables, "they got at this one here pretty good."

From where Kurt was standing, the smashed balsa wood construction resembled a pillaged miniature Oz. "What is it?" he asked, walking over for a closer inspection.

"You mean, 'What *was* it?' " Gill said.

The officers gathered around the table, staring at the destruction. The centerpiece was a replica of one of those glitzy hotels Gill had mentioned, its roof crushed by a furious blow. Fragments were scattered on the street layout around the hotel, tiny houses swept aside, apartment buildings sheared in half. The plastic support towers of a ski lift and its wire cable had been stripped from the papier-mâché mountain range above the resort village, if that's what it was. The only feature that hadn't been wrecked was the snow-white range itself, a veined mass of peaks enwrapping the village like nurturing hands. It wasn't Aspen or Snowmass, but there was something familiar about the simulated landscape.

Kurt picked up a tiny piece of balsa not much larger than a matchbox. It was a commercial shop, painted with impressive detail, the minuscule sign above its door saying BOUTIQUE.

"Whoa, people," Muffin said, joining them at tableside, "this is classified stuff. I'm sure these architects would load their pants if they knew a bunch of yahoos like us were poking through their confidential megamillion-dollar projects."

"Right," Kurt said, setting the little shop back down on a foundation of dried glue. "When the college boys get here, drool a little, scratch your nuts, and show them you're too dumb to violate anybody's privacy."

The men laughed.

Muffin pulled Kurt aside. "All right, wise guy," she said, "I'm taking you to your Jeep. We've got other things to worry about, like a trunk full of porno tapes. These boys don't need our help to write up a friggin' break-in."

He had parked his Jeep near Doc Brumley's house in the West End neighborhood on the other side of Main Street. On the drive over, Muffin radioed the deputy stationed outside Kurt's home on Red Mountain.

"It's quiet now," Mac Murphy said. "The TV van left about one o'clock. A couple of meathead reporters hung around another hour and then blew it off for the night. They threatened to be back at daybreak. Tell Kurt he'd better find himself another crib till this thing dies down."

She pulled up next to his Jeep. The small overpriced bungalows rowed along Bleeker Street were dark and somnolent, their ice-beaded trees glittering in the cruiser's headlights. "You can stay at my place," Muffin offered. She lived in a narrow, claustrophobic mobile home in a trailer park at the foot of Smuggler Mountain.

"Last time I did that," he said with a tired grin, "there wasn't much room for both of us in your bed."

She dropped her chin, cutting her eyes at him. "You can take the first shift," she said. "You need the sleep more than I do, old fella. I've got to round up Linda and start looking through those tapes."

"Use the A-V room in the jail," he said, serious now. "Lock yourselves in."

"There's no microwave. How are we going to pop the popcorn?"

"Ha ha," he said, opening his door to the chilly night. "Beep me if you find something."

"Don't you want my key?"

He stood in the brittle snow, his hand resting on the cruiser's cold roof. "Hold that offer," he said, closing the door.

The window hummed, lowering halfway. "Kurt, where are

you going? You need to get some sleep. You know what the doctor told you."

"I'll sleep when I'm dead."

She rolled her eyes. "Okay, macho man, suit yourself. But
you'd better be ready to meet the press first thing in the morning, right after their vodka and Malt-O-Meal."

"They have to catch me first, don't they?"

"They've got nothing better to do with their time. And neither do the Bauer brothers and their lawyer."

He inhaled the crisp wintry air. How much longer could he
run from them all? "Beep me when you find something," he
said. "I won't be far away."

23

JOEY FLORIO WAS on duty, sitting in a Pitco cruiser nosed up to the wrought-iron gates of Nicole Bauer's mansion. Burglar lights irradiated every square foot of her property, turning night into day. The lighting was so bright, the deputy was reading a magazine without using the interior dome. Kurt tapped on the window. "Bang, you're dead," he said, aiming his index finger and raised thumb like a pistol at the side of Joey's head.

The window whirred, releasing radio music and the aroma of coffee. "Your point being?" Joey said with a surly smile.

"Good thing Son of Sam is locked away."

"Like I didn't see you park your Jeep down there by that big ugly monstrosity."

Kurt turned and stared back down the road at the neighboring villas. "Has Starwood Security been by?"

"Every half hour like clockwork. Two knuckleheads in a marked Volvo. They have instructions to shoot anybody on the street with less than six figures on their check register." Joey opened the door and got out to bounce on his toes, wake himself up. "What's in the bag?"

Kurt handed him a tall, steaming cup of coffee, courtesy of

the night clerk at the Snowflake Inn. "Anybody home?" he asked, nodding at the mansion.

Joey shook his head. He thumbed the lid off the cup and took a cautious sip, his entire face swirling in smoke as if his mustache were on fire.

"Have you seen that kid Kyle? The chauffeur with the blond hair."

Joey shook his head again. "I came on at midnight. The place was empty."

Kurt looked through the gate spears at the mansion glowing like the showcase stop on a Christmas tour of homes. She had fortified her castle, taking all the right precautions, state-of-the-art lighting and sensor alarms. The place was invincible. No crazed intruder could breach her walls now. So instead someone had gone after a deeper frailty, the old worm turning inside her.

"I need to get in," he said.

Joey shrugged. "Be my guest," he said. "I've got the gate opener. And the guys left the patio door unlocked."

IT WAS THE same glass door the young junkie had shattered with the butt end of her kitchen knife. Kurt slid the door a few inches, expecting the alarm to sound. When nothing happened he entered the house and passed quietly through a long dining area cloaked in shadow, making his way into the great room with its flagstone fireplace and high-arching windows, an impressive view of the bright-lit, opulent dwellings arranged along the lower hillside. Upstairs, in the hallway outside Nicole's bedroom, he stopped to gather courage before opening the door. Something was preventing him from going inside, and after a moment he realized it was an overpowering sense of dread. When finally he turned the knob and gave a push, the room lay silent before him in the soft amber of a single night-light. For an instant he imagined her lying on the four-poster bed in her silk nightgown, smiling at him expectantly. *What took you so long, darling?* But the bed was empty, still unmade from this morning, the covers mussed exactly as he remembered them. The telephone receiver sat in its cradle. He sagged against the doorjamb, considering the magnitude of what had happened here. Someone had stalked her, preying on her fragile nerves, scaring her to death. The coroner was mistaken if he declared this a suicide. She had been driven to it by someone's sadistic torment. He wished he felt blameless and professionally detached from this case, free of guilt, but her death bothered him on some deeply visceral level and it was time to make amends.

He forced himself to enter the room. Standing perfectly still in the dark center of her close, familiar world, he thought he smelled a faint scent of jasmine. His eyes traced the passage she had taken to the glass doors, secured now and untroubled by the calm night. The police tape had been removed. Out on that icy deck two people had gone to their deaths. So many secrets and lies. This house was forever doomed.

Gazing toward the ceiling, searching the white space above the hall door, he tried to calculate the precise angle of vision from the video camera as he'd witnessed it on tape. There was a central air grate in plain view, a small rectangular metal plate positioned a few feet above that painting entitled "Territory," the battle between bear and bighorn ram.

Standing on a chair, Kurt used the screwdriver on his Swiss Army Knife to loosen the four screws. When he removed the plate he discovered that Lyle had left the camera behind, no doubt because the deputies parading in and out of the bedroom all day had ruined his access. It was a simple Magnavox camcorder, braced firmly in place on what looked like the base of a tire jack. He pulled the flashlight from his hip pocket and checked the tape compartment. Empty. Two cords trailed away from the camera. They were plugged into extension cords that ran for four or five feet and then disappeared down a hole in the sheet metal.

You sick little prick, Kurt thought. Why were you doing this to a woman who had been so good to you?

He screwed the plate cover back in place and left the room. Downstairs he turned on the light in the room directly underneath Nicole's suite and discovered that it was Lyle's bedroom. There were signs that the young man had been in a hurry to leave. Bureau drawers were flung open and emptied out; hangers dangled in the closet like wire wind-chimes. Discarded clothing was scattered across the bed. Lyle had packed most of his worldly possessions into the trunk of Nicole's Saab.

As Kurt crossed the room to a computer terminal resting on a glossy white desk, he recalled what he'd asked the young man at the hospital: *Who were you running from? The law? Or was somebody else after you?* It was still a good question. Maybe Lyle was involved in a blackmail scam that had gone sour. Or maybe he was afraid of the same lunatic who had frightened Nicole to death.

Kurt switched on the computer and waited for the glowing screen to stutter and load. On his knees under the desk he found a mess of cables plugged into a power strip. There were two cords issuing from a discreet hole drilled in the wall, feeding directly into a converter box of some sort, which in turn was connected to the computer. These were the cords trailing down the wall from the video camera in the air duct. Lyle had rigged it so he could watch Nicole and company on his computer screen in the cozy comfort of his own room.

He sat in the chair and clicked the mouse, opening the computer's hard drive. The folder labeled MY DOCUMENTS was completely empty of files. Lyle must have dumped all of his dirty little secrets in the trash before he fled. Kurt clicked on the trash icon. It too was empty.

He started opening desk drawers, examining whatever Lyle had left behind. It was like digging through the hidey holes in Lennon's bedroom, a mayhem of colored pencils and sketch pads and glue tubes and old *Gamepro* video-game magazines with ripped covers. He found 3-D glasses, sticks of incense, Zig Zag rolling papers, baseball cards, a rubbery action figure from a Japanimation TV series. At twenty-two years old Lyle Gunderson appeared to be stunted in some strange larval state between childhood and adolescence.

The bottom drawer contained the young man's stash of porno magazines, a parade of specialized tastes: bondage, bisexual, S&M. Rifling through the collection Kurt came across a tattered copy of something called *Groovin' Groupies,* the same early '70s vintage as the yellowing mags they'd found next to the sleeping bag in the Wheeler attic. This one featured the groupies attached to various music groups from that era, band names Kurt had forgotten or had never heard. *Lemon Fog. Fever Tree. The Moving Sidewalk.* The girls were unremarkable, by and large, stretched out in pseudoartistic poses on threadbare couches and stained mattresses, their emaciated pale bodies neither erotic nor tantalizing. Every one of them looked melancholy and deeply wounded, the prevailing affectation of the times. On their knees, staring dazed at the erect object of desire, they seemed oddly detached, disinterested, elsewhere. Kurt remembered those days and the seedy crash pads where these poses were struck. Sunless, smoky, castaway digs, an endless drift of bodies coming and going, lurking around the edges of the action. He didn't know how he could ever explain that crazy scene to his son, the impulses and excesses, the careless abandon. Lennon's generation would probably discover these things for themselves.

Flipping through the pages he found an article entitled "The Rhodes Crew," its short introduction stating that "these ladies are working double shifts, night and day, to keep the Rhodies happy." There were a half-dozen photos in the spread, allegedly the women involved with "the great bluesmaker" Rocky Rhodes and his band. In one picture Kurt recognized the young Amanda giving oral pleasure to a hairy, potbellied man cropped off at the shoulders. It could have been Gahan, or Rocky himself, or Henry Kissinger, for that matter.

Kurt wasn't prepared for what he discovered when he turned the page. A young woman who looked very much like Nicole Bauer lay on a polar bear rug with her head cast to one side and her eyes squeezed shut in convincing sexual ecstasy. Her long thick auburn hair fanned out across the white fur and her arms were flung back above her, one hand gripping the other wrist. In the soft hollow beneath each shapely bicep, wisps of reddish hair curled with perspiration. Amanda, nude, was kneeling beside the prone madonna like a supplicant in prayer, her mouth parting above an erect nipple. There was another young woman in the picture, her face buried between Nicole's legs. She was cropped off at the waist, a small woman with a ridge of spine prominent down her back, an outline of ribs. Coal-black hair, brushed behind her ears, hung low on her neck. The butterfly tattooed on her left shoulder blade looked real enough to flitter off the page.

An old polar bear rug. Amanda and two other women performing for the camera. It didn't take much imagination to figure out who had been standing behind the shutter, directing the scene. More than twenty years later Gahan's tastes hadn't changed.

But who was the small dark-haired woman with the butterfly tattoo? Was this Mariah Windstar? *You flutter your pretty little wings until you get noticed,* Amanda had said about her. *When you're in their net you turn into an ugly flesh-eating grub.*

And what about the young video freak who had collected these magazines? Where did Lyle fit in? Had he been supplying Gahan Moss with tapes of Nicole? Did Gahan want them for himself or for an old friend who had been hiding out for twenty years?

There were too many unanswered questions. Kurt carefully folded the magazine and slipped it into his leather jacket, then turned off the computer and closed the desk drawers. He glanced at the digital clock beside the bed. Four forty-seven A.M., over twenty-four hours without sleep. He didn't care what time it was or how tired his body felt, he was going to wake somebody up and make them talk.

24

HE BELIEVED IN giving a man five minutes notice before pounding on his door in the dead of night. When the toadstool mailbox appeared in his headlights, glowing like an acid-rock poster, he dialed Gahan's number on the cell phone. There was no answer, only Amanda's recorded voice: "Greetings. Say the word and you'll be free." They were asleep, like every sensible couple on Buttermilk Mountain. Kurt parked in the clearing at the foot of the stone steps and checked to make sure the pepper spray was still in his pocket. He got out of the Jeep and strapped on his shoulder holster with its fully loaded Smith & Wesson .45, then slipped on the insulated vest. Digging around in the boot of the Jeep he found a rusty tire tool and tested its swing in the frigid air. If the rottweiler was prowling the premises, playing dutiful watchdog, Kurt was going to need every deterrent he could get his hands on.

He thought his ankle was strong enough to make the climb without a crutch, but by the time he reached the top of the hill he was out of breath, light-headed, and his ankle was nagging at him. The Magic Mushroom House looked like a dark fungoid growth clinging to the edge of a precipice. In the blackness beyond, snow clouds drifted across a field of icy stars. It was freezing cold and his body felt worn down and weak. He asked himself what he was doing here at this ungodly hour. Why wasn't he sleeping peacefully in Muffin's warm trailer?

He heard something stir off in the bushes near the house and gripped the tire tool firmly, ready to crack the dog on the nose if he had no other choice. He remained motionless for several moments, anticipating a growl and quick movement. All was quiet, the only sound a stiff breeze gusting through the hillside woods. Halfway down the cobblestone walkway he heard something again, and this time it sounded like an animal whimpering. He stopped abruptly, trying to read its location in the underbrush. The whimpering was louder now, a wounded lamentation.

Switching on his flashlight, Kurt waded through a thick hedge and shined the beam into the bushes at the bend of the circular house. The dog lay on her side, limp and panting, bathed in blood. She had tried to burrow into a mound of old snow to die, and the pawed-up chunks around her body were as bright red as a cherry Popsicle. Kurt approached the animal cautiously, one slow step at a time, speaking in a low consoling voice. "Take it easy, girl. You need some help? What happened to you?"

He thought she might have been attacked by something wild, a raccoon or bear, but when he came closer he could see that her front leg was crushed in a steel-jawed bear trap chained to the bottom of a stone bench.

"My god," he said, crouching down to direct the light. The dog's throat had been slashed from ear to ear. This was human work, someone with a knife.

There was nothing he could do for the animal. She was gasping now, her final breaths. She had lost the strength to whine. "Go gentle, girl," he said, remembering the lines from an old schoolboy poem. When her breathing stopped he reached over and patted her bloody head.

Furious, Kurt stood up quickly and slammed the tire tool to the ground, sweeping the area with the flashlight beam, searching for footprints in the light snow. He saw them now, a large waffle-soled boot and long stride angling into the hedge. The man had set a trap for the dog and then finished her off with his knife.

The prints picked up again on the other side of the walkway and followed the curved wall of the house down toward a wood-pile silted with snow. As Kurt neared the stack he could see that a window had been smashed by one of the split logs. The dog killer had slipped into the house.

Kurt had no doubt who it was. He jerked the radio from his belt carrier and called for backup. "Everyone on duty," he said, speaking to the dispatcher in a near whisper. "Bring 'em heavily armed."

He opened the window wider, broken glass tinkling every-where, and dragged himself up into the dark house. His fall was muffled by the thick bearskin rug he landed on. The room was pitch-black and he had no idea where he was or how to find his way to the more familiar realms of this strange place. He with-drew the .45 from his shoulder holster and followed the flash-light beam down a winding hallway, feeling like a rat trapped in a maze. Just as he was about to give up and turn back, retrace his steps, he stumbled upon one of those Dalíesque dreamscape portals, which delivered him into the bar area where Gahan had poured his drinks. The half-empty bottle of Bushmills remained exactly where Kurt had last seen it. His business card floated nearby in a circle of condensation. Sweating now, trembling with uncertainty, he shone the light out over the dark open spaces, the volcanic rock steps and dry fountain, catching a glimpse of the piano in the pond room farther on. He wanted to call out their names—*Gahan! Amanda!*—issue a dire warning, but he knew the man with the hunting knife was lurking some-where within these walls and he didn't dare open his mouth.

Where were they sleeping? He was struggling with indeci-sion, trying to determine which direction to take, when he heard a dog bark somewhere, followed by a high mournful howl. It was the other rottweiler. Kurt moved off toward the sound, groping his way down the stone steps and into another bizarre corridor that could have been from the set of *The Cabinet of Dr. Caligari.* Several paces down the hallway he caught sight of a tall bulky man rushing up beside him. He pivoted quickly, aiming the pistol. Flashed in light, the man aimed back, surprise and horror widening his eyes. It was Kurt's own reflection in a long row of mirror panels. He swallowed hard and lowered the gun, his heart banging against his rib cage. The face staring back at him was blanched with fear.

The dog howled again, distant and grieving. Kurt hurried down the corridor and soon found himself engulfed in a cloud of warm steam swirling from an open doorway. He stepped into the room, pointing his flashlight into the fog. Several seconds passed before he realized it was a large bathroom and dressing area. Heavy steam was billowing up from an overheated Jacuzzi in the far corner. Someone was sitting in the water. Waving an arm through the smoky vapor he pressed farther into the room, approaching the figure with his gun raised. "Gahan?" he said, the word a faint note beneath the loud gurgling water.

Gahan Moss sat facing the wall. Kurt could see the back of his head, the rat tail clinging to his neck like a curl of lost hair on a shower drain. His arms were spread wide, resting on the flagstones at the edge of the recessed pool. He could have been a man relaxing in his Jacuzzi after a long taxing day at the office. Except for the fact that the water was now a boiling cauldron of blood.

"Jesus, Gahan," Kurt said, kneeling down to check for a pulse on the man's neck. The body keeled over into the hot water and Kurt had to haul him back up by the rat tail. Gahan's eyes were still open and blood was flowing freely from the gash across his throat. He had also been stabbed once in the heart.

Kurt felt it coming. He resisted, but his stomach heaved. He hadn't eaten all day and there was nothing to puke up. After two more gut-wrenching heaves, dry and involuntary, he pulled himself together, took a deep breath, and rose from his knees. With the flashlight as his guide he searched the murky room for Amanda, but she wasn't anywhere in view. *Find her,* he told himself. *She might still be alive.*

Leaving the body in the Jacuzzi, he batted his way through the steam and lurched back into the corridor. After fifteen yards or so, the passageway swerved sharply to the left and ended at a closed door. Water was seeping out through the bottom crack. When he turned the knob, pressure forced the door toward him, a warm wave washing over his boots, wetting the cuffs of his jeans. He held his breath and pointed the light into the bedroom. The killer had slashed the king-size waterbed, creating a lagoon that was now draining past Kurt's feet and down the corridor. His beam ranged quickly over everything, finding slippers and a newspaper adrift in the gentle current, a bathrobe spreading slowly on the surface of the water. Amanda's nude body bobbed facedown near the bed, her long yellowish-white hair floating like duckweed around her head. Even at this distance Kurt could see that she had been stabbed repeatedly in the back.

"If you're in here," he said in a loud angry voice, his arm extended with the Smith & Wesson, "I'm going to shoot you on sight. This is your only chance to drop your weapon and come out where I can see you!"

Silence. The sound of water trickling around his boots.

He probed the room again with the flashlight, exploring every dark corner. The word *betrayed* had been smeared on the wall in blood. Unnerved and trembling, he sloshed through the lagoon and knelt down at Amanda's side. When he turned her over, blood bubbled from her nostrils. Her body was still warm, perhaps because of the heated water. She had been knifed in the chest and belly, a savage attack. Kurt searched for a pulse, some sign of life. The woman was dead.

He settled her on her back in the receding water and slogged his way across the room to an open window. A cold wind blew dancing snowflakes into his face. The killer had left blood on the sill while making his escape. Kurt stuck his head out the window and raked the grounds with his flashlight beam. Large footprints curved down the rocky hillside and disappeared into the woods.

There was a noise behind him and he whirled, training the pistol on a nearby door. A dog began to bark, scratching wildly on the wood. Somehow the killer had managed to lock the other rottweiler in a closet.

"Hold on a minute, fella," Kurt said. The latch bolt was rattling violently inside the striker plate. "Help will be here soon. We'll get you out."

There was nothing he could do now, not by himself. He waded over to Amanda and draped the soggy bathrobe across her body, then radioed the dispatcher to send EMS. He could hear panic in his voice, the edge of hysteria. Whenever he stood still, his body began to shiver.

Returning down the corridor to the bathroom, he dragged Gahan's heavy, water-logged body out of the Jacuzzi and arranged him on the flagstones. When he was finished he walked over to the wide dressing mirror and rubbed his hand across the fogged glass, managing only to mess his pale reflection with four red finger-streaks. He turned on the tap and filled the basin, staring at his slick fingers before submerging them. Rocky's ring was soaked in blood. When he tugged at it, pulling as hard as he could, the ring slipped over his large wet knuckle and came free.

Kurt washed off the ring and studied the *I Ching* symbols embedded in gold. Yin-yang, harmony and balance. The eight meditations, Shocking Thunder, Lake in the Valley, the others he couldn't recall. Could it really be Rocky Rhodes? Could the old rocker have become a stone-cold psychopathic killer? In the mirror Kurt could see Gahan's bloodied body lying behind him. Given the chance, the man would have butchered Nicole the same way. He would have plunged the long hunting knife into Kurt's heart.

25

WRAPPED IN AN army blanket, his wet boots drying beside him on the polar bear rug, Kurt hunkered in a window seat and watched his deputies carry the slumbering rottweiler, bundled in a Persian rug, to a cage truck parked on the patio. They had used the department's Cap-Chur rifle to shoot the dog with a tranquilizer dart.

"Better hope he doesn't wake up anytime soon," Kurt said.

Muffin materialized from the back of the house, where the team was still gathering evidence, and walked over to speak with him again. Her khaki pants were wet to the knees.

"Talk about up close and personal," she said, peeling off her surgical gloves. "That eight-inch hunting knife did some serious damage."

A dozen years in law enforcement, Kurt had never encountered anything this gruesome.

"You really believe it was Rocky Rhodes?"

He nodded. "I don't know what else to think."

"Why would he go after his old friend? I mean, hell, they made some classic songs together."

Kurt inhaled deeply. "He's out of his mind, Muffin," he said. "Who knows what's tripping through his head."

"Did you see what he wrote on the bedroom wall? BETRAYED."

"That's what the letters to Nicole were all about," he said. "She'd betrayed him. Everybody had betrayed him. He was going to kill them all, starting with her."

"You think he's got a list?"

Kurt shrugged. "It's possible," he said, wondering what he'd done with that list of names from the 1977 police report.

Muffin turned and gazed back over the pond room, dark and fenlike and tracked with mucky footprints. She seemed to be looking for something everyone else had missed. "So you were here yesterday," she said in a distant voice. "You talked to them about Nicole."

It felt like a hundred years ago. "If they'd played it straight with me, I could've helped them," he said solemnly. "Maybe saved their lives."

"You figure they knew about Rocky all this time?"

Kurt glanced at the baby grand piano sitting in shadow. "Some of it doesn't make sense. If they were in contact, why didn't he just give them a call and ring the doorbell? Why did he have to kill the dog and break in a window?"

They watched two grim EMS medics wheel a gurney from the back of the house. A body bag was strapped to the table. Kurt asked who it was.

"The guy," one of them said. "We'll have the lady packed up in half an hour, Sheriff, give or take."

Muffin worked her head back and forth, loosening the tension in her neck. When she looked at Kurt again he saw a fierce, unforgiving anger burning deep in her eyes. "We've gotta stop this crazy fucker," she said. "Any idea who might be next on his list?"

"Yeah," Kurt said, hesitant to admit it. "You're looking at him."

They stared at each other, calculating what that could mean. She didn't blink for several moments, not until the beeper sounded on her belt. "It's Linda," she said, reading the number. "Is there a phone in this nutty place?"

When she returned he was waiting for her down in the pond room, where he had gone to browse through the awards and framed photographs on Gahan's vanity shelf. Without explanation he handed her the photo of the two women kissing beneath the Hawaiian waterfall.

"Mm-hmm," she said, studying the picture. "Is this supposed to turn me on, Kurt?"

"I'm pretty sure the redhead is Nicole Bauer. I think the other one is a young woman named Mariah Windstar. Apparently Rocky was jealous of their relationship," he said, nodding at the photo. "The letters said Mariah was there with Nicole the night Rocky died and that she'd caused the fight that ended in his death. My guess is Rocky discovered them together and lost it."

Her eyes flicked upward, meeting his. "Is there anything else you've failed to clue me in on, Sheriff?" she asked, quickly irritated with him. "I feel like I'm playing catch-up here."

"This information comes from the letters, Muffin. It's the word of a madman. Who knows if it's true?"

He withdrew the folded magazine from inside his jacket and thumbed through the pages to the place he'd marked with a crease, then handed it to her. She held the framed photograph in one hand, the printed image in the other, her eyes darting back and forth between them. "This case is turning into a regular pornfest," she said.

"It's the same girl," he said, pointing to the butterfly tattoo in each picture.

"Meaning what?"

"I think I know who she is."

"You just said. Some chick named Mariah Starbuck or something."

"No. Who she is today."

"What difference does it make, Kurt? There's a butcher on the loose and you're showing me chick pix from Larry Flynt's old photo albums."

"She's the connection," he said, scratching his stubbly neck. "We've got to find her. If it's Rocky, she's probably on the list, too."

Muffin shoved the magazine and framed photograph against his chest. "Look, that was Linda on the phone," she said. "She's been staring at Lyle's videos for three hours and she's finally found something. She wants us to come take a look right away."

Kurt glanced at the groupie magazine. At least two of the women in that photograph were dead.

"Those hairstyles," Muffin said, taking a final peek at the picture and rolling her eyes. "Come on, we'll take my unit."

ON THE DRIVE into Aspen she reported what she and Linda Ríos had discovered about Lyle's video collection. "More than half of his tapes were commercially produced. He's into the usual adolescent boy stuff, with a sweet tooth for S&M. There are some hiddens, mostly shot from motel closets. They seem pretty phony. You wonder why nobody ever walks over to hang up a coat. I don't think he filmed them himself. You can download all that stuff from the wonderful world of Web sleaze, if you know where to search."

"What about shots of Nicole's bedroom?"

"We're still looking through it. Lyle's been working for her since February, eight or nine months, but who knows when he installed the camera. It could've been last week."

"You're telling me you haven't found anything solid from Nickie's room?"

"Well," she said, pausing for reflection, clearing her throat. "We found *you*."

Heat rushed into his face. When he'd made the decision not to withhold the tape from their inspection, he knew this moment would arrive all too soon, but he hadn't prepared himself for how awkward he would feel.

"What else?" he asked.

"Nothing nearly as good."

He gave her a dark look.

"I'm sorry, Kurt. What I meant was, we haven't found any other tapes with that kind of detailed"—she groped for the word—"action," she said with a straight face.

"The kid lives nine months in her house and there's nothing else on tape?"

She shrugged as if to say *Don't blame me.* "There's lots of dead time, Kurt. Nicole pacing back and forth in front of the camera. Nicole sitting in bed filing her nails. Nicole curled up with a thick book. Nicole drinking herself to sleep."

It was a scenario Kurt didn't want to dwell on: Nicole's world shrinking, diminishing into greater solitude.

Muffin made a left turn off Main Street and cruised into an empty space at the side entrance to the courthouse. "From the evidence I've seen, the woman was leading a very quiet life, Kurt. Her nights were lonely and boring, and she drank enough Scotch to eat up a kidney," she said, staring ahead over the steering wheel. "But maybe we're in luck. It sounds like Linda has found something."

To ensure absolute privacy, the two deputies had set up shop in a windowless, underutilized audiovisual room located in the county jail facility behind the courthouse. The door was locked and they had to knock and identify themselves before Linda opened up. The room lacked ventilation and smelled of strong coffee, pastry, and roll-on deodorant. The women had systematized the tape collection, arranging boxes according to category.

Although pleased to see them, Linda Ríos appeared weary and drawn, as if she'd just walked away from an all-night poker game. Her khaki sleeves were rolled haphazardly to her elbows and the long sweeps of her dark hair were piled on top of her head, clasped together with something that looked like a kitchen bag clip. She was clearly tired but elated by her discovery. "I'd just about given up on finding something like—hey, you know, like—" She dropped her eyes, forcing herself to address the man standing a few feet away. "Like the one you star in, Kurt."

"It might help," he suggested modestly, "if we all agree that what you witnessed was my reckless twin."

He and Muffin dragged folding chairs close to the VCR. Linda rewound the tape to the place where a well-groomed man crossed the screen from left to right in a blur of motion, disappearing so quickly it was impossible to see his face. A conversation began off camera, male and female, muddled fragments, lilting laughter, a low sultry coupling of voices. Kurt recognized Nicole's throaty laugh, her seductive rhythms. He tried to distance his own feelings from what he knew was happening somewhere in the room—the delicate negotiation of lips, the game of buttons. Like a college boy again, he felt the familiar dull constricting pain in his chest he'd felt every time a girl had told him there was someone else.

"Should I fast-forward through this part?" Linda asked, retrieving the channel selector.

"What is it you want us to see, Linda?" Kurt asked with a sharpness that surprised even him.

"I think there's a pretty good look at his face," she said. "It's coming up."

"Okay, get to it," he said, folding his arms.

Linda thumbed the button and the tape sped forward. Nicole brought the man to her bed, leading him by the hand, and they jerked like silent movie actors through the ceremony of undressing. His back remained toward the camera. It must have been summer. He was wearing a short-sleeve polo shirt, Bermuda shorts, expensive Nike jogging shoes, shedding everything in twitchy motion onto the floor. A well-built man, shorter than Nicole, his skin tone the evenly applied bronze from a tanning lamp. On top of her, his back rippled with the kind of muscle definition middle-aged men purchased by the month in health club weight rooms. His dark hair gleamed with oil and retained its stiff sculpted shape even when he burrowed his face between her breasts.

"Bear with me," Linda said, pressing on. "There's something near the end."

Kurt stood up and walked over to one of the boxes. He picked up a videotape and pretended to read the description on the back. He wasn't going to watch any more of this until Linda found what she was looking for.

He was still shuffling through the video titles when Linda said, "Here it is, Kurt. Come take a look."

The man was sitting naked on the edge of the bed, smoking a cigarette, paused in a jittery freeze-frame. Nicole was partially visible, lying on her side under a sheet, her legs curled halfway to her chest. They had finished with each other.

"Holy shit," Muffin said, leaning forward, truly surprised. "Is that who I think it is?"

Linda rubbed a knuckle against her chin, uncertain and perplexed. "He looks familiar but I can't make him. Who is he, guys?"

"Roll it back a few seconds and then let it run," Muffin said, her eyes fixed intensely on the TV screen.

Kurt stood behind his empty chair, watching the tape replay. The man took a drag from his cigarette, blew smoke, and turned to rub a mound of sheet, Nicole's soft hip. Kurt didn't need to see any more to know who he was.

"Good god, Kurt," Muffin said, gazing upward at him. There was a look of utter astonishment in her eyes. "It's Ben Smerlas."

26

IT HAD BECOME a clear, crisp autumn morning, with a residue of snow on the lawns of the suburban cul-de-sac. Kurt parked the Jeep at curbside, strode up the shoveled walkway, and rang the doorbell. The Sunday newspaper was lying neatly on the welcome mat. Someone at last night's party had left a champagne glass in the flower box by the door, and a cigarette butt floated in the grainy gray liquid. He picked up the newspaper and rang twice more before a Latina housekeeper finally appeared. She might have been the same young woman who had raced outside with the coats. This morning she was wearing jeans and a baggy Broncos sweatshirt instead of the prim black-and-white domestic's uniform.

"Yes, please?" she said, looking put out by this early intrusion. It was shortly after eight A.M.

"Pitkin County Sheriff," Kurt said, showing her his badge.

"Señor Smerlas, he is not home. He is gone to the club for his exercise."

"I'm not here to see the *señor*," Kurt said, an edgy adrenaline rush fueling his words. "I would like to speak with Mrs. Smerlas, please."

The young woman seemed a little frightened by him. Perhaps it was his disheveled appearance. She shouldered the door, blocking the meager open space with her body as if she expected him to force his way in. "Missus Smerlas is in her bath, *señor.* You must come back later."

"I'll wait," he said. "Tell her the sheriff is here to see her."

She closed the door in his face. He rang the bell immediately. When she cracked open the door, showing only one eye, he said, "Tell Mrs. Smerlas this is official police business and I'm not leaving until she speaks to me."

She closed the door without a word.

Prepared for a long wait, he slipped the Aspen newspaper out of its plastic sheath and sat down on the entrance step, glancing at the front page. Nicole's death had made the headlines. An apparent suicide, the article said. Alcohol mixed with a prescription drug. Distraught. Disoriented. "Earlier in the evening Bauer had won the bidding for an auction date with Sheriff Kurt Muller at a nonprofit gala held at the Hotel Jerome. The two had returned to her Starwood residence by limousine. It is unclear at what time the sheriff left her home. Muller has avoided reporters and was unavailable for comment."

He wondered how much longer he would be able to play cat and mouse with the press.

There were two articles below the fold on the front page, one headlined MULLER DISAPPEARS FROM DEBATE and another loudly proclaiming SMERLAS TO RUN FOR HOUSE SEAT. Its lead began "Surrounded by a crowd of enthusiastic supporters after a bizarre town-hall debate that ended in controversy (see MULLER DISAPPEARS, same page), Pitkin County Commissioner Ben Smerlas took advantage of the occasion to announce his candidacy for the U.S. House of Representatives, Third District."

Kurt was thinking about lighting the newspaper with his Bic and sticking it in the mail slot when the door opened suddenly. "Follow me, please," said the housekeeper, inviting him into the foyer. "Missus Smerlas say come, have coffee in the sun room."

She walked ahead of him into the large den where he had

seen guests milling about the party. The life-size poster announcing Ben Smerlas's candidacy remained against the wall near the fireplace. Patio doors were open, airing out the reek of wine and saucy hors d'oeuvres. Water was running in the kitchen, plates clinking. The party must have lasted far into the night. The maids were only now cleaning up.

The housekeeper directed him through French doors into a sun-filled room exuding a botanical Pacific Island ambience. Bamboo furniture, exotic birds swinging in wicker cages, the glass walls fitted with roll-down curtains that resembled grass mats. Plants with long green tendrils and spearlike leaves spilled out over their pots. Although the morning chill had fogged the glass, the smells inside this room were as wet and earthy as a tropical arboretum.

A service of steaming coffee waited for him on a round glass-topped table. "How do you take it?" the young woman asked, pouring coffee into a china cup.

"As dark as it comes."

Though he hadn't eaten since dinner on Friday night, he still had no appetite. Not after his discovery in the Magic Mushroom House.

"She will see you," the housekeeper said, taking her leave.

Kurt brought the cup of coffee to the glass wall and rubbed his fist against the condensation, clearing a view to the sun deck where he'd seen Jay Westbrook with his arm around Tanya. Last night there had been three people at this party with intimate connections to Nicole—an ex-husband, a surreptitious lover with political ambitions, and a woman who had known her years ago, perhaps an old lover as well. It was clear to Kurt that Nicole's death had conveniently solved a number of their problems, and maybe a few of her brothers', too. An illicit affair, a family embarrassment, a failed marriage. Without Nicole, their world had become a tidy place once again.

Sipping the strong coffee, he gazed out beyond the Smerlas

property line toward the snow-rimmed golf course in the distance, where the commissioner had dispersed an entire bucket
of balls in his party mood. Kurt could remember when that
course was nothing more than a grassy prairie off the old two-
lane highway, a field full of plump quails luring him and his
brother with their pellet rifles. As teenagers the two boys had
spent many a gilded summer afternoon dragging golf bags behind their father and the other aging entrepreneurs who had
mowed and graded and irrigated those wild acres for their own
personal recreation. *You're raping the wild,* Kyle Martin had
screamed at him in the Opera House. But it wasn't rape, Kurt
knew after nearly fifty years of living in this mountain wilderness, observing what the masterbuilders had done to the land. It
was a slow, relentless seduction, a calculation of compromised
positions leading to surrender.

"Would you like a warm-up, Sheriff?"

He turned around to find Dana Smerlas pouring herself a
cup of coffee at the glass table. Raising the silver pitcher, she
beckoned him with the lilt of an eyebrow. She was wearing a
pearl-gray bathrobe and the silk clung to her moist skin, revealing small firm breasts and a trim waistline. He walked over
and held out his cup, studying her face as she poured. She had
applied light eyeliner and lipstick, just enough to waken her features. Her short red hair, graying at the temples, was still wet
from the bath and curled around her ears. He could easily picture her as the young woman in the photographs with Nicole.
Small, black-haired in her youth, the same delicate jaw. The two
images he'd seen had not revealed a full view of her face, but he
knew this was her. He was certain that if he peeled back her robe
he would uncover the butterfly tattooed on her left shoulder
blade.

"So what brings you to our door so early on a Sunday morning?" she asked with a sly smile, her eyes drifting toward the
front page of the newspaper he'd left by the service tray. "Don't

tell me you've come to pledge your personal endorsement of Ben's campaign."

He could smell her shampoo, a fruity tropical fragrance that matched the palmy room. Her freshness made him aware of his own body odor, a full day without a shower or change of clothing. He felt like a ripe hunter who had wandered home after a week in the woods.

"I came to ask you some questions about a double homicide," he said, watching her pale blue eyes widen. "Gahan Moss and his wife were murdered in their home early this morning."

"My god," she said, frowning. "The musician?"

"Did you know him?"

"No," she said, puzzled by the question. "As you can imagine, we didn't run in the same social circles."

"You've never met Gahan Moss?" he persisted.

She gave a slight shrug, brought the coffee to her lips. "Not that I recall," she said, speaking into the cup. "Perhaps in a group of friends at one of the clubs. You know how small that scene is here. But like the song says, I don't get around much anymore. Ben doesn't go for the Aspen nightlife."

You'll think otherwise about Ben's nightlife, Kurt thought, once you've seen the videotape.

"If you didn't know Gahan Moss, Mrs. Smerlas, why did you meet him in Red Butte Cemetery last night around ten o'clock?"

She blanched, a look of surprise and dismay. "I have no idea what you're talking about," she said, tightening the folds of her robe. "I hosted a party for my husband last night. Here, read about it yourself," she said, sliding the newspaper across the glass surface. "A hundred people will tell you I was here by my husband's side."

Kurt smiled at the shrewdness of her cover. "I tailed Gahan to the cemetery, Mrs. Smerlas. I watched you walk over and meet with him by the tombstones in the dark. I followed you back to this house."

Her face hardened. "You must have me confused with some other woman," she said.

"You joined a crowd of people heading down the sidewalk to the party. If I go through your guest list, somebody's going to confirm that. They're going to admit it seemed odd that the hostess was out for a long walk while her party was at full-tilt boogie."

She banged her cup against the saucer, a flare of temper. "I invited you into this house of my own accord, Sheriff. I have been as hospitable as I can be. But now you're grilling me about a man I've never met. I'm sorry he was murdered, but I haven't the slightest idea what that has to do with me. If you persist with these questions I'll have no choice but to call my husband at the club, and he will contact our attorney. You can address any further questions to them."

Kurt finished the last sip of his coffee. "Okay, fine, lawyer up—it's your right," he said. "When you call your husband, tell him and your lawyer to meet you at the Pitkin County jail. Because that's where I'm taking you for booking, Mrs. Smerlas."

"You're *what*?" She was indignant.

"You met in secret with the homicide victim at ten o'clock last night. You had an angry exchange, which I personally witnessed. A few hours later he and his wife were brutally murdered. You're my number one suspect, lady."

"Surely you're joking!"

"Am I? Unless you start talking to me about Gahan Moss, you're taking a ride to jail. Now what's that going to do to your husband's political future? The day after he announces he's running for Congress, his wife becomes a suspect in a bloody double murder."

Dana Smerlas gripped the edge of the table and pulled herself halfway out of the chair, crouching like a small, sinewy animal ready to spring from the brush. "You can't do this," she fumed. "The public will see it for what it really is—a desperate man

smearing his political enemy by taking a cheap shot at his wife."
She straightened her shoulders and flashed small white teeth in
a cynical smile. "When is that recall vote coming up, Sheriff?
Two weeks? Is this some kind of diversionary tactic? There isn't
enough time left in your career for the ink to dry on these silly
charges."

Kurt smirked at her. His career. He'd never put much stock
in the concept. The only time he gave any serious thought to
holding onto his so-called *office* was when someone accused him
of being incompetent. The Ben Smerlases of the world.

"You've got ten minutes to get dressed," he said. "My Jeep is
out front. I'll be waiting for you."

He was halfway across the large den when she called his
name. There was a note of exasperation in the way she addressed
him: "Sheriff Muller, *wait*."

He stopped and turned to face her. She was standing in the
open doorway to the sun room, backlit by the room's sea-green
glow. They studied each other for several moments without
movement or speech. He knew she wanted him to appreciate
her natural beauty, the diligent care she had taken to maintain
her small, taut, forty-five-year-old body. When she left the
doorway and sauntered down the steps toward him she dis-
played plenty of leg, showing off her muscular calves and the
hardness of her thighs stretching against the silk robe. He suspected that she was the product of some personal trainer named
Lars or Sven, one of those young muscle boys from the Nordic
Club. Weights, rowing machine, treadmill, laps in the pool.
There was a social set of Aspen women who spent their entire
days being pampered by long-haired Romance-cover models
passing themselves off as gym instructors.

When she was close enough to touch him, Dana Smerlas
paused to study Kurt's large, unkempt body. "My husband was
right about you," she said, her breasts rising as she sighed.
"You're persistent."

He was in no mood for compliments.

"Will you come with me, please," she said, solemn now, conceding. "The walls have ears. If we're going to discuss this, I don't want the help to overhear."

With some misgivings about propriety he escorted her upstairs and down a long sunny hallway past several open bedrooms. At the end of the passage a pull rope dangled from an attic door in the ceiling. With one good tug she lowered the door and unfolded the attached stepladder.

"Where are we going, Mrs. Smerlas?"

"Come now, Sheriff, you aren't losing your nerve, are you?"

"I always like to know what I'm getting into."

"Really? That's not what I've heard about you."

She was teasing him now, trying hard to turn on the charm, but it wasn't working.

"You want to discuss private matters with me," she said, gathering the robe at her knees and stepping up the ladder, "you'll have to come into my private lair."

He watched her disappear into the rectangle in the ceiling, where buttery light shone down over him. He hesitated, then climbed up after her.

To his surprise the attic had been converted into a spacious art studio finished out with pine paneling and a polished wood floor stained here and there with dried oil paints. A large skylight and a ventilation window at the end of the house provided strong natural lighting for her work. Three easels were located around the studio, each bearing an unfinished canvas. A supply bench was cluttered with rolled tubes of paint and Mason jars stuffed full of soaking brushes.

"So you're a painter, Mrs. Smerlas?"

"I dabble," she said, standing before one of her easels, studying the canvas with great concentration as if planning the next stroke. "And please call me Dana. *Missus* makes me sound like a schoolteacher." She folded her arms across the thin robe and smiled at him. "And that, I assure you, I am not."

He turned a slow circle, amused by the bohemian messiness

hidden atop her perfectly ordered ranch-burgher life. She had carved out a secret place of her own. "Okay, you've got me up here," he said. "The *help* can't hear us now."

She walked over to a corner of the studio furnished with an old couch and a small table rowed with liquor bottles. "Would you like a drink?" she offered.

"It's just past eight o'clock in the morning."

Her hand trembled slightly as she splashed brandy into a glass. "You're not going to make this easy for me, are you, Kurt?" she said, speaking his name with an uncomfortable familiarity.

"Why don't you make it easy on yourself and tell me why you met Gahan Moss last night in the cemetery."

She tasted the brandy and gazed out the window in silence. He knew that small sensuous body, the shoulder blade where butterfly wings imprinted the white skin beneath her robe. He could trace its shape with his finger.

"Gahan and I once had a very brief affair," she said with a breathless reluctance. "Four or five years ago, before I met Ben. I was coming off a divorce and behaving badly. Closing down the clubs, snorting coke in the ladies' room, that whole Aspen scene. I didn't know Gahan had been a famous musician once upon a time, and it wouldn't have made any difference. He was charmingly British, he treated me like a princess at first, and he had great blow." She paused to sip her brandy. "The fling lasted about a month. I found out he was living with someone. And then things got a little too weird for my taste. He wanted me to meet his wife or girlfriend, whatever she was." She turned with a wary look. "You can imagine where that was leading. I didn't want to go there. I'm not into that kind of thing."

Kurt thought about the photograph in the groupie magazine. Three young women together. "Let me guess," he said. "You're going to tell me that after you married Smerlas, Gahan started becoming a nuisance."

She frowned at him. "He wasn't after money, if that's what you're implying, Sheriff. Gahan was angry about a tape he'd given me when we were together."

She stepped over to another easel and studied her work, the sketchy outline of a reclining female nude.

"It was some songs he'd written. Just him on the piano and his voice. They were his only compositions in fifteen years, or so he told me. I'm not much of a music critic, Sheriff, but they sounded pretty lousy to me. After we broke up I tossed them in the trash. A couple of weeks ago he started calling me and demanding the tape back. He said he'd come across a bootleg of the songs for sale on the Internet and he accused me of selling them to some pirate producer in L.A."

Kurt ventured over to have a look at her drawing. He suspected that the nude was a self-portrait in progress. "And you expect me to believe that's why he was yelling at you in a cemetery at ten o'clock last night?"

"He wanted the tape back. When I told him I'd thrown it away, he didn't believe me. He accused me of selling him out."

"So why couldn't you and Gahan have discussed this problem in broad daylight over coffee?"

"Because I didn't want to be seen in public with Gahan Moss," she shot back. "My husband doesn't know about the affair. It was a period in my life I'm not particularly proud of. I live in a very different world now, Kurt. With certain expectations. Can't you understand my dilemma? Haven't you ever been involved with someone you shouldn't have?"

It was the way she said it that gave her away. A sympathetic arch of the brow. She knew about him and Nicole, and not simply from allegations in the newspaper. Perhaps she and Nicole had remained in touch for all these years. Confidantes. Lovers.

"They were butchered, Dana," he said flatly. "Would you like to see the photos?"

With an irritated sigh she turned to study the canvas again.

He came up behind her, staring at the wing of shoulder blade protruding through the silk. He wanted to see the butterfly with his own eyes.

"Their throats were slashed. He even killed one of the dogs."

She shuddered and took a long drink of brandy, emptying the glass. "My god, that's terrible," she said with the drop of her chin.

"He's out of control, Dana. He'll kill *you* if you aren't careful."

She turned quickly, glaring at him, panic flooding her pale blue eyes. "What do you mean?" she asked.

"You know what I mean. Don't play dumb with me, girl. Your story about Gahan is bullshit. Yeah, there may be a bootleg tape somewhere on the Net, but that's not why Gahan was angry. You've known him and his old musician pals for at least twenty years. You used to hang with them pretty tight."

"That's absurd."

He pulled Rocky's ring from his pocket and offered it to her in his open palm. "Gahan was pissed at you because he'd seen this," he said, spinning out his suspicions. "He called you and threatened to show up and make a scene at your big announcement party if you didn't meet with him."

She glanced at the ring. "I have no idea what this is about," she said.

"Come on, Dana. He called you out of your party because he wanted to know if you were the one who'd stolen this ring off the body at Canyon de Chelly."

When she raised her eyes to meet his, he saw fear and anger and a tenacious defiance. "These ridiculous accusations have gone far enough," she said. "I'm going to ask my husband and our attorney to join us for the rest of this conversation."

Her sudden haughtiness made him smile. "I know who you are," he said, his words matching the intensity of her glare. "Or at least who you were twenty years ago. I even know the name you used back then. Have you forgotten there's a photograph of you in the Rocky Rhodes book?"

It was a gamble. A wild bluff. The only kind that ever worked. He would either win on this hand or go home with empty pockets turned inside out.

"A *photograph* of me?" she said with a bemused expression. "In a book? Imagine that."

"Rocky and his Aspen friends, 1976," he said. "On a page in the photo section. Would you like me to show it to you?"

It was her turn to smile. "Nineteen seventy-six," she said, raising a dark eyebrow. "That was a long time ago, Sheriff. People change. Hair comes and goes. So do the pounds. Age makes us a different life form. Have you been to your high school reunion recently?"

"Some things change," he said. "Tattoos don't."

"Tattoos?"

"A butterfly, for instance," he said, moving closer. Her eyes followed him, suspicious. "Like the one right here."

He touched the silk robe with his index finger, drew it lightly across her bony shoulder blade. "I have two photos of you," he said. "They both show the butterfly."

She blushed, smiling coyly. "A butterfly tattoo, Kurt? What a cliché."

"I know you and Nicole were once very close. Back when Rocky went through the railing. How close were you these past few weeks, when she was falling to pieces again? Do you have any idea what she was going through?"

Her laugh surprised him. Low and guttural, mocking. "If this is all a guessing game," she said with a triumphant gleam in her eye, "you lose."

She turned her back to him and lowered the robe to her waist. She wasn't wearing a bra. Two thin white strap lines ran vertically down the smooth tan sway of her back. Her skin was rich and flawless, as tight as a teenager's. There was no tattoo.

"Don't be shy," she said. "Have a closer look. I understand that removing a tattoo creates a nasty scar."

He stepped closer. There was a light spray of freckles underneath the tan. No signs of scarring anywhere on her back or shoulders.

"You can touch me if you like," she said, turning her chin to observe his stunned expression out of the corner of her eye. "I don't want you to go home wondering."

He studied her thin feminine neck, the sensuous narrowing V of her back, feeling too foolish to speak. She held her pose for a moment longer, then pulled the robe to her shoulders.

"Sheriff Muller," she said, rearranging the collar, tightening the sash, "I hope this will conclude your little witch-hunt." She turned to confront him face-to-face with a firm, unyielding expression. "I'm not the woman you think I am."

27

THERE WERE FEWER mourners than usual for a Sunday morning, perhaps because of the light overnight snow. Thurman Fisher, the old gent who owned the pool hall in town, was visiting a daughter who had died twenty-five years ago in a kayak accident on the Colorado River. Stooped Mrs. O'Carroll, recovering from recent cataract surgery, puttered around her husband's marker, replacing the plastic flowers in a permanent vase. When Muffin's cruiser pulled up to the ornate iron fence, Kurt was standing at his father's grave, staring at the name and dates etched in stone and wondering what desperate urgency had brought Gahan Moss and Dana Smerlas to this secluded place on a cold dark night. Maybe it was more than the ring. Maybe Gahan had demanded to know if Rocky was still alive. It may have been the question that had cost him his life.

Muffin had brought breakfast from McDonald's and a change of clothing from Gill Dotson's department locker. "A little while ago two TV satellite trucks tried to sneak past the guard station up in Starwood to film the Bauer mansion," she said. "And the reporters are camped outside your yard again. Now they've got a bloody double murder to chew on, too."

He settled into the passenger seat and turned up the car's

heater to warm his legs. After the first bite of food he discovered that he was ravenously hungry. "You want that hash brown?" he mumbled with a mouthful of egg and processed cheese, pointing to the white sack on the dashboard.

"Jesus, Kurt," she said, watching him devour everything in sight. Food steam and their collective breath clouded the windows. "You're eating like a Dumpster diver. Here, take this sausage biscuit thing."

She surrendered her entire bag except for the tall paper cup of coffee. "What did you find out about Mrs. Smerlas?" she asked.

"She doesn't have a butterfly tattoo."

Muffin held the coffee with both hands. "What is this fixation you have with a friggin' butterfly tattoo?"

He knew now that it had been absurd to hang everything on a couple of twenty-year-old photographs. Tattoo=Pariah= Dana Smerlas: a poorly formulated equation. The woman with the tattoo could have been anybody. A passing flirtation, here and gone. What was it Gahan had said about the women in Rocky's circle? *All the pretty birds have flown. You and I wouldn't recognize them anymore.*

He needed to find the photo of Mariah Windstar printed in the biography. It was the only certain way to eliminate Dana Smerlas as Pariah. He would call the book publisher tomorrow morning.

"She told me she'd had an affair with Gahan Moss," he said, relating Dana's story between bites of food. "I don't believe her, but there's nothing solid to charge her with."

"Did you tell her we have a videotape of her husband with Nicole?"

He shook his head, spilling crumbs in his lap. "The timing wasn't right," he said.

"Whose reputation were you trying to protect—his or Nicole's?"

He stopped eating and gave her a hard look. "This is not

about marital fidelity. They'll have to deal with that on their own time," he said. "This is about seeing Dana Smerlas right over there by those headstones last night. She had an argument with a man," he said, "and a few hours later the man was murdered. That's my interest here."

"Oh how I admire your powers of separation."

"I don't care what you think. I'm not trying to bring down Ben Smerlas."

"Excuse me? Did anyone say you were?"

Kurt knew he had to be very careful. If the tape's existence was leaked to the media, Smerlas would accuse him of waging a vengeful smear campaign, as his wife had suggested. It would win Smerlas more sympathy at the polls.

Like a bored child on a family car trip, Muffin leaned forward and drew a large tic-tac-toe board on the steamed windshield. "Okay, Sir Galahad, what have we got so far? Nicole Bauer's where this whole thing started." She swirled an O in the center square. "And now there's Dana Smerlas," she said, marking an X in one corner, "and Gahan Moss." An X in another corner. "And let's not forget our boy Lyle Gunderson." An X in a third corner.

Kurt studied the drawing. "Or a killer who might be Rocky Rhodes," he added, slashing an X in the last corner.

She sipped coffee and smiled at her clever composition. "One more square and we can draw a line," she said.

They sat in silence, watching the sketch dissolve slowly into long cold trails of water. "It's all falling apart," Kurt said finally. "We don't have dick."

Wadding up the empty McDonald's bag, he got out of the car, opened the rear door, and climbed into the backseat. There was a large manila envelope, 24 × 17, lying next to the neatly folded pile of Gill's clothing.

"Put a couple of our people on the horn to every mental hospital in the state," he said, slipping off his leather jacket. His clothes smelled like a rabbit cage. He was happy to exchange the salty flannel shirt for Gill's forest-green uniform. "Let's give their staffs a profile—age, physical description, the works. Mention that our man may have shown some musical talent, especially with the guitar. If Rocky's been locked away all these years, he hasn't been using his real name."

Muffin caught his eye in the rearview mirror. "If Rocky's been locked away on a rubber ranch," she said, "that means somebody put him there, Kurt. It means somebody's been responsible for his care."

"Find out if his mother is still alive down in Texas. Maybe she knows something."

Muffin sighed heavily. "It's a needle in a haystack, boss. He could've been locked up anywhere. Sitka, Alaska, for all we know."

"Start with Colorado and Texas," he said. "Recent releases with Rocky's profile. Escapees with a history of violence. This guy hasn't been out more than a month or two, I guarantee."

He was shedding his jeans now, stuck with Gill's goofy boxer shorts designed with lipstick kisses all around the crotch snaps. He noticed Muffin's eyes still watching him in the rearview mirror. "If Rocky's been released into the population after being locked away for a long time," she said, "wouldn't the hospital put him into some kind of halfway house program to ease him back in?"

"Maybe," he said. "Keep going."

She thought it over. "Wouldn't there be a shrink assigned to him? Somebody like a probation officer?"

"Good possibility. A local contact wherever he's gone to live."

Muffin looked over her shoulder at him, saw that he was indisposed, then turned to stare ahead at the windshield. Lost in thought, she smeared a final X onto the watery tic-tac-toe board and slicked a line through the row. "Your favorite head doctor," she said. "Dr. Jay Westbrook."

He grinned. "I knew there was a reason I hired you."

He remembered seeing a man sitting on the cabin steps underneath the distant spruce trees. "Visitor cabins are spread all over that property," he said. "He could be holed up in one. Let's get a search warrant."

"Judge DuPrau is probably at home this morning," Muffin said. "It's Sunday and there's snow on the golf course."

"Type up something quick and get it over to him. Tell him we suspect a murderer is hiding out in one of the cabins. He'll sign it."

He was dressed now, his funky clothes rolled up next to the large envelope lying on the seat. "Is this for me?" he asked.

"Oh, yeah," she said, glancing over her shoulder, remembering. "That came for you at the courthouse early this morning. Nobody saw who delivered it. We figured it was some asshole reporter trying to grab your attention. It's probably stuffed with interview money."

He opened the envelope and glanced inside. No money, only a ream of paperwork. He didn't have time for paperwork, not now or for the rest of his life.

"Where will you be while I'm dogging the judge?" Muffin asked.

"Waiting for you at the Elk Mountain Lodge."

She turned around in the seat. "Don't talk to Westbrook until I get there," she said emphatically. "I don't want you blowing the warrant."

"Bring Gill and Florio with you, fully armed," he said, slipping a boot over his tender ankle. "The fucker killed a rottweiler with a knife."

28

DRIVING DOWNVALLEY IN his old Willys Jeep he lowered the window and listened to the Roaring Fork River rippling alongside the highway in a temperate mood, its shallow October waters streaming through fragile crusts of ice. If he followed this road north through the valley, he would find his son feeding a young gray-eared Himalayan rabbit in its hutch behind the farmhouse, the two passing quiet company on a lonesome Sunday morning. In a perfect world he would drive that child and his rabbit as high up Mount Sopris as the ancient four-wheel Jeep would carry them and they would sit on a log and watch the creature frolic in the white wilderness she knew from ancestral Tibetan dreams. She would zigzag and leap and race the wind, her tiny paw prints looping far into the distance, patterned seams in the snow. In a perfect world there would be no predators and no hunters and no end to her pleasure and theirs. Like a faithful pup she would always return when they whistled.

But today was another day, another world.

He nudged the brakes and turned off Highway 82 onto Elk Mountain Road, heading west through the ponderosas toward Snowmass Creek. The CB radio hawked like someone with a bone in his throat, seizing Kurt's attention: "Come in, Sheriff, are you there?"

He unclipped the mike speaker and responded. "Go ahead, Toni."

"You've got an emergency call, Kurt. Some guy desperate to speak with you," the dispatcher said. "He's at a pay phone in the Denver airport."

"Who is it?"

"He won't identify himself. But he says it's extremely urgent."

He was passing the padlocked gate to Star Meadow, the small village of geodesic domes and solar-heated cottages that had been a popular center for holistic studies throughout the 1980s. Waning interest and financial mismanagement had forced Matt Heron to close the institute last year, and now the place looked abandoned and bereft, like a New Age ghost town with weed-grown bike paths and loose brush blowing past the boarded-up yerts.

"It's probably just another reporter hustling an angle," he told the dispatcher. "Dump him. I don't have anything to say to the press right now."

A short time later he rumbled across the wooden bridge over Snowmass Creek and coasted through the wrought-iron archway marking the entrance to Bauer land. Off to the south a herd of elk was sunning in the hoof-trampled snow of a large open pasture, a hundred shaggy beasts and their calves milling about aimlessly. Snow melted on the tin roofs of the cabins rowed along the creek. Kurt wanted to drive over without delay and inspect them one by one, but he knew he'd risk blowing the case if he didn't wait for Muffin and the search warrant.

He continued down the muddy road to the parking lot of the Elk Mountain Lodge and pulled off into a small picnic area underneath a stand of spruce trees. There were fewer vehicles this morning. He sat in the Jeep and watched smoke curl from the lodge's fieldstone chimney and wondered what would lead a successful doctor to destroy a woman who had trusted him and depended on his care, and who had once loved him as a wife. After a few moments he got out of the Jeep with his binoculars and framed the windows of the lodge, fingering the delicate focus until he could see far into the lobby. No one was moving about. He slowly veered direction, spying the dense treeline hugging the base of the mountains farther west. There were a handful of cabins back there, where he'd observed that man yesterday morning. He found one small structure, then another, but they appeared dark and unused, curtains of snow pressed against the windowpanes.

A vehicle slushed into the parking lot and he lowered the binoculars to see who it was. A large black GMC Yukon was edging into a space near the front walkway to the lodge. The door opened and a woman stepped out wearing a familiar brown suede jacket with a fur-fringed hood lying back on her shoulders. He raised the binoculars and followed her up the split-log steps and into the shadows of the covered porch.

Isn't this cozy? he thought. Dana Smerlas coming to Jay Westbrook for counseling.

The CB radio crackled loud enough to wake a coma patient. He slid behind the wheel and snatched the mike. "It's the guy at the Denver airport," the dispatcher said. "He's blowing a fuse. Says he needs to talk to you before he catches a plane."

"Tell him to fuck off."

"He says he left a large manila envelope for you that contains important information about the Nicole Bauer case."

Kurt glanced into the rear of the Jeep, where a corner of the hand-delivered envelope stuck out beneath his bundle of dirty clothes. Whoever he was, he'd been in Aspen earlier this morning.

"You still don't know his name?"

"He says he won't talk to anyone but you."

Kurt reached for the envelope. "I'll call you back in sixty seconds, Toni. It's probably a line of bullshit."

The thick ream of paperwork turned out to be architectural blueprints, drawings, rough sketches. Taped to the first page was a sheet of elegant stationery imprinted with the words *From the desk of Nicole Bauer.* A hasty message had been scribbled in ballpoint ink: *This is why they killed her. She was the only one who could stop them.*

The words, the personal stationery, startled him. He rubbed the paper between his fingertips, brought them to his nostrils. Jasmine. Nicole had written several desperate notes to him on this stationery when he'd stopped seeing her last fall.

"Toni," he said, thumbing the CB mike. "Is he still on the line?"

"Yes, sir."

"Patch him to my cell phone."

Waiting for the phone to ring he shuffled through the documents, each one stamped with the logo of Guerin and McCord, architects. This was stolen property. It had been taken from their burglarized office in the middle of the night.

The phone chirped. Kurt lifted the receiver. "Okay," he said solemnly, "you've got my attention."

There was a slight delay, then a young man's voice: "I did it for Nickie. She woulda wanted you to see them for yourself."

Kurt thought he recognized the voice but he wasn't sure. "Who am I talking to?" he asked.

"You know who I am." He could hear a loudspeaker in the background, a generic tape reminding passengers that smoking was not permitted in the terminal. "I couldn't let 'em get away with it, man. But who was gonna believe a two-time loser like me? That's why I had to break in and liberate that shit."

Kyle Martin. Fence-sawer, mink farm vandal.

"I just opened the envelope," Kurt said, knocking askew his rearview mirror as he unfolded an unwieldy blueprint. "I need time to look this over, Kyle."

"Give me a number. I'll call you back in ten minutes. Get with the program, dude."

Careful not to rip the creases, he unraveled the largest document, smoothing out its cool surface on the passenger seat. It appeared to be a design plan for something called The Elk Mountain Ski Resort. He recognized it instantly as an early study for the vandalized scale model he'd seen in the architects' office. Reading their handwritten inscriptions and geographical guide, he knew now why the damaged model had seemed so familiar when he'd examined the broken pieces on the table. He raised his eyes, taking a hard look at the old lodge and the white mountains rising beyond, where those young Dartmouth skiers had perished sixty years ago. Someone was planning to build a new state-of-the-industry ski resort on the very ground where he was parked.

He shifted in his seat and studied the details. The proposed village would cover 150 acres, the entire parcel of Bauer land from Elk Mountain down to the county road and Snowmass Creek. A 300-unit hotel would replace the old lodge. The plan called for several condo high-rises and private health clubs and a shopping district with bars, bistros, and fashion-wear shops. The rusting T-bar would succumb to a towering new ski lift and modern high-speed gondolas.

Printed boldly at the bottom of the sheet was the name of Guerin and McCord's client: THE BAUER COMPANY, Denver, Colorado.

Kurt straightened up and looked around at the untouched acres of snow. The Bauers envisioned another Snowmass or Vail at one of the last great unspoiled corners of the Roaring Fork Valley.

He glanced down at the note scribbled on Nicole's stationery. *This is why they killed her. She was the only one who could stop them.*

He emptied out the packet and scattered the remaining documents across the blueprint. One of the smaller sheets caught his eye, the sketch for a proposed monorail system that would link five major ski areas, sleek futuristic capsules zipping across the mountaintops between this new resort and Snowmass Village, Buttermilk, Highlands, and Aspen. One great big happy interconnected ski bonanza, making all of the investors obscenely rich.

The cell phone rang. Kurt grabbed the receiver.

"You see what's going down?" the voice said. "Now that Nickie's dead there's nobody to stop them. They can do whatever the fuck they want."

"Your note says they killed her, Kyle. What makes you say that?"

"They're all in it together, man. It's a fucking conspiracy."

"*Who*, Kyle? Her brothers?"

"They hated her. She embarrassed them too many times, dragged the family name through the mud. They hated everything she'd done with her life, and everything she stood for. She told me they tried to cut her out of the family money but their old man wouldn't go for it. He loved his princess, no matter what. Before he died he fixed it so she had a vote and veto power, like the other two."

Kurt remembered what Nicole had said to him in their final moments together: *Decisions, decisions. They can't piss away all the money unless I let them.*

"This ski resort deal was the thing that finally drove them to the wall," Kyle said. "They wanted it real bad. You got any idea how much they stand to pocket if that shit gets built? Billions, man. But Nickie didn't give a damn about the money. She wanted to keep the land undeveloped. The whole goddamned valley's getting paved over by assholes like her brothers and there's no place for the critters to go. She had her own plans to make the place an animal refuge. So she said *fuck you* and refused to okay the deal."

Kurt knew that many years ago Nicole had insisted on removing the fences around the Bauer property because the land had always been a major elk run. If this resort was built, it would destroy the animals' migratory patterns. And a rail system across the mountains would drive every last bear down into civilization, where the Mike Marleys of the world were waiting with their .38s.

"Look, man, I've got a plane to catch," Kyle said. Flight numbers were echoing in the background. "I gave you that stuff because Nickie trusted you and woulda wanted you to know about it. Maybe you've got the balls to do something, I don't know."

"Hold on, Kyle. Where are you going?"

"A place where there ain't no fences and the wolves outnumber the people. I'm not hanging around to face a felony break-in. This time they'll send my scrawny ass to the meat factory in Cañon."

"You've got to sit down and talk to me, son. I need to know everything Nickie told you. I can't build a case without your help."

"Sorry, dude. They're boarding my plane. I've told you everything I know. The rest is in those blueprints."

"Kyle, don't go!" he said. "We can work out a deal. I'll get the D.A. to grant you immunity in exchange for your testimony."

Kyle laughed bitterly. "Nickie may have trusted you with her life," he said, "but I sure as hell don't. So long, chief. I've got your number if I get lonely."

"Stay right where you are! I'll come get you and put you up in a safe house till something's worked out."

Cabin rows were being announced by microphone.

"You can't stop them," Kyle said. "Nickie tried and look what happened to her. They'll do the same to you and me."

"Are you saying somebody murdered her?"

"They didn't have to stick a knife in her, fool. They worked on her head. Check out what that asshole mind doctor gets out of the deal."

"Westbrook?"

"Like I told you, it's all in the blueprints. Later on, chief. I gotta bolt."

"*Kyle!*"

The line went dead. Kurt slammed the cell phone against the dashboard and cursed. He pounded the steering wheel. After a few moments he calmed down and gathered the papers together, refolding what he'd already seen, searching now for something that might implicate Jay Westbrook. If the Bauers intended to tear down the lodge and build a ski resort on this site, what would happen to their former brother-in-law—the man they had hired to save their sister from life in prison?

It didn't take long to find his answer. One of the documents was labeled STAR MEADOW RENOVATION. Unfolding the squares, he saw that the architects had drawn up remodeling plans for the bankrupt New Age village five miles down the road. Apparently the Bauers had bought Star Meadow and intended to restore it along with their ski development.

Kurt climbed out of the Jeep and spread the blueprint on the hood to have a better look. The design showed that many of the institute's permanent structures would be left intact. There were plans to add more first-class sleeping accommodations and a new conference center. Additional classrooms, tennis courts, a heated pool. And a director's private residence, 8,000 square feet. At the bottom of the sheet Kurt discovered the proposed title for the new place: The Alpha Institute, Rocky Mountain Campus.

The Alpha Institute, he thought. Wasn't that name on a diploma hanging in Westbrook's office?

Kurt remembered the shrink and Walt IV standing shoulder to shoulder on the Smerlas deck last night, toasting with their wineglasses. One big happy family now that Nicole was out of their way. The resort would be built. The old Star Meadow would become a glorified summer camp for Jay Westbrook's clientele. Peace and wellness in the Rockies. His thirty pieces of silver.

* * *

SITTING ON THE warm, bug-spattered hood of the Jeep, arms folded, Kurt stared at the entrance to the lodge, mindful of Muffin's words not to go in without her. He glanced down the road toward the creek, where the elk were slowly herding off toward an aspen grove in the distance. No sign of his deputies. It might take Muffin another hour to find Judge DuPrau. And if he was in a bilious mood, as he often was, he might not authorize the search warrant.

Kurt knew he had to seize this moment before Dana Smerlas finished her business and drove away.

When he entered the lobby, Tanya was speaking quietly to three elderly women warming themselves near the stone fireplace. Her eyes locked on to him as he strode toward the corridor where Westbrook's office was located. "May I help you, Sheriff Muller?" she called out in a brisk voice.

He had nearly reached the man's door when he felt a strong tug at his jacket. "I'm sorry, Sheriff," she said, hanging on to him with a dogged determination. "Dr. Westbrook is with someone. If you'll have a seat in the lobby . . ."

"Let go of my sleeve," he said. She recoiled a step, chastened by the anger in his voice.

He pounded on the office door and opened it without waiting for a reply. Westbrook and Dana Smerlas glared at him, startled and offended by his intrusion. The psychiatrist rose from his regal chair. "I am in the middle of a private session, sir," he said indignantly. "Tanya, what's going on here?"

"I tried to stop him but—"

Kurt took hold of Tanya's arm. "Step back out of the room, young lady," he said, showing her the way. "This is police business. I'll call you if somebody needs a foot rub."

He closed the door in her face and turned to acknowledge Dana Smerlas. She looked perfectly at home here. She had tossed her coat onto a chair, kicked off her snow boots, and nestled comfortably on the couch with her jean legs curled underneath her taut buttocks. Her expression slowly softened into a coy smile. "Still chasing butterflies, Sheriff?" she asked with a raised eyebrow. She seemed as blithely amused by his sudden appearance as Westbrook was incensed.

Kurt's eyes shifted from one to the other. "Where is he?" he demanded.

"This is outrageous," Westbrook said. Behind the rimless glasses his small hard eyes looked like hollow-points in the chambers of a revolver. "I must ask you to leave immediately or I will file charges."

"Tell me where he is," Kurt said. "I'm going to put him away before he kills somebody else."

Westbrook and Dana Smerlas exchanged glances. "I have no idea what you're talking about," the psychiatrist said.

"Then you're in serious denial, my friend. Isn't that what you tell your patients?" Kurt said. "It's too late to go simple on me, Westbrook. We've got Lyle. We've got his tapes. Pretty boys don't enjoy the prison experience. Sooner or later he'll spill his guts in a plea bargain."

"I'm aware of the young man's situation," Westbrook said, standing behind his chair now, resting his small freckled hands on the high back. "His parents called me this morning and asked if I would visit him. They said he's been bullied by the police. I should have guessed it was you."

"He's under arrest and he's not seeing anybody but the lawyer he hires to save his sleazy ass. You've done enough talking to that poor fucked-up boy."

"I don't believe you're qualified to make that judgment, Sheriff Muller."

"Agreed. Which is why I'm turning you over to the state licensing board for *their* judgment. Let's hear what they have to say about it."

"What do you mean?"

"Your ex-wife and longtime patient comes to you and confides that she's afraid to be alone and she wants live-in company, so you set her up with a sick young voyeur with a history of secretly videotaping women. That ought to catch somebody's attention in Denver. I'm also curious what the board will say about a doctor who prescribes strong antipsychotic medication for a woman he knows has had a drinking problem for at least twenty years."

"You're way out of line," Westbrook said, his face flushed with anger. "Nicole needed domestic help, Lyle needed a job. I was doing them both a favor."

"You knew he would show you the tapes, didn't you, Doctor? You were like a father to him and he wanted to make you happy, so he shared them with you. And then you shared them with other people, didn't you?" he said, turning to Dana Smerlas. "Which is how Mrs. Smerlas found out about her husband and Nicole."

The sound from Dana Smerlas's mouth favored a Pekingese yelp. Sudden, unexpected, irritable. She closed her eyes, composing herself.

"I'm sorry, did I touch a nerve, Mrs. Smerlas? Your friend the good doctor did show you the tape, didn't he?"

"These assertions are insulting, to say the least," Westbrook said, his neck stiffening at an awkward angle. "You have no right to come into my private office and make wild allegations about Lyle Gunderson or Mrs. Smerlas or any of my patients, Sheriff Muller."

So Dana Smerlas was his patient as well.

"You two make quite a team," Kurt said, again looking from one to the other, his smile carrying a dark edge. "How did you find each other? Did Nicole introduce you?"

Dana Smerlas was staring back with seething abhorrence.

"You've got that one big thing in common," he said. "Nicole hurt you both and you hated her."

Westbrook laughed insincerely. "That's absurd," he said.

"You're beginning to sound delusional yourself, Sheriff. May I recommend a good shrink?"

It was then that Kurt noticed the gun on Westbrook's imposing walnut desk. The doctor had made no attempt to conceal the weapon. It rested on a stack of manila folders next to the telephone. An odd thing for a psychiatrist to keep in his office. From where Kurt was standing, the pistol looked like a sheeny black .45, enough firepower to stop a crazy man with an eight-inch hunting knife.

"Mrs. Smerlas, would you excuse us for a moment," he said. "I would like to speak with Dr. Westbrook alone. Please go have a seat in the lobby. I'll talk to you when I'm finished here."

With a sullen reluctance Dana Smerlas rose from the couch, fetched her fur-lined coat, and slipped an arm into one sleeve, her eyes riveted on Kurt all the while. "I'm due to meet my husband at the club for lunch," she said, checking her watch. "I hope this doesn't ruin my plans."

"This is a police investigation, Mrs. Smerlas. Call your husband from the lobby and tell him whatever you want, but don't leave the building. I'll speak with you as soon as I can."

After she left the office Kurt walked over to the desk for a closer look at the gun. It was a Colt 1911-model .45 semiautomatic, not a discreet gentleman's pistol but the weapon of choice for Marines and macho paramilitary types. It could probably stop a rhino in full stride. He also noticed an old cleaning kit with its lid open, the bore rod and pads and oily polish rag ready for use.

"What made you drag this old hog out of the closet, Doctor? I didn't realize that counseling was such a high-risk occupation. Are you expecting trouble from one of your patients?"

"I have a permit," Westbrook said with a furrowed brow. "I don't need your permission to own a weapon."

"Gahan Moss probably had a weapon and a permit, too, but it didn't keep him from getting his throat slit in the middle of the night."

Westbrook approached his desk, opened a drawer, and slid the .45 inside. "What do you want from me, Sheriff?" he said, slamming the drawer.

Kurt wanted to punch him in the face. "Where is he?" he demanded. "Has he been under your care all these years?"

The psychiatrist shrugged. "I haven't the slightest idea who you're talking about."

"You've lost control of him, haven't you, Doctor? You didn't expect him to kill anybody, but you were wrong. And now you're a little nervous about the whole situation," Kurt said, nodding at the drawer that housed the gun. "He's gone ape shit on you. You probably don't even know where he is right now. Hell, he might break into *your* place tonight with his nasty hunting knife. He might sneak up on Tanya while she's sleeping and cut her pretty little throat."

Enraged, Westbrook threw up his hands. "I refuse to acknowledge these sadistic fantasies of yours. In fact, I'm going to call my attorney before this goes any further. You can take out your frustrations on him."

He lifted the telephone receiver and furiously punched a set of numbers. Kurt reached down and ripped the phone line out of the wall outlet. Then he grabbed Westbrook's padded shoulder and shoved him into the swivel chair behind the desk. "Sit down," he said, bracing his hands on the chair arm and leaning into the man's face close enough to see a toast crumb in his beard. "Let's discuss you and Nicole, shall we? It's never too late for marriage counseling."

There was sudden panic in Westbrook's eyes. Sweat greased his forehead. He wasn't used to being on the other end of the questioning.

"She rejected you, Doctor. Isn't that why you hated her? She was the one who filed for divorce. That had to be tough on your ego. It's tough on any husband, especially one who's always in control of the relationship."

"I advise you to refrain from using any more physical force

against me," Westbrook said, staring at the ripped-out phone cord. "I'm going to report your behavior to my attorney."

Kurt straightened his shoulders and glanced across the room at the aquarium sitting on a table underneath the psychiatrist's diplomas. Only one fish was visible in the tank, that willowy golden beauty swimming gracefully near the glass. He watched the fish waggle into the underwater greenery and reappear seconds later in a long gliding motion.

"Fifteen years together, holy matrimony," Kurt said. "And then she finally figured it out. The only reason you married her was to play watchdog for the Bauer family. It was your job to keep her medicated and shut off from the public so she wouldn't embarrass them again. That's why she left you, isn't it, Doctor? She woke up one morning and realized you weren't her husband, you were her caretaker."

"Your pronouncements are getting more surreal by the minute," Westbrook said, shaking his head in disgust.

"And then there were the other lovers," Kurt said. "The ones she took to bed instead of you. It made you unhappy, I'm sure. Even after the divorce. You hated the fact that you'd lost control of her. The Bauer brothers were unhappy, too. My god, she was on the loose again, free to ruin their name. Which is why you set her up with Lyle. You knew he would keep an eye on her for you. Literally."

"Are you finished with this nonsense yet, Sheriff?" Westbrook asked with a sour expression. "Because I have clients to attend. A schedule to keep."

He stood up from the chair but Kurt gripped his shoulder, shoved him back down, and leaned in close again. Westbrook turned his head away like a child refusing to accept a scolding.

"It didn't take much to get the crazy bastard worked up, did it?" Kurt said, his voice rising. "You're a goddamned professional at this. You know all the right buttons to push. So you showed him Lyle's videotapes of Nicole in bed. Maybe you let him read some of those letters you say she'd written to herself over the years. Enough to light a fire under the man, get him stoked. You knew the voices in his head would take over and tell him to do the things you didn't have the guts to do yourself."

Indignant, Westbrook removed his glasses and tossed them onto the desk blotter. "If you persist with these ludicrous accusations I will sue you for slander," he said, jabbing a finger in Kurt's direction. "You won't be able to buy a stick of gum with what you're worth."

Kurt had made him furious and slightly off balance, which is what he wanted to do. He backed away from the man and ambled over to the sliding doors that opened onto the deck. Dana Smerlas was standing at the railing outside the lobby. She was smoking a cigarette and gazing up the snowy mountainside.

"Nicole was in everybody's way," Kurt said, his eye following the old T-bar passage out of the spruce trees and up through the snow-filled draw. He saw what Dana was looking at, three bundled men standing around a tripod high along the slope, and two others with a second tripod at some distance farther above. Surveyors taking measure of what was to come.

"She was mocking the Bauer name, she was holding up their plans, and she was sleeping with a man they'd handpicked to carry water for them in Washington, if he could keep his pants zipped and avoid scandal."

He turned around to find Westbrook studying him with utter contempt, his arm and balled fist supporting his bearded chin.

"And so you went to work fixing the problem, Dr. Westbrook," Kurt said. "Like you always did. You were the expert on neutralizing Nicole's damage. You were the one who knew how to shut her down."

The psychiatrist dropped his fist on the desk and issued a low scoffing sound. He seemed determined to remain silent until he was allowed legal representation.

"But I have a hunch, pal, it didn't turn out the way you wanted it to," Kurt said, feeling the sunlight prickle the back of his neck. "You thought you could soften her up with those drugs and sic a madman on her from out of her past—drive her over the edge and put her away someplace non compos mentis. My guess is you didn't want her to die, you just wanted her under control again and out of the game. Diminished capacity, incapable of signing her own name."

Kurt made his way toward the walnut desk and the seated man. "But you got more than you bargained for, Doctor," he said, picking up a gold letter opener lying on a pile of envelopes. "You misjudged your boy. You didn't know how crazy he really is." He touched the sharp tip of the letter opener against Westbrook's hairy Adam's apple. The man froze, closed his eyes. "You didn't realize if you pumped him up and set him loose, he would tear the house down."

Beads of perspiration pimpled the psychiatrist's forehead. He was breathing heavily.

"I hope for your sake you know how to use that Colt," Kurt said, dropping the letter opener onto the desk. "I don't blame you for keeping it close at hand."

A loud knock on the door startled them both. An urgent female voice shouted something from the corridor. Tanya, Kurt thought. "What is it?" he said, raising his voice impatiently.

The door swung open. Muffin Brown was flanked by two armed deputies, Joey Florio and Linda Ríos, with Gill Dotson looming behind. The team was geared in bulletproof vests and cammo clothing. Muffin frowned at Kurt, annoyed to find him with the man she'd told him not to interrogate.

"Enjoying yourself?" she asked in a low voice as she marched past him.

"Enormously," Kurt said.

She handed a document to the psychiatrist. "We have a signed warrant to search your premises, Dr. Westbrook," she said, glancing back at Kurt with the skillful trace of a smile. "The lodge and all outlying property. I hope we can count on your cooperation."

29

WHEN HE SLID open the glass door and stepped onto the deck, Dana Smerlas gave him a haughty sidelong glance and blew smoke out of the corner of her small glossed mouth. As he drew near she refused to acknowledge his presence, her arm poised in the air, thin white fingers curled around the cigarette. She was leaning into the pine railing like a pensive voyager gazing starboard out to sea.

"What an amazing coincidence, Mrs. Smerlas," he said. "You and I have a heart-to-heart talk and the very same morning we meet again at Westbrook's office. Was there something urgent you needed to discuss with him?"

"Jay Westbrook is my therapist," she said in a cool, distant voice. "Do you have a problem with that?"

"I didn't realize shrinks met with their patients on Sunday mornings. Will I find your name in his appointment calendar?"

A small wooden bird-feeder was mounted on the railing near her arm, its seed tray plugged with soft snow. She poked her cigarette into the tray, making a hiss, and left the butt to smolder and darken the ice. "If you're going to charge me with something," she said defiantly, "charge me. Otherwise I'm walking out of here to meet my husband for lunch."

Kurt studied her face, ageless and tinted with makeup, the fur-lined coat open at the neck, and tried to imagine how she'd looked that wintry night in Canyon de Chelly when she'd stolen the ring off a dead man's finger. It was difficult to picture this well-heeled woman stoned and grieving, fumbling around a corpse on her hands and knees in the desolate darkness, her young face streaked with tears and her long tangled hair whipped by the desert wind.

"I don't know how deep you're in this, lady, but if I were you I'd put some distance between myself and Jay Westbrook," he said. "You can start by telling me what you know about Nicole Bauer and Rocky Rhodes."

A clever smile tugged at the corners of her mouth. "Only what I read in the newspapers," she said. "She pushed him, he died. End of ancient history."

"No, the history goes on, Mrs. Smerlas. And I think you may be a part of it. Maybe you're not as involved as Westbrook, but you're carrying some dirt. Are you sticking by him because he's your shrink, or because he's got juice with the Bauer boys?"

"You're guessing again, Sheriff. Here, there, and everywhere."

"At the very least you knew your husband was having an affair with Nicole. I understand your interest in wanting her out of the way. You had your marriage to protect, and your husband's future. Politicians need to be careful who they're caught sleeping with."

She narrowed her eyes, and Kurt felt the full force of her resentment. "Half the men in this town were sleeping with that woman," she said bitterly. "There's a long list of angry wives. If you're looking for her enemies, I suggest you start with the *A*'s and work your way through the Aspen phone book."

Heavy boot steps were approaching from the lobby. Muffin

and Linda Ríos appeared at the patio doors. In their bulky vests and strapped-on gunbelts they looked like combat soldiers trained for door-to-door fighting. "We're ready to roll when you are, boss," Muffin informed him.

Dana Smerlas gave him a cunning smile. "Well, *boss*," she said, offering her limp wrists, "cuff me or kiss me. What's it going to be? If you don't want to play anymore, I've got a lunch date with another man."

Kurt had no cause to detain her and they both knew it. "You're free to go, Mrs. Smerlas," he said without hesitation. "But don't go far. We will continue this discussion another time."

"I can hardly wait."

She hitched her handbag strap onto her shoulder and sauntered directly toward the two female deputies, forcing them aside as she passed between them and walked through the patio doorway into the lobby.

"Mrs. Smerlas!"

Kurt called her name but she didn't slow her stride. He followed after her across the golden pinewood lobby and called her name again just before she reached the Bavarian door. She stopped and pivoted to face him.

"What now?" she snapped. The shrewd defiance was gone from her eyes. At this moment she seemed only restless and tired.

"Smerlas doesn't know any of this, does he?" Kurt said. "You've kept it from the poor dumb bastard. Your past, everything. He doesn't know you've watched a video of him and Nicole having sex and it made you mad enough to want her dead."

She closed her eyes and inhaled deeply before she spoke. "I realize you hate my husband and what he stands for, Sheriff Muller. And I know you'd do anything to stop him from becoming the next Colorado congressman from the Third District. But let me assure you there's nothing you or anyone else can do to prevent that from happening. Your pathetic little bedroom scandals won't work, no matter how low you stoop."

"This isn't about your husband's career, Mrs. Smerlas—"

"No, you're right," she said, cutting him off angrily. "It's about male ego, isn't it, Sheriff? My husband was sleeping with her, too, and that's been eating you alive."

She saw the surprise on his face and bore in deeper, searching for an open wound. "Did you think you were somebody special, lover boy? The only rabbit going down that hole?" she asked with a cruel smirk. "It's killing you that she was fucking your old rival, isn't it? 'How could she do that to a prince like me?' But hey, don't get down on yourself, Romeo. That's what every man wonders when a woman makes a fool of him."

She shrugged indifferently, the smirk spreading across her lips. "Imagine that story when it hits the press. 'Enemies clash over sex partner.' You come after me and my husband, that's all the public will hear, mister. 'Sheriff's probe motivated by sexual jealousy.' Everything else will be buried on page eight."

He knew she was right. It would be too easy for the media to spin this as simply a clash of alpha males.

"What's the matter, Sheriff? Cat got your tongue?" she said. "I feel your pain. Let's continue this discussion another time, when you're in a better mood to talk dirty."

She turned and opened the heavy door and walked across the lodge's front porch and down the steps to her GMC Yukon. A small, graceful woman who was doing everything in her power to protect her secrets and cover her tracks. And maybe someone else's as well.

"Want me to bust that chick for you, Kurt?" Muffin was making her way across the lobby behind him. "We'll figure out what to charge her with later on."

He shook his head. "Let's give her a little more rope," he said.

He turned to find Muffin and the three other deputies standing together near the reading chairs, staring at him, embarrassed by the conversation they'd overheard.

"What are we waiting for, Kurt?" Gill asked him with a stern expression. "We've got a search warrant. Let's go find that killer."

30

KURT ASSIGNED LINDA Ríos to baby-sit Westbrook while he and the other deputies teamed up to search the cabins. Dotson and Florio drove down to those near the creek, and Kurt and Muffin hiked up a snowy trail to the woods at the foot of Elk Mountain. As they made their way out of sunshine and into the spruce forest, the light faded into deep blue shade and the air felt arctic and sealed. With their weapons locked and loaded they followed a worn path that meandered alongside a dry runlet clogged with scree. When they came upon the first cabin, Muffin ducked behind a thick spruce trunk with her pump twelve-gauge and Kurt crouched in the icy underbrush a few yards away, focusing his binoculars. There was no movement inside the cabin, no light.

"I want this guy alive," he said. "I want him to talk."

"Let's not get too cute about taking him, Kurt. He's a stone killer. God knows what else he's packing besides that hunting knife."

She raised her shotgun and covered him while he hobbled on his bad ankle to the backside of the small wood structure. The windowpanes were iced over and dirty. He wiped a clear circle with his jacket sleeve and peeked in. The interior appeared dark and empty. He holstered the .45 and cupped his hands around his eyes, pressing his nose against the glass for a better view. He could make out an old iron woodstove and a small bed with a bare mattress. The place looked as if it hadn't been occupied in months. He walked around to the front door and signaled for Muffin to join him.

Untrammeled snow crusted the steps and small entry porch. No one had entered or left the cabin since the snowfall two days ago. The door was unlocked, and when he gave it a nudge with his boot he heard rats scurrying across the floorboards. He could smell their feral nest.

"Nobody's home," he said as they stepped inside and looked around.

The cabin wasn't as rustic as it appeared from outside. The walls were bare cedar and there was no electricity, but the furnishings included a table and two chairs and a writing desk with an empty bookcase on either side. Dust layered every surface. There was a kitchen nook with shelves, a cutting block, an aluminum sink and faucets. A kerosene lamp sat on a side table next to a rocking chair. The bed's mattress had been chewed down to the stuffing by the little critters that had vanished at the sound of the creaking door.

"Who stays in these places?" Muffin asked, resting the shotgun across her shoulder.

"Westbrook's patients, I imagine. Weekend navel-gazers. The ones who need their own space."

"If I holed up in this little dump for very long I'd need therapy, too."

"Let's check out the other one," he said. "It's a hundred yards farther back."

He led the way silently along the rocky runnel as it curved westward through the forest, climbing steadily toward its ancient dry source somewhere high in the mountains. Sunlight slanted through the thick overhead limbs. Soon they caught sight of the second cabin deeper in the woods, unassuming and bark brown, concealed by surrounding foliage. They huddled in the brush, trading turns with the binoculars. The undergrowth made it difficult to see anything clearly.

"I know you want him in one piece," Muffin whispered, "but watch your step, okay? I've got a bad feeling about this."

With his deputy stationed behind a tree, her twelve-gauge raised aloft, Kurt lowered his shoulders and fought his way through clinging vines for twenty yards or more before he could gain a better angle of vision. From his hiding place he scanned the front of the cabin with the glasses and noticed something that made him swallow hard. Footprints tracked the snow on the steps leading up to the door. Someone had been here recently. And maybe he was still inside.

Kurt waved to her, nodding his head emphatically: *He's here!* He motioned for her to approach the left side, he would take the right. She gave him the thumbs up and sprinted to a tree closer to the cabin, the shotgun braced in both hands.

As he moved off quickly through the wet vines he snagged his foot and began to slide downhill over a mat of soggy spruce needles, snapping twigs in the chilly silence. Halfway into the slide he lurched to his feet in a running stumble, sounding like a bear crashing through bamboo. When he reached the side of the cabin he dropped to his knees and rolled underneath a snarl of wild bushes for cover. His jeans were wet, his hands were numb-cold, and he couldn't catch his breath or slow his pounding heart. He worked his fingers, blowing into cupped hands. If he had to use his gun right now, he wouldn't feel the trigger.

The air around him was ripe with decay. A few yards away, pegged to the frozen ground by a railroad spike, lay a steel trap that had snapped off a small animal's leg, possibly a raccoon. The animal was gone but its blood-dried stump protruded from the jaws, teeming with maggots. All Kurt could think about was that poor trapped rottweiler with its throat slit from ear to ear.

The .45 gripped in both hands, he rose slowly on his aching ankle and peered into the cabin window. It had been shrouded by a white sheet, denying him a view inside. He edged along the wall until he reached the corner of the cabin, only a few feet from the porch. Muffin was kneeling on one knee underneath a front window, her shotgun aimed at the door. She gave him a damning look that said, *Where have you been?* He signaled that he would take the lead, and in four long strides he was on the porch yelling, *"Pitkin County Sheriff! Open up!"* He jiggled the doorknob but it was locked. Stepping back he kicked the door with the sole of his good foot. The frame split away after three hard blows and the door jarred open.

"Look out!" Muffin shouted, grabbing his jacket from behind and pulling him down.

The knife blade swung through the open door, carving the air above their heads, then arced back inside. Kurt aimed his pistol but saw that the weapon was tied to a trip cord. It swung at them again, the second time with less velocity. The pendulum had lost its momentum and the knife retracted into the cabin, where it dangled harmlessly from its cord looped over a rafter. If Muffin hadn't reacted quickly, the blade would have struck Kurt squarely in the chest.

"Police!" he shouted, pointing the .45 into the darkness. He could smell the man, the same rank, piss-soaked body odor from the sleeping bag in the Wheeler attic. *"Give it up, Rocky. Let me see your hands!"*

They both crouched in the doorway, Muffin beside him with the shotgun set against her shoulder. The windows were covered by sheets and tattered blankets. Rising slowly, hip to hip, they scanned the dark room for movement. The only sound was the buzzing of flies. Kurt took a step to his left and ripped down one of the blankets, pouring daylight across the enclosure.

"Jesus H. Christ," Muffin said, sighting down the barrel of the twelve-gauge. "What the hell is *this*?"

The cabin was cluttered knee-deep with piles of magazines and catalogs and cardboard boxes stuffed with what appeared to be years of collected junk mail. Satisfied that no one was hiding inside, Kurt holstered his weapon and inspected one of the boxes. Grocery flyers, coupon packets, contest entry forms, credit card offers, subscription renewals, political endorsements, notices bearing the snapshots of missing children. He checked the mailing labels and discovered that every item was addressed to a box number at the Aspen post office.

"I guess his momma never made him clean up his room," Muffin said, looking around at the mess.

"Be careful," he said, glancing up at the knife slowly twisting at the end of a long strand of mailing twine. "The whole place may be booby-trapped."

"You figure that's the knife?"

"Same kind," Kurt said. The blade was certainly long enough.

He noticed an old Underwood manual typewriter pushed to the back of the writing desk. Taking cautious steps through the deep drifts of cut-up magazines, he made his way to the clunky machine. On the desk two drip-streaked bottles of Elmer's Glue-All and a rusty X-acto knife lay atop a stack of glossy pages slit from a Victoria's Secret catalog.

"It's our man," Kurt said.

A page torn from a book was taped to the wall above the typewriter. The page missing from the library book. Photographs of Rocky and his friends.

"This is disgusting," Muffin said, her footsteps shuffling across littered paper. "The crazy loon left some food out over here and it's crawling with flies. I can't even make out what it was."

Kurt scratched at the taped edges with his blunt nail, carefully extracting the page from the wall. He held the sheet in his flattened palms with a nervous delicacy, as if it might smudge or deteriorate at his touch. There were two photographs on each side of the sheet, a rogue's gallery of Rocky's entourage from that hip bygone Aspen of twenty years ago. Studying the faces in one group shot, the surly body language and self-conscious posturing, he was nearly certain he'd found the young Dana

Smerlas. Her coy smile hadn't changed in two decades. She was lounging in a circle of hippies on Nicole's Starwood lawn back before the walls and floodlights and laser eyes were installed. They were all laughing and mugging for the camera. A joint was making its way from one hand to another. Dana's hair swirled in the breeze, long and thick and darker than Kurt had imagined. She was wearing a loose Mexican peasant blouse and jeans, her legs tucked underneath her the same way they had been on Westbrook's couch. The young freak with his arm around her shoulders wasn't Rocky but one of the band members whose name Kurt couldn't remember now, maybe that drummer Jack something-or-other, the guy with the blond ponytail on all the album covers. In this picture he was shirtless and clearly enamored with his own physique, showing off his wildly tattooed arms and muscled upper body.

"What's he doing with all these magazines?" Muffin asked.

Kurt opened the cover of a dog-eared spiral notebook lying on the desk and turned the pages. "He likes to cut out pictures and words," he said, examining the images of women glued to each page. "Looks like he's got a hang-up with the opposite sex."

"Hey, here's some old clothes and his stash of weed," she said. "God, it stinks."

Kurt turned around to caution her, but before he could open his mouth she had taken another step and the floor collapsed underneath her, a funneling commotion of paper and cracked wood. Powerless, he watched her go down, her legs giving way and disappearing through a hole in the floorboards. There was a loud steel snap, metal on bone, followed by her scream and the roar of the twelve-gauge blowing out a window.

"My leg!" Visible only from the waist up, she pounded the floor with her fists, trying to pull herself out of the hole. "It's a fucking leg trap!"

Kurt ran for her, toppling the mounds of magazines in his way. Halfway across the room his boot found the soft give of a loose board and in that moment he knew what was coming next. He flinched and deflected the upswinging board with his forearm, and the six-inch nail driven through the board only grazed his jacket, ripping leather.

"Don't come any closer!" Muffin cried. "The floor's a tiger trap!"

The son of a bitch had set crude booby traps all over the cabin. Kurt stopped abruptly and knelt down in the magazine debris and began crawling on his hands and knees, testing the floor's firmness foot by foot as he pressed his way toward her. She was grimacing from the pain, her face bathed in sweat. She had managed to pull one leg out of the hole but the other one was pinned in a steel-jawed animal trap chained to the concrete slab underneath.

"Hurry, Kurt," she moaned. "I'm gonna pass out."

Digging away the scattered pages that had been sucked into the hole, he saw that the trap had snared her between the ankle and calf, metal teeth chewing into bloody cammo. He forced his large body down into the hole, no more than five feet in diameter, three feet deep, a dank, earth-smelling space beneath the cabin. Using both hands and all his strength, he pried back the jaws, feeling the steel claws rip away from her skin and bone.

"Oh, Christ!" she screamed.

"Can you lift your leg?" he asked, forcing the tight jaws apart with wobbling hands.

"No," she said. "I can't move it!"

"Grab your knee and lift!"

She gripped her cammos and dragged her leg upward, shrieking in agony. He released the jaws and they snapped together with a wicked ring.

"Oh, god, Kurt!" she cried, scooting away from the hole. "God, it hurts!"

He peeled back her ragged pant leg and stared at a splinter of exposed white bone. She raised up on her elbows, took one look, and fainted dead away, her head thumping against the magazines. Kurt jerked the radio from his belt and called the deputies searching the cabins near the creek.

"Officer down!" he said, breathing quickly. "I need a chopper here pronto. Do you read me, Gill? I need a medevac team!"

"Copy that, Kurt."

"There's a snow field between the lodge and these woods. Tell them to put the chopper down there."

"Will do."

"Get over here, Gill. Muffin's hurt bad."

"Copy that. We're on our way."

He took a deep breath and examined Muffin's leg again. There wasn't as much blood as he'd expected, not enough to warrant a tourniquet. The jaws had struck solid bone, fracturing the tibia. Using his Swiss Army Knife he slit her pants up to the knee, releasing pressure. Then he removed the department cap from her head and smoothed her sweaty hair with his shaking fingers.

"You're gonna be all right, champ," he said, staring into her slack face, praying she could feel his hope on some deeper level. He looked again at her leg, a hash of torn flesh and exposed bone, and feared that the injury would end her career in law enforcement.

Kurt peeled off his jacket and placed it across her chest. The flies were beginning to swarm around them and he knelt over her, batting his arms to ward them off her face and damaged leg. It was impossible to stanch the anger that overwhelmed him right now. He wanted the psychopath who had done this to her. And the people who had set him loose.

31

AFTER TWO HOURS of surgery Muffin lay recovering, semiconscious and heavily drugged, in a private room at Aspen Valley Hospital. Her tibia had been nearly severed by the steel jaws. The surgeons had done what they could to pin and stabilize the fracture, but they informed Kurt that she would have to be flown to Denver for extensive orthopedic reconstruction.

After the attending nurses had left the room he remained at Muffin's bedside, holding her hand in the antiseptic silence. She didn't know yet the magnitude of her injury and he wasn't going to be the one to tell her. He was having enough trouble keeping his own emotions under control.

"The pain was so bad I wanted to die, Kurt," she said in a hoarse whisper, her eyes fluttering when she spoke.

"I wasn't going to let that happen."

"I know," she smiled palely, squeezing his hand. She didn't have the strength to crush a grape.

He had broken his leg playing football in high school and had crutched around for two months, never regaining his original speed. Her recuperation would take even longer. Hospital, rehab, home care. She would never be as agile as she once was—the expert skier and leader of the Search and Rescue rappel squad, the point guard on the department's basketball team. He suspected that if she returned to law enforcement, she would see limited duty for the rest of her career.

He studied her wan face. Even under these conditions there was pride in the set of her jaw. A desk job would destroy her. "The guys found two more tiger traps underneath all those magazines," he told her. "I'm lucky I'm not in here with you."

Her eyelids blinked open, then slowly sagged of their own weight. "Find him, Kurt," she mumbled. "Bring him in."

They didn't speak for several minutes. Eventually her hand went slack, the first sign she'd fallen asleep. Tears had pooled in the corners of her eyes. He found a Kleenex on the bed stand and gently daubed them dry.

SLOUCHING IN HIS Jeep in the hospital parking lot, surrounded by the long chill shadows of late afternoon, he picked up the cell phone and called Meg. "It's been a helluva weekend," he grumbled in a voice racked with fatigue. "Things are crazy here. I can't come after Lennon right now."

"I read the newspaper, Kurt. You should've told me about the mess you're in."

"I didn't realize that Buddhists read newspapers."

"Are you going to be all right?" She sounded genuinely concerned.

"There are a bunch of reporters following me around. They've got the house staked out. Why don't you bring Lennon to Carole and Corky's tonight?" he suggested. Otherwise it was a twenty-mile drive on a traffic-crawling two lane from the Basalt farmhouse to their son's school. Forty minutes one way every morning, as bad as Denver at rush hour. "He can stay with them this week until everything dies down."

"I don't want him to get caught up in your problems, Kurt. You know how I feel about that. I don't want the ugliness to rub off on him."

"The world has its ugly side, Meg. We can't keep him from seeing it," he said. "Look, he'll be fine at the Marcuses'. I won't bring him back home until things are perfectly normal again."

He heard the exasperation in her sigh. "Things are never going to be perfectly normal if you keep behaving the way you do."

"Don't judge me until you hear the whole story."

After a long, awkward silence she said, "When this is all over, Kurt, and things are perfectly normal again, I want to sit down and talk with you about our custody arrangement. I would like more time with Lennon."

This was not the moment to start this discussion. "Fine," he said dismissively. "You can explain to the judge why you left your son and holed up in an ashram for two years while I was left here running the county sheriff's department and taking care of him by myself."

"I don't want a fight, Kurt. I want an understanding," she said. "A fair arrangement."

"Sorry, gotta go catch a killer. But I'll meditate on it when I have some downtime," he said, "and get back to you. In the meantime please bring Lennon to the Marcuses'. If it's no inconvenience to you and *Bhajan*."

"You're being an asshole."

"Well, now. Is name-calling one of those steps on the path to inner bliss?"

"You're carrying a lot of anger, Kurt," she said with another sigh. "I wish you would see a therapist."

"I have been seeing a therapist, Meg," he said dryly. "I'm going to put him in jail."

After hanging up, he dialed the district attorney's office and found Donald Harrigan at his desk on a Sunday afternoon. "How did it go?" Kurt asked, inquiring about the D.A.'s interview with Westbrook and his lawyer.

"I had to let'm walk, Kurt," Harrigan said in his slow country drawl. He was the only Texan Kurt had ever liked. "Dr. Westbrook claims he had no knowledge of anybody staying up there.

He insists that those cabins were strictly off-limits to his guests because they needed repair and hadn't been used in a couple years."

"He's lying, Don."

"I believe you but it's gonna be hard to prove in court. I'm sorry, Kurt, you don't have a strong case here."

"Talk to Lyle Gunderson. Offer him a deal. He's the weak link."

"I'm driving to Glenwood first thing in the morning."

"If we can get him to admit he showed the tapes to West-brook, it's a start."

"I don't know how that will shake out," Harrigan said. "So Lyle cops to giving his shrink some tapes. The shrink will say he studied the tapes to diagnose the young man's illness and offer a proper treatment. All very professional. He'll scream doctor–client privilege to justify why he didn't turn the tapes over to the police."

"Goddammit, Don, three people are dead and my best deputy may never walk right!"

"Stop yelling at me, Kurt. We're on the same side, remember? But you've gotta give me more to work with. Why don't you go find the cutter you say is causing all this grief?"

After a few moments of staring at the dead phone Kurt dialed the squad room in the basement of the county courthouse. Mac Murphy picked up the call. He was the only deputy in the building. "How's Muffin?" Murphy asked. "She gonna be all right?"

"No, she's not, Mac. They've got to take her to the Denver Medical Center."

"Son of a bitch." Everyone in the department was fond of Muffin Brown. "I feel like kicking somebody's ass."

"Hold that thought. Right now I want you to do me a favor," Kurt said. "Locate Walter Bauer. He's probably at his crib on Red Mountain. I want to meet with him as soon as possible."

"Roger, boss."

"Call my beeper when you find him."

He pitched the cell phone into the glove box and sat watching the sky over Shadow Mountain soften into a beautiful amethyst hue. The air was cooling rapidly in this shoulder season between the golden waning days of autumn and the cold dead arrival of winter. The prospect of seven months of snow no longer cheered him, as it had when he was a younger man with his skis waxed and ready. At this moment he felt worn down by memory. Like a fool he had tried to save so many people in his life, recover the best parts of his past, and in the end he hadn't saved his brother or his partner lying in a hospital bed with a crushed leg or his marriage to the mother of his child. He had less to show for his years than Gahan Moss and his paltry shelf of mementos. He hadn't saved a goddamned thing.

The Sunday newspaper lay on the seat beside him. He stared at the front-page photograph of Ben Smerlas and his wife cutting a cake at his announcement party. She had survived the long strange trip from rock groupie to dutiful Republican wife. Anyone who could pull that off deserved everything that was coming to her.

He peered into the rearview mirror to see if his eyes were as bloodshot as they felt. He looked wasted. His skin appeared puffy and red, the tiny white L-shaped scar in his brow shining like a fresh scrape. He smiled about the silly fishing accident that had produced that scar many years ago and about the old doctor who had stitched him. And then he glanced at the newspaper photo of Dana Smerlas again and realized that Doc Brumley might be in serious trouble.

32

KURT BANGED THE knocker and pounded on the door of the old Victorian home but there was no response. Somewhere in the house a television was blaring so loudly he could hear the narrator describing the nesting patterns of bald eagles. He stood on his tiptoes and peered through the fan of beveled glass into a quiet living room awash with evening light. When the doctor didn't appear after several more knocks, Kurt tried the knob and discovered that the door was unlocked. He stepped inside the living room and called Brumley's name. Again, no answer. The house still nursed its ancient odors, only now Kurt detected urine and a trace of something that smelled like copper. He slipped the .45 from his shoulder holster and held it near his ear as he slowly approached the parlor off to the left. Through the doorway, pale gray light flickered from the television set.

"Doc?" he said, nearly shouting.

From the parlor door he could see the old man slumped in a large overstuffed reading chair. His head was lying to the side, his eyes were closed, his half-moon reading glasses clinging to the tip of his nose. A section of newspaper was spread across his lap, the rest on the floor near his slippered feet. On the television screen a pair of eagles soared high in the Sierra Nevadas.

Kurt quickly scanned the small room. There were no signs of struggle. "Doc," he repeated, "are you all right?"

He walked over and touched the man's shoulder.

"Hunh?" Brumley said, stirring, licking his dry lips. "Whu? Who is it?"

He opened his eyes and stared at Kurt and the gun in his hand. The glasses dropped from his nose onto the newspaper in his lap.

"It's me again, Doc. Is everything okay?" he asked, restoring the .45 to its holster.

"Say what, now?" Brumley asked in a croaking voice. He squinted at Kurt, trying to comprehend who he was. "Oh, it's you, Bert. Goodness alive. I didn't know you were back in town. Have you come to see Timmy?"

His son Tim was nearly fifty years old and lived in California with his wife and three children.

Kurt stepped over and turned down the TV set. "Sorry to wake you, Doc. I need you to look at a picture."

"A picture?" Brumley said. He sat up straight and worked his stiff neck. "Gracious sakes, your brother was here the other day asking a lot of questions, too. He's the sheriff now, you know."

Kurt smiled at the old doctor. "Take a look at this photo and tell me if you've ever seen this woman before." He handed Brumley the photograph of Ben and Dana Smerlas he'd torn from the newspaper. "Does she look familiar?"

Brumley rubbed the sleep from his eyes and found his reading glasses. Breathing raggedly, he stared at the photo for at least two minutes without moving a muscle, his gaze frozen on the Smerlases. "I don't know her," he said finally. "Was she one of Martha's schoolmates?" Brumley's daughter.

"Are you sure you've never met her?"

The old man raised his eyes to regard Kurt. "Not that I re-call," he said. "She's a nice-looking gal, though."

"Look again," Kurt said patiently. "Is this the woman who came to visit you last week?" He stooped down to study the photo with Brumley. "Late at night, remember? She reminded you of a Frankie Laine song. Her name was Mariah Windstar."

"Yes, of course I remember the lady," Brumley said, staring at the picture in his wobbly hands. "But this isn't her. I can see why you might think so. They're both attractive, both small and brunette."

"You're sure it's not her?"

"I'm positive, Bert. I never forget a facial structure."

Kurt stood up straight and looked around the parlor. Embers smoldered in the quaint fireplace. The heavy, dust-stiff curtains had been drawn against the dying light. A stuffed blue grouse and the owl Brumley had repaired yesterday were the other occupants of the room, mounted on driftwood and staring black-eyed from their corner perches, silent companions overseeing the old man's final preoccupations. Kurt thought he heard a noise and turned toward the doorway, his eyes searching the twilit corners of the living room and the stately dining area beyond the arch. There was too much unaccounted space in this house, an entire floor upstairs, too many rooms and closets and unopened doors.

"Doc, how would you like to spend the next couple of days at the Hotel Jerome?" he asked. "The county will pick up the tab."

"Why on earth would I want to do that?"

Kurt could hear wind rustling the trees outside the windows. The front porch creaked. This place was beginning to give him the creeps. He didn't want anything to happen to the old coroner.

"Mine tailings," Kurt said. "There's a problem with lead in the soil. It goes back to the silver mines a hundred years ago. The entire West End is being analyzed by the EPA this week."

"Lead, you say?"

"The agency has sent a team out from Denver. They want you to leave for a couple of days while they conduct some tests around your house and in the basement."

"Good god. Lead! They'll stir everything up."

"We'll put you up in the Hotel Jerome. Three meals a day, courtesy of my department. Room service. Saunas. Whatever you want, Doc."

Brumley removed his reading glasses and stuck the curved tip of the arm in his mouth, thinking it over. "I've read somewhere that they have a masseuse on duty," he said.

"Yes, sir, I believe they do."

"How many days did you say?"

"Two or three, tops."

"Make it four and I'll go get my toothbrush."

33

Kᴜʀᴛ ᴡᴀs sʜᴏᴡɪɴɢ Doc Brumley how to order a pay-per-view movie in his posh hotel suite when the beeper went off. It was Mac Murphy calling from the courthouse. "Walt Four and his brother are at the Nordic Club, racquetball court number three," the deputy informed him over the phone. "They have dinner reservations afterward at the Caribou."

"What did you do, Mac? Break into their office and peek at the calendar?"

"I know a guy whose girlfriend is pals with somebody whose sister is their secretary."

Aspen.

The Nordic Club was the most prestigious, celebrity-infested health facility in the Rockies, an unobtrusive structure sprawling into the meadows and brushland on the east side of town. It was dark when Kurt parked among the BMWs and four-wheel sport utility vehicles gleaming under the halogen safety lights. As he crawled out of his old Willys with the envelope tucked under his arm, he felt giddy and loose. There was music in his head. He could smell the silent snow dancing in dark currents a thousand feet up the mountain. He wondered if this was what the doctor had warned him about, messages from the shaken eight ball.

He hadn't been to the Nordic Club for at least a year and didn't recognize the two well-scrubbed young greeters stationed behind the marble sign-in desk. They didn't seem to know who he was, either. "Police business," he said, flashing his badge. "Nothing to be concerned about. I need to speak with one of your patrons."

Outside the glass walls of the racquetball courts a comfortable seating area was provided for curious spectators and players awaiting their turn. Tonight the chairs were unoccupied at court number three. Kurt placed the envelope on a table and sat watching the two brothers thwock the hard rubber ball off the black-scuffed walls. Jeffrey Bauer was poor competition for his tall athletic brother, who pounded each return with impressive force and skill, sending the overweight accountant into deep corners of the box to chase his next shot. In spite of the obvious mismatch, Walt IV showed no mercy in punishing his brother swing after swing.

Kurt understood the competition between brothers. He and Bert had gone at it hard for an entire lifetime. Bert was faster, more agile; Kurt was stronger. Their rivalry had hung in that balance. But when all was said and done they had loved each other and it was Bert who had slowed down that day and waited for him, pointing to the cutoff with his ski pole, saving his younger brother from the avalanche. Bert would never have left him behind. Jeffrey Bauer couldn't say the same thing about his older brother.

Behind the glass wall Jeffrey was bent double, gripping his knees, the racquet lying on the court next to his Reeboks. Waiting for him to recuperate, Walt IV stood near the service line bouncing the ball rapidly up and down between his racquet and the floor. He looked disgusted with his younger brother's lack of stamina and conditioning. Kurt could tell by his impatient demeanor that the man didn't tolerate weakness of any kind.

"There you are, you son of a bitch!"

Kurt turned in his chair to see Ben Smerlas storming toward him with a racquet swinging freely in his hand.

"What's the fucking idea picking on my wife?" Smerlas said, wagging the racquet at Kurt. The commissioner was dressed in a loose orange nylon gym-suit that made him look like a Vegas hood. "You wanna pick on somebody, whyn't you pick on me, motherfucker?"

Kurt stood up. "You don't know what's going on, do you, you dumb bastard?" he said.

"Izzat so? I know this. When I get through with you in this recall, you won't have a pile of shit to crawl back under. You're done, hoss."

Kurt smiled meanly. "Did your wife tell you she'd seen the tape of you and Nickie? I've got the original if you'd like to watch it sometime," he said. "By the way, you might want to try Viagra for that weak little hard-on of yours."

Smerlas swung the racquet at him full force, overhand like a tennis serve, but Kurt caught the handle and swung the commissioner against the glass wall of the ball court with a thunderous boom. His legs buckled and he slid to the floor, but he recovered quickly and lunged at Kurt, tackling him around the knees and dragging him off his feet. Smerlas had surprising upper-body strength and powerful arms, and they wrestled around on the carpet until Kurt finally struggled to his knees, grabbed the man by his oily hair, and smashed his face against the glass.

"You stupid prick!" Kurt huffed. "You're assaulting a cop!"

"Not the *nose!*" Smerlas pleaded as his face met the glass a second time. "Please! The nose ain't paid for!"

Walter Bauer was standing in the court doorway with a look of horror on his face. "Stop that!" he said in a loud nervous

voice. "You've got witnesses watching you, Sheriff! He's not re-
sisting. Let him go!"

Kurt thought about banging Smerlas's face against the glass
one more time for luck but shoved him aside and stood up.
"Your candidate could use some grooming, Mr. Bauer," he said,
straightening his leather jacket, breathing hard. "You want him
to be your pony, you better brush him up a little. 'Cause the next
time he attacks a cop, he's going to jail."

Jeffrey Bauer was watching everything from the other side of
the see-through wall. Without his glasses he had the squinty,
perplexed expression of that solitary fish in Westbrook's aquarium.

Kurt retrieved the large envelope from the table and tossed it
at Walt IV's feet. The blueprints spilled out the open end. "I believe these belong to you," he said. "They were stolen last night
from Guerin and McCord."

Walt IV glanced at the packet on the floor. "How convenient
they've shown up in your hands, Sheriff," he said.

"I didn't steal them, Bauer, but I've taken a look at them,
all right. I know what you're up to. I know you need the
commissioner here to push your big plans through the
county zoning committee. And when you buy him a seat in
Congress he'll make sure the Forest Service doesn't slow you
down."

Smerlas was on his feet now, studying his reflection on the
glass wall, gingerly probing his nose as though it were made of
putty.

Kurt nodded at the blueprints on the floor. "I can see why
Nicole had become a problem for you and why you wanted her
out of the way," he said.

Walt IV glared at him through ice-blue eyes. "If you dare to
dishonor my sister again—"

"Spare me the phony outrage," Kurt said with a tired sneer.
"You despised your sister and you did everything you could to

destroy her. Well, congratulations, mister, you and your cronies finally broke her down."

Walt IV's handsome face hardened. "My sister was a deeply disturbed woman," he said, his voice dripping with pity. "She destroyed *herself*, Sheriff Muller. Day by day—slowly—over a long period of time. Those of us who loved her had the misfortune of witnessing her deterioration. We tried to intervene many times but she wouldn't let us in."

Kurt smiled sadly at Nicole's defiance and courage. "She knew if she let you in," he said, "you'd stick a knife in her heart."

Walt IV held Kurt in his angry gaze for several moments, then dropped his eyes to the blueprints on the floor. He stooped down and shoved them back in the envelope and rose again, measuring Kurt with palpable contempt. "I'm going to ask my attorney to investigate that break-in," he said. "I'm curious to know who stole these plans and why they wanted them."

"It doesn't matter now, Bauer. I know the truth about you."

"The truth, Sheriff?" he said with a cunning smile. "Many people grasp a small corner of the truth and think it makes a difference. You can't change anything, my friend. You're a small-time loser in a big boys' game."

Kurt wanted to smash Walt IV's face against the glass, too. He stared at Smerlas, still patting his nose with light fingertips, a cocky smile emerging from under his hands. Behind the court wall Jeffrey Bauer stood motionless, watching them, his racquet lying on the floor at his feet. He looked like a scared little boy calculating where to run and hide.

Kurt nudged Walt IV aside and stepped through the doorway onto the court. "Jeff," he said, "I've been told you're very upset about your sister's death. I have a feeling you really cared about her. When you get tired of being bullied by your brother and want to talk, here's my card."

Jeffrey Bauer took the card and stared silently at the printed information as if it were as useless as a losing lottery number.

"You know better than anybody else what your big brother is like," Kurt said, looking back at Walt IV. "Someday he's going to get upset with you, too—like he did with your sister. You'll do something to piss him off and he'll find a way to cut you out of what's yours."

Jeffrey Bauer's soft round face went colorless with fear. He glanced at his brother, then handed back the card. "I have no idea what you're talking about, Sheriff Muller," he said, swallowing hard. "Please leave me alone."

Kurt scratched the card against his bristly jaw, a two-day beard. "I think you know something about your sister's death," he said. "You want to live with that the rest of your life, be my guest. But it'll eventually eat a hole right through you. Because you cared about her."

Jeffrey Bauer lowered his eyes. He refused to look at Kurt.

"He'll turn on you, Jeff. Maybe not real soon—he needs your silence right now. But it'll happen, you can count on it. Just like it happened to Nicole. When it does, give me a call. I don't care if it's ten years from now, give me a call. I'll help you do the right thing."

He turned and walked out of the racquetball court past Walt IV and the scowling Ben Smerlas and marched down the quiet Sunday-evening corridors of the Nordic Club. When he reached the lobby he whooshed through the automatic doors into a dark outside world gently afloat with snow. Silent, heavy clouds were rolling in from the north, a smell of frost. Soon it would all come down.

34

FOR ANOTHER HOUR he cruised the streets of Aspen in his drafty Jeep, trying to calm down and concentrate on what had to be done. He drove up to his home on Red Mountain and counted two satellite trucks and four other vehicles parked near the sheriff's department car stationed outside his ranch fence to keep the media at a respectful distance. The snow was forcing the reporters to stay in their vehicles. He pulled over to the side of the road and radioed Linda Ríos, the deputy sitting in the Pitco unit.

"Don't let them see your Jeep, Kurt. They're a pretty gnarly bunch," she responded. "Unless you want to play Princess Di in the Paris tunnel."

"Any chance they'll just go away?"

"I wouldn't count on it. Not tonight."

"Who's inside the house?"

"Stuber," she said. Fully armed, waiting in the dark for Rocky Rhodes to break in again with his eight-inch blade.

"Tell him not to take any chances," Kurt cautioned.

He drove back down Red Mountain Road into town, checking on the other stakeouts by radio. "Creepy," said Mac Murphy, hiding in the Opera House attic with another deputy.

"Cold," said Gill Dotson from the pup tent he and Florio had set up out in the icy woods near the cabin. Kurt had assigned every remaining unit to patrol the county roads around the Elk Mountain Lodge and on Buttermilk Mountain in the vicinity of the Magic Mushroom House. And there were Aspen city cops on foot watching the pedestrian streets surrounding the Wheeler Opera House. If that bastard made a move tonight, they were going to nail him.

Worn down and edgy, Kurt needed to get out of the cold for a short break, stretch his legs, and infuse some caffeine into his system. He made his way along Lone Pine Road as it swerved upward across the river from the county jail, and soon he wheeled the Jeep into the trailer park where Muffin lived. There was light and motion in the other mobile homes, but hers remained dark and lifeless, like a huge shell shed by some prehistoric creature that had crawled off somewhere to die. He parked in her space next to an empty planter box and trod up the steps onto a small entry porch. He had taken the house key from her jeans at the hospital and used it now to open the front door.

When he turned on the lights he saw that the place hadn't changed since the last time he'd been here, probably a few years ago. Same old lady's furniture, same barnlike aroma of grains she kept in glass jars on the kitchen counter, same photo clusters of her five brothers from their Wyoming ranch family and the new wives and children. She was the only daughter of Fred and Millie Brown, the only child living outside the state. He had talked to them this afternoon from the hospital and the entire family was now on its way to Colorado in a caravan of camper trucks.

He slipped off his boots near the door, turned up the thermostat to heat the chilled rooms, and wandered into the cramped kitchen–dining area looking for coffee. There was a dark hallway beyond, leading to the bedroom where he had once slept with her, four years ago, the evening he'd won his last election. The victory party had been wild and jubilant. On that festive night Kurt could not have imagined that someday he might be recalled from office by those same voters.

He found a half cup of tepid coffee sitting next to the sink. She'd taken a few gulps before rushing out on one of their emergencies. He didn't have the energy to brew his own so he spooned off the floating film and heated the cup in the microwave. There was a Felix the Cat clock on the paneled wall, its tail and eyes wagging back and forth in a syncopated rhythm, watching him. He sipped the coffee and stared back at the clock and tried to put himself inside Rocky's head. Where would he go tonight to get out of the weather? Was the hurt inside him satisfied now, with the deaths of Nicole, Gahan Moss, and Amanda, or did he have other scores to settle?

He dragged the ring out of his pants pocket and placed it on the Formica countertop. The yin-yang symbols looked like two interlocking sperms with single eyes. He reached into his jacket for the page that had been torn out of the Rocky Rhodes biography and unfolded the creases, carefully flattening the paper on the counter with both hands. The young Dana Smerlas smiled at him from a lotus position, loose peasant blouse, her hair blowing in the wind. Sitting beside her, with a proprietary arm around her shoulders, was the tattooed, ponytailed drummer of the band. Studying the photograph, Kurt saw something he hadn't noticed at the cabin. The drummer was carrying a hunting knife in a handmade leather sheath, the handle resting against his bare waist. Kurt skimmed the caption below the picture. *Jack Stokes.* He remembered the name now: Rocky's old buddy from Texas, the only musician who had stayed with him from the beginning.

In the chaos of the cabin Kurt hadn't taken time to read the names in the caption. There were four or five from the list scribbled on the 1977 police report. *Crescent Moon. Boogie Downes. Wolfgang P. Gursted. Maggie Mae Turner.* And a couple he hadn't come across before. *Dana Word, Jack Stokes.* And the one he'd been looking for all along: *Mariah Windstar.* He counted quickly, three from the end. There she was, the small, slender woman with dark hair and an intriguing smile, someone altogether different from Dana. It was the same young woman standing under the waterfall, kissing Nicole. The girl with the butterfly tattoo.

"My god," he said aloud. He reached up and turned on a lamp hanging over the sink. This was the first time he had seen a full view of her face. He lifted the page and studied her closely. Mariah Windstar. Pariah. He couldn't believe his eyes.

There was a wall phone next to Felix the Cat. His fingers raced over the numbers he knew by heart. After three rings a man answered.

"Bhajan," he said, "is Meg there, please?"

"No, Kurt. She's probably on her way back from Aspen by now. They left well over an hour ago. She drove Lennon to his friends' house."

"Jesus," Kurt said.

"You sound stressed. Is something wrong?"

"Can we contact her? Does she have a phone in the car?"

"We're not a high-tech household, Kurt," he chuckled. "We don't even own a television."

"Listen to me very carefully, Bhajan. If you hear from her, tell her to go straight to the courthouse in Aspen and wait for me in my office. Tell her to make sure she goes straight there. Do you understand?"

"This sounds serious, Kurt. What's going on?"

"Just do what I ask, please. Tell her to go to my office. There's no time to explain it now. I've gotta run."

35

IT WAS A large house with many rooms, all black now at this late hour except for a somnolent glow somewhere deep within, like a lantern burning in a closed barn. The snow had stopped falling but the lawn was frosted with a white crust that dissolved under each footstep. He made his way quietly up the outside stairs to the redwood deck. She was sitting alone in the hot tub, her eyes closed and her head pitched back on her shoulders above the roiling water. There was an empty wineglass near her hand, which dangled over the lip of the tub. She didn't hear the tread of his boots until he was close enough to slit her throat.

"Is that you, sweetie?" she asked in a sleepy moan.

Steam billowed up between them. The only light glowed from the hot tub itself, a swirling white incandescence.

"The kids are asleep. Why don't you come join me?" she said, a sexy invitation.

He hesitated, remembering their night together in the tent. He wondered what would have happened to their lives if they had gone too far.

"It's me, Carole," he said. "Where's Corky?"

"Kurt?" she said, startled by his voice. She splashed upright and ran her hands through her short wet hair. "I wasn't expecting you."

"Come on out of there. Where's Corky?"

"He's at his office, working late. I thought you were him."

"Come on, get out," he said, handing her the towel draped across a deck chair. "Is Lennon here?"

"Sleeping in Josh's room. What's the matter? You sound angry."

Kurt gazed out across the dark lawn where he'd left tracks in the brittle snow. He could hear Castle Creek hissing nearby, cutting off a corner of their property only a stone's throw from this deck. A hundred feet away the woods began, a dense grove of fir trees undergrown with snowberry and yarrow. The killer could be out there in the darkness right now, watching their every move.

"Let's go inside and get the kids," he said. "We've got to take you someplace safe."

"Would you mind telling me what's going on?"

When she stepped out of the tub he grabbed her wet arm and turned her body so he could see the butterfly tattoo for himself. He slid off her bathing suit strap and stared at her shoulder blade. The tattoo was there, small and delicately rendered and slightly faded now in the hazy light.

"What's the matter with you, Kurt Muller?" she said, slipping the strap back in place. She jerked away from him, irritated by his rough behavior. "Why are you acting so strange?"

"It's Jack Stokes," he said, gazing into her deep brown eyes. "He stalked Nicole. He murdered Gahan Moss and his wife. And now he might be coming after you."

She patted her neck with the towel and looked away. "I don't know what you're talking about." Her words should have sounded more convincing.

"No more secrets, Carole," he said, fetching a robe from the chair and placing it around her warm wet shoulders. "I know about the young woman named Mariah Windstar."

He expected another denial but instead she whirled around and seized both of his arms. He felt her nails pressing through the leather jacket. She searched his eyes before she spoke. "Don't do this to me, Kurt," she said with a startling vehemence. "I have Corky and the kids now. Don't do this, goddammit!"

Glass shattered somewhere in the dark house. They looked at each other, a moment of sudden fear. He drew the .45 from his shoulder holster, latched one hand around her wrist, and dragged her stumbling barefoot across the deck to the patio doors. He aimed the pistol into the darkness as they entered the high vaulting grand room of the Marcus home. Silhouettes loomed all around them, furniture and lamps. With Carole clinging to his hand they maneuvered awkwardly toward the soft gray light of the kitchen. Broken glass was spread across the Mexican tile. The side door had been smashed.

"He's in the house," Kurt whispered above the sound of his own pulse.

Carole released his hand and ran through the darkness toward the stairway leading up to the floor where the children were sleeping. He was three steps behind her, grabbing at her robe to slow her down, but she flew up the stairs ahead of him. When he reached the top landing he heard her gasp somewhere down the dark corridor. Her bare footsteps had ceased their slapping on the hardwood.

"Carole?" he said in a low voice.

The corridor between the bedrooms was cast in a ghostly green hue, weak and diffuse, a single night-light in a wall socket. He saw her outline not twenty feet away, motionless in the white robe. When he heard the laugh, raspy and choked with phlegm, he knew what had stopped her. A man was standing at the far end of the corridor near the doorways to her children's rooms.

"If you touch any of them," she said, her steady voice echoing off the walls, "I will tear your heart out and stomp on it. Do you understand me, Jack?"

The man shuffled his feet and Kurt cocked the hammer on

the Smith & Wesson. He couldn't see him well enough in this poor light. Carole was standing between them. Four children were sleeping on the other side of these Sheetrock walls. He knew there was no way he could fire his weapon.

"Give it up, Jack," Kurt said. "That was my trigger cocking."

He heard the sound of stainless steel sliding through leather. The man had withdrawn his knife.

"Don't call me that name," he said in his tortured voice. "You know who I am now. He lives inside me. He whispers in my ear."

"Lay down the knife," Kurt said. "We'll get you some help."

Ragged footsteps shuffled across the hardwood. He was coming toward her. "I know what you and the other bitch did to him. What you did to me. She's dead now and you're going to meet her in the worm world."

Kurt stuffed the .45 in his holster and dashed for Carole.

"You killed the music, you little cunt."

Kurt grabbed her shoulder and pulled her to the floor just as the man sprang at her with the eight-inch knife. His momentum carried him stumbling over their bodies into the shadows and for an instant Kurt lost track of where the knifer was. Carole screamed and scrambled to her feet and bolted through a doorway into the master bedroom with the man scurrying after her. In a dead run Kurt tackled him from behind and they rolled through an open sliding door onto a small balcony where Carole had tried to escape. The man slashed at Kurt but missed, slashed again, the blade carving air near his face. Kurt seized his cutting arm with both hands, battling him for the knife, but in their scuffle a sharp knee caught him in the groin. He groaned, losing his hold. A wild swinging elbow cracked his chin and everything went black for an instant. When he opened his eyes he saw Jack Stokes crouching over him, laughing his vile laugh, the long gleaming knife drawn back behind his ear in that final savage motion before he thrust the blade into Kurt's chest. He crossed his forearms, hoping to deflect the blow. Then suddenly Jack was jerked backward toward the balcony railing. Carole had collared his loose duster and was dragging him away from Kurt. The man stumbled against the low railing, almost toppling over the side, but quickly caught his balance and lashed at Carole with the knife, drawing blood across her shoulder. She cried out, and in that moment Kurt leaped at the man and slammed him against the railing. Nails groaned and the wood gave way. With long flailing arms Jack Stokes tried to take Kurt with him, but Kurt slipped his hold and grabbed on to the rail as Jack tumbled into a free fall. The broken section swung outward like a ranch gate but held Kurt's 220 pounds. Clinging to the rail, dangling above the deck, he watched the man plummet twenty feet toward the hot tub. There was a long, heaving moan when his body hit solid redwood.

"I've got you," Carole said, kneeling over him at the edge of the balcony, clutching his shoulders. He glanced up and saw blood trailing down her arm.

A few minutes later, when he had finally dragged himself to a standing position on the balcony, they held each other trembling in the cold night and peered down at the body sprawled on the deck below. The drop alone may not have killed him. But the hunting knife was embedded in his rib cage. Blood spattered his gray beard and long silver hair.

"Mom, I heard a noise."

Her twelve-year-old was standing in his pajamas at the patio door, rubbing sleep from his eyes.

"Everything's okay, sweetie," she said, leaving Kurt to embrace her son and turn him away from the sight below. "Let's get you back in bed."

"You're bleeding, Mom. What happened to you?"

"It's just a scratch. Come on, now. Back to bed. Tomorrow is a school day."

Kurt watched them disappear into the darkness of the house, a doting mother comforting her sleepy son. He tried to imagine her as the young woman called Pariah, wild and reckless and strange, doing the things he knew she'd done back in those days when they'd all run so hard and burned so bright. He tried, but he couldn't see her playing that part. She was someone else now. Pariah was as dead as the man lying in his blood on the deck below.

36

AFTER A LONG night with the coroner's team and three hours of sleep on a couch in Corky's study, Kurt drove back to the Elk Mountain Lodge and hiked into the woods to have a look around the cabin one more time. His deputies had cleared the floor, raking catalogs and mail-order debris into two-dozen fat brown storage bags stacked in orderly rows against a wall. They had also removed five loose floorboards with punji-like nails and had placed orange traffic cones next to the tiger-trap holes. Kurt walked over to the nearest hole and discovered that one of his men had used a tree branch to spring the leg trap spiked in the ground underneath the cabin. A quick inspection showed him that the two other traps were also inoperative now. But he wasn't prepared for the rush of dread he felt when he saw the trail of dried blood near the hole where Muffin had gone down. He stared at her blood and wondered if she would ever walk without a limp.

Opening one of the storage bags he found a sheet of pizza coupons labeled with the Aspen P.O. box number that appeared on every piece of mail. He pulled the cell phone out of his jacket and dialed directory assistance for the number of the Aspen post office. His old poker buddy Bruce Davis, twenty-five years in the postal system, was now the head supervisor.

"I need to know who's renting one of your boxes, Bruce," he said after a short round of pleasantries. "Can you help me with this?"

"Tell me it's police business," his friend suggested, "and I'll act properly intimidated."

"It's a murder investigation. Does that qualify?"

Kurt read the number and Bruce put him on hold, then returned a few minutes later with a name Kurt didn't expect to hear. The box account fee was paid up until the end of the year and currently rented to a Mrs. Alvina Stokes of Houston, Texas. Possibly Jack's mother, Kurt thought. His friend volunteered the woman's phone number in area code 713.

"Thanks, man," Kurt said. "I owe you one."

After five rings he had decided to try again later but the line finally clicked. There was a long awkward silence, followed by a feeble female voice saying hello.

"May I speak with Mrs. Alvina Stokes," he said.

"Speaking."

She sounded very old and possibly in poor health. He identified himself as the sheriff of Pitkin County, Colorado. "Are you any relation to Jack Stokes, ma'am?"

"I'm his mother," she said, her voice warbling. The weak phone connection wasn't helping their conversation. "Is my son in some kind of trouble, Sheriff?"

In his kindest manner, saying the words slowly and with profound regret, he told her that her son was dead.

"Dear Jesus." He expected her to cry, but instead she took a deep breath and raised her voice. "I've been waiting for this phone call for a long time, Sheriff. It comes as no surprise. How did it happen?"

He told her that her son appeared to be mentally disturbed and that he had tried to kill someone, and that in the process he had died in the hands of law enforcement. He did not tell her that Jack had murdered two people, or that he himself was involved in Jack's death.

"Have you been in touch with him, Mrs. Stokes? When was the last time you spoke with your son?"

"Ohh," she said, struggling with memory and resignation. "He called here about three months ago asking if I would rent him a postal box up in Colorado, where he wanted me to forward his mail. It was the first time I'd heard from him since he left the state hospital in Rusk. I didn't know where he was."

"Maybe you'd better tell me about Jack," Kurt said. "Had he been under psychiatric care?"

"Oh, dear me, yes. That poor boy had a rough go of it. He was disturbed, like you said. The drugs did that to him. Burned a hole in his mind. He was never the same after he lost his best friend, a boy named Rocky that played in his rock 'n' roll band when they were kids."

She told him that after Rocky's death her son had disappeared for several years, sending postcards from India and other faraway places. "For a while he lived with some hippies in Amsterdam, Holland," she said. "And then lord knows whereall. Then one day—oh, I don't know, maybe ten years ago—I heard a knock on my front door and there was this bum standing there, long stringy hair and a nasty beard, his teeth half rotted out. I started to call the *po*lice. I didn't recognize my own son. He was homeless and half dead from malnutrition and babbling like a loon."

She took him in, she said, and watched his mind slowly deteriorate over the next few years. The doctors diagnosed him as schizophrenic. He seldom left the house and made no attempt to communicate with his old friends or the outside world.

"My poor crazy boy thought all the junk mail that came every day was letters from his music fans. He started sending autographs to the return addresses. He liked to cut out pictures and paste them in his scrapbooks. Brassiere ads, mostly. Pretty girls. He wouldn't let me throw anything out and his room got so cluttered up we had to start using the garden shed to keep his catalogs in."

Kurt glanced over at the row of storage bags. "Is that what the Aspen P.O. box was for?" he asked, trying to understand this. "You were forwarding junk mail?"

There was a long delay on the line, then the old woman spoke again. "He was my son and I did what I could for him," she said. "Getting mail every day, making his scrapbooks—that was the only thing that gave him pleasure." She paused, then asked, "Do you have children, Sheriff?"

Kurt smiled. "A son," he said. "Eight years old."

"You sound like a gentleman. I bet you're a good father to that boy. You know what I'm talking about. We do whatever it takes to make our children happy."

Kurt walked over to the empty writing desk. The deputies had confiscated the typewriter, the scrapbooks, everything. The only sign that Jack Stokes had worked at this desk was the crisscross of X-acto knife lines in the soft wood.

"You said he'd been in a mental hospital, Mrs. Stokes."

"Oh yes. The doctors put him there," she said. "It nearly broke my heart. I'd been taking care of him a long time when he got in trouble with the law and they wouldn't let him stay with me no more."

She explained that Jack had been convinced that the local children were spying on him, mocking him behind his back, so he set animal traps in the bushes around their house and along the fence, hoping to catch them at it. Instead he had snared a neighborhood dog, and the dog had bled to death. "The authorities figured it was time to put him away before he hurt some kid," she said.

Kurt thought about the rottweiler with its slashed throat, dying in the snow. "Why did they release him from the hospital?" he asked.

"He was there two years, Sheriff. They said he'd behaved real good and was well enough to go. My lawyer told me it was the overcrowding. They needed the room for somebody worse off than Jack."

"And that was how long ago?"

"Ohh," she said, that sigh again. "About March, I believe." Six months ago. "My brother drove up to Rusk to bring him home but Jack wouldn't get in the car. He didn't want anything to do with us anymore. So Glenn gave him some money and said good-bye and we didn't hear from the boy again for maybe three months, when he turned up in Colorado."

Kurt reached inside his shirt pocket and retrieved the page torn from the book. He placed it on the desk and unfolded the creases with his free hand, staring at the image of the young ponytailed Jack Stokes with his arm around Dana. "Mrs. Stokes, did your son ever talk about an old girlfriend?" he asked. "Specifically a young woman named Dana. He knew her when he was in the Rocky Rhodes band."

He could detect a change in her voice. "Jack was a looker back in those days," she said with a mother's pride. "Tall and built like a ballplayer. He had lots of girls, Sheriff. They followed him all around. Dana, you say? I didn't know their names. The last time I went to Rusk he told me one of his old girlfriends had paid him a visit. Maybe it was that Dana, I don't know. You never knew if it was Jack's imagination. His mind was all awhirl and he couldn't get a good grip on the things of this world."

Kurt studied the old photograph of Dana Smerlas with her boyfriend the drummer. Maybe she was the reason Jack had found his way back to Aspen after his release from the mental hospital. Maybe she had invited him. *There's a cabin up in the mountains, Jack, where no one will bother you.* Aspen may have been the last place where he could remember being young and happy and in love.

"Thank you for talking with me, Mrs. Stokes. I'm very sorry I had to call you with such bad news."

"Will you help me make arrangements to send his body back home, Sheriff? I will pay for it. I have some money in the bank."

Kurt smiled sadly. "That won't be necessary, ma'am. Pitkin County will take care of the expense."

"I'm going to bury him next to his father," she said, her voice expressing emotion for the first time since their conversation began. "They never spent much time together. Maybe the two of them will get along now."

After Kurt hung up he took one final look around the cabin and then stepped outside into the raw morning air. He stood on the steps and smelled the scent of pine and wondered if the Bauer brothers would level these woods to build their new ski resort. He thought about poor Jack Stokes, a '60s casualty they had used to their advantage, playing the crazy bastard like a toy drum. Dana had known where he was and lured him back, and Westbrook had done the rest. By the end the old rocker was so screwed up he'd thought he was his best friend and idol, Rocky Rhodes. He had assumed a lover's rage and gone after Nicole and done their dirty work for them. And now that Jack was dead everyone could walk away with what they wanted. Westbrook had his new facility and Dana had her husband back. Walt Bauer could build his resort. *Tra-la-la,* Kurt thought, what a wonderful world it would be.

37

MONDAY AFTERNOON KURT met with the D.A. in his office at the courthouse. Don Harrigan was a short, chipmunk-cheeked man prone to expensive haircuts and humorous ties. Today he was wearing one that looked like a salmon hanging from his neck. He was Kurt's age, nearly fifty years old, but he'd taken better care of himself and looked ten years younger. There wasn't a gray hair on his sandy blond head.

"Come on, Kurt, you know how it works," Harrigan said, reacting to Kurt's impatience. "It's one thing to know something, it's another thing to take it to court. Ask Marcia Clark."

"Here's a photo of them together when they were young," Kurt said, slapping the torn page onto Harrigan's desk. "He's got his arm around her."

"So what?" Harrigan shrugged. "Frank Sinatra appeared in photos with half the underworld. It doesn't mean he conspired to commit murder."

Kurt raised an eyebrow.

"Okay, but you know what I mean," Harrigan said. "We still don't have a conspiracy case. And maybe we never will, Kurt. Maybe this is one we'll have to live with. 'Drug-fried loon comes back to take revenge on all his old druggie friends.' I'm not un-happy with that."

"Except it isn't the whole story, Don, and you know it."

"Spit in one hand and wish in the other, Kurt, and see which one of 'em gets wet." He held up his palms. "So far they're bone-dry."

Kurt made a face. "I hate it when you go southern on me."

He ambled to the window with his hands in his pockets. There was snow in Spar Gulch and higher up Aspen Mountain, and snow plowed to the street curbs. This early snowfall prom-ised a long white winter. The tourists and merchants were going to love one another again.

"You haven't told me about your visit with Lyle Gunderson this morning," Kurt said. "I guess that means it didn't go well."

Harrigan remained seated behind his desk. "When I got to the hospital Lyle was talking with a lawyer from Ross, Ewing, Jordan, and Smith. Same Denver firm that represents West-brook. Same people who've made a fortune off the Bauer family for the past fifty years."

Kurt turned to face him with a smug smile. "And that's why you know I'm right about this thing," he said.

Harrigan nodded. "Follow the lawyers," he said.

"So what are they advising our boy to do?"

"Cop to a simple invasion-of-privacy charge," the D.A. said. "He isn't admitting he showed the tapes to Westbrook or any-body else."

"God damn," Kurt said, shaking his head. "Can't you threaten him with serious jail time?"

"How?" Harrigan asked. "It's pretty clear to me that Lyle and Westbrook have cut a deal with each other, through their law-yers, to concede absolutely nothing. So how do we prove the videos changed hands? And even if we do, what does it mean?"

Kurt paced back and forth across the office, taking mental stock of what they had. No proof that Westbrook had been nursemaiding Jack Stokes in a remote cabin on Bauer land. No proof that he had shown Lyle's lurid videos of Nicole to the crazy bastard. And not one shred of proof that Westbrook and Dana Smerlas had done all of this to make Walt Bauer happy.

"What time is the press conference?" Harrigan asked.

Kurt glanced at his watch. It was three-thirty. "Half an hour," he said. "What do you suggest I tell them, Counselor?"

Harrigan stood up from his desk and came forward with his hands in the pockets of his pleated tweeds. His brow was furrowed in serious contemplation. "Tell them Jack Stokes was a deranged man who hounded Nicole Bauer to death, murdered two of her old friends, and then went after an innocent family," he said. "Tell them you stopped him, Kurt. You did your job. Isn't that enough?"

It wasn't enough and they both knew it.

"Corky's a very shrewd man," Harrigan said. "He'll spin this so you come out looking like the hero. And you know what, Kurt?" he said with a warm smile. "You *are* the hero. So quit beating yourself up. You stopped the bad guy from killing again."

Kurt rubbed his face and the back of his neck. "Then how come I don't feel like a hero, Don?"

The D.A. was too short to put his arm around Kurt's shoulder. He contented himself with gripping an arm. "Look, buddy," he said, walking Kurt to the door, "we can't get at those people right now, and maybe we never will. It's going to take time and a shovelful of luck. Make your peace with that."

Kurt didn't know if he could ever accept that version of peace.

"But believe me, stranger things have happened," Harrigan said with a cavalier shrug. "Old partnerships sometimes dissolve in acrimony. People spill their guts to get even. You never know."

Kurt stopped at the office door and gave the D.A. a hard

look. "I know this, Don. I'm going to do everything I can to help their sweet little partnership dissolve."

Harrigan held up his hands, a gesture of caution. "Do us both a favor, Kurt. Play it by the book, okay?"

"Donnnn," Kurt said with a sly grin. "Have I ever played it any other way?"

38

THE PRESS CONFERENCE was an intense but surprisingly civil exchange. Afterward Kurt drove Corky Marcus home and thanked him for fielding the questions and for offering his own comment and support.

"I'm the one who should be thanking you, Kurt," Corky said. He was standing in the gravel parking area outside their double garage, still absorbed with what had taken place at his home last night. "My god, if you hadn't come by to say good night to Lennon . . ."

His sentence lingered. This is how Carole had explained it to him.

"We were all very lucky," Kurt said grimly.

Corky exhaled and stared at the automatic doors slowly rising to reveal their two vehicles and a neatly arranged wall full of garden implements. "Are you sure you and Lennon can't stay for dinner?"

"Thanks, Corky. Not tonight. We're going for a ride. And then we're going home to sleep in our own beds."

Kurt stopped at Little Annie's and bought take-out food, the hamburger and fries Lennon desperately craved, and they drove downvalley in the frosty blue twilight while his son ate from the greasy bag and listened to the radio. Before long they crossed the small bridge over Snowmass Creek and passed through the Bauer archway. Kurt parked the Jeep facing south across the white meadowlands toward the old lodge and the mountains beyond. They finished their burgers in silence, waiting for the elk herd to appear.

"Have I ever told you about the time your Uncle Bert and me and a friend of ours almost died in an avalanche?"

"I don't think so," Lennon said, mayonnaise smeared at the corners of his mouth.

"It happened right up there in that range above the lodge."

He began to tell his son the story of what had taken place that day in 1964, a lifetime ago. "There were wild and beautiful slopes like I'd never seen before. So wild no one could tame them," he said with a storybook flourish.

Men had landed on the moon since then. London Bridge had been moved to Arizona. With enough money you could alter anything, he thought.

After he finished the story they sat watching the darkness descend around them. There was no moon and a frigid wind blew across the snowy pasture where Kurt had seen the herd yesterday.

"It's dark, Dad. How long are we going to stay here? I'm getting cold."

"I guess we'd better go."

"I don't think the elks are coming."

"Doesn't look like it."

"I wonder what happened to them?" Lennon asked.

Kurt wondered, too. Maybe they already knew.

39

ON THE DAY of Nicole Bauer's funeral he flew into Denver and rented a car. He drove downtown to the Denver Medical Center, where Muffin Brown lay awaiting further orthopedic surgery in the trauma unit. One of her brothers was sitting with her in the room while the rest of the family had gone to lunch. He rose to shake Kurt's hand.

"How's my best deputy?"

"Tough as wahr," said the brother, a tall rancher with a wind-blown face. "She's gonna be jus' fine." He looked at Kurt with one eye half squinted. "I taught her how to swing a baseball bat."

Muffin was heavily sedated. She opened her eyes and smiled at Kurt, gripped his hand. Someone had washed and dried her hair and applied blush to her pale cheeks. "I heard you got him," she said in a weak, druggy voice.

He nodded and squeezed her cool hand.

"Anybody get hurt?" she asked.

"Carole Marcus needed six stitches on her shoulder. It could've been worse."

She closed her eyes, drifting in and out of sleep.

"They aren't telling me very much, Kurt. Am I going to use this leg again?"

He looked down at the sheet across her lower body. "Of course you are. In a few months you'll be dribbling up and down the basketball court."

"You wouldn't lie to me, would you?"

"Absolutely not," he said with a boyish grin. "A little rehab and you're gonna be good as new."

He held her hand and gazed around the room. The place was filled with flowers and potted plants and so many get-well cards her family had taped them to the wall across from her bed.

"What about the others?" she asked. "Are you going to get them, too?"

He smiled at her. "Sooner or later," he said.

She tried to return the smile, but her face darkened suddenly and a single tear raced down her cheek. "Kurt Muller," she said, wagging his hand, "you're the biggest liar I've ever met."

THE FUNERAL SERVICE was held at St. Paul's Lutheran Church near the state capitol. News cameras clogged the sidewalk out front and Kurt had to fight his way past a melee of reporters rushing at him with microphones. Inside the venerable old church only three pews were occupied on both sides of the aisle. Kurt sat far in the rear and listened to the cavernous echoes of the pastor eulogizing a woman he hadn't known. He lofted words like *beloved daughter and sister* and *revered family of the parish* and *torn with grief at her untimely death*. The two Bauer brothers sat in the front row with their wives and college-age children. The grief-stricken ex-husband, Jay Westbrook, was accompanied by a young woman so primly dressed it took Kurt several moments to recognize her as Tanya. And the Smerlases were present, too, shoulder to shoulder in their formal condolence. It was a disgusting pageant of hypocrisy. Kurt wished he had stolen Nicole's broken body from the morgue in Aspen and cremated her somewhere out in the desert.

After the final prayers he remained seated while the ornate coffin proceeded slowly through the long narrow church, followed by the small congregation. Jeffrey Bauer was the only mourner with tears on his cheeks. Kurt caught their eyes one by one as they passed by, Walt IV and Westbrook, Ben and Dana Smerlas. None of them showed surprise to see him there. He nodded to each in turn and smiled. It was his way of letting them know he would be watching them for the rest of their lives.

There was no snow in Denver, only clear autumn skies and fallen leaves and the hint of another season passing. The funeral procession crept down Alameda to the old Fairmount Cemetery in the princely Cherry Creek neighborhood. It was the cemetery where Denver's elite were buried, a hundred years of governors, railroad barons, mining magnates, cattle kings.

A private security guard was posted at the cemetery gate, waving the limousines through. When he saw Kurt's rental car he raised a hand and stopped him.

"May I have your name, sir?" he said, consulting his clipboard.

"Sheriff Kurt Muller. You won't find me on the list."

The guard acknowledged the word *sheriff* but was slow and clearly conflicted in his response.

"I was a friend of Miss Bauer," Kurt said, showing him his badge. "And I'm in charge of the investigation into her death."

The young man glanced back at the short line of cars waiting behind Kurt. "Technically your name is supposed to be on the list, Sheriff," he said reluctantly.

"I won't tell anybody if you won't."

The guard considered this, then waved him on. "Go ahead, sir."

He followed the limos down a long, winding lane through the bucolic grounds to the Bauer family monument, a massive red granite shrine located several acres away in an older section reserved for the wealthiest gentry, the elite of the elite. Nicole was being laid to rest beside her parents, Walt III and Sophie Bauer. Kurt witnessed the ceremony from a distance, standing in the shade of an ancient cedar. Only a handful of friends and family members had made the trip to the grave site. They gathered under a canopy and prayed aloud with the pastor, then issued past the casket, placing flowers on the lid before strolling back to their limousines. He saw Walt IV check his watch and confer quietly with the secretary at his side.

Kurt caught up with the lead entourage as they huddled near the door of their limousine, speaking in hushed voices, embracing one another. "Well well," he said. "Now that that's over I suppose it's Miller Time for you folks."

They all turned to glare at him. Walt IV, the Smerlases, Westbrook and Tanya. "If you don't mind, Sheriff Muller, we're having a private moment," said Walt IV, crisp and conventional in his chalk-striped three-piece suit.

Kurt was amused by their charade of dignity. "Hey, what's a party without a few presents," he said, reaching into his trench coat. "Here, Dana, this is for you."

He handed the woman a small rectangular package neatly wrapped in shiny silver paper. "I know you've already seen the movie, but maybe you'd like to watch it again with your husband," he said.

Dana Smerlas looked at the package in her hands and blanched.

"It's a copy of the video of your husband and Nicole in bed together," Kurt said. "Enjoy."

There was a Band-Aid across the bridge of Ben Smerlas's nose, a souvenir from their fight at the gym. He stepped toward Kurt with doubled fists but Westbrook extended an arm and held him back.

"Don't feel left out, Doctor," Kurt said, shoving another package against Westbrook's chest. "This one's even better. It's Nickie's last few minutes before she died."

Linda Ríos had found the footage at the end of the tape of Kurt and Nicole making love. Nicole was sitting on the edge of the bed in her nightgown, listening to the phone pressed to her ear, two calls only twenty minutes apart. She looked exhausted and disoriented and deeply frightened. Tears streaked her face. Her body rocked wildly as she listened and cried and screamed into the receiver. Most of the audio was unintelligible, but Kurt had made out the words *Leave me alone, you son of a bitch!* and *You were choking me!* In the last heartbreaking moment of her life she dropped the receiver and stood up pulling at her hair and screaming in horrific anguish. And then she ran. Out of the camera's fixed range. He could hear the glass doors bang open. He could hear her final scream.

"Consider it documentation of the job you did on her," Kurt said, staring at each of them. "It ought to make you proud of yourselves."

Walt IV stared back with outrage in his cold blue eyes. "I won't forget your behavior today, Muller," he said.

Kurt smiled at him. "I don't want you to, Mr. Bauer," he said. "Every year on her birthday, when another gift arrives in the mail from me, I want you to remember that the party isn't over until I say it is."

He noticed Jeffrey Bauer watching the confrontation from the open door of a limousine parked second in line. Kurt forearmed Ben Smerlas out of his way and walked directly toward the accountant, searching the inner pocket of his coat for another gift he'd brought along. "Jeff," he said, "I've got something for you, too."

The younger Bauer recoiled a step and glanced nervously into the back seat at his wife and two daughters. His face looked flaccid and beleaguered. He sank away from Kurt with the cowering disposition of someone who always expected a blow.

"Here," Kurt said, extending his hand. Nicole's earrings, the amber bears. The ones she'd worn Friday night and left on the night table. "They're Nickie's. I'm sure she'd want you to have something of hers as a keepsake."

Jeffrey stared at the earrings in Kurt's palm. His brow was creased, a wary suspicion. He was prepared for another cruel prank. When he realized that Kurt was sincere, something softened behind his eyes. "Thank you," he said, reaching out to take the miniature bears.

"It won't work, Jeff," Kurt said. "You have no idea what kind of fight you're going to have on your hands."

Jeffrey squinted quizzically, confused.

"The ski resort," Kurt said. "The green groups all over Colorado will drag you through hell before they let you carve up another mountain."

Jeffrey shrugged indifferently. "It's Walt's baby," he said. "I just balance the books."

Kurt had suspected this. He patted the man on the shoulder. "If you ever want to talk about your sister and what happened to her," he said with a sympathetic smile, "you know where to find me."

HE SAT IN the rental car until everyone had gone. Two grave attendants and a smartly dressed supervisor were waiting under the canopy for him to drive away, too, so they could lower the casket and fill in the dirt. After half an hour of idleness they decided to ignore him and proceed. He got out of the car and walked down the sloping green hill toward the grave. By the time he arrived, the casket was in place six feet below the earth and the men were removing the hydraulic equipment. They stopped working as he approached.

"May we help you?" the supervisor asked. He was a middle-aged black gentleman with a red carnation in his lapel.

Kurt gazed down into the hole at the casket settled in its final resting place. He reached into his pocket, withdrew the ring from among his coins and car keys, and studied the yin-yang symbols and the eight trigrams one last time. The Wind in the Woods. The Receptive Earth. He said two silent prayers for her, the Hail Mary his father had taught him when he was a child and a few half-remembered phrases from the Kaddish he had heard his mother recite. And then he dropped the ring into the grave. The heavy gold band clanked against the bronze casket lid and rattled off to the side.

"Sir, is there anything we can do for you?" the supervisor asked, visibly uncomfortable with Kurt's presence.

Until this moment Kurt had never understood the verse *Let the dead bury the dead.*

"Yes, there is," he said, wiping his eyes with the loosened cuffs of his starched white shirt. "You can hand me a shovel."

ON THE DAY of the recall vote, Kurt and Lennon invited the two youngest Marcus boys over for pizza after school. It was Kurt's way of distracting himself, of ignoring the inevitable. He also wanted to show off the elaborate rabbit hutch he had finally completed, and the children were the only ones who would appreciate his hard work.

Although it had snowed two days before, the afternoon was clear and bright and perfect for a picnic. Kurt shoveled and swept the deck and spread the pizza boxes and soft drinks on the outdoor table. The boys ate quickly, abandoning their crusts to play with the rabbit inside her new home. Kurt had built the hutch in a sheltered corner of the deck, twenty square yards of floor space covered in spongy green indoor-outdoor carpet, screen walls reinforced with heavy-gauge mink wire, an eight-foot ceiling roofed in tinted Plexiglas, electric heater lamps for the single-digit winter. He had also provided a cozy cage for the rabbit's waste and her nighttime safety. Patchella was the luckiest bunny in the valley.

The boys were sitting on the floor of the hutch, petting and fussing over the small white creature, when the patio door slid back and Carole Marcus stepped onto the deck. She smiled at

Kurt and said hello to the boys, who shouted greetings of *Hi, Mom!* and then promptly returned to their play.

"You're just in time for the last two slices," he said, opening a box lid to show her what was left.

"No, thanks, I'm fine," she said. "I've had enough pizza to last a lifetime."

She looked wonderful today, effortlessly appealing. She was wearing a sleeveless down vest over a black pullover sweater tucked trimly into her jeans. The afternoon light caught the copper strands in her short dark hair.

"Sorry I'm late," she said. "The line at our voting precinct was longer than I expected."

"So you finally made up your mind about me?"

She smiled slyly. "Do I have to say which way I voted?"

He offered her a deck chair next to his recliner. "I couldn't face the newspaper this morning," he said. "What was their prediction?"

"Too close to call," she said. "Your numbers have improved in the last ten days. It could go either way."

He expelled a weary sigh. "It'll all be over in a few hours," he said.

"True enough," she said, squeezing his hand. "Corky is coming by in a little while with the champagne."

"I didn't know your husband was such an optimist."

"He's not. But he figures it's time to get wasted one way or the other."

For several moments of silence they watched the boys scoot around after the rabbit. He reached over and rubbed her arm just below the place where Jack Stokes had cut her, a few inches from the butterfly tattoo. "How's the wound?" he asked quietly, not wanting the children to hear this question.

"Healing nicely," she said, patting his hand. "The stitches come out next week."

The three boys banged through the screen door one after the

other, announcing that they were tired of the rabbit and were going inside the house to play a video game. Once they had disappeared, the solitude was so sudden and intense that Kurt found himself at a loss. This was the first time he'd been alone with Carole since the incident and he didn't know where to begin.

"I talked to Jack's mother," he said, disrupting their silence. "She told me he'd been screwed up for years. A serious mental case. They had to lock him away for a while. Was he like that when you knew him?"

She narrowed her eyes, trying to remember. "Looking back twenty years, yeah, maybe there were signs. I don't know," she said. "All the guys in the band were mental. Obnoxious . . . macho . . . in love with themselves. They threw tantrums like two-year-olds. I can't explain why we put up with them."

"The times, I guess," Kurt said with a jaded smile.

Her eyes danced over him. "And where were you when all this was going down in my life?" she asked.

He shrugged. "Skiing," he said. ". . . naked. I wish you could've been there."

She tossed back her head and laughed. After a few moments of awkward silence she touched his hand again. "You haven't told anyone, have you? Not even Corky. You've kept my dirty little secrets to yourself." Her cool smile was tempered with suspicion. "When a man does that, it usually means he expects something in return. Are you expecting something, Kurt?"

He remembered what Muffin had once told him. *You need to find yourself a nice stable lady who loves dogs and children and putters around in her garden. Somebody who isn't beaten up by her past.*

"Your secrets are your business, Carole," he said. "You're the one who has to live with them."

She stood up and sauntered to the railing and gazed down the slope of Red Mountain toward the gingerbread village of Aspen. "I tried out a lot of things when I was younger," she said with her back to him. "I guess we all did, didn't we? Some of them took, some didn't. You remember how it was."

He remembered. "How about you and Nicole?" he asked. "Did that take?"

She hesitated, then shook her head. "No, it didn't. She married Westbrook, I found other partners. I wasn't into women for very long. Like you said, it was the times."

"Did you stay in touch with her?"

"We didn't see each other for years," she said. "The trial was too scary to hang around for, so I left town. I couldn't have helped her, anyway. The Bauer family locked her up to keep her away from all her old friends. The marriage to Westbrook was Papa Bauer's bright idea. After that none of us could get near her."

"When was the last time you saw her?"

She paused, calculating. "About nine months ago," she said. "We met for lunch." She turned around to offer him a sad smile. "She knew that you and I were friends, and she wanted my advice. She wanted to know what she should do to get you back."

Kurt dropped his eyes. He had been cruel to a good woman.

"She called me again a few weeks ago, when the letters started coming. She was convinced Rocky was alive. She wanted me to tell her it wasn't so."

He stared at her. "Because you would know for certain," he said. "Because you were there the night he died."

Her face betrayed the truth. She made no effort to deny what he had said.

"And that's why you went to see old Doc Brumley," he said. "You had to be sure yourself."

Without answering him she slowly crossed the deck to the patio doors and peered through the glass. Her children were somewhere in the house, lost in a fantasy world of their own. She tested the door, closing it tightly. She didn't want anyone to hear what she was going to tell him.

"He was beating and choking her, Kurt," she said, turning to face him with her hands behind her back, clutching the door latch. "I was asleep on a couch downstairs and I heard her screams. When I got to the bedroom they were fighting out on the deck. It was slick with ice. She kept slipping down and he kept kicking her and calling her horrible names." The memory brought tears to her eyes. "I thought he was going to kill her."

He rose from his recliner and walked toward her and took her in his arms. "It's okay," he said, rubbing his hand up and down the back of her vest. "It was a long time ago."

"I didn't know what to do," she said, her voice husky and breaking. "I ran out onto the deck and grabbed him from behind and, and—"

"Shhh," he said, touching his finger to her lips. "That's enough, now. Everyone knows what happened. He slipped and went through the railing and it was all an accident."

"No, Kurt," she cried. "That's not exactly how it happened."

"Hush, now," he said, holding her close. "Don't say another word. It doesn't matter. It's ancient history."

Looking over her head he saw Corky approaching the glass doors with a champagne bottle in his hand. The door slid back quietly and Kurt's old friend stood watching their embrace with a pained expression. He seemed hesitant and confused. When Carole turned and saw him she pulled away from Kurt and rushed into her husband's arms.

"Hey, is everything okay?" Corky asked, stroking her hair with his free hand.

She was crying too hard to speak.

"Delayed reaction," Kurt explained with a warm smile for his friend. "It's going to take her a while to get over what happened."

He patted them both on the arms and went inside the house to give them some private time together. He checked on the boys, who were jabbering away, taking turns with the joysticks, oblivious to his presence. They wouldn't need him until they got hungry or wanted a ride somewhere.

He walked into the study and closed the door behind him. Sitting at his father's old desk, staring at the heavy Underwood typewriter, his thoughts turned fondly to Nicole Bauer. Whatever else she had done with her life, however distraught and unstable she had become, she had never betrayed her old friend. She had borne the burden of guilt and spared Carole from an indictment for homicide, and she had carried their secret to the grave. Nicole had been a woman who valued loyalty and friendship, no matter how poorly she was treated in return.

He opened a desk drawer and searched through the clutter. Somewhere in there he had stashed the notes Nicole had sent him last fall. A faint scent of jasmine led him to her stationery, buried in the back behind the unpaid bills and loose rubber bands and box of paper clips. He dragged out the small stack of envelopes and opened one. *Darling Kurt,* the note began. *Why don't you call? I know you're a busy man but I would love to see you for a few hours, if you can spare the time. Have you forgotten me?*

No, he hadn't forgotten Nicole Bauer. And he promised her he never would.

Acknowledgments

I WISH TO thank my wife, Annette Carlozzi, and my friends Rick Roderick and Jim Magnuson for their careful reading of the manuscript and their generous support and encouragement. I am equally grateful to my editors, Susan Kamil and Carla Riccio, who asked the hard questions that made this a better story.

Though I no longer live in Aspen, it occupies a special place in my memory. There were many good friends who enriched our life there, too many to name in this space. They know who they are. I will always cherish them and the town where our son was born.